About the Author

Faith is an avid reader, and lives in London with her husband and cats. Remarkably, they all manage to get on well.

Here is a picture of Faith making friends with an owl, who wisely seems to be looking for an escape route.

THE FAIRY'S TALE

The Pathways Tree, Book One

This book is dedicated to Jon, without whom Bea would still be stuck in the forest.

F. D. Lee

Glossary: The Major Fae

Adhene

Small and slight-boned, adhenes are traditionally extremely beautiful, mischievous fae. Before the Great Redaction, they made their stories through misleading women, stealing babies or seducing wives away from their husbands. According to the rules of their tribe, if you ask an adhene for help on a mission of mercy, they will offer you genuine advice and aid.

Boggart

Part of the trio of hobgoblins, brownies and boggarts. Boggarts are usually quite malevolent, causing milk to sour, dogs to lame and crops to fail, if not appeased. Creatures of swamps, lakes and bogs, they have delicate, iridescent scales covering their bodies and were extremely good at curating belief before the Mirrors began to break.

Brownie

Part of the trio of hobgoblins, brownies and boggarts. Brownies are household fae, usually coming out at night. Unlike their cousin tribe, the boggarts, brownies are helpful creatures, often performing small acts in exchange for food. Prior to the Great Redaction, their status was low, as good works do little for belief. However, since the Great Redaction, the brownies' status has risen significantly, mostly due to how quickly they adapted to the Teller's rules and regulations.

The Cerberus (The Beast)

The Cerberus is a large creature with three canine heads, strong jaws and an extremely adept ability to hunt. The first servant of the Teller, the Cerberus was instrumental in bringing about the Great

Redaction and the creation of the General Administration. Not really a tribe, as there has only ever been one Cerberus. The creature is genuinely unique, and as such has always held a position of distrust amongst the fae.

Dwarf

Generally stocky, dwarves are a robust tribe that have always found a place in the stories. Usually perceived as heavy drinkers (strong in the arm and thick in the head), dwarves are in fact very thoughtful and meditative.

Elf

Elves are often shorter than average human height, and more slender and graceful. They have pointed ears and pale skin. Before the Great Redaction, the elves lived in forests, spoke with the animals, and played games with the lives of the characters. Elves particularly loved a love story, and would often interfere with human events for their own amusement and gratification. Now the elves enjoy an uneasy alliance with the GenAm—they generate a lot of belief, but they greatly resent the limits placed on them by the Teller.

Fairies

The fairy tribe is divided into three clans: the flower fairies, the garden fairies, and the house fairies. Only flower fairies have wings. In general, the flower fairies are the most successful of the tribe as, due to their beauty and the fact they can fly, the characters believe in them for longer than house or garden fairies. Many house fairies are employed as tooth fairies due to their small size and practical nature. Garden fairies are the lowest of the three clans because of the minimal belief they generate.

With the exception of the house fairies, fairies are rarely employed by the General Administration, a fact that only adds to the stereotype of them as useless. This prejudice is based mainly on the notion that the characters quickly grow out of believing in fairies.

Gnarl

Little is known about the gnarls. It is understood that, along with the orcs and ogres, gnarls now live in the wastelands beyond the Sheltering Forest. They fought for Yarnis in the Rhyme War and are said to eat other fae.

Gnome

A cousin tribe to the imp, gnomes are small, bony, grey-skinned creatures with questionable hygiene. Before the Great Redaction, they tended to spend their time in Thaiana, living in caves or other dark places, frightening humans. They liked to ask riddles, especially on their birthdays. Now they mostly stay in Ænathlin.

Goblin

Technically, a goblin is a type of fairy. However, this is not a connection either tribe likes to acknowledge. Goblins are small, agile fae with large saucer-shaped eyes. They are also mean spirited and do not like dealing outside their own tribe. They did well before the Redaction, but since then they have, unsurprisingly, fared less well. A large number of goblins left the Land completely and have spread over Thaiana. They remain mostly undisturbed by the Cerberus and the GenAm because they tend not to interfere with the stories or the characters.

Hobgoblin

Part of the trio of hobgoblins, brownies and boggarts. A small, orange-skinned, knavish fae, hobgoblins tend to be very changeable in attitude and easily offended. There are many attributes associated with hobgoblins, such as their speed and quick wit.

Imp

Green-skinned and blonde-haired, imps are followers rather than leaders and will change allegiance at the drop of a hat (or crown). As a result, the tribe survived the Redaction without any real change in their lifestyles. They are popular with the characters, and so are generally employed by the GenAm.

Kelpie

A water horse with dripping manes and smooth, seal-like skin. The kelpie are the same size as regular horses, but cannot be tamed in the way a 'regular' horse can be. Before the Redaction, the kelpie made their stories by luring mortals, especially children, into the water and then drowning and eating them. Since the Redaction, they have been mainly employed as workhorses, an insult they feel very keenly. The kelpie can be any colour, though they tend towards black, and need to be kept wet at all times.

Ogre

Ogres are a very rare fae, possibly belonging to the same tribe as trolls. Ogres, however, are much larger than trolls, and more prone to violence. Incredibly honourable in their own way, ogres believe in the beauty of a clean death, and respect strength. They come from a tradition of warfare and fought with Yarnis during the Rhyme War.

Orc

The orcs, along with the gnarls, sided with Yarnis during the Rhyme War. They are ugly, ill-tempered creatures. None have been seen since the Teller took control.

Tompte

Tomptes are a tiny, winged tribe, with cherubic faces. Before the Redaction, they cleaned houses for characters in return for food and shelter. However, the tompte are vengeful, and when they felt that a character had not kept up their end of the bargain, they would blind babies, sour milk or free herds in revenge.

Troll

A large fae, trolls are often assumed because of their size to be cruel or stupid, though there is no evidence for this. Before the Redaction, they lived quietly, usually isolated from the other fae, who have a tendency to bully them. They have never been known to live under bridges, nor are they made of stone.

Witchlein

Given their yellow, scaled skin and hissing voices, it is surprising that the Witchlein did not join Yarnis during the Rhyme War. Perhaps even more remarkable is how well they have done under the Teller. The Redaction Department is always able to find a use for these frightening, sharp-scaled fae. They are small, light, and fast.

Chapter One

Bea watched anxiously from the hill as the handsome hero fought his way into the thorns, trying to reach the castle where the heroine lay sleeping.

Everything would be fine, she told herself. The hero seemed a strong lad. And that armour was serious stuff. And it was only a *plant*, for goodness' sake. What harm could a plant do?

It was quite a bit bigger than she'd expected, though. In hindsight, she probably shouldn't have left it alone for so long.

Bea started to chew her thumbnail.

Ten minutes passed.

There was no sign of the hero. By now the briar should have retreated and the hero awoken the heroine with True Love's Kiss.

She squinted at the tower. The story should finish at sundown, and the sky was darkening as the sun sank lower on the horizon. If the godmother returned before the hero had reached the tower...

Bea swore.

Puffing and holding her skirts up, she ran down the hill, skidding to a stop in front of the barricade that imprisoned the castle. It was undoubtedly impressive up close. Green branches wove in and out of each other, each one edged with sharp thorns. She glanced to her left, at the horizon. The sun bobbed low, a half-circle of brilliant orange.

From somewhere inside the briar, she heard a scream.

Rolling up her sleeves, Bea plunged her arms into the mess of branches, ignoring the pain as the thorns ripped at her skin. She closed her eyes and began to have a serious discussion with the plant.

Plants don't really have language—they don't have mouths or tongues and teeth, so producing words is, understandably, something of an impossibility. But that isn't to say they can't communicate. And Bea was a cabbage fairy, which, while offering her no status at all in fae society, did mean she had the trick of communicating with plants.

And so Bea proceeded to tell the briar, in no uncertain terms, exactly what she thought of its enthusiastic interpretation of her request to keep the castle and the heroine safe. And that, if it wouldn't mind, could it please stop killing the hero and, right now, retreat back to the rose garden where it belonged.

Days, weeks and years passed while Bea waited for the briar to respond. The sun was little more than a sliver, hugging the horizon.

The briar pulled back, adding a cross-section of tiny cuts to the ones already on her arms. The branches twisted and turned on themselves as they retreated back across the castle, Bea's chest heaving as she tried to catch her breath.

The hero was revealed, waving his sword around and thankfully without any serious harm having befallen him or his horse. He hacked at the already greatly diminished briar, a determined and, Bea felt, somewhat constipated look on his face. The courtyard cleared, he jumped off his horse and dashed into the tower. The briar returned to the rose garden, and, perhaps by way of apology, started to flower.

Dropping heavily to the ground, a cold sweat making her skin clammy, Bea fixed her eyes on the tower, watching the hero run past the narrow windows. He reached the turret just as the sun went down.

Bea fell backwards, exhaustion and relief flooding her body.

A shadow fell across her.

"What are you doing down here? You should be watching from the hill."

Bea scrambled to her feet.

"You look a state," the newly arrived godmother said.

Bea glanced down at her homemade dress. It was covered in tiny thorns and bits of leaf, and one of the patches she had attempted to sew on was coming loose.

"I fell," she said, brushing away the worst of the evidence. "From the hill, I mean. Yes. I fell down here."

The godmother, a pixie, rolled her eyes. "Sleeping on the job, I suppose?"

"No, no, I was just, um——"

"I need you to take this and drop it off with the Indexer at the Grand; if you think you can manage, that is," the godmother said, shoving a large, leather-bound Book into Bea's arms.

"But—"

"Please don't make a fuss. I've got a new Plot starting at midnight. I don't have the time to get back to Ænathlin, fight my way through the Grand, drop off the Book, and then get back here again."

"Yes, but—"

"Honestly, I'd have thought you'd want to help, to be given a bit of extra responsibility. Isn't that what you're always banging on about?"

"I am, I do," Bea said.

"Well then, stop gulping at me like a half-dead fish. There are plenty of others who can watch my Plots, you know. I didn't have to take a fairy on."

Bea looked down at the Book, and then at the rose garden. There was no reason to be worried. Everything had ended the way it should. And they never checked small Plots like this—it was barely a three-acter.

"Alright," she said. "Of course. I'd be happy to."

"I should think so too," the godmother said, her expression shifting from one of focused annoyance to a more general exasperation. "You should count yourself lucky you've *not* been accepted to train as a Fiction Management Executive, quite frankly. I'm not a fairy-hater, but I doubt one of your tribe could keep up with the workload, not if you can't stay awake to watch a simple Happy Ever After. Right, wait here while I do the conclusion, and then you get that to the Indexer."

She looked Bea up and down, taking in her round, flushed face, her silver hair that never seemed to want to stay in its bun, her tatty dress and the cuts running up her forearms.

"Fairies. You don't help yourselves, do you?"

The godmother bustled off to finish the story.

"You've got no idea," Bea said to herself.

Bea had learnt several things about travelling by Mirror between worlds, such as not eating immediately before stepping through. At least, not unless she wanted to spend the rest of the day feeling like her stomach was both sickeningly full and painfully empty. Nausea went hand in hand with transworld travel, and Bea always carried a sprig of mint in her bag to counter it.

But life is the kind of teacher that revels in pop-quizzes, and Bea was about to learn a new lesson. Namely that the sudden appearance of a short, fat fairy in a space already full to bursting point would result in a face full of armpit and the fervent wish she'd held her breath.

She'd stepped through one of the few remaining Mirrors, leaving the characters' world behind and entering Ænathlin, the last surviving city in the Land of the Fae. She had also stepped into pandemonium, confusion and, best of all, sweat.

No wonder the godmother hadn't wanted to return the Book herself.

The Grand Reflection Station was the home of the Mirrors and the commuter hub of Ænathlin. Instinctively, Bea hugged her bag to her chest, the weight of the Book against her, and joined the queue to get out. She stood on her tiptoes and was rewarded with the ominous sight of a checkpoint barring the exit, causing the bottleneck. The GenAm were out in force, which usually meant something bad had happened.

Or was about to happen.

Pulling at the fleshy arm of a troll lumbering along next to her, Bea said, "Excuse me, do you know what's going on? Why's the checkpoint up? Is anyone in trouble—I mean, are they looking for someone? Specifically?"

The troll looked down. For a moment, it seemed he wasn't going to reply. Still, he overcame his initial reaction at being accosted by a fairy.

"You been in Thaiana?" the troll rumbled, not bothering to iron out the look creasing his face.

Bea nodded.

"Huh. They can send fairies through, is it? Been picking flowers, have you?"

"I was on official business. And I'm not a flower fairy."

The troll snorted. "Fairy's a fairy. What business?"

"Plot-watching—but it's still official," Bea added quickly. "What's happened?"

"We've lost another Mirror—cracked straight down the middle. The Anties are at it again."

"Bloody Anties," Bea said automatically. "How many Mirrors have they broken now?"

"The GenAm won't tell us, but they keep closing sections of the station. Reckon there'll be no Mirrors left soon. Then we'll be in real trouble."

She frowned. "It can't be that bad?"

"Well, it ain't looking particularly good, is it? How old are you?"

Bea pulled herself up to her full height. She realised it might have been more impressive if she hadn't been talking to a troll.

"What's my age got to do with anything?"

"Coz you're too young, that's what. You don't know what it was like when we nearly lost the Mirrors. You ever seen a siege?"

"No."

"Yeah, well, you better hope you never do. What do you think will happen when we ain't got no Mirrors to get into Thaiana? When there's no food to be had? If the Anties keep messing up the Plots, that's what'll happen."

"It won't get that far," Bea said. But there was a question in her voice, and she knew it.

The troll shrugged, an action akin to two fat men colliding. "Yeah, well. Better hope so, that's all I'm saying."

Bea glanced up at the high, vaulted ceiling of the Grand Reflection Station. Above her, the General Administration's giant red banners, repeated every few hundred yards, carried their slogans:

"The Teller Cares About You"

"Carelessness Creates Crossed Plots"

"Anti-Narrativists Operate In Thaiana"

"The Redaction Department: Protecting Your Safety"

She shivered, for once not because of the reminder of the Redaction Department. After all, it would be a pretty poor state of affairs if the state weren't interested in your affairs. But listening to the way the troll talked, it sounded almost as if the GenAm didn't know how to stop the Mirrors breaking. Which was ridiculous. The General Administration's whole reason for being was the Mirrors. Of course they knew what to do.

Nevertheless, Bea's grip on the Book tightened until the cover bit into her pudgy fingers. The Book was her way past the checkpoint. With it, she wouldn't have to queue up or face being randomly pulled out of the crowd and questioned.

On the other hand, if the GenAm was nervous, would they be *more* likely to check it...?

Bea was being slowly herded towards the checkpoint, and beyond that freedom and fresh air, or at least what passed for both in Ænathlin. If the fae had ever thought of employing canaries to check the air quality of their city, the little birds would have unionised in a wingbeat. She jumped up and down as she walked, looking for the Indexer she had to hand the Book to, desperate to get rid of it, when something caught her eye.

Ahead of her was one of the now many defunct Mirrors, a black cloth shrouding it from view, and in front of it was a small circle of fae in clean, white suits.

Redactionists.

Redactionists from the Redaction Department, all dressed in brilliant white, glaring beacons illuminating the GenAm's control, its rule... its ire.

The kind of ire that was always, inexorably, inevitably, directed at those who jeopardised the smooth running of the Plots. And the crowd was going to push Bea right past them. In a few moments, she would be standing next to the Redactionists.

Bea's lungs burned, full with unspent air. Physiology is a strange thing. It holds onto life when it thinks it's about to lose it.

The white suits were next to her, talking in hushed urgency.

And then they weren't. Nothing had happened.

Bea breathed again.

She glanced around, worried her sudden fright might have been noticed. But no one was paying her any attention. In fact, everyone else was staring resolutely ahead, carefully ignoring the white suits. Before she knew what she was doing, Bea shifted slightly in the flow of commuters, so she could see over her shoulder. She stumbled a bit, but the Grand was so densely packed she wasn't going to fall.

The white suits were deep in discussion, only the hard set of their shoulders betraying their intensity. One of them, a blonde imp with a stern, pale green face, was tapping her fingers against her hip. She didn't say a word, and yet the other white suits kept glancing at her in the manner of school children who knew that the teacher was in a bad mood and just waiting to share it.

The crowds continued to trundle forward, carefully ignoring the Redactionists' dispute. All but Bea, whose eyes were fixed on the blonde imp. There was an air of grim authority surrounding her, so intense Bea could feel it pulling at her, even from so far away. She shouldn't be staring, but it was impossible to drag her eyes away.

Of course, the Redaction Department would say such behaviour was dangerously similar to that of the Anti-Narrativists.

Coming to her senses, Bea turned back towards the exit, looking for the Indexer. It took her a moment, but eventually, she spotted her. The Indexers, or the grey suits, always gave Bea the impression that if she were to touch them, they would feel cold and clammy. She supposed it was all the time they spent deep below ground in the Indexical Department, sorting and categorising the Books. The GenAm didn't like its Books outside the safety of the Index for long once a Plot was finished.

Bea shoved her way through the crowd.

"Hi, hello, hi. I've got this Book to drop off." She shoved it into the Indexer's hands and turned to leave.

"Wait! Where do you think you're going?"

Bea froze.

"The Book needs to be signed in."

"Ah. Right. Of course." Bea answered, smiling madly. "Everything's here, safe and sound, no need to worry about *that.*" She realised her voice sounded too high and coughed.

"Worry about what?" the Indexer asked over her clipboard.

"Nothing."

The Indexer inspected the Book.

"What's this?" she said, flipping open the cover.

"I can explain—"

"You're just the Plot-watcher. Why isn't the FME handing this in?"

"She had another Plot. But I'm the official Plot-watcher for the story, and—"

The Indexer shut Bea down with a glare and flipped over the sheets of paper on her clipboard in the manner of one who knows that the whole system would fall to pieces if it wasn't for them.

"Sign here."

"Thanks. Um. So another Mirror's gone down?"

"Sign here."

"The Anties are getting worse?"

"Sign here."

"I mean, I hope they catch them all soon, huh? That Robin Goodfellow, who does he think he is? Redact the lot of them, that's what I say! Messing up the stories! Who would do such a thing? Ahaha?"

The Indexer looked at her blankly and then pointed at the paperwork. "Initial here, here and here."

Five minutes later, and all the paperwork was complete. The Indexer laid the Book in a heavy chest, slammed the lid and locked it. Bea felt her shoulders drop, aware suddenly that she'd been holding them tight. She'd done it. She'd handed in the Book, and nothing had happened. It would be sent off to the Index and never seen again. Oh, the Plot would get reused, naturally, but *that* Book was finished.

She'd got away with it—no one would ever know about the wall of thorns, that she'd changed the story, broken the rules. Broken *the* rule.

And then Bea paused. She glanced back to the covered Mirror.

She should get out. She was so nearly free and clear.

But the Mirrors were breaking…

Perhaps this time…

"Are the Plot Department issuing anything?" Bea asked, all good sense incinerated in the white heat of optimism.

"Only Fiction Management Executives can run official Plots. You're just a Plot-watcher."

"I know that, but—"

"If you know that, why are you asking?"

Bea stared at the grey, drab gnome in front of her. "It doesn't matter," she said, cursing herself for her own stupidity. "I was just wondering. Right. Well. Until next time, then."

The Indexer looked puzzled. "Until next time then, what?"

But Bea had already made her escape into the city.

"What do you think she meant?" the Indexer asked, turning around.

A tall figure stepped out of the shadows. He had brown hair and tan skin, the same warm shade as a hunting dog's coat, and was wearing a well-cut suit and a thoughtful expression.

"She was just saying goodbye. It was rhetorical," he answered, knowing from experience not to try to explain. The grey-suited members of the Indexical Department weren't retained because of their understanding of the complexities of social interaction. "Did anything about her strike you as unusual?"

"She didn't sign her name very clearly," the Indexer muttered in a tone that suggested that, of all the strange and quite possibly nefarious actions of the fairy, this was the most serious. She passed the offending paperwork to the man.

"Mmm." He looked up at the covered Mirror and the blonde Redactionist. His eyes narrowed.

He glanced at Bea's receipt.

He blinked.

"Buttercup Snowblossom? That's not actually her name, is it?"

The Indexer sniffed. "It's a fairy name. She calls herself 'Bea'. I had to adjust the filing system."

"Bea…" He looked again at the Redactionist. "Have her brought to the GenAm. Tonight. What kind of person stares at the Redaction Department, I wonder?"

The Indexer looked panicked.

"That was rhetorical too," he sighed.

Chapter Two

Bea, unburdened by the knowledge that someone had finally taken notice of her, walked from the Grand Reflection Station towards the centre of Ænathlin, where the GenAm buildings sat like a headache on the city.

She should have gone straight home, but instead, she'd decided to go to the Contents Department and the Notices board. She'd pick up a short story, nothing like the last one, and she'd do it by the Book.

No more changing the Plot.

It wasn't like she'd set out to break the rules. The changes she'd made were only little ones. Nothing serious, nothing that would derail the story. Just a few small—very *minor* really, when you weighed it up—tweaks here and there to the Plots she'd been watching. Well, at least until the last one. Bea couldn't deny that asking a rose bush to surround a castle was, *perhaps*, more than a little amendment.

But it wasn't like she was an Anti. The Anti-Narrativists' intention was to stop the Plots altogether and cause the Mirrors to break, blocking off all access to Thaiana and destabilising the city. Seen in that context, it was easy to understand why changing the Plots was one of the most serious crimes anyone could commit. But all Bea had tried to do was make the Plot better.

Still, it was unlikely the white-suited Redactionitsts would see the distinction…

The very first time Bea had changed a Plot, it had been so small, and it had seemed so sensible, that the significance of it hadn't registered until long after she'd returned home. When she'd finally put two and two together, she'd fled the city in panic. She'd packed up her meagre possessions, wrapped a thin cloak over her shoulders, and was deep in the forest before she stopped herself.

She'd stood in the darkness, the threat of orcs, ogres and gnarls ever present, and realised she simply couldn't do it. She couldn't run away, not again. She couldn't fail and prove them all right.

Let the Redaction Department come for me, Bea had thought. Better that than slowly falling forwards into her grave, every day watching someone else get their Happy Ever After. Better to be punished for touching the story than to return home and have to explain, have to apologise, have to admit she'd been wrong.

At four in the morning, this kind of thinking always seems logical.

She'd returned to Ænathlin, and for the next week sat in her apartment, eyeing the door, waiting for the Beast to burst through and haul her off to the Redaction Department.

Nothing had happened.

So she'd had to face a completely different truth: no one noticed because no one cared what she did.

It should have ended there.

But she'd got away with it, so she'd done it again. And again. And then just once more because it had worked so well the last time. And before she knew what was happening, she'd taken to adding little touches here and there almost without realising what she was doing. But nothing big. Nothing noticeable, not unless you knew what you were looking for.

At least, not until now.

Bea supposed she should be grateful no one was interested in her.

Not exactly cheered by this thought, she arrived at the General Administration buildings. She darted across the central square, carefully ignoring the Redaction Block in the centre, to where the Notices board stood, hidden in the shadow of the Teller's spire.

There was a crowd around the Notices board. Bea swore under her breath. It was hard enough finding something interesting to watch; with so many others pushing and shoving their way forward, she doubted she'd find anything.

She stood on the edge of the scrum, weighing up her options. It was unusual for so many fae to be picking up Plot-watches. No one liked the tasks, they were underpaid and boring. Hells, Bea only did them because they were supposed to be the best chance of getting recommended to the Academy where the Fiction Management Executives—including the godmothers—were trained.

"I don't know why you're here," said a sweet voice.

Bea felt a great wave of exhaustion overwhelm her. As if her day couldn't get any worse. "I'm looking for a new Plot to watch, just like everyone else," she said, turning to the imp who had appeared next to her.

Carol looked up at Bea. Her golden eyes, bright against her green skin, were flecked with disgust. "Still relying on the Notices? How long has it been now?"

Bea didn't answer.

"Gosh," Carol giggled, "you were here before I began, I know that. I must say, you fairies are persistent, aren't you? You're almost like one of the characters—Believe In Your Dreams, And You Can Achieve Anything!"

Bea clamped her mouth shut. She started to walk away, preferring the crowds surrounding the Notices to the sweet, soft voice of the imp next to her.

"There's nothing for you," Carol announced.

And Bea made the same mistake she always made:

"Says you," she answered, turning back to the imp.

"Why would they give a Plot to you, cabbage mother? None of the grown-up characters believe in fairies. They've got farms and steam engines to run them. Now me, they believe in imps. We're fun. We're pretty. They like that," she finished, smiling smugly.

"Belief's belief," Bea said. She had seen the way Carol shuddered affectedly when she spoke the cruel nickname and hated her even more. "True Love, Rags To Riches. You don't need to be popular to manage a Plot."

She sounded confident enough, but Bea knew Carol had a point. Ænathlin was full, and the Mirrors were breaking; the stories created belief, and belief powered the Mirrors. Without the Mirrors, the fae had no way to support themselves. The land beyond the Sheltering Forest was a useless desert, ruined in the Rhyme War.

Thus, to be a Fiction Management Executive was a great honour—being an FME meant you mattered. And if you were a godmother or a witch, you were directly involved in the Plots, interacting with the characters and everything. But the only way to get into the Academy was to be recommended by an official FME, and so far none had wanted to put a cabbage fairy forward.

"I don't know why you bother," Carol said. "You'd do better to work in the markets, importing plants or whatever you cabbage fairies do. No FME will ever recommend you. Not like me."

Bea's heart sank. "You've been accepted into the Academy?"

"Didn't you hear?"

"Oh. Well. Congratulations."

"Thank you. Of course, *I* could recommend you once I've graduated."

Bea let the kite of hope fly, only for it to be struck by the lightning of Carol's viciousness.

"I won't, of course," the imp said. "It wouldn't exactly help my career to be associated with you, would it? Hah, 'cabbage mother'. I do like that name. I won't have time for these little catch-ups anymore. But I'm glad I got to see you today."

"Yes, I can tell."

"Now, now. Don't be bitter. I only stopped to say hello. Well met." Carol bowed and sauntered away.

Bea looked up at the Notices board, her eyes stinging.

Surely nothing else could go wrong?

Dusk settled like dandruff on the shoulders of the night.

The air in the Indexical Department, so far removed from anything approaching life, was cold and tasted stale. It hung in little clouds whenever the tall, tanned man from the Grand breathed out. Thankfully, he didn't need to go far into the Index. The Books he was looking for weren't important and didn't need to be kept hidden, deep in the cold darkness of the earth.

The Index was quiet—not because of the lateness of the hour, but because it seemed somehow to demand silence. The weight of all the Books, stacked neatly in orderly lines for miles and miles, worked to repress any noise foolish enough to venture down here. It was said only the Indexers could find their way around the maze-like aisles. Once, during the Great Redaction, a group of Anties had apparently tried to break in and steal the Books. The story went that they were still down here somewhere, lost and alone.

The man, his feet tip-tapping softly on the stairs, hated it. He avoided the Index like a gambling addict avoids the tic-tac-tac of the dice table. But, like an addict, he was *always* aware of it: of the pull of the Books, and the darkness, and the silence.

He quickened his pace.

A few Indexers looked up from their cataloguing when they heard him, but when they recognised the colour of his suit, they went back to their tasks with the urgency of a thousand bees making ready to swarm. The Mirrors were breaking.

Without any discernible change in the shelves that surrounded him, he stopped. He focused his senses, turned off the staircase, and walked, slowly now, carefully, down a narrow aisle. Shelves of Books towered over him, making him seem small and insignificant.

He came to an intersection, dimly lit and narrow, more rows of shelf-filled aisles spanning out around him.

He closed his eyes.

Sniff.

He turned left.

He was breathing faster now. Little puffs of his breath were visible in the chill air, escaping him like steam from a funnel, chaining him to the world. He stopped in front of a section of shelving that was in design no different from any other. He ran gentle fingers along the spines of the Books, noting that none of the Plots were particularly complex ones, even allowing for the Teller's enforced simplicity. If he had been so inclined, he might have thought this was luck, but he recognised the reassuring predictability of Narrative Convention.

He reached out well-manicured fingers and, tipping the spine, careful not to damage it, selected a Book. He sat on the floor and began to read. An hour later, he closed it and stared at the shelves opposite. It was clear he had a *lot* to discuss with this Buttercup 'Bea' Snowblossom.

Mistasinon smiled in the darkness. And then he went to find another of the Plots Bea had watched.

Chapter Three

Depressed and without a new Plot to watch, Bea arrived home. She lived in a one-room apartment on the fourth floor of a building that gave the impression time had started demolishing it when it had become clear no one else was going to. It was square, crumbling and carried in its design the nightmares of a thousand bored architectural students.

Bea's home was situated near the wall that surrounded Ænathlin, an area of the city that was considered seedy even by the low standards of the fae. As a result, she found herself stepping over a puddle of what looked like vomit and smelled like pure alcohol to get into the reception.

She walked over to the desk where Ivor, definitely a gnome and technically the building's supervisor, was listlessly flicking marbles into a cracked pint glass. He was as Bea remembered him: hunched over some lonely game, swaddled in a thick woollen coat, collar up and sleeves hanging long over his bony hands.

"Back again?" he asked, disinterested.

"Back again." It seemed pointless to deny it.

"Heh," he snorted, reaching under the desk for her key. "Turned down again?"

"Just give me my key, please."

"You got your rent?"

Bea handed over one of her ration tokens, which Ivor snatched up. He pulled his lips back in what was probably meant to be a smile but instead resembled the rictus grin of a corpse. "Don't know why you bother. They ain't gonna take the likes of you."

"Rags To Riches, Ivor," Bea said, reaching across the desktop to take her key.

"Right, right. And you think you're legit now, do you? Think they'll let you into their little club?" Ivor replied. "You know the Teller, *whocaresaboutus*, don't get me wrong, but he don't like to give us choices."

"Maybe. I don't need a choice, do I?"

"What is it you need then?"

"A chance, Ivor, just a chance."

The gnome stuttered out a laugh. "A drink before you go up?"

He reached into the black hole that seemed to exist under the counter and pulled out a cheap-looking bottle of tobacco-coloured liquid. He popped the cork with the ball of his thumb, not trusting his rotten teeth to manage the task, and waved it at her. The smell that reached Bea made her eyes water in a manner that was both terrifying and deeply tempting.

"What is it?" she asked, already knowing she didn't want an answer.

"Just a drink," Ivor shrugged, passing her the bottle.

"Where's it from?"

"Here."

"Ænathlin?" Bea whistled through her teeth. "Things must be bad."

"Just don't ask me what it's made of. Can't get hold of anything from Thaiana now, s'too expensive. I don't suppose...?"

Bea smiled and reached into her bag. She pulled out a set of playing cards, their edges frayed. "How could I forget you?" she said, handing Ivor the cards. "I took them from a pub while all the background characters were asleep. Mortal gods, I *hate* Plot-watching."

"Least you get out of Ænathlin," Ivor said, flicking through the cards. Bea had long ago given up on him ever thanking her for the games she smuggled in for him. She didn't mind. Ivor gave her somewhere to live at a rent she could afford, and he wasn't a fairy-hater.

"Go on. Drink up," Ivor said, putting the cards away. "Where were you, anyway? Been gone long enough."

"Nowhere, really," Bea gulped, swallowing the burning liquid with the expertise of a sword-swallower—careful not to let it touch the sides. "Just watching a girl sleeping. It was a stupid story. I made—I could have made it much better. If they'd let me."

Ivor grunted, which Bea took for encouragement.

"What I mean is," she said, taking another quick sip, "I know you've gotta pay your dues. But exactly how many dues need to be paid? I work harder than all of them. Just because I wasn't born here, just because of *how* I was born. They all sheem to think I'm stupid." *Sip sip.* "They all act like if I was given a Plot, I'd messh it up before the end of the First Act." *Sip sip.* "I bet I've *watched* more Ploshs than any of them. I bet that's why they won't recommen' me." *Sip sip.* "Because they think, they think I'd be goo tood. They don't want t'be shown up by a cabbage fairy. I *hate* them."

"It's the King and Queen you should hate. Was them that gave up the Chapter to the Teller. Them that gave you fairies a bad name."

"Yeah, but *I* wasn't around then. S'not fair blamin' all of us because of them."

"Time was you'd've gone into Thaiana and done it by yourself," Ivor said mildly, having heard it all before. "That's the trouble nowadays. It's all about them Plots. None of you got no initiative."

"I have," Bea protested. "I just need t'initiate my initiative. I need a'ninitiation. Hah."

Ivor rolled his eyes.

Bea leaned forward on her elbows, slipped and tried again. The alcohol was strong, but, she reasoned as she fumbled another sip, she was stronger. "Tell me a story."

"Go pay a Raconteur."

"Ashhif," Bea snorted. "Can't afford it. Go on. Ish just you an' me."

Ivor took the bottle and pulled on it, enjoying the momentary sense of power. "You ain't worried about the informers? The Beast is out tonight, so I hear. What about your fine career?"

"My career ish about as fine as your eshtablishment."

"Good enough for the likes of you then," Ivor said, not exactly unoffended. "You really wanna hear one?"

 Bea snatched the bottle back. "Yeah. Why not? Like you say, no one'sh botherered with us."

"I said they don't like to give us a choice, not that the white suits won't have us dead-headed," Ivor replied sharply.

"Tell me the one, the one, the one about the girl, only she's underground, but she married him, even tho' she didn't know him, shomethin' like that, and her lover comesh to rescue her, he looksh at her, right, and then she's stuck there because ish cold. No, she makesh the cold? She'sh got a cold…"

"You're drunk, girl."

"'m not," Bea hiccupped.

"Then you're suicidal. No chance I'm telling a tale with the Beast in it on the very same night another Mirror goes down."

Bea thought about arguing or trying to cajole a tale out of him, but suddenly it didn't seem worth it. It was just another disappointment in an already disappointing day. And she liked Ivor, despite his efforts to make himself unlikeable. Why bother upsetting him and frustrating herself?

So instead Bea smiled and bowed with unsteady sarcasm and climbed up to her room, trying not to acknowledge the leaden weight still sitting heavy in her gut, which the alcohol had failed to wash away.

There was an angry knocking at her door.

Bea, groggy and stuck to her table by a pool of drool, tried to frown it into silence without causing her head to explode.

The banging continued, immune to her glares.

Resigning herself to yet another failure, she shuffled over to the door. It didn't have a spyhole and was made of solid wood—but it was thin. She pressed her ear against the splintery surface and listened. She could hear breathing, laboured and straining.

She stood undecided for a moment but figured it didn't sound like the Beast. This was a conclusion based on nothing more than a vague idea of what a three-headed, giant dog-monster might sound like when it was waiting outside one's home.

She inched the door open and peered into the dark hallway.

The next thing she knew, she was being frogmarched down the stairs, through the dirty reception and past Ivor, who sat with an affected interest in his new playing cards when he saw the brown uniform of her assailant.

Bea was dragged over the puddle of 90 per cent proof regurgitation towards a polished black carriage with two kelpi bound in leather bridles and reins, their unshod hooves stamping at the ground in angry impatience. Painted in gold on the side of the coach were the letters 'G. A.'.

"What's going on? I didn't do anything—" Bea cried, but the troll only sneered and pushed her unceremoniously into the carriage. The troll slammed the door, and a moment later the vehicle began to move, knocking Bea backwards onto the small bench, winding her.

The air tasted dusty and... she frowned... of juniper-spirit? As her eyes adjusted to the darkness an entirely different—yet equally unpleasant—notion formed in her mind. She wasn't alone.

In the dark were two brownies. Judging from their uniforms, they worked as morals, managing the kinds of Plots in which, usually, the character learns to be more generous or to love their family. Morals' stories were short and needed frequent repeating to keep the belief up, but even so, they were *official* FMEs. Thus, they were more important than someone who just watched Plots to make sure nothing went wrong during the off-pages.

And, of course, Bea was also a fairy.

She could tell the brownies were thinking exactly the same thing as they looked at her, their faces screwed up like they were swallowing cod liver oil. Bea fought the urge to smooth out her dress. She was not a natural seamstress. She told herself it was because she didn't want to give into stereotype, but the truth was she didn't have the patience. Still, she'd done her best. But now, sitting opposite these two real FMEs in their real uniforms, she wished she'd taken a bit more care over it.

"Er... hello?"

The first brownie's lip curled. "Why have they picked a fairy up? Has there been a mistake?"

"I don't know—" Bea began, but she didn't get very far.

"Mortal gods, you're not an Anti?"

"What? No!" Bea said, shocked.

Anti-Narrativists believed the Teller's stories weren't working, and that it was time for a new Narrator and a new Chapter.

'If,' they said, or rather whispered, 'belief keeps the Mirrors working, and the Teller's Plots are supposed to be the best at making the characters believe, well then. Ipso facto, isn't it? The Mirrors are breaking. So either the belief isn't working, or the stories aren't.'

Which was the normal ebb and flow of a free-thinking society. This was what freedom was about: the freedom to say what you wanted, and then the freedom to explain to the Redaction Department, in any way you liked, exactly *why* you thought you should be allowed to say that.

"I am not an Anti," Bea said, adding for good measure: "The Teller Cares About Us."

"The Teller Cares About Us," chanted the two brownies automatically. It wasn't enough, however, to distract them from their horror at sharing their carriage with Bea.

"So why are they bringing you with us?" the first brownie whined. "You're just a fairy. Not even an FME."

"Don't encourage it, Maeve," the second brownie chided.

"Anyone can be an FME," Bea said. But it was no good.

"Listen to her, Dot," Maeve said. "Where do they find them?"

The brownie identified as Dot inspected Bea over the end of her nose. "Being a Fiction Management Executive is a very important role. The Mirrors are breaking."

"Absolutely," Bea said, "that's exactly why—"

"That's exactly why one has to be recommended," Dot snapped. "The Plot Department doesn't take just anyone. What tribe are you?"

"I'm a garden fairy, but—"

"A garden fairy as an FME? Well. I suppose it takes all sorts." Dot said this in a manner which stated very clearly that, while it may indeed take all sorts to make a world, it was not the kind of world that she, a decent and upstanding citizen, wanted any part of.

Bea fell silent. Ignoring the tightness in her throat, she twitched the heavy curtain on the door aside. There was no point trying to explain. The brownies had already switched her off, chatting happily to each other, not even bothering to make a point of ignoring her.

I'm not even worth being deliberately rude to, Bea thought as she stared unseeing at the narrow, night-time streets of Ænathlin.

Ænathlin was almost beautiful in the orange glow of the oil lamps. The coach had to be nearing the wealthier centre of the city. The lanes were getting wider, and the buildings were more ornate and individual than those by the wall. Even the bars and dragon's dens were cleaner, with names that didn't require the speaker to be over 18 to utter.

The shops were better fronted, too. Some actually had window displays, with Thaianan-made glass in the frames. Once, when all the Mirrors were working, it had been possible to bring through decorative materials like glass, but the Teller had banned such frivolous items long before Bea was born.

The GenAm posters were nicer in the centre, too. Where Bea lived, they were cheap woodcuts, mass-produced by the Contents Department and spread over any available surface. They carried simple slogans: 'The Teller Cares About You', 'Carelessness Creates Crossed Plots', that kind of thing. Here the posters were fewer, but they were also much larger and more beautiful.

Some showed stylised images of the Teller smiling benignly down at his city. Others depicted grossly deformed caricatures of the imp and Anti-Narrativist leader Robin Goodfellow. In these posters, Goodfellow stole food from homes or burned Books, his small face twisted in a spiteful smile. There were also delicately painted scenes from the Teller's Plots, reminding the fae how important his stories were.

There were even some depicting the Beast, the Teller's three-headed, dog-like pet, black blood dripping from its fangs as it clawed at a nameless Anti. The Beast worked with the Redaction Department, sniffing out Anties, delivering them to the white suits to be interrogated and then Redacted. They said there was no escaping the Beast once it had your scent.

All of this was lost on Bea, however. She stared through the little coach window, going over the same old mantra:

Just because I'm a cabbage fairy... One day, they'll see they're wrong...

The carriage sped on, bouncing her up and down. Bea realised suddenly how fast they were moving. Ænathlin was many things, but one thing it was not was easily navigated. Yet now the roads were almost empty, and they were making unnaturally good time.

"It's so quiet," Bea said without thinking.

"Curfew," snapped Dot, "the GenAm's cracking down. The Beast is out."

"The Beast? They've released it?" Bea's attention jerked back to the window, now expecting to see the Beast stalking the streets, its three heads low to the ground as it searched for Anties.

Or those who'd changed the Plots.

"What do you expect?" said Maeve. "Another Mirror broke today. Don't you know anything?"

"Of course, I—"

"Then why act so surprised? The Anties are sabotaging the stories. Without the stories, the Mirrors don't work. Without the Mirrors, the city dies—*we die*. How are we supposed to gather goods, to find food or drink without access to Thaiana? You might as well suggest we farm the wastelands. I can only assume you have something more to offer the blue suits than your keen intellect."

Bea stared at her. "Blue suits? We're going to the Plot Department?"

Maeve rolled her eyes at the stupidity of fairies.

Chapter Four

It was, in fact, to the Contents Department and not the Plot Department that Bea had been led, and where she now remained.

She had been waiting for hours. Only the fact the room was filled to the rafters with other fae kept her from being swept away under waves of anxiety.

She focused on her surroundings. Never having been so far into the GenAm before, Bea wasn't sure what she'd expected. Now she was at long last here, she realised everything was, paradoxically, very busy and yet also mind-achingly dull.

She supposed she had always thought the inner offices of the GenAm would be calm and luxurious, with golden chandeliers and velvet sofas. Instead, she'd found herself being led through a series of dull, beige corridors, and then unceremoniously dumped in this waiting room, a space that was for interior design what the plague was for a healthy complexion.

What *was* interesting, however, were the other occupants.

She tried not to stare, but the room was so full that wherever she looked, she would be watching someone. And, sitting far away from her, was a group that absolutely had Bea's attention: real, actual Fiction Management Executives. And not just any kind of FMEs—godmothers, all dressed in the famous purple uniform with the little cape. They sat in a huddle, gossiping and sharing boiled sweets and, Bea couldn't help noticing, sly nips from a silver hipflask. Needless to say, she hadn't been invited to join them.

Besides the godmothers were other FMEs, including the two brownies Bea had shared the coach with. There were also some misks, who tended to work on young belief and tradition, and a handful of clerks dressed in the dull brown uniform of the Contents Department. Finally, there was a group of elves, probably drunk and certainly loud.

Elves were often pulled in by the GenAm to get them off the streets and away from the trouble that invariably followed them. A lot of the elves were said to be Anties, or at least have sympathy for their cause. They didn't like the boundaries the Teller's Plots placed on them and pined for the older Chapters, when they had been free to do what they wanted.

And yet, even elves were more highly respected than fairies. They were beautiful, elegant creatures with pointed ears and creamy skin, and the characters loved them, believing in them well into adulthood.

Elves helped the Plots. Fairies didn't.

Fairies were the first tribe the characters stopped believing in. And there were too many fairies in the city, or at least that's what everyone said. But most damningly, the King and Queen had loved the fairies.

The thought of the King and Queen brought back an image of the crisp, white-suited blonde Redactionist from the Grand. Bea bit her lip. They'd have had time to read her Book by now…

"I didn't know you were back!" cried a shrill voice, causing the whole room to turn.

Bea looked down. "Well met, Joan. I got back tonight—well, yesterday now."

She smiled at the long face and short, haystack hair of her friend. Bea was used to Joan turning up unexpectedly. After all, tooth fairies were extremely adept at being stealthy, and Joan, as short and small-boned as a child, with her warm cape, well-heeled boots, rope and little bag of crampons, was typical of her kind.

Bea was happy to be surprised by a familiar face, and tried not to notice the way the godmothers were the first to start up their whispered conversation again, shooting them dirty looks.

"Do you know what's going on?" she asked. "I got pulled out of my flat and brought here. What're you doing here?"

"Dropping off the teeth. What do you mean, 'pulled out of your flat'?"

"Oh, I'm sure it's nothing," Bea said airily, managing to convey a lot more certainty than she felt. "I had to share the coach with two FMEs, though."

Joan groaned in sympathy. "Still up in arms?"

"I don't think they'll ever be *down* in arms. It was only a few written requests, you'd think I'd murdered a character. This whole recommendation thing is rotten." Bea thought about Carol. "I'm sure it encourages some very underhand methods. Anyway, so you don't know what's going on?"

"Only that another Mirror broke, but everyone knows that." Joan dropped her voice. "I heard the Beast's been released."

Bea leaned down, so she was level with Joan. "I saw the white suits today at the Grand. I thought for a moment—but there are so many people here. You don't think anyone's in trouble?"

"Why would anyone be in trouble?"

Bea straightened. "No reason. Have you seen any Plotters?"

"Why? You don't think you're going to be invited to meet one?" Joan asked, her eyes widening as realisation dawned.

"I don't know, but listen," Bea said, trying to keep her voice down. "Another Mirror's broken, and they've called all these people in... I reckon they're going to need to get some pretty big stories going to fix the Mirrors, and if they need stories, then they must also need—"

"Fiction Management Executives!"

"Shhhh! Maybe. Possibly," Bea said, worried that if she spoke too loudly, someone might overhear and take it upon themselves to disabuse her of her hope.

"Just imagine!" Joan said. "What story would you choose if you could? Journey of Discovery? Lost and Found? Oooh! Girl Meets Boy Who At First Seems Rude And Arrogant, And Then She Meets Another Boy Who Seems Really Nice But Actually He's Not, And Then The Girl Realises The First Boy Is Really Nice But She Thinks It's Too Late Because He Appears To Have Found Someone Else, But At The Last Minute It Turns Out He Hasn't, And He Actually Loved Her All Along And They Get Married And Live Happily Ever After?"

"Honestly, if I got the chance to be a godmother, I'd take anything. A story where I actually get to *do* something," Bea sighed, encouraged by Joan's enthusiastic grin. "Which do you think is best?"

Joan opened her mouth to answer when a frayed-looking imp in a crumpled brown suit walked in and began to call Bea's name.

Bea jumped up, a blush already sweeping across her face at the dreaded first syllable. "That's me," she admitted.

Bea saw the brown of his suit and tried not to be disappointed. She and Joan had spent hours imagining the types of stories she would one day manage; there was no reason to get upset now, just because she'd thought for a moment she might be about to meet a Plotter.

And the suit wasn't white. *That* was what was important.

The imp spun mechanically on his heel and walked back through a door marked 'Private', assuming Bea would follow.

She looked down at Joan, who gave her a wide smile and waved two crossed fingers. Bea smiled and then followed the imp out of the waiting room and down a long, bustling corridor decorated with the same lack of style as the room she'd just left.

"I thought it would be a bit more glamorous," she said.

"i do not understand" the imp intoned, coming to a halt. He turned around slowly, looking at Bea with a face that, with no emotion to animate it, hung slack. "do you need me to change something"

Bea stared in horror.

The imp in front of her had been Redacted: erased and emptied. Even the green of his skin seemed diluted, like everything about him had been made grey.

She'd seen a few fae dead-headed like this, but always at a distance. Up close, the vacant, foggy eyes of the Redacted were as disconcerting to behold as the blood-spattered scene of a violent murder. Although you couldn't see it, you knew that in this space, not long ago, something barbaric and incomprehensible had occurred.

"Er…no, no thank you. I was just thinking aloud."

"if you would like me to alter the halls i am able to do so"

Bea glanced around at the other brown suits rushing past, carrying their clipboards and piles of paper. No one was paying them any attention, and she'd never actually met a dead-head before.

"Do you… do you know who you are?" Bea asked the imp, watching his face as he listened, looking for any kind of reaction. There was none.

"i am godwyve i work for the teller The Teller Cares About Me"

"Yes. Yes, he does. And, um, do you know who you were?"

Godwyve's eyes remained unfocused, but he spoke a little more slowly when he answered as if the question required great thought.

"i am godwyve yesterday i was godwyve tomorrow i shall be godwyve"

Bea started to ask another question but stopped. He'd been Redacted; there was nothing left of him. She wondered what he'd done to deserve it, and hoped it was more serious than her own misdemeanours.

"That's great," she said, a brittle smile scratching her face. "Thank you for explaining."

"you are welcome now i must bring you to meet mistasinon he is waiting"

"Mistasinon? That's an odd name."

"The Teller Cares About Him."

"Yes, of course. The Teller Cares About Us."

Godwyve led her to a row of four beige chairs. He waved her onto one before walking back down the hallway, presumably to move more people from one thinly upholstered seat to another.

Bea wiggled, trying to find a way to sit that didn't make her realise that, despite its padding, her bottom also consisted of quite a large amount of bone. It wasn't any use. Whoever had designed these chairs had obviously been a very malignant, evil creature—Bea suspected an elf. She sat up and turned around, attempting to rearrange the cushion into a more comfortable shape. It resisted her advances, so she swore at it, loudly and imaginatively.

And so it was that she was found using language best not repeated to berate an innocent chair cushion.

Mistasinon coughed politely.

Bea turned around to see a willowy, dark-haired man with large brown eyes and skin the warm brown of ripe wheat, holding out a slim hand with neat fingernails. His hair was slicked back in a style that was just a bit too tidy, like the unnatural cleanliness of a house after a teenager's party but just *before* their parents come back. He was staring at her from behind a clipboard with a faintly bemused expression.

But Bea, cushion still in hand, was too horrified to notice anything more than the colour of his beautifully cut suit, which was the dark blue of the Plot Department.

Not brown, not grey, not white: *blue.*

She jumped to her feet and held out her hand. "I'm Bea. Just Bea. Bea will do, I mean."

She'd found when faced with clipboards, it was best to introduce herself before the paperwork got a chance. He lifted an eyebrow as thick as her finger and glanced down at his notes. And yet, in a move that instantly guaranteed him her eternal gratitude, he refrained from using her full name.

"Nice to meet you, Bea," he said, taking her hand and shaking it. "I'm Mistasinon. Yes, I know—the first thing we have in common, eh? Let's get on, then. My office is just down here."

Bea followed, making the right kind of noises to the dribs and drabs of conversation the Plotter made, while her mind reeled.

Here was a Plotter, and he was leading her, Bea, to his office. She was going to a Plotter's office!

Chapter Five

When they arrived at his office, Bea began to doubt her excitement.

This Mistasinon had brought her to little more than a box room, cluttered and crowded by Books and filing cabinets. He pulled out a chair for her and then attempted easing himself around both her and his desk, but only managed in difficulting himself into his seat.

"So, I gather you've just finished a story?" he asked, placing his clipboard on the desk, an action akin to the most violent of land-grabs and resulting in several pens being displaced. Bea reached down to rescue them from the asylum of the floor.

"Um, yes," she said, trying to find a place to put the pens. "The heroine had to be woken by True Love's Kiss, so it was my responsibility to make sure she wasn't disturbed before the hero could come."

Mistasinon watched as she tidied up his desk, making both the pens and his empty cup fit around the folders and Books.

"I know the one. It's a long wait, isn't it?"

"Yes."

"How did you pass the time?"

Bea felt a twinge of warning. But, she reasoned, if they knew, she wouldn't be sitting here with a Plotter. Still, better play it safe. "I watched the Plot diligently, making sure nothing untoward happened."

Mistasinon gave her the kind of look that said *'I know the cookie jar's empty, and incidentally you've got chocolate all over your face.'*

Bea replied with a little smile.

"You've been quite prolific since you started with us," Mistasinon said, glancing at his notes.

"Yes. I enjoy working."

"So it seems," he answered, indicating his now tidy desk. "Idle hands write poor verses."

Bea sensed he was laughing at her. She brought her hands up and folded them on the desk in front of her.

"If you say so," she replied coolly.

Mistasinon looked confused for a moment. He closed Bea's folder. "I see from your records you moved here six years ago and have been Plot-watching all that time. Most people do it as a hobby, or as an excuse to get to Thaiana, smuggle in goods—but for you, it seems to have become something of a career. No one has recommended you for a Plot, despite your obvious drive. I wonder why?"

Bea realised he expected an answer. "I think they probably thought I couldn't do it. But I can, I assure you. I can do most things when I set my mind to it."

The Plotter continued to look at her, his large brown eyes still. Bea tried to fill the silence.

"I work very hard. I've done almost all the Plot Types, and certainly all the romances."

"But only Plot-watching?"

"Well, yes—"

"So you've never spoken to a character?"

"…No. But I could. They all want to be in a story."

"And what about you?" Mistasinon asked, but before Bea could answer, he waved the question away. "You were born in the Sheltering Forest?"

"Does that matter?"

"Not to me. Difficult time to try to make it in the big city, though. I also understand that you took matters into your own hands. With the Plot."

Bea froze.

"More than once it seems," Mistasinon continued. "Though the Book you handed to my colleague at the Grand seems to represent your masterwork. Did that particular story require what I can only describe as a wall of thorns?"

Bea could feel the blood draining from her face. She thought about Godwyve and wished she hadn't. He'd read the Book. No one ever read the Books she worked on. They weren't worth it. But he had. What could she do? Could she deny it? No, no, he'd read it. He knew. There was only one thing for it.

Bea swallowed.

"Yes, I think it did," she said, moving from sentence to sentence with the careful hesitancy of an Arctic explorer stepping from drifting ice slab to drifting ice slab. "You see, there was only a very weak Plot holding the heroine... and it's a devil if the wrong person stumbles on her, and I just thought... I just thought it would help the story... which it did, I think..."

"The *stories,* I think, is more accurate," Mistasinon corrected.

Bea understood then that she'd never really thought she'd be caught. The realisation landed like a hundredweight. She'd tried and failed and changing the stories had been her rebellion. She swallowed, her mind racing. She'd changed the Plot. She was going to be Redacted.

"Are you alright?" Mistasinon asked.

"Am I—no, I mean, this is it, isn't it?"

"I'm not sure about that. It doesn't seem to have done any harm. In fact, we need a little more ingenuity."

Bea gaped at him.

"Sorry?"

"Whatever for?"

"I'm not going to be Redacted?"

"Not if I can help it," he said with a smile. "You're not in any trouble. I've been reading good things about you."

"Really?"

"Cross my heart."

"So the, uh, thicket isn't a problem?"

"No. The 'thicket' isn't a problem." He was grinning now.

"Are you sure?"

And then he laughed. "I'm sure I'm not bothered in the least."

Bea stared at him. He knew she'd changed the stories, and he didn't care. Like a painful boil on the side of her nose, she couldn't stop herself from squeezing the situation until it burst.

"Are you really a Plotter?"

"I'm new to the Department, certainly," he said.

"But you know I changed some of my stories? And you're not angry?"

"A little more than some, I think. Anyway, you more adapted them than changed them."

Bea tried to see the trap. But he just smiled at her. Veteran Generals would have clapped Mistasinon on the shoulder and shaken his hand, so good was his technique, and then retired in disgust at how dishonourable war had become.

"You haven't told the white suits?"

"What business is it of theirs?" Mistasinon replied.

It was pretty much the Redaction Department's only business, but Bea decided not to push that line of enquiry any further. "You know, uh, who I am?" she said instead.

"I believe I do, yes."

"And there's nothing that worries you about me?"

He looked at her levelly. "Why should I be worried, Bea?"

"So you know I'm a... garden fairy?" For some reason, she couldn't bring herself to say cabbage fairy.

"I try to make it a point not to judge people. That's the Teller's job, not mine."

"I didn't mean—"

Mistasinon made a dismissive sound and reached across the desk, placing his hand over hers. Bea looked down, startled by the gesture.

"Look," he said, "I can imagine what it's like to be a fairy in this city. And I know how difficult it can be trying to change, to be something else and having everyone looking over your shoulder, waiting for you to foul it up." He squeezed her hand. "I'm not trying to catch you out. I like your ingenuity. I think in the circumstances you did the right thing."

"You do?" Bea asked, conscious of the feel of his hand. She glanced up at his face and was surprised to see he was looking at her with genuine concern. She was used to attracting the interest of others, certainly, but interest in her experience did not equate to kindness.

In fact, there was something about him that didn't add up. Bea had seen Plotters before, at official ceremonies. Like Mistasinon, they'd been dressed in blue, but that was as far as the similarities went. Where the other Plotters had simply been workers in uniform, Mistasinon looked... Bea searched for the right word but couldn't find it, and then realised it wasn't one thing.

Unlike the fae, whose skin, depending on their tribe, tended towards cool tones of colour, Mistasinon's skin was a warm brown, making him look like one of the characters after a day in the sun. The second odd thing about him was his build. He was much taller than any fae tribe Bea knew, but he was slender as an elf. This, coupled with his large brown eyes and heavy eyebrows, gave him an air of fragility that was only enhanced by his shabby office and obviously lowly status.

And yet, his suit was better made than anything Bea was used to seeing. The material must have come through the black market— there couldn't be any Ænathlian shopkeepers with enough influence to import something so beautiful when necessities were so hard to come by.

But for all his unusualness, he was certainly not ugly. The more she looked at him, the more Bea began to suspect he was, in fact, quite attractive.

His hand was still holding hers across the table. This was not how she had imagined her first meeting with the Plot Department would go. She could feel a blush creeping up her neck.

"Well, the story finished, and perhaps we might suggest a thicket for future versions," Mistasinon smiled, answering the question Bea had forgotten she'd asked. He brought his hand back to his lap. Bea fought the urge to flex her fingers.

"So," he continued, "your Books read very highly of you."

And Bea lost the battle against the blush. She wasn't used to being complimented, least of all by the GenAm.

"I'd like to put you on a slightly more involved story," he said, rubbing his neck absently. "As I'm sure you're aware, we're having a few... issues... at the moment. It's vitally important we get the Mirrors running again. So it's all hands on deck, as it were. I don't mean, of course, that we're only advancing you because we're desperate," he added quickly, seeing the look on Bea's face, "but, well—"

"You're desperate?"

"Eager to pursue new avenues." He had the grace to look embarrassed. "You won't be an FME, not as such, but you will have an official Plot to follow, with characters and a Book. If you finish it well, engender some belief, we'll see about sending you through training. Oh yes, it'll be a godmother assignment, only a small one, but I think that's what you said you wanted in your letters? Does that sound alright?"

Bea didn't even need to consider it. She'd been waiting years for this opportunity. And he'd said he was impressed by her. He didn't mind the fact she had revised—ever so slightly—the stories. He said they needed people like her. He wasn't at all what she had expected a Plotter to be like. He was nice, approachable, sympathetic.

He liked her ingenuity.

She liked his eyes.

"What story did you have in mind?" Bea asked in a professional-sounding voice.

"A classic," Mistasinon answered, looking relieved. "It's only a short one, I admit, but there's direct involvement with the heroine—I think you'll be very pleased."

Bea, in fact, wanted to jump for joy but judged the room unable to accommodate it. "Of course, of course. You can count on me!"

"I'm sure. I'll be the one handling you." A look of panic darted across his face. "Um. Not... I don't mean with my hands... Not that there's any reason I wouldn't... Er. I just I mean I'll be looking at, over, *after* you."

They stared at each other.

Mistasinon coughed.

"That is, I'll expect you to report back to me at regular intervals. As you can imagine, it's not usual to have untrained individuals working on a Plot."

"Yes, of course. I understood what you meant," Bea said kindly.

He gave her a grateful smile and then continued, with painful deliberateness, "I've chosen you, Bea, because I think you've got what we need to help save the city. I don't think I have to tell you how important it is that the story finishes well. It's not a difficult Plot, but your main priority is to get some belief coming in—no matter what. Do you understand?"

"Yes, absolutely. 'No matter what'. Got it," Bea said, surprised. She had expected a Plotter to be more precise with their language, but then she remembered the comment about 'handling' her.

"Good!" he said, clapping his hands together. "Go and pick up the Book from the Contents Department. You can begin tomorrow. You should have it wrapped up in a few days, but if there are any problems come straight to me. Don't be shy. It's my job to help you, Bea. And, um…"

"Yes?"

"…Never mind. Just don't be a stranger."

"Oh. No. No, of course not." She stood up to leave. Her hand was on the door handle when she turned around and said, "Thank you."

"You really don't need to thank me," he said, surprised.

"No one else's given me a chance before. And you've not reported me."

"Well, I hope I won't regret it," he replied, smiling at her. "Now, if you'll excuse me…"

Bea nodded and left his office, her thoughts focusing on her first-ever Plot before the door had hit the frame.

This was it, the moment when everything would change.

Chapter Six

While Bea was collecting her Book from the Contents Department, another meeting was unfolding in the characters' world.

Llanotterly was one of the many smaller, semi-independent fiefdoms in Ehinenden, the Third Kingdom of Thaiana. Llanotterly lay in the north-west of Ehinenden, near the mouth of the river Ehi, for which the country was named. The Ehi was a good basis for the name, as in the old language, *Ehine* meant strength and love.

Llanotterly was named after a small local water ferret that, upon hearing of the death of the first King, left the Ehi and travelled to the fledgeling town centre, where it spun around three times before falling down dead. No one was quite sure what the animal's intentions had been, so it was assumed that the event was mysterious and therefore significant. The locals still nodded a respectful hello whenever they saw an otter, causing no end of mirth in the rest of Ehinenden.

Llanotterly had recently been undergoing some significant difficulties, partly due to the growth of The Imperial City of Cerne Bralksteld to the west, and partly due to the death of the old King. Its new ruler was not having a good day. John was, as he would say, manifest with the blue devils and decidedly un-chipperoo.

He pressed his knuckles into the table, crumpling the map that was spread out below his hands. He glared at it, trying to bully it into showing him something other than what he was seeing. It was proving to be annoyingly resistant to intimidation.

"Where're the blighters now?" John asked.

"To the north, m'lord. 'Ere, near the river." Harold, the Overseer, pointed at an area near the top of the map.

John sighed. "Can't we work over that area post-script, as it were? Begin elsewhere?"

Harold was not an unkind man, John knew, but he was a traditionalist. He drew a long whistling breath in past his teeth, shaking his head at the sheer magnitude of what John was asking of him.

"Could do, could do. The only problem, m'lord, is we need access to that water," he said, jabbing the map. "Gotta water the horses and cattle. Need steam t'run the engines."

John rolled his eyes. "Blasted steamers. Be a sight easier if we could just keep on farming and whatnot. World's changing, Harold, and we've got to keep up. I don't mind the idea of change, course not. My cousin went through one once, and now we're all expected to call him DeMenTor and ignore the fact he always wears black, even when it's hot."

John sighed. Sadly, the changes facing Llanotterly were somewhat more dramatic than a dash of lipstick and a summer letting your hair grow.

Llanotterly had survived for hundreds of years through agriculture and farming, but the new steamships were changing everything. The world was getting smaller, and it was almost—not yet, but almost—cheaper to buy imported goods from far away. Especially when cities like Cerne Bralksteld relied on slavery. John was forced to admit that, while obviously being dash unsporting and generally a rum job, slavery certainly guaranteed low production costs.

"Dunno 'bout that, m'lord," Harold said, interrupting his thoughts. "But the men won't like workin' if they're constantly waitin' t'be jumped on by a load of in-ser-gents. We'd hafta pay 'em danger money, on top of the rest."

"How much danger can a gaggle of chits, bounders and chota-wallas actually pose?"

"Couldn't say, m'lord. But a lot of the lads... well, it's their sons and daughters out there or their wives. S'not nice havin' t'go up against family. To be honest, m'lord, it's a bit of a problem," Harold added, winning the prize for understatement.

"What do you suggest, S.?" John asked, glancing into the corner of the room.

Llanotterly's new Adviser detached himself from the shadows and approached the table, bracelets jingling as he stepped into the light.

John had never met a man who wore jewellery before, but this one was a magpie for sparkling metals and precious stones. Rings ran up the shells of his ears and bands jangled around his wrists and ankles, causing him to jingle like a dancer whenever he moved. But it was the golden snake that wound its way around his neck, its head pressed against his collar bone like it was about to sink its teeth in, that really gave John the heebie-jeebies. He had to remind himself it was just a torque every time he saw it, it was so sinister.

On any other man, so much jewellery would have been feminine and out of place. On Seven, his Adviser, it looked both beautiful and extremely male. John didn't know how he managed it. But then he was foreign, something which surely explained a lot about his fashion choices, not least the jewellery. Seven wore gloves, even when he was indoors, and loose, white linen tunics and trousers—something no native of Llanotterly would be caught dead in. He also liked to wear a white silk hood that totally obscured his face.

John could forgive the impractical clothing, but he found the hood to be the height of bad manners. And even though Seven would remove it when John ordered him to, the King couldn't help feeling the other man was resentful. Which was, in fact, also damnably odd.

When John had first ordered Seven to remove his hood, he had been half-expecting some kind of monster to reveal itself. Instead, John had been presented with a pair of knowing, sapphire-blue eyes set in a brown face that might have been sculpted from marble, all framed by a mop of tightly curled hair, so black it was almost blue. Why he wanted to keep himself hidden was anybody's guess.

Still, despite his unusual customs, Seven at least spoke well, his accent as rich as treacle, and he had the air of a gentleman, or at least as John understood the term. Seven conducted himself not with the confidence of the newly wealthy—an arrogance that had to be earned and as such was tainted by the need for consent—but with the absolute assurance that anything he did would be correct simply because he was the one doing it. A *real* gentleman. Not only that, but Seven had so far proven himself to be an extremely good Adviser. John was beginning to wonder how he'd ever managed without him.

"It is difficult, my Lord," Seven said. "The forests number among your most valuable resources. Yet so too do your people. Unfortunately, you need the latter to make use of the former."

"Blast it! What's a fella supposed to do? Only got to meet Cerne Bralksteld's Baron to know that everything they say about him's true. As slippery a devil as I ever met. Can't this lot see I'm trying to keep Llanotterly safe? Why can't they just do what I'm telling them to do?" John said, voicing the question that has plagued rulers, managers and cat owners across time and space.

"They do not understand, my Lord," Seven said. "They are afraid of the threat posed by the Baron and Cerne Bralksteld. They fear that by expanding you bring undue attention onto Llanotterly. They are mistaken. But this is their fear."

John sighed. He knew his Adviser was correct. For years the two other counties of Ehinenden, Marlais and Sausendorf, had done nothing as The Imperial City of Cerne Bralksteld grew larger and more powerful, taking slaves and investing heavily in steam engines and infrastructure.

Now they were beginning to take notice, it was too late.

Cerne Bralksteld to all intents and purposes ruled Caer Marllyn, the county that housed Llanotterly. Marlais and Sausendorf sent half-hearted ambassadorial parties—the political equivalent of going door to door trying to sell religious absolution—and hoped the problem would go away, or at least remain outside their borders.

John, newly enthroned, was worried. Traditionally, as long as Llanotterly kept in line and paid its dues, it was considered a friend of the Baron and left in peace. But how long this arrangement would last once Llanotterly ran out of money—a fate that was perilously close to becoming a reality—John didn't want to find out.

"So what can we do, S.?"

His Adviser ran his gloved hand over the map, tracing the outline of the camp with his fingers, lost in thought. The movement caused the bracelets on his wrist to tinkle softly.

John waited. He had spent his life longing for someone handsome, well-bred and articulate to look up to him, and suddenly, with the arrival of Seven, his wishes had come true. And it was good to feel respected. Not because he was King, because everyone respected *that*, where 'that' was, of course, the crown but not, crucially, the person wearing it.

"My Lord, we must ascertain what it is they want," Seven said at last. "Everyone desires something."

"What they desire? They want the woods! You got fluff in your ears?"

"I am sure they do not require the woods, your Majesty. There is, after all, plenty of wood to go around. Cannot you think of something else that might be motivating them?"

John thought for a minute. "There's a woman. The one that started all this. She'd know what they want, wouldn't she?"

Seven watched the King carefully and, with the kind of controlled casualness normally encountered in high-stakes card games, said: "Oh?"

"Ooh *yes*. She's quite possibly the worst specimen of womanhood. A real stinker, you know the type. Rude, disrespectful, snotty. Always thinks she's right. Nose the size of... of... a really big thing, I don't know," he waved his hand around, searching for a word that would truly capture the majesty of the woman's nasal region. "A cannon! Nose the size of a cannon. And her voice, ye God, her voice. Girl sounds like she's just digested a hedgehog, sans hog and with double helpings of hedge. And she smells. You know, not of flowers or vanilla or the usual…"

The King drifted off for a moment, the expression on his face conceding that, perhaps, smelling clean and natural might just be preferable to smelling like an explosion in a florist's.

Seven interrupted his musings. "If you were to speak with this harridan, encourage her to see the wisdom you so clearly behold, common ground may yet be found."

John looked horrified. "Been at the sauce, S.?"

"At the very least, you may uncover any demands she has for the cessation of her activities."

The King slumped in his chair. He was tired, and now he had to talk to the only person in the whole of Llanotterly who—to his face, at least—showed him no respect? It was too much.

"Blast it all, S. Can't you just tell the girl what's what? Give her her marching orders? 'Off to Penqioa with you' and all that?"

Seven took a deep breath, and, accompanied by his background jingle, knelt by the King. He pulled his hood back and fixed John with a steady gaze.

"Your Highness, please do not let my stupidity cause you to lower your own intellect. Were not you the one who said plans never see completion when founded upon a wish?"

John wasn't entirely sure he remembered saying any such a thing, but he nodded along anyway.

"My Lord, it is my very life's purpose to aid you," Seven continued smoothly, "but you have to trust me. It is of equal import to me as it is for you that this situation is resolved satisfactorily."

John looked into Seven's eyes, now revealed, and felt an unpleasant sensation, not unlike when one stands on the edge of a cliff and some urge from the darkness whispers '*jump*'.

It's something to do with his eyes, John thought. *There's something there that pushes back, somehow.* For just a moment, John was certain he was looking into eyes that were blue from lid to lash, as cold and obdurate as the end of time. His eyes began to water, straining to see what couldn't possibly be there.

Seven blinked. "My Lord?"

And then his eyes were just eyes. Admittedly, they were still lined with the strange black kohl he insisted on wearing, but otherwise, they were normal and full of the respect and admiration John had spent his whole life longing for.

"'Xcuse me, gentlemen," Harold interrupted, raising his hand with all the enthusiasm of a lingerie salesman at a nunnery, "but there's still the issue of finances. It's cost a packet keepin' them men on, and we're behind now."

Seven stood. "I see. And when exactly were you planning on sharing this piece of fiscal information?"

Harold, who was watching both men with the kind of intensity often reserved for those with the power to see you hang, did not miss the look that passed across the Adviser's face as he pulled his hood back over his head.

"Um... now?" Harold said, looking for all the world like he would rather be anywhere else.

"Now, now, S.," John said, "can't shoot the messenger. Seems we'll have to put the girl on the back burner. Focus on money matters."

Seven paused and then turned back to the King.

"Lord, what about the Ball you plan to host, in order that you might attract investment? Were you not this very morning considering using it as a means to broker an agreement with the insurgents? Of course, at the time, I could not understand your brilliance and foresight. Now I am agog at your mastery of thought and action."

John smiled, pleased with himself. "Ah yes, jolly good memory, S. So much on my plate I'd forgotten that one. So... the Ball, eh? Don't suppose you can remember exactly what I said...?"

Seven bowed low and, it couldn't be denied, elegantly. He'd promised to teach John exactly how it was done.

"As fortune would have it, my Lord, I can..."

Chapter Seven

The cottage was almost sickeningly adorable.

It nestled into the garden as happily as a warm cup of tea in a pair of chilly hands. Roses climbed the honey-coloured walls and twisted around the stable door and over the charmingly mismatched windows. A crooked chimney stuck up merrily from the thatch, and, judging from the smell drifting out of the open window, a cake had been baked in the not-too-distant past.

Bea, however, was not in the right frame of mind to enjoy the twee prettiness in front of her. She had woken early to get started on her Plot. Today was the introduction, and introductions were important. The girl had to meet the boy in an equal setting—if they met any other way there'd always be a question about whether it was True Love or a more financially motivated desire that awakened the passions.

It was also very important that the heroine got to see the hero being, well, heroic.

He couldn't just introduce himself and start a conversation about the weather. He had to do something to impress her, and Bea, eager to get off to a good start, had spent hours setting up an introduction that would guarantee a Happy Ending. Now she just had to get the girl out of the house and into place. She put her hand on the strap of her bag, making sure yet again that she could feel the weight of the Book inside it, set her shoulders and steeled her nerves.

She ran through the garden in a crouching, hopping sprint as she fought to a) not be seen by the girl, b) get to the safety of the back of the cottage as quickly as possible, and c) not fall over her skirts and land in the pigsty. The course of True Love was certainly circuitous.

She peered through the cottage window and was relieved to see her heroine still at home. The girl was young, with shoulder-length, ash blonde hair and the kind of figure most men would gladly go to war for. She was, of course, singing to herself as she swept the floor.

Bea slipped away from the window and snuck around to the back of the cottage and the kitchen door. Now she just needed to get the heroine out of the house. According to the Plot, the girl was supposed to buy some fruit to bake a cake. Bea peered in at the window. The fruit bowl was empty, and cooling on the table, quietly mocking her, was a rich, brown cake.

The problem was that the Plot said it had to be the necessity of baking a cake that called the heroine out of her house and into the path of the hero. But Bea had taken too long setting up, and now the cake was baked. She bit her thumbnail, weighing up her options.

The thing she should do was go back, admit she'd missed the cue and try to convince Mistasinon to give her another go. The thing she should absolutely not do was go into the cottage, rummage around the heroine's drawers and cupboards, looking for a way to re-engineer a meeting.

Bea gave the conundrum due care and deliberation for all of three seconds before opening the kitchen door and sidling into the heroine's house.

She tiptoed over to the cupboards and quietly opened them one by one, looking for anything that might help. In the end, it was an absence of something that gave her an idea. She padded over to the cake and knocked it off the table, so hard it landed with a crash. She dashed out of the kitchen and ducked under the open window, her heart pounding. It was a risk. The heroine might just give the whole thing up as a bad job. But she had to try.

Bea heard footsteps, closed her eyes and hoped for the best.

"Oh... *poot!*" exclaimed the voice of the heroine. "It took me hours to bake that cake! I suppose I'll have to make another before they all get home, which means I'll have to go out again. Isn't that just the most rotten luck?"

Bea heaved a sigh of relief. And then froze when she heard another voice. A man's voice.

"You're the best cook I know, Sindy. Can't you do something with this one?"

Bea felt a tingle in her chest. There wasn't supposed to be a man in the house. What was going on? She delved into the Book to check the Plot, quickly thumbing through the pages. The heroine's voice drifted out from the kitchen.

"No, no. It's ruined. Look, it's got bits of broken plate in it. And I daren't not have one, not on *her* birthday," Sindy said darkly. Or as darkly as she was able.

"No, I suppose not," came the man's voice again.

The pages of the Book turned furiously as Bea skimmed through it. It was no help. There was definitely not meant to be a man here. The tingle in Bea's chest started to sting. She closed the Book and put it carefully back in her bag. So... the cake was already baked. And there was a man. But she could manage, couldn't she? She had ingenuity. She'd seen hundreds of these stories.

Bea started chewing her nails.

This was her chance.

Once the girl met the hero, it would all work out.

True Love couldn't be denied.

"Would you mind finishing tidying up for me?" Sindy said. "I'll have to pick up some more flour from the miller. It shouldn't take me long, but...."

"Don't be daft, Sindy, of course I'll help. I'd always help you, you're... we're friends, after all."

"Oh, yes! Thank you! I'll be back soon, I promise."

The girl might have missed the telltale note in the intruding man's voice, but Bea hadn't. Something was very wrong here. This man, whoever he was, spoke to the heroine in a way that he definitely shouldn't. *That* tone was reserved for the hero, and him alone.

Bea's panic was interrupted by Sindy dashing out through the door, basket in hand, and into the woods. She gave up trying to work it out and ran after her heroine.

An hour later, Bea traipsed behind Sindy as she skipped through the forest on her way back from the miller. A less experienced person might have raised a few questions regarding the health and safety implications of prancing through an environment almost

F. D. Lee

solely designed to trip one up. But Bea knew about heroines even if she'd never had personal dealings with one.

She'd come to the conclusion that one of the lesser-known attributes of heroines was an extremely adept sense of balance. Possibly it was genetic—a well-honed inner ear or particularly wide toes. Either way, she wasn't surprised to find herself puffing through the woods as quietly as she could in her patchwork dress, trying to keep the girl in sight whilst not, and here was the tricky bit, actually revealing herself.

According to the Plot, the hero and Sindy would meet in the forest, the hero rescuing Sindy from some kind of mild peril. They would share a tender moment and part, to be reunited in the Second Act.

Bea had set it up that morning, although she'd had to be quite ingenious. Normally a troll would be contracted in, but there was no way she was going to risk the GenAm attributing her success to someone else. It had taken some doing, but she felt confident she had a pretty special danger for the hero to save the heroine from. One that she would be able to take full credit for.

There was nothing to worry about. Of course, the addition of an unknown male character wasn't an ideal beginning to her first-ever Plot, but Bea had by now convinced herself that it wouldn't matter in the end. Sindy would Fall In Love the minute she met the hero, and any amount of second cakes and mystery men would be forgotten.

In fact, nothing really had gone wrong, had it? The heroine was on her way to meet her hero, just like the Plot demanded. All Bea had to do now was observe and perhaps gather a few key details to use later, when she would officially meet the heroine before the Ball.

The sound of hoof-beats clip-clopped across Bea's inner monologue.

This was it.

Bea gathered up her skirts and settled behind the nearest bush to watch the story begin.

Sindy paused to pick some flowers, humming to herself. She looked, Bea was pleased to see, absolutely beautiful. The sun was floating through the leaves in ribbons, catching her golden hair and making it shine. Birds sang sweetly, and little rabbits hopped around the glade. It was perfect.

Bea took a deep breath. There was nothing she could do now but watch…

One day, as the fair maiden walked through the forest, she was chanced upon by a tall, handsome stranger. He rode a white stallion, the dappled sunlight catching in his hair. The maid gazed into his clear blue eyes and realised she had never before seen such a man. It was love at first sight.

…or at least, that was what was supposed to happen. What actually happened was this:

Bea, from her vantage point, saw the handsome King ride ever closer to the glade in which Sindy so charmingly stood, his stallion prancing beneath him. He looked magnificent. Bea smiled. She'd always known she could do this. She didn't know why she'd been so nervous. In just a few moments, the King would burst forth and see Sindy looking beautiful. They'd walk a spell, trip the trap Bea had laid, he'd save her in a dashing fashion, and they'd Fall In Love.

Bea covered her mouth to stop herself squealing with excitement.

Everything was going perfectly.

And then it all went wrong.

"My lord," called a voice from somewhere behind the King. It was a voice more musical than even the most talented elf, softer than the most seductive adhene, more convincing than the most persuasive imp. The trouble was not the voice. The trouble was what it said next:

"We appear to be headed in the wrong direction. The camp is far east of here."

Bea watched helplessly as the King pulled his horse up and turned back the way he had come, away from Sindy and his destiny. Sindy finished picking flowers, took her bag of flour and walked off in the opposite direction, back to her house.

Bea swore. She didn't know what to do, but she had to do something. She watched Sindy disappearing into the forest and made a choice.

She swept up her bag and ran after the King. She had no idea what she would do when she found him, but she'd cross that bridge when she came to it. The most important thing right now was to get the introduction back on-Plot. And, she added, to find out who had ruined it in the first place.

It didn't take Bea long to catch up with her hero. He was sitting astride his horse, talking to a tall, broad-shouldered man who was holding a map and wearing a hood that completely obscured his face. She ducked behind a tree and listened.

"Look here old bean, the map clearly states the damnable thing is here," the King said, leaning over his horse's neck to indicate a point on the map.

"Indeed, Sire, you are correct. We, however, are here," the hooded man said patiently.

"What's that? We can't be there, S. We left the castle out of the north gate. We're here, blast it."

Bea bit her lip. Her whole Plot was being jeopardised because neither one could read a map? If it wasn't so horrendous, she'd laugh.

"Sire," the hood sighed, "I assure you we are moving in the wrong direction. Her house is… yes, her house is about a mile in that direction, but if we are *here,* the encampment must surely be *here*."

Bea continued her attack against her lower lip. Things were really going wrong now. She should go straight back to the GenAm and report everything that had happened to Mistasinon. It would be alright. He'd give her a new Plot to work on, surely? The GenAm needed the stories running. She should do the right thing.

But…

He *might* not put her on another Plot. If the stories were so desperately needed, maybe he wouldn't risk her fouling up another. Especially if she couldn't even get the introduction right. The introduction, for mortal gods' sake. It practically told itself.

She could fix it.

No one would ever know.

'*No matter what*'. That's what Mistasinon had said.

Bea stepped out from behind the tree.

"Um. Hello."

The two men looked up.

Bea managed a smile. It was absolutely imperative to the Plot that she, as the godmother, didn't meet the King. She needed to play this very carefully.

"What what? You alright there, gel?"

Bea's smile froze. It suddenly occurred to her she had no idea how to talk to the characters.

"Er. Marry. I wish ye good morrow? Lawks."

The two men stared.

"Ah? Well. Good morrow to you, too," the King said.

"I have come, cometh, to this place, here, I mean, to make merry…er…" Bea faltered as her brain pointed out that her mouth had just said 'make merry', "…make merry, that is, with the, um, the tidings. Merry tidings. I am hererereth"—that didn't sound right—"to guide you, for I am a humble…woodcutter, going about my humble wood cutting, here in these humble woods." That was better.

The King smiled at her. The other man, the one in the hood, cocked his head in a way that made Bea relieved she couldn't see his face. For some reason, she had the feeling his expression, hidden behind his cowl, was not a friendly one.

"Gosh. That is a bit of luck. Me and my Ad—"

"*John,*" the hooded man said, a note of warning in his voice.

"Ah, yes, right-ho. Nearly had cats everywhere! My friend and I appear to have got turned around. You don't know where the traitors' camp is, do you?"

Out of the corner of her eye, Bea saw the hooded man drop his face into his hand.

"The traitors' camp?" she asked, and then, remembering herself, added, "oodalally."

"Oh right, no, no, sorry. I meant the rebels' camp, of course. Good old rebels, what? Voice of the people, etcetera."

Bea, a person for whom the phrase 'impulsive' was too well thought out, was tempted to ask what he meant, but she was too preoccupied with her Plot.

"Yea, there's a house, um, just down that way, I faith. You could ask there. That's what I'd do. If I were lost. Ask at a nearby house.

Marry." She'd better get the hero and the heroine together quickly, she was running out of words.

The King turned to the hooded man, who was standing with his arms folded.

"What say you, S.?"

"Had not you intended your visit to be conducted with the minimal amount of notice possible?" he replied. "It is troublesome enough to have met with this 'woodcutter'."

"It's only just a little way," Bea said, noting the way the hooded man said woodcutter and not liking it one bit. "I knoweth the maiden who liveth thereth. She's very, sorry, verily pretty. And she can sing and cook. You're bound to like her."

"Well... that's... spiffing," John said, clearly not up to speed on why singing and cooking made her better able to give him directions. "Now, S., I don't see what harm it'll do to go find this cottage and sort this whole mess out. I am the K—that is, I am the one with the map, and so I think it's down to me to call the shots."

The hooded man stood silent.

Bea held her breath.

And then he nodded.

"Jolly good," John smiled. "Lead on then, miss."

Bea couldn't believe it!

She'd done it!

And they all said fairies couldn't do anything more important than tidy houses or pick up teeth! Well, this just showed them—

"Madam, if it *verily* pleases you," the hooded man said, picking up the reins of his horse and leading it by hand.

"Oh, yes, sorry."

Bea started towards Sindy's house. The hooded man walked next to her, keeping a distance between her and the King. Bea found herself wondering if he wasn't some kind of bodyguard. There was something about the way he moved that seemed to suggest he was wary of her, like he thought she was suddenly going to assassinate her hero.

Well, when he saw that she was leading the King to his rightful destiny, he'd have to swallow his words. Though he hadn't actually said very much to her. Well, he was certainly thinking some pretty unkind things, if his body language was any clue. She supposed she shouldn't let it upset her. She only wished that, just once, someone might not instantly assume she didn't know what she was doing.

"I suspect you know very well what you are doing. Therein lies the problem," the hooded man said.

"Excuse me?"

The hood snorted and then muttered something in a language Bea didn't recognise.

"Oh yes, very brave. Why not say it so I can understand it?" Bea snapped, forgetting her role as a humble woodcutter.

The hood turned to face her. "Happily. I—"

A scream filled the forest.

"Mortal gods!" Bea cried out, breaking into a run. "The bear!"

"The bear?" the hooded man said. But Bea was already running ahead, her feet pounding against the leafy carpet of the forest.

She'd forgotten about the bear. The bear she'd set up to frighten Sindy, the one that John was supposed to save her from. The one which she'd secured with a rope and a clockwork release, the trigger of which Sindy must have stepped on. The very same bear she'd decided to use because she didn't want to get in a troll and risk sharing her success.

Another scream rang out.

Tears stung Bea's eyes as she ran. She hurtled through the forest, the trees blocking her like prison bars, causing her to slide and stumble. The ground began to climb, and Bea to slow.

She wasn't going to make it in time…

And then suddenly John was overtaking her, his stallion churning up the ground as it galloped.

Bea pushed forward as another scream filled the forest and then, abruptly, cut off. Still running, she grabbed a large, heavy stick and charged over the brow of the hill.

John was on his horse, his sword half out of its scabbard, about to face down the bear, Sindy on the ground next to him. The bear was standing on its hind legs, its great paws raised to swipe, its claws long and sharp.

John's horse, panicked, was mid-buck. There was no way he would be able to keep his seat, not with his right hand freeing his sword and only his left to hold the reins. The two characters didn't stand a chance against the creature.

Except they were all frozen, mid-action, like statues.

Chapter Eight

It was the strangest thing Bea had ever seen. She reached out and touched Sindy's nose, which was so cold her finger tingled with the contact.

"I know not what you imagined you might achieve with that stick."

Bea spun round, bringing her branch up. The hooded man stepped out from behind a tree, his left hand pressing tight on his stomach as if he were trying to avoid being sick.

"I was going to save them," Bea said. "Obviously. But when I got here, they were like this."

"You appear to have misplaced your accent. I trust you will make no great effort to locate it?"

Bea coughed. "Yes. Well. Do you know what's happened to them?"

The hooded man leaned against the tree. He seemed unsteady on his feet. Bea was about to ask him if he was feeling alright when he said, "the more pertinent question is how such a creature came to be in the forest, bound and ready to attack."

Bea looked around the clearing, but there was no help to be found.

"I note with interest that it appears to have consumed a mixture of datura stramonium," the hooded man continued. Bea was really beginning to hate the sound of his voice, melodic as it was.

"Oh, well, you know what bears are like. They'll eat anything."

"Indeed. They are voracious. Though I admit I had not, before this moment, known one to travel across the Shared Sea in order to find a plant that grows only in Sal Dorma. And yet even this does not represent the most intriguing aspect of this mystery."

"It doesn't?" Bea said weakly.

"No. For such a culinary beast, I am shocked it did not know that datura stramonium, if not diluted with milk, is an extremely potent hallucinogenic."

"Oh."

"I would imagine the poor creature was ill-prepared to be woken by a skipping blonde with flowers entwined in her hair."

"Oh."

"Such things are, I am given to understand, the cause of far-reaching psychological trauma. It is a wonder no one was killed."

"Fine, alright," Bea said. She looked again at the frozen characters. "Are they alright?"

"They are perfectly safe," he answered, stepping carefully away from the tree. "You are from the General Administration, are you not? This is how they manage their affairs now?"

"You're not a character? Wait. Were you sent here to check up on me?"

"I am not. I was not."

Bea sighed with relief. "Ah. You must have misread your Book. Still, I'm glad you were here. So how'd you freeze them?"

"Magic."

"Magic can't do that. It's not strong enough. Everyone knows that. Anyway, the Teller, *whocaresaboutus*, banned magic. I've never seen anything like this before. You're sure they're alright?"

The hood turned to John, still fixed like a statue. "They will survive what I have done. Would you be able to claim the same?"

Bea opened her mouth to answer, and realised he was bloody well right, wasn't he? If he hadn't done whatever it was he'd done, she almost certainly would have killed her characters. She felt a sudden stab of guilt.

"And what would your Plotter say if he knew you'd done that?" Bea snapped, waving her arm at the tableau.

"I beg your pardon?"

"In fact, if you hadn't interfered in the first place, none of this would have happened anyway."

The hood stared at her.

"I suppose it's not entirely your fault," Bea relented. "And you did help, so, you know. Thanks. But clearly, there's been a mistake."

"The General Administration is wont to make mistakes," he replied, the shadow of his face, hidden by his hood, paying her very close attention.

"Yes, well... sometimes, maybe," Bea said, uncertainty creeping into her voice. "So, I guess you'd better unfreeze them and then I'll sort out the introduction. Really, what have you done to them?"

"Magic, as I have told you." The hooded man stepped further into the clearing. He still moved carefully, but he seemed to be recovering from whatever sickness had overcome him.

"Why exactly are you here?" Bea asked.

He stopped, staring at her until she began to feel very uncomfortable. Bea put her hands on her hips, steeling herself for what she was certain was going to be some kind of tirade. Instead, when he spoke his voice was gentle and conciliatory, slipping past her defences like greased silk.

"I am here to help these people," he said. "Perhaps I may also be of assistance to you. Would you not rather leave all this to me? Would you not prefer to be far from all this, somewhere quiet, where there is no call to struggle so? Maybe... with your family, your mother and your brother? Away from all the hatred and anger and fear? Are you not tired of running?"

Bea realised she was. Why couldn't she go home? What would they say, really? So she'd run away, and since then everything had gone wrong... There was nothing for her in the city. What was it about her that always insisted on pushing forward?

She pinched the bridge of her nose.

Something wasn't right.

"Who *are* you?"

"You do not behave like one of them," he said, dodging her question. "You are not in uniform—or perhaps the costume has changed?"

"I—they're making my uniform," Bea lied. She'd asked for a uniform, but the Contents Department had refused. She still wasn't really a godmother. Not yet, anyway.

"What did you say your role was again?" Bea tried. It was getting harder for her to ignore the possibility that this person might not, in fact, be another FME. Which left only one other alternative, something Bea wasn't prepared to acknowledge. It would be too awful—her first-ever Plot...

No, mortal gods damn it, whoever he was, he wasn't going to take it away from her. She'd work it out later. Right now, she had to protect what was hers.

Bea stepped between him and the King.

"Exactly why are you here with *my* characters?"

"Your 'characters'? You are certainly one of the General Administration, uniform or no."

"What in the worlds are you talking about?"

The hooded man closed the space between them. Every muscle in Bea's body told her to run, but she couldn't stop staring at him. She had often encountered what she would have thought, before this moment, to be disgust. She now realised that the way the other fae treated her was, in fact, very low on the spectrum of abhorrence.

"You wish for transparency?" he said, each word like chipped ice. "Very well. I neither condone nor tolerate your presence here. You are abhorrent, a vile, sour little fairy, living vicariously through those who know no better."

"Riiiight. I see." Bea almost felt relieved. At least she knew where she stood with fairy-haters. "Well, you're not anything special, you know? You all think you're so great just because the characters believe in you for longer—but you know what, they stop believing in all of us, sooner or later."

The hooded fae seemed confused. Whatever it was, he shook it off, walked over to the King and began untangling him from his horse. "This is only the beginning," he said, lifting the King with a grunt.

"What do you mean 'this is only the beginning'?" Bea said.

He turned to her.

"Let me gift you with some advice. Resign your post. You are not welcome here."

"What? No! This is my story!"

"We shall see." He held up his gloved hand and snapped his fingers.

Sindy screamed.

Chapter Nine

"What about the bear?" Joan asked, her seemingly mild words masking the desire for high drama that her tone conveyed.

Bea ran a finger around the rim of her wine glass. She'd arrived home and immediately sent a tompte with an urgent message for her friends to come around. They were now sat at the small table in what might, by a particularly unscrupulous liar, be called her kitchen.

"He didn't wake the bear up. He was there with the hero over his shoulder, clicked his fingers and disappeared, and then the heroine was screaming. So I thumped her on the back of the head and carried her home. Oh, don't look at me like that," Bea said, trying not to sound guilty.

It is perhaps worth noting that there are many expressions of horror available to a face blessed with forty-two muscles, and Bea was experiencing two of them. Joan's was skating in the grey area between disbelief and excitement. Melly's, on the other hand, had more of a classic air about it, with accents of dismay and shock.

"I can't believe you did that," tutted Melly, an elf by tribe and a witch by trade, between pulls on her cigarette.

She smoked voraciously, although Bea was pretty certain she didn't actually enjoy it. She'd told Bea once it was expected of a villain, along with the black dresses and the penchant for red wine and evil laughter. When they'd first met, Melly had worn green face paint, but it had made her skin itch, and after a while, she'd given up. That was when she'd started smoking.

There was also the crown. For someone who went to such great lengths to look witchy, Bea had never understood why Melly wore it. The crown was small, ornate and antlered, the startling white of the polished bone softened by silver and mother-of-pearl, though not enough to detract from the fact that the ends of the antlers were viciously sharp. She said it was a gift, though from whom Bea had no idea.

Witching wasn't a traditional job for an elf. They were too vain and, often, too feckless for such a demanding position. But Melly had been doing it for years—longer than Bea had known her—and she was obviously good at it since the GenAm didn't seem to put any demands on her, even with the Mirrors breaking.

"Well, honestly, I can't believe that's all you did," said Joan.

"What should I have done, then?" Bea asked and immediately regretted it. Joan had a very active imagination and a love of mysteries. The little tooth fairy tended to see everything in terms of a crime scene.

"Well," Joan began, taking a deep breath. Bea caught Melly's eye and tried not to laugh. "Firstly, right, I think you should have tackled this hooded man. Suspicious, wearing a hood. Shows he's hiding something, doesn't it?"

"Well… yes. I guess so. But he pretty much admitted that he didn't want me on the story. Not much hiding there."

Joan waved the comment away. She was in full flow now and wasn't going to be pegged in by boring little things like what actually happened. "Fine, fine, fine. So, firstly, I'd have tied him to a chair—"

"Were there any chairs in the forest?" Melly asked casually.

"Not many," Bea admitted, trying not to grin.

"Oh, for goodness' sake," Joan said, glaring at them. "Alright then. To a tree. Yes. I'd have tied him to a tree and then begun the interrogation. I don't suppose you had any thumbscrews on you? Or some kind of torch? Torches always work well for questioning," Joan said with all the authority of an overactive imagination. "You can shine the light in their eyes, and they get so nervous they give up on the whole thing. Of course, you need to be careful you don't singe their hair. Did you really not get a chance to see his face?"

"No," Bea answered miserably.

"You didn't get anything out of him at all?"

"Only what I've told you. He said he used magic, which is nonsense. If we had magic like that, we wouldn't need the Mirrors. Oh, and he spoke really strangely."

Melly frowned. "What do you mean?"

Bea thought about what she meant. Now she had to, it was hard to explain.

"I guess… He sounded like he'd been dead for hundreds of years. The way he spoke, his sentences were all backwards. 'Have not you descended the staircase', that kind of thing. And he had this accent, it was lovely. I mean, if you didn't actually listen to what he was saying, his words sounded wonderful. Like he was talking directly to you."

"But weren't you the only one there?" Joan asked, puzzled.

"I don't know, it's hard to explain. It just seemed like he knew all this… this stuff."

"Stuff? You're not being a very good witness, Bea. What did he say?"

"Oh, nothing really. I can't remember now."

Joan rolled her eyes, obviously giving up on Bea for any answers. She turned instead to Melly, who was staring up at the ceiling, her expression clouded. "What do you think?"

Melly pulled her attention back to Joan and Bea. "He's an Anti," she said simply. "He'll have to be reported. Better he meets the white suits than you."

"She's right there, Bea," Joan said. "Why haven't you given the whole thing over to the GenAm? You didn't mention Mehta— Mitas—your Plotter. You have told him about this, haven't you?"

"Mistasinon. And it's complicated," Bea said in the convincing tone of someone who knew it wasn't.

"Exactly how is it 'complicated'?" Melly asked.

Bea glared at Melly across the little table. If looks could kill, Joan would have had her very first, real-life crime scene to investigate.

"You said it, not me," Melly said, drawing on her cigarette for emphasis. The effect was ruined somewhat by her squinting through the smoke.

Bea shuffled in her seat. "You're just assuming he's an Anti, but he quite clearly said he *didn't* want to stop the story. He's just another fairy-hater. I can deal with one of those by myself, I don't need the GenAm."

Melly nearly choked. "You're seriously considering not reporting all this?"

Bea wanted to say, '*Of course I know I should involve the GenAm. But then they'd take the story from me, and maybe I'd get a new one, but probably I wouldn't. And I'd have to tell Mistasinon I wasn't able to finish the 'simple' Plot he gave me. And all the other FMEs would know I'd failed before I'd even begun'.*

But instead, she said, "I don't think there's anything to report."

The witch stubbed her cigarette out. "They don't mess around anymore. I've heard the Beast is out every night."

"Well, that's true enough, but the Beast wouldn't be called out for a simple mix-up," Joan said. She looked at the expression on her friends' faces. "Would it?"

"Not if she reports it now," Melly replied, her eyes fixed on Bea.

"If I report it, I'll lose my story!" Bea shouted, frustration overwhelming her. "Look. It's a short story," she continued, aiming for calm but landing in patronising. "Ball, Kiss, Happily Ever After. Easy. Anyway, I've got to finish it, no matter what."

"No matter what?" Melly parroted. "And does 'no matter what' include engaging with an Anti? Does 'no matter what' include being Redacted?"

Bea ran her hands over her face. "No, of course not. But I'm not giving up my Plot. Not for a little hiccup."

"But if he is an Anti, it isn't really a hiccup," Joan said. "We're worried about you, that's all."

"Yes, but he's not an Anti, is he? He didn't actually do anything wrong," Bea answered slowly, testing the idea. "He just said that I was to drop it."

"Oh, right," Melly snorted, letting her beautiful face crease. "Because he didn't suddenly launch into the Anti-Narrativists' manifesto he's somehow legitimate?"

"I only mean that you're assuming he's on the other side, which, really, is a bit of a jump. Why would an Anti even bother with this Plot? It's tiny."

"He used magic," Melly said.

"He said it was magic," Bea countered quickly, "but obviously it must have been some kind of drug, like the one I used."

"So you admit he lied?" Melly said triumphantly.

"Look, I'm not defending him, I'm just saying there's no reason to go jumping to conclusions."

"To be fair, Bea, you did say he threatened you," Joan said, taking a sip of her beer, ignoring the rising tension. When you grew up in a house full of sisters, you learned not to pay attention to disagreements, no matter how serious.

"He...well, I mean, that could be open to interpretation."

The witch and the tooth fairy shared what only could only be described as a Look. Bea began a detailed study of her tabletop.

Melly broke the silence.

"Mortal gods. You're serious, aren't you? You're actually not going to report him. The Beast will be the least of your problems. They'll get the white suits involved, mark my words. Why are you being so stubborn?"

"I'm not being stubborn—it's just the thought of all those bitter-faced FMEs, whispering about me, about how they'd always said I couldn't do it. I came all this way, I left everything behind, and now it's almost going to have been worth it. Can't you understand? The Beast won't be called out, not if I get everything back on track. It's only the introduction. And anyway, Mistasinon said he wanted me to use my initiative."

"This is madness, Bea," Melly said. "There has to be a moment when you accept that some things just aren't meant to—"

"Wait! Wait!" Joan cried, "the Plotter! Blue suit! You can talk to him!"

Bea looked at Joan like she'd suddenly taken up shark wrestling. "Haven't you been listening?"

"I'm not saying you should tell him everything. Only, well, it seems like your main point is that this hooded man could maybe *not* be an Anti, right?"

Bea nodded, glaring at Melly.

"So, why don't you try to find out from him exactly what an Anti might look like, or what they might do to stop a story?" Joan said. "You pop over and, you know, just sort of casually ask about Anties in general. Like a character précis."

"Actually, that's not a bad idea," Melly said after a pause. "He said you could ask him for help, didn't he?"

"Exactly," Joan said. "What harm could it do?"

Bea drummed her fingers on the table. She was pretty certain it could do a lot of harm, but she had to admit that her friends had a point. There was no way she was going to go to the GenAm and tell them that she'd been accosted by a *possible* Anti, and *potentially* lost control of her story—not yet, anyway. But it would be good to get some information.

"Fine, fine," she said, hands held up in defeat. "But I'm still not going to report it."

Joan beamed. "Why don't you go now? It's still early, I'm sure he'll be there."

"And if nothing else," Melly added, stubbing out her cigarette, "if you speak to this Plotter now, you can argue later that you told the GenAm."

Melly and Joan walked away from Bea's squalid bedsit, winding their way through the honeycomb of narrow lanes. There was something heavy in the air. Although it was hours until evening and the streets were busy, there was a sensation that Ænathlin was slow and watchful, like a wounded animal. Joan also noticed there was an above-average number of brown-suited workers from the Contents Department out. No white suits, though.

"Well, that was a little fraught," she said.

Melly pulled a cigarette from her onyx case and tapped it against the lid. Joan waited while she lit up, politely ignoring the way the witch spluttered on the first inhalation. When she decided Melly had recovered, she said, "I understand that she doesn't want to lose the story—not after working so long to get one."

Joan let the comment hang in the air, but Melly only flicked her cigarette with her thumb, letting the ash answer for her as it dropped to the cobbles.

"It was a bit weird though, wasn't it? All that stuff about not wanting to go back? Go back where—the Sheltering Forest? Go back to orc and gnarl attacks? That's obviously not what would happen."

Melly glared ahead.

"She gets by on Plot-watching. Even if she did lose the Plot, she wouldn't have to give up her flat," Joan said.

Glare. Puff. Glare.

"I think she expected it to be easier."

Puff. Puff. Glare.

"You can't say this isn't a good opportunity for her. She couldn't have waited much longer, I think."

Glare. Puff. Puff.

"And, you know, fair enough, she probably should report this hooded man, but the chances of him being an Anti must be a million to one."

"Hah," Melly said, finally breaking her silence.

Joan looked sidelong at her friend. "Do you really think Bea can't manage her Plot?"

"She can't let it go." Melly sighed. "It'll hurt her, sooner or later."

"Oh, I see," Joan said, though she didn't.

"She just doesn't want to risk her 'career'," Melly continued. "She should report it and get as far away from the whole thing as possible. This is real life. It doesn't have a Happy Ending."

Joan looked up at her friend. There was a look on the witch's face that suggested she was not, despite her physical location, actually here at all.

"Her Plotter seems alright at least," Joan offered. "Between you and me, from what she said he said, I think he was quite taken with her."

"That's hardly any great help. People do stupid things when there are feelings involved." The end of Melly's cigarette burned white. "But not nearly as stupid as the things they do when all their choices are taken away."

Chapter Ten

The bronze doors of the Plot Department shone painfully in the autumn sunlight.

The Teller had had the General Administration buildings constructed early in his Chapter, and for reasons only he could answer, had chosen to build in a style that was not reminiscent of any of the Five Kingdoms of Thaiana. This was a show of architectural deviance wholly uncommon in Ænathlin, a city founded on an almost schizophrenic plagiarism of the characters' world.

On the streets of Ænathlin, red stone from Ota'ari jostled for space with Penqioan marble and Ehinen wood. Whatever could be stolen from Thaiana was put to use, one way or another. Ænathlin, therefore, had no uniform style, and as such, the Teller's deviation from the norm should not have jarred as it did.

And yet the design of the General Administration buildings was wholly indicative of the Teller, a Narrator who had changed everything: the Plots, the city, the rules; the lives, hopes and dreams of all the fae.

And, as Bea stood on the shallow steps leading into the Plot Department and looked down at the open space in front of the GenAm, she could see another example of the changes the Teller had wrought.

Once, the fae used executions.

Now they Redacted.

Bea hated watching Redactions. She'd always found it too easy to imagine what it would feel like to sit in front of the screaming crowds, knowing this was the last thing she would ever experience, knowing that in a few moments there would be nothing left of her. But this time she couldn't tear her eyes away.

The Redaction Block sat in the square outside the GenAm. It was old, the wood almost black and as hard as stone. It rested on the top of a raised dais, big enough to accommodate the criminal and the Redactionist who would carry out the sentence. The square was wide and open, unusual in the overcrowded city, to allow people to watch.

Redactions always drew a crowd, something the Redaction Department encouraged. Food and drink were handed out, and a few Raconteurs were paid to retell the tale of the Great Redaction, being sure to highlight how the Teller Cared About Them. Redactions were exciting, and an excuse the fae rarely needed to laugh and dance and celebrate. This time, however, no one was cheering. There was instead a terrible expectancy in the way the crowd stood and whispered, in the recrimination that hung over the square.

Bea pushed her way through the throng until she could see the gnome being led up to the platform, her tiny hands tied tightly behind her back, a gag biting into the corners of her mouth. The gnome sat gently on the block, resigned to her fate. A lock of hair brushed against her cheek. Bea realised that was probably the last thing the gnome would ever truly feel again.

Her stomach lurched, but she couldn't move. She was trapped in the crowd. She hadn't noticed how far forward she'd pushed herself, and now she was stuck. She didn't want to be here. She didn't want to see the bravery and the sadness in the eyes of the gnome any more than she wanted to acknowledge the fact that there was a part of her, hidden behind the horror, that was ever so slightly jealous of the prospect of never having to think or worry again.

The Redactionist stepped forward and addressed the audience, stating the words quickly:

"Once upon a time, there was war and starvation and death. Once upon a time, we would kill our brothers and sisters, fearing for our own lives. Once upon a time, the characters turned from us, and we wept. Now we do not war, nor do we fear, nor do we weep. We Redact. The Teller Cares About Us."

"The Teller Cares About Us," Bea echoed with the crowd.

The Redactionist placed the white, stone Eraser on the gnome's forehead. The little body went rigid at the touch and then limp. He knelt down in front of the newly Redacted gnome and asked, "Sister, what do you know?"

The gnome blinked slowly. Bea was close enough to see the difference in her saucer-like eyes.

"The Teller Cares About Me," the gnome replied, her voice hollow.

"And what else?"

"i care about the teller is there something you would like me to do"

The Redactionist nodded. He turned back to the waiting crowds and announced that, due to the current situation with the Mirrors, the GenAm would only be providing beer and bread, but as many who wished were welcome to partake of the Teller's kindness. The audience relaxed, and small bubbles of conversation began to rise from the general malaise. But it was not joyful or celebratory, as it usually would have been.

Bea shivered and pushed her way out. The crowds milled around like a circle of spirits, observing a world they couldn't affect, taking it all in, waiting.

Bea hesitated outside the door to Mistasinon's tiny office. She was having doubts—not exactly surprising given that, if she wasn't careful, she could very well end up losing her Plot.

The possibility of *the other thing*, fresh in her mind, was one she was trying not to acknowledge. Oh, it sat there in her consciousness with all the subtlety of not only the hoolalump but the entire circus in the room, she was just working extremely hard at pretending it wasn't. It would be difficult to say whether she was succeeding.

She could also hear him talking to someone.

His office was little more than a broom cupboard and, though it was clear that he had attempted to lower his voice, the sound didn't exactly have far to travel. As a result, although she couldn't hear what he was saying, she could quite easily make out his tone of voice, which sounded worried and very tired.

As she dithered outside the door, she felt a wholly new pang of unease, one that hadn't occurred to her until now. Mistasinon had shown a lot of trust in her. He had chosen her, despite her background, her lack of experience, and the general dislike towards the fairies, and she was about to lie to him.

You're about to put him at risk of Redaction, she corrected, eyeing the door at the end of the corridor. *If I lie now, there'll be no turning back. I'll have to finish the story Happily Ever After.*

She started biting her thumbnail.

It was one thing to believe in yourself, but quite another to bet. Could she do this? Perhaps she simply wasn't capable of managing a Plot. Maybe there was a reason why so many people didn't trust the fairies.

Mistasinon's voice drifted, too exhausted for anything more strenuous, through the door and down the hallway. Bea felt the soft resistance of flesh between her teeth and the metallic tang of blood filled her mouth. Startled, she looked down at her hand. She'd bitten her nail down to the quick. A small bead of heavy, black blood sat neatly on the tip of her thumb. She lifted her hand up and watched as the shiny bead began to trickle towards her wrist. It looked like a teardrop.

She heard the door open and swore under her breath.

"Bea! Hi," Mistasinon said, smiling conspiratorially as he said her name.

"…Hi."

"Were you waiting to see me?"

Bea glanced at the exit, all the way down the corridor.

Beyond that door was safety. Beyond that door was her regular life, with her friends and her little flat and every single day being exactly the same as the last. Beyond that door were the other fae who would tut and smile and express their sympathies in such a way that held minimum empathy and maximum delight. It was also where the taunts of her childhood waited for her, her home and, still raw after so many years, The Argument that forced her to leave.

Beyond that door was her life: empty and pointless, exactly like everyone said it would be.

She looked past Mistasinon, who was smiling at her in confusion. "Is everything alright?" he asked.

Behind him was the door to his tiny office. Bea realised that if she walked through *that* door, she very seriously faced Redaction.

They would make her empty and hollow, locking her away from everything she had ever known, including herself.

But if she could finish the story…

Mistasinon would let her join the Academy. She'd basically be recommended by a Plotter, which had to be a thousand times better than an FME. Everyone would have to take her seriously. She would finally *be* someone.

The hooded man was probably just an over-enthusiastic FME. He was probably not so different from herself. In fact, had they met under different circumstances, they'd almost definitely have got on. It would have to be the worst luck in all the Five Kingdoms and The Land to have her very first Plot attacked by a real Anti-Narrativist.

Bea looked up at Mistasinon.

"I was hoping you had a few minutes…?"

"Of course. Please, after you," he said, holding the door. "This is a nice surprise," he continued with admirable sincerity, given the fact he'd been about to leave for the day. "Take a seat, won't you? What can I do for you?"

Bea looked around, surprised. "I thought you had someone in here with you," she said as they took their seats.

Mistasinon stared at her.

"I heard you talking," Bea clarified. He rubbed his neck. She remembered he had done the same thing when she had asked him if he was desperate.

"This is a little embarrassing. Sometimes I, uh, I talk to myself. Not all the time. I suppose you think I'm mad."

"Not at all—I expect it's the only sensible conversation you get, right?"

Mistasinon gave her a grateful smile. "Exactly. So, what can I do for you?"

Bea took a breath. "I was just wondering if you could give me some advice. I've never had a Plot before, and I want to get it right." So far, so good—no lies there. Perhaps this was a good idea after all.

"I'm sure you'll be fine, Bea," Mistasinon said. "I understand I might have given you the impression that you don't have the full confidence of the General Administration behind your selection, but that was my fault entirely. Really, you wouldn't have been recommended if you weren't up to it."

"Recommended?"

"I mean, your work recommends you. I have every faith in you," he corrected quickly, seeing the hope flash across her face. "You're going to do exactly what I want you to do."

Bea dropped her eyes. "Um, thank you, but still… There's just a couple of things I'd like to ask if you don't mind?"

Mistasinon leant on his elbows, his chin balanced in the palm of his hand. He nodded encouragingly, perhaps feeling guilty for raising her hopes a moment before.

"Alright then, I certainly don't want you having any trouble finishing the Plot. If nothing else, I'd never hear the end of it from all those crumpled old FMEs who think they run everything here. By the mortal gods, they're awful. Oh, dear. I suppose I shouldn't have said that," he added, looking worried.

There was no escaping it, he really was lovely. Bea grinned at him. "Please don't apologise on my account. I wouldn't have put it half as gently as you just did."

"I'm sure you would've thought of something," he replied, returning her smile. "I've read your Books, remember. You strike me as being quite inventive enough to describe your more, er, staid co-workers."

Bea laughed, and then immediately wished she hadn't. She shouldn't be making friends with a Plotter, especially not given her reason for being here. "So," she began again, trying hard to keep her voice level, "I was actually wondering about the Anties."

Mistasinon's smile wilted for a moment, but he revived it well enough that it only suffered a little. "The Anties? I'd have thought anyone who hasn't been living under a rock would know about them."

"I just wondered what you'd like me to do if I were to come across one. In my story."

"Have you?"

Bea could have cried. "Not that I'm aware of," she said, hoping he wouldn't notice.

"Well, there's plenty of literature available from the Contents Department," he replied. "They're really the ones you should be speaking to, you know."

"I just thought... you said if I needed any help I could come and see you."

Bea concentrated on not fidgeting under the look Mistasinon was giving her. It was, she was worried to note, not dissimilar from the one Melly and Joan had subjected her to.

"And nothing's happened to prompt this?" he asked.

"I really think I should be ready for any eventuality, that's all. We need to protect the Mirrors."

"Of course. I'm sorry. I didn't mean to seem distrustful. Things have been..." he trailed off, searching for the right word.

"Trying?" Bea offered.

"Hmm. I was going to say 'bloody awful'," Mistasinon replied, making Bea feel even guiltier. He had a certain smile that, no matter how often or how sincerely he gave it, managed somehow to carry with it a sense of melancholy, like a dog that, although happy to see you, longs for its master to return.

"I'm sorry, I shouldn't be bothering you," Bea said, standing to leave. She wasn't sure if she was relieved or disappointed when he stood up with her. He seemed as surprised as she was, and equally unsure what to make of it.

"You don't have to go," he said. "I'm new in the Department, that's all. I was reassigned, and I don't think anyone knows what to do with me. Or I with them, to be honest. It's difficult, learning how to be something else. I keep getting it wrong."

"Well, I can certainly sympathise with that."

"Oh?" Mistasinon asked, sitting back down. Bea noticed that he had to stretch his legs out to the side of the desk in order to fit behind it. She found herself not only sitting down again but volunteering the one subject she always tried to avoid.

"Well, you know my mother was a cabbage fairy," She said, giving a painful little laugh that only the most self-involved of people would mistake for humour. "I mean, even now I can remember all the jokes the other children made. It didn't take a lot of imagination. Cabbages are comedy gold, really, aren't they? Anyway, there was, well... my mum and I argued, and I left. And now I'm here, and it isn't really any different. Once a cabbage fairy, always a cabbage fairy."

The tiny office seemed only to become smaller.

"Life can be cruel," Mistasinon offered.

Bea's face hardened. "Life isn't cruel. Life never did anything to me. The other fae did."

Mistasinon regarded her carefully.

"I suppose it's never easy, going against expectation. Whether you choose to do it or not," he said, picking up one of the pens that once again lay haphazardly on his desk, letting it slip through his fingers to bounce against the surface and back into his grip, his gaze fixed on it. Bea felt sad suddenly, and she didn't want to think about why.

And then he looked up from whatever thoughts he had been inhabiting, and his face broke into a smile of such genuine warmth that she had to resist looking behind her, just to make sure no one else had come in.

That was part of the magic of Mistasinon. His face was not really a handsome one, not by the standards of the story. His forehead was too high, and his eyebrows too thick, but he had large brown eyes that looked at the world with almost uncensored feeling. For Bea, a person used to the device of True Love and Happily Ever After, it was a strange and fascinating thing to see true emotion.

"Well then, Bea," he said, clapping his hands together, "I guess we'll have to look after each other, won't we? So, let's start as we mean to go on. What's worrying you about the Anties?"

Bea managed a smile. "Ah. Yes. Well, I mean, nothing serious, of course. I guess, firstly, I was wondering what they might, uh, look like?" She tried not to wring her hands. Could she sit on them? Would he notice?

Mistasinon was silent for a moment, thinking. "Honestly, they look much like anyone," he said finally. "They tend towards the elven, and more of the imps, adhenes and such are going over. Fairies of course—they're disenfranchised anyway, so why not go one step further? But I suppose anyone could be an Anti, in theory."

"Oh. Right."

"You seem disappointed?"

"No, no. Of course not. I just thought… Actually, sorry, one more question: if they could be anyone, how does the Redaction Department find them? Is there, I don't know, a tell? There must be some way to recognise one?"

"It's not a secret," Mistasinon said. "The easiest way for the Redaction Department to find anyone is with the Mirrors."

Bea tutted. It was such an obvious, thoughtless lie it was hard not to be insulted by it. Everyone knew that the Mirrors didn't pick up sound—all it took was the judicious use of a tea towel for the GenAm to have no idea what you were doing.

But she shouldn't have shown her frustration, and now, despite his long day, Mistasinon had found the strength to furrow his impressive eyebrows.

"The Mirrors, yes, of course, sorry," she said. "I knew that. I must have forgotten. You know how it is. Forget my head if it wasn't sewn on." She attempted a friendly smile, but she felt it sliding down her face the second she put it there.

Mistasinon stared at her levelly. And then he said something that, in all her wildest imaginings, Bea would never have expected a GenAm official to say.

"You're right to disbelieve me. It's nonsense that we use the Mirrors to find the Anties. Even if the Redactionists could use the Mirrors, there simply aren't enough left for us, that is, the GenAm, to waste by watching them."

Bea stared at him, shocked and fascinated, and ever-so-slightly delighted. What Mistasinon had just said to her was impossible. No one admitted to weaknesses on behalf of the GenAm. It was like listening to a politician hold their hands up and admit they were only in it for the bribes. Everyone knew it was true, but no one ever owned up to it.

"So how do the Redaction Department find the Anties?"

"Informers. Double agents. And we have the Cerberus, of course. Nothing escapes the Cerberus. Or so they say."

Bea shivered.

"You're frightened of the Cerberus?" Mistasinon asked.

"And you aren't? Can you imagine what the Beast must be like? I've heard it's the most pitiless, evil creature ever writ. A savage monster only the Teller, *whocaresaboutus,* could tame. You know they say its teeth are permanently black now, from all the blood? And they say it's got eyes like hellfire, and that its breath carries the stink of a thousand rotten corpses. It's a monster. Everyone says the King and Queen are to blame for the Teller, but I mean, really, it was the Beast that caught all those fae. It's irredeemable."

Mistasinon began tapping his fingers on the edge of his desk. It was like Bea had said something wrong, which didn't make sense. It was only right and proper to hate the Beast. The Teller wanted people to hate it.

"Is everything—"

"The Cerberus," Mistasinon said, his fingers drumming faster and faster, "is a loyal and faithful servant of the story, the Teller and the Land."

"Of course, I didn't mean to—"

"I know what you meant. I'm not interested in idle complaints, Bea. I'm only interested in the Mirrors and the survival of the city." He met Bea's eyes. "I've given you this story because I have reason to believe that you can complete it. You're a thinker, and that's what we need—someone who can deal with anything that's thrown at her and still get the story finished."

"I am, I can."

"Good. Because if you can't complete the story, say so now and I'll give it to one of the other FMEs. But I must say I'd be disappointed. You remind me of an old friend, someone I... well I miss a lot, and who I trusted. He was someone who could get things done, and I think you're the same. But I need this story finished, Bea, Happily Ever After. Can you do that for me?"

Chapter Eleven

Bea sat in the pub, staring at the greasy sheen on her wine glass.

She'd left Mistasinon's office hours ago and still hadn't managed to find her way home. She'd walked around the city centre, trying to work out why she felt so unhappy. When it became obvious she wasn't going to find an answer there, she'd decided to head back to the wall and see if a glass of white wouldn't prove more forthcoming.

Bea took another sip. She wished she had enough for a second glass, but she'd already had to lay down a not inconsequential bag of salt for the one in front of her, and she'd left her ration tokens at home.

Things were definitely getting harder in the city. Of course, that was the reason Mistasinon had given her the Plot, wasn't it? They were desperate. It wasn't really because he thought she could do it. Even Melly, who was supposed to be her friend, didn't think she had what it takes.

It occurred to Bea that if she stayed any longer, she was going to cry. She abandoned her wine and stood up to leave when the doors were pushed open, and a group of fae marched in.

Normally this wouldn't have had any effect on the other customers, but there was an air around the group that seemed to radiate danger. Perhaps it was something in the way they moved, or in their tone of voice. But it was probably the fact they were loudly singing one of the old songs, and that the ring-leader was an elf, still beautiful despite his matted hair and filthy clothing.

"A man of words and not of deeds," they sang, *"Is like a garden full of weeds, and when the weeds begin to grow, it's like a garden full of snow…"*

Bea put her glass down, her eyes fixed on the gang, who had got their drinks and were waving them to the tune of their forbidden song. In addition to the scraggy elf, there were a couple of imps, a gnome and two pretty adhenes, who were giggling maniacally and flicking their long hair over their shoulders in a way that managed to accentuate their slender necks and petite frames.

"And when the bird away does fly, it's like an eagle in the sky, and when the sky begins to roar, it's like a lion at the door…"

The whole bar had dimmed to a murmur, all eyes on the group.

"And when the door begins to crack, it's like a stick across your back, and when your back begins to smart, it's like a penknife in your heart…"

Bea inched towards the door. She was nearly there when the elf shouted across the room.

"Wherefore are you leaving, sister?" He said the word 'sister' in a manner not inclined toward familial good feeling.

Bea swore under her breath but turned around. "I'm going home. I'm tired."

The elf stepped forward, looking her up and down. His pretty lip curled.

"And when your heart begins to bleed, you're dead, and dead, and dead indeed," he sang softly.

"I'm just going home," Bea repeated. She could feel the pull of the door behind her, so close she only had to turn around and take a couple of steps. But elves were fast, and Bea knew without needing to be told that he would like it if she had her back turned.

"Marry, sister," the elf spoke gently, but the bar was so quiet everyone could hear him. "Are you not going to dance with me?"

Bea took a step backwards.

"By the moon, you are afeared!" the elf laughed, stepping further into the room. The adhenes squealed in delight. "I shouldn't expect more from you, servant of Titania. Yea, you sneer at me for saying what's true. Mayhap we shall discover if dirt doth grow behind your ears…"

He lunged at Bea, his lovely face warped by the cruel smile stretched across it.

Bea did the only thing she could.

She hit him.

The elf fell to the floor.

For once, Bea was grateful she was a garden fairy. Cabbage fairies were built sturdy and strong, and Bea hadn't felt the need to pull her punch. She realised too late her bag had fallen off her shoulder, spilling her Book. She grabbed it and held it tightly in her arms.

F. D. Lee

"Hark, friends. She does not want to dance with me, for I am not bound to her master," the elf proclaimed, climbing to his feet. Even wiping black blood from his face, he managed to be beautiful. "Look you at this serf, this slave, this whore of the General Administration." He turned back to Bea. "Without your kind, I'd be free—we'd all be free."

His voice grew louder as he realised that the majority of the room were nodding along with him. Someone, hidden in the safety of a dark corner, shouted, "Hear, hear".

Bea turned around and dived for the door.

"Aye, run away! You can't stop it! The 8th Chapter is dying!" the elf cried, banging his fist into the palm of his hand, overtaken by his own rhetoric. "Long live the story! Long live the story! Long live the story!"

The other fae took up the chant, and the last thing Bea saw was the elf jumping onto a table, fist raised to the ceiling, mouth open wide as he decried the Teller and the GenAm.

Chapter Twelve

Bea had barely slept the night before, but she wasn't tired. She'd spent hours planning how to get back on Plot and wondering exactly how far it was she was prepared to go in order to do so—a question which, alarmingly, she was still no closer to answering.

What she needed was information. If she could find out what tribe this strange, hooded man came from, she might be able to do something about him. At the very least she'd know what he was capable of.

Mistasinon hadn't been any help, but Bea conceded he'd tried to cheer her up, and he did seem to genuinely think she could work a Plot. And the incident in the bar had shown her that he was right to be worried about the Mirrors. She didn't want to let him down any more than herself. So she'd decided to try another avenue.

She put on her dress and brushed her grey hair until it shone like silver. Finally, she applied a touch more make-up a little more carefully than usual. She was about as ready as she'd ever be.

She walked down the crooked stairs to the ground floor of her building, took a deep breath, and stepped into the reception.

Ivor was sat where he always did, playing a complicated game involving a gridded board and small bone tiles. Bea never knew which Kingdom he got these games from. She suspected even Ivor didn't know, and that he made up the rules to suit himself. Like most of the fae, his life had become crushingly mundane since The Great Redaction and the introduction of the Plots. And yet, again like most of the fae, he was too terrified of the Teller to rebel. He was, quite simply, trapped.

Bea reminded herself of all this as he looked up and gave her a dirty brown smile as if he hadn't watched her being dragged off by the GenAm to a fate only the mortal gods knew what.

"Thought we'd lost you," he said with something approaching real warmth.

"Would you have missed me?" she asked, trying her best to purr.

Ivor shot her a puzzled look. "You got a cold coming on? And what's all that muck on your face?"

F. D. Lee

Bea flopped down onto one of the stools that lined the counter, defeated. She had heard once that all women had in their possession the weapon of their sex. She wondered if whoever had said that had ever tried to launch said sexuality at a gnome. She suspected not.

"I've got a new story. A Plot actually," she offered in explanation. Ivor looked her up and down, his face drawn in an expression that showed it was clear that he was reluctant to receive her elucidation.

"And that's part of your uniform, is it?"

"I just thought it'd be nice."

"Hum." Ivor turned back to his game.

"Actually, I was wondering if I could ask your advice?"

Ivor looked up from his board. "You want advice from me?"

"If you don't mind," Bea answered, trying to appear casual.

Ivor tapped one of the bone tiles against his muddy teeth, weighing up joys of being able to condescend against the dangers of being asked something he didn't know the answer to.

"I really can't think of anyone else to ask," Bea said. "But only if you have the time. I know you're busy."

Bea and Ivor tried to ignore the almost ceremonial stillness that permeated the reception of the dirty boarding house.

"Yeah, well," Ivor coughed. "What y'wanna know?"

"I wanted to ask you about a man."

The gnome leered. He had a face written for lewdness, and to date, he'd had very little chance to avail Bea of what was his pièce de résistance. He now revelled in his opportunity, and with good cause. Every feature was incorporated: his bushy, tangled eyebrows jumped up and down on his forehead like a cat dancing on hot coals; his large, yellowing eyes darted left and right in their sockets; his lips pulled back over his brown, pitted teeth in what was the worst smile Bea would ever experience.

"Men, is it? You wanna know what to do with one in the morning?"

"No, thank you," Bea answered firmly. "I met someone the other day. I think he's one of the fae, but I didn't recognise him from any of the tribes I know."

"And you want t'see him again, that it?"

"I'd certainly like to know what to expect if I do."

"If you didn't recognise him why d'you think he's one of the fae?"

"Intuition?" Bea said hopefully. If she gave too much away, Ivor would work out she was asking about someone who was quite likely an Anti, and then the best Bea could hope for would be that he'd evict her—more probably he'd report her.

She held her breath while the gnome eyeballed her.

"Don't put much stock in all that stuff meself, but alright," he said after a moment. "You'd better tell me what you can."

Bea breathed again.

"There's not much. I didn't see his face or anything. But he was tall, strong. I think he was wearing jewellery, or possibly some kind of plate. Something that made a noise when he moved. And he spoke strangely. Like from the old stories, the banned ones."

Ivor scratched his chin. "S'not a lot to be going on. If he speaks funny, might be he's been off on a long Plot."

"It's more than that, but I don't know how to explain it."

"Go on."

Bea licked her lips. This was the moment. If she said this wrong…

"When he spoke, he made me want things. Things only he could give me. Not sex," she said, seeing the look on Ivor's face. "Other things."

The gnome picked his nose thoughtfully.

"There's not many as I can remember like that. It rings a bell, though. There used t'be a group of fair folk who could make the characters trust 'em, believe in 'em, a long time ago."

"What happened to them?"

"What do you think? They got Redacted. What's all this about? I ain't gonna risk a visit from the Beast for you, missus."

Bea picked up one of the tiles from the board and spun it on the countertop, trying to think what to say when inspiration struck.

"How about a game? A game's just a game. No rules against games."

Ivor's mouth twitched. "You know I love a game."

"A guessing game?"

"Alright. Old house rules. Three guesses."

"Naturally. So, number one. I reckon that these fae, the ones who made the characters believe, were very powerful? Famous?"

Ivor glared at her, angry to have been so easily tricked into continuing the conversation. But rules were rules. "Dunno. Don't remember. But even if they were, they ain't now. The GenAm seen to that."

"Alright. Second guess. You said they could make the characters believe, so shouldn't their stories still be popular?"

"Not necessarily," Ivor said sullenly. "Belief weren't always in something popular, nor in something nice. That was the whole problem, weren't it? The stories got too close to the bone, and the characters turned to their machines instead of to us. Anyway, this is all before The Great Redaction."

"Final guess. You know more than you're telling me?"

Ivor squealed with delight. "Stupid fairy—you wasted that guess! Course I know more than I'm telling you. There's your answer. Now the game's done, and you can go bother someone else."

Bea swallowed her disappointment and got up to leave.

"Why d'you really wanna know all this, anyway? You never shown any interest in a man before, least not for long. Who's this one to you?" Ivor asked, magnanimous in victory.

"It's nothing. I just… he might be important. To my story. I'm sure I won't see him again, anyway."

And then something very strange happened.

"Here, hang on, girl. I got some post for you," Ivor said, head bobbing on his shoulders like a chicken's.

"Post? But you don't collect our letters."

"Just started this week. Ain't you read the notice?"

"What notice?"

"Stupid fairy, never paying attention," he continued at top volume, diving under the counter. Bea heard him scrabbling about.

"What are you talking about?"

Ivor reappeared, a crumpled piece of paper in his hand. He shoved it at Bea.

"There. *Your post*," he said again, now adding a wink to the waggling of his eyebrows.

"Oh? Right. Yes… my post. Thanks."

"Now get lost. Can't you see I'm busy?" Ivor snapped, returning to his lonely game.

Bea walked out of the building, the note held tight in her fist. The streets were at that strange neither-nor time when last night's revellers were crawling into their beds and the morning's workers crawling out of them. More often than not, it was the same bed, Ænathlin being a city of opportunity; in this case, the opportunity to share lice.

She unfolded the paper Ivor had given her and looked down at his spidery handwriting.

"D(2)1-102."

Bea frowned, recognising the shorthand for the 2nd Chapter.

She, like most of the fae, didn't really know anything about the very early Chapters. The GenAm controlled the histories, and most fae only really knew about Oberon and Titania's Chapter, which was the 7th, and the Teller's, which was the 8th and current Chapter. She wondered if she could go back and try to find a way to get the gnome to explain, but she knew he wouldn't.

The note fluttered softly in the palm of her hand. She tore it into tiny pieces of confetti and dropped them into a puddle of acrid yellow liquid, watching them dissolve slowly.

Chapter Thirteen

Sindy sat in her room, brushing her hair and watching Will as he worked in the garden.

She liked watching Will. She'd known him all her life. He was friendly and familiar and kind. He didn't lose his temper, and he always listened to her chatter about the things she liked to talk about. He and Sindy just seemed to understand each other, which was more than she could say for the rest of the people she met.

Sindy was beginning to have very unkind thoughts about the people that made up her immediate universe. The type of thoughts that made her feel mildly ashamed and then annoyed with herself. Why shouldn't she be cross—no, no, *pissed off*, thank you—with everything? But Sindy couldn't help it. She didn't like arguments, even though she knew she should stand up for herself a little more.

Take her stepsister, for example. Ana was so passionate about things. It didn't seem to matter what the thing was, somehow she always managed to find a way to make a fight out of it.

Sindy could remember when Ana and her mum moved in. She'd wanted to make a good impression on her new family, so she'd spent hours in the kitchen, making a lovely roast dinner. She had dug up all the vegetables herself, killed and plucked the chicken and had, after hours of hard work, produced a meal fit for a king.

But Ana had taken one look at it, told Sindy off for wasting perfectly good food (there was no need, she'd said, to have all those vegetables and both roast potatoes and roast parsnips) and then announced she was vegetarian and told Sindy off again for cruelty to animals.

Sindy had tried to see Ana's point of view, but she didn't think she'd been wasteful, or cruel to the chicken. She had fed it and watered it and looked after it all its life, and now it was its turn to feed her. She thought that was fair, not cruel. And her dad had always loved her roasts, although he had sat quietly while Ana scolded her, doing nothing.

Sindy had wanted to cry but knew she shouldn't make a fuss. Everything had changed. Her dad had remarried, and he hadn't even asked her what she thought about it. He had just come home one day and told her he'd met someone, and she would soon have a new mother and sister. Sindy had thought *that* was unfair, but she'd never said anything about it.

She watched as Will went to the shed to get the small hoe. Everything was certainly a lot simpler with Will. He often came over in the evenings, since his own family had been taken by the 'enza. He'd survived, but at the age of fifteen had found himself alone in the world. Sindy admired that in him. She thought it was awful he had lost his mum and dad and brother all at once. He must be very lonely in their little house. He was quite possibly the bravest person she had met, and so when she felt sad or lonely, she tried to be like Will.

He had found her the night Ana had moved in, in the kitchen by herself, cleaning up all her hard work. She'd been trying to sing a song because her mum had told her once a happy song meant a happy heart. But she hadn't been happy, and every time she opened her mouth, she'd had to bite back the tears.

Will had sung along with her and made her laugh. He helped her wash up and clear away, and valiantly stepped in and ate both chicken legs and taken some home for sandwiches.

So Sindy liked Will very much. He was simple and friendly, and he didn't make her feel ashamed or angry or helpless. He wasn't a very rich man, and she supposed he wasn't very handsome. But then she wasn't rich, and everyone said she was pretty, but it didn't make her any happier, so what did that matter?

Sindy was pulled out of her thoughts by a knock at the door. Her father was at work, her stepmother in bed with her nerves, and Ana with her friends in the woods. Ana was rarely at home. She said that sitting doing nothing was an insult to the thousands of slaves forced to toil for hours every day in the underground manufactories in Cerne Bralksteld.

Sindy liked it when Ana said things like that, as it was clearly aimed at their mother, a woman for whom the merest thought of lifting a finger brought on a bout of nervous indigestion and necessitated a long sleep. Sometimes Ana was alright.

She wandered downstairs to see who was at the door. Simple as she was, no one could blame her for being surprised to find her liege, lord and master, his Royal Highness, King John of Llanotterly on her doorstep, flanked by a broad-shouldered, hooded man, a dozen palace guards, a butler, a master of the hound and about ten beagles.

There were a number of rules that should be observed when meeting royalty, ranging from what one can say and when, to where one should stand, when one can sit, even where one should look.

Sindy bobbed a nervous curtsy and, before being introduced, blurted out an invitation to come inside whilst looking John directly in the eye.

The King followed her into the cottage, the hooded man behind him. Thankfully, the remaining entourage waited outside.

"It's, um, it's an honour to meet you, Sire," Sindy said as she showed them into the front room.

"Yes, yes, quite so, miss, uh…" The King faltered. The man in the hood leaned forward and whispered something in his ear. "Ah, yes, of course. You're the sister."

"Excuse me?" Sindy said, confused.

"The stepsister, what? If my Adviser here has it right," he turned to the hooded man for confirmation, but the moment the King's eyes landed on him, he seemed to lose his temper. "Blast it, S.! Remove that damnable puggaree! It's bad enough hiding away like that in the castle, but you're a guest in this young lady's hovel. Bad show, bad show."

Sindy cast a sympathetic look at the hooded man, but he didn't seem concerned to be shouted at by the King. He pulled his hood back, revealing himself to be quite possibly the finest-looking man Sindy had ever met, with dark blue-black hair and a golden snake coiled tightly around his neck. He smiled at her when he caught her staring at him.

"Oh, oh," Sindy flustered, turning quickly to the King and then realising she had no idea what to say to him, either. Somehow her house had been invaded by two men with whom she had no idea how to communicate.

"Um… My father's not here," she settled on.

"Do not fret," said the handsome man. "It is not for your father that his Highness visits. Nothing is amiss." His voice reminded

Sindy of melted butter. The butterflies in her stomach began to settle.

"Oh. But then why…?"

"His Highness requires—"

And then something awful happened.

"I say, is that a picture of me on the mantel?" John interrupted.

Sindy went pink. "No… Um… It's… Um…."

It was too late. John had walked the short distance to the fireplace and was studying one of the woodcuts Ana used for her political pamphlets.

"I see," he said.

"It's not meant to be—"

"I think the teeth are a little unfair. My aunt paid quite the sum to get them fixed."

Sindy gulped.

"And I'm not fat, I know that. Still, the eyes aren't bad. And he's caught the shape of my head." John turned back to Sindy. "I assume this belongs to your sister? It's Miss Ana—"

"Ms, your Royal Highness," Sindy corrected without thinking. Her hand flew to her mouth, but it was too late.

"What's that?"

She didn't know what to say. She turned to the other man for help, but he was making a show of looking around the room with polite curiosity.

"Er. Ms, Your Royal Majesty," she answered, curtsying to be safe. "You see, Ana says that there's no reason why you should get to know if she's married if she doesn't want you to know."

"Why shouldn't she want a fella to know if she's hitched?"

"Well… I think it's just that she'd rather men were also called 'Mrs', too."

"But then how would you know who you're writing to?"

"I'm sorry?"

"When you write a letter, and you haven't met the person you're writing to," John tried to explain.

"But you don't need to know if they're married?"

"But you do need to know if it's a lady or a fella."

"I… I mean, maybe? But instead of Mr and Mrs, we could say, um, Sher and Shim?"

"Sher and Shim?" John asked, an edge of panic in his voice. "Isn't that just the same as him and her?"

"But you could be, um, Shim John, for example," Sindy said.

"Think I'll stick with 'King'."

"Shouldn't you be a Prince if you're not married?"

"Prince? My father's dead, gel. I'm King. You think I should get all my letters addressed to 'That Fella With The Dad What's Popped His Clogs'?"

"But that's Ana's point, you see."

John blinked. He, too, looked to the handsome man for help, but he had his back to them. His shoulders were shaking.

"So is sher, *she*, married or not?"

"No, my Lord," Sindy replied. "She, I mean sher, just doesn't want you to know that."

The only noise in the room was the wheezing sound of stifled laughter coming from the man in the corner.

"Righto," John said. "*She* about then? Just a 'yes' or 'no', if you'd be so good."

Sindy shook her head, hoping that the King would leave now that he knew Ana wasn't home. But misfortune favours the hopeful, and both men failed to exit.

"D'you know when she'll be back?" John asked, taking deliberate care over the pronoun.

Sindy looked again at the other man, who had recovered enough to nod encouragingly at her.

"No, I'm sorry. But honestly, you're welcome to wait for her," she said bravely. "I'm sure if she knew you were looking for her, she'd be here. I've made some Battenberg. Would you like a slice?"

John glanced over at the Woodcut. The belly was very prominent. "No, ta."

"Oh. Perhaps a cup of tea?"

"I've not travelled all this way for tea and cakes, surrounding myself with fizgigs!" John glared meaningfully at Sindy, who, happily, wasn't all that offended as she had no idea what a fizgig was.

"My lord," said the handsome man gently, "you decided after yesterday's misadventure, it would be wiser to try a new approach."

Sindy stared at him. She had never heard such a wonderful voice in all her life. Somehow it reminded her of the times she and Will had spent together. She found herself wishing they saw more of each other. But since his family died, he was so busy and, since her dad remarried, so was she.

"No point hanging around, S. I'm off. Waste of a perfectly good morning," the King announced, making for the door.

Sindy caught the look that swept across the other man's face, and suddenly she was offering to take a message, her voice ringing with uncertainty, her eyes fixed on the curly-haired man. He shot her a grateful smile, and for the first time in her life, someone other than Will managed to make her feel like she'd done something right. She smiled back at him.

John paused in the doorway. "Yes, alright. Capital. Tell her… what was it?"

The man moved to the King's side and muttered a few words in his ear.

"Ah yes: I'm hosting a Ball this Saturday. You've probably seen the posters. Fundraising, meeting and greeting various dignitaries and whatnot. Dreadful bore, but needs must. Tell her she can come in exchange for giving up this nonsense in the wood. Pretty dresses, dancing and all that rot. That ought to do the trick."

"I'm not sure Ana really likes Balls," Sindy said, every note in her voice saying that she was actually very sure, and the answer, in fact, was no, Ana did not like Balls one little bit.

"Course she does. All gels love a Ball. All in?"

"Pardon?"

"You get all that?"

"I think so…"

"Marvellous."

The King flounced regally out of the house, leaving behind him a strange ringing in Sindy's ears. The handsome man, however, remained.

"Might I introduce myself? I fear his Highness has forgot his manners, so heavy is his burden. My name is Seven, and sadly it would not be wise for me to linger," he said with a low bow. "However, I would like to thank you for your assistance."

"I didn't do anything," Sindy said. All of a sudden, she couldn't think what to do with her hands.

"Not at all," he replied seriously. "Thanks to your quick thinking, your sister has the opportunity to discuss terms."

"Oh... well, I don't know..." Sindy said, caught in a tempest of unusual pride and familiar confusion.

Seven smiled at her again. "The Ball will begin at..."

Sindy tried to concentrate as he told her the details of the Ball, but she just couldn't pay attention.

There was a game she and Will used to play when they were children, before death had touched their lives. They would lie on their backs in the fields and stare up at the sky, looking at the clouds as they drifted past. The game was won or lost based on how many different things they could see in the same one. Sometimes Will would win, but more often than not Sindy would. She just had a knack for seeing all sorts of possibilities in the soft compliance of the clouds.

She turned the same skill onto the Adviser. He was tall and muscular, with dark, corkscrew hair. He wore a lot of jewellery, and impractical, loose-fitting clothes, but other than that he was... yes... he was normal.

Yet looking at him stung her eyes, like trying to keep them open when something had burned in the oven. She tried to make him out, her vision fogging with tears. But she knew somehow that if she wiped them, she would lose sight of it, whatever *it* was.

As she stared at Seven, she realised what she was seeing was just one of the possibilities: there was something else, a different man, hidden in the same shape...

She bit her lip against the urge to blink.

"You're... you seem... there's something I need to ask you— could you...?" she said, trying to make sense of the need she was suddenly, urgently feeling.

Seven pulled his hood up, and the spell was broken.

"Excuse me. I must attend to the King. Perhaps you would inform your sister of what has transpired here?"

"Oh, yes. Of course."

"Once again, Sindy, you have my thanks."

The Adviser bowed and exited the room, leaving it somehow emptier than before he arrived.

Sindy stood, breathed out, and wondered if he wasn't right. She could cook, after all, and sew and clean and do first aid. Maybe she wasn't as simple as she thought. Maybe she *could* speak to Will about how she felt...

And then she thought about the trouble Ana was about to get into, and her burgeoning confidence faltered.

She wasn't at all sure she had done the right thing now that she was the one suddenly responsible for telling Ana that the King was somehow cross with her while, it seemed to Sindy, inviting her to a Ball in order to spend time with her.

She walked into the hallway, pulled her cloak from its hook and, fastening the ribbons below her chin, went to find her stepsister.

Chapter Fourteen

Ten years ago…

Ana was twelve and about to learn her father was a pirate and a slaver.

She was never supposed to find out, of course. With hindsight, she realised she'd picked up on the signs, but at the time, she'd just assumed people liked her father. After all, she loved him more than anything else in the world, so why shouldn't other people like him just as much? Why shouldn't he be popular and respected, the kind of guy everyone bought a drink for and loudly said what a stand-up bloke he was?

It was always a grand adventure, going to the docks with her dad. Normally, they would watch the steam-powered ships coming into the harbour, and she'd listen quietly as he told her how the pistons were kept moving, how much coal and wood was needed, and how fast they could travel despite their immense size.

But not today. Today, Ana was kicking around the port in Sinne, waiting for him to finish a business deal in one of the many bars that disfigured the harbour like plague sores. Usually, she liked hanging around when her father did business. Harbours were interesting places if you didn't mind the dirt and the smell and the ear-piercing whistle of the steam engines. There was always something to do or someone to speak to, and people were nice to her because they liked her dad.

Today, for some reason, the docks were quiet, and she was bored. A twelve-year-old girl with a quick mind and nothing to occupy it is always going to find trouble. It was almost a natural law, only the fact it hadn't been boiled down to letters and numbers holding it back.

Ana idled her way along the jetty, wishing she had brought a book with her. She didn't like dolls. Dolls were only good toys if all a girl wanted was to be a housewife, and she had no intention of settling down to a life of dishes and babies and laundry. She was also, in the spiteful quiet of her mind, beginning to notice that boys weren't that interested in her, anyway.

She pulled at her nose, annoyed by the fact that she had once again dredged up the memory of Simon's cruel jibes and that she hadn't been able to think of a cutting reply quickly enough. She knew her nose was too big and her arms and legs too long and skinny. Her mother, in her laziness, had tried to convince Ana his maltreatment was because he secretly liked her, but she knew that was a lie.

And anyway, what good did telling her he was only mean because he liked her actually do? Was she expected to chase after any man who treated her like dirt?

There had been a girl in one of the other villages who'd had a baby out of wedlock. The story went that she had been 'done wrong' by a rich man. Ana didn't know what that meant, but if the man was rich, she didn't see why he couldn't just give the girl some money for the baby and let that be an end to it.

Still, from what she'd heard, it didn't matter. The girl's baby had died, and she'd run away. Only something bad had happened... Ana stamped her feet on the wooden boards as she walked, trying to remember what she'd overheard. The girl had fallen in love and married. That was it. But her new husband had found out about the baby and had thrown her out.

The girl murdered the rich man in the end, and then she'd been hanged. Ana thought she could understand why the girl had done it and, to her mind, there was no reason to hang her. But everyone else said the girl had deserved it.

At least her dad didn't think like that. He didn't care what she did, and Ana was too young to realise this was not the evidence of his love that she thought it was.

The jetty ended abruptly, as they were wont to do. Ana looked up from her shoes to see the boat her dad worked on in front of her, its beautiful, rich brown body curving invitingly. The gangplank was down.

So she snuck aboard. Not because she particularly expected to find anything exceptional, but because it was something she was expressly forbidden from doing unaccompanied, and so was the most exciting thing she could possibly do while unaccompanied.

She darted onto the boat and threw herself down quickly to avoid being seen. She grinned. She was somewhere she shouldn't be!

Ana scurried below deck and into her father's cabin. She was always surprised how small it was, especially for such a large man. She liked being in here. He kept souvenirs of all the places he'd visited, and she knew that one day, he would make room in his cabin for her, and she would travel with him. She poked around, but there wasn't anything new. She picked up his compass and spun herself around a few times, trying to trick it into confusion, but it bested her each time, and after a while, she started to feel sick.

She left her dad's cabin and walked further through the lower decks. She remembered suddenly that in the big steamers, there was an engine room right at the bottom. This was a sailboat, but maybe they had an engine as well, and she'd like to see a steam engine. Ana wasn't exactly optimistic, but she was here, alone, and she thought it was worth a try.

She climbed down the narrow ladder to the next level, hoping to find something wonderful.

What she found was the ship's hold. And with it, she discovered that her daddy was storing massive amounts of grain and salt, provisions that were in short supply and very hard to get hold of. Ana had never heard the word 'profiteering', but it didn't take her long to work out the significance of the crates.

She moved through the hold, running her fingertips against the rough hessian sacks and smooth barrels that held, like disgustingly gorged gluttons, the food and supplies so desperately needed by the people of Caer Marllyn.

Ana could feel something growing in her stomach, a kind of queasy sickness, like when she ate too many sweets. The air under the ship had a strange smell; it was hot and fuggy, but underneath that was a sharpness that reminded Ana, she wasn't sure why, of a farmyard. Ignoring her nerves, she followed the path down the centre of the hold, past the bags and barrels, until she got to the cages.

The thing Ana remembered most, the thing she would always try to forget and would never be allowed to, was the smell.

Not the stench of the people, though forty slaves kept in close conditions, far away from any ventilation and with what was the beginning of a dysentery outbreak is certainly a smell that lingers in the mind as well as the nose.

No, what Ana would always remember is that someone, perhaps her father or one of the numerous 'uncles' who sat her on their knee and joked with her and gave her little nips from their mugs of sticky, dark rum, someone she most certainly knew, had tried to cover the smell with a pomander.

A few years later, her father had died or vanished. No one knew, and Ana didn't care. The man she had loved had disappeared for her the moment she had seen that dried-up orange, stabbed through with cloves and hanging from the beam on a piece of pretty silk.

That little touch of humanity in a space of cruelty and greed.

Chapter Fifteen

"Right, what's the matter?"

Ana could see there was more to Sindy's request to return home than the claim that her mother and stepfather missed her. She doubted very much her mother had even noticed she'd gone, and as for Sindy's father… Well, he was a kind enough sort of man, but it was clear he regretted the marriage. Either that or there was a greater need for a travelling cobbler than Ana had ever imagined.

"Oh, oh, oh," Sindy cried, her normally lovely face screwed up with anxiety. She looked around at all the people milling about the encampment. "Please, Ana," she whispered, "*he* came to our house. *He* was in our living room!"

Ana paused. She had known Sindy for a few years now, and although she couldn't for the life of her understand why her stepsister didn't stand up for herself more, she had learnt not to completely disregard everything she said.

"He?" she asked, a shadow of realisation darkening her expression. "Let me guess: Prince Charming?"

Sindy nodded.

Ana, scowling furiously, grabbed Sindy's arm and pulled her into a nearby tent. Inside it was warm and cosy. A small fire burned in the centre, and the air tasted of sap and smelled of apples. Ana flopped down onto the rug-strewn floor, as graceful as a sack of potatoes, and waved for Sindy to do the same—which she did, and yet somehow Sindy performed the exact same action with about half the density.

Ana was not a big girl; in fact, she was quite far over the slim horizon and entering the plains of skinniness, but she managed to carry herself in such a way that she gave the impression of being larger than she was. Sindy, although much plumper than Ana, looked like a warm breeze might unsettle her delicate balance.

Ana and Sindy, Sindy and Ana.

For every golden hair that fell in shimmering waves of liquid honey over Sindy's creamy white shoulders, Ana had lank, muddy brown strands that hung in tresses which always seemed to have been dried in a hurricane. Sindy saw the world through eyes of the brightest blue, so wide and serene that when she blinked, one felt for a moment that the oceans had suddenly dried up. Ana observed it through a layer of suspicion that she desperately wanted life to counter, all hidden behind eyes that were the sludgy green of wet bark. Sindy was pale, Ana was pasty. Sindy was naïve and simple and kind. Ana was an idealist, a fighter and a hardened cynic.

But this did not mean that they hated each other.

So when her stepsister showed up, waving her arms around as she tried to encapsulate the full horror of opening her front door and finding the King on the other side of it, the King who, *by the way*, had only come to see a sister who wasn't even there, and who, *coincidently*, was causing him no end of grief, and *also* the very same King seemed to be more annoyed than he should have been that the first sister, that is the *missing* sister, wasn't there, and *anyway*, he was inviting said missing sister to his Ball, which was to raise money for the deforestation that sister number one was fighting against, and he would very much like the absentee sister to come, but *only* if she would stop, *please*, squatting in his wood and specifically stopping him from accessing his water supply, Ana decided to listen.

Ana digested this information. From the rather pained expression on her face, it didn't seem to be going down well.

"He wants me to go to his Ball?" she asked, an entire orchestra of disbelief in her voice, including the triangle.

"Yes," Sindy said.

"To his *Ball*?"

"Yes."

"To *his* Ball?"

Sindy, apparently deciding to make things even more simple, nodded.

"Of *all* the nerve! I mean, seriously? Can you just...? Really? Does he honestly think I'm that shallow? That *we're* that shallow? I knew he was a megalomaniac with about the same moral compass as a, a, a, wheel of cheese, but I can't believe he would try to...! Right, well, you know what he can do with his bloody Ball? He can just damn well stick it where the sun doesn't shine!"

"Is that somewhere in the north?"

Ana deflated. "No… I just mean… I mean he can forget it. That's all. There's no way either of us are going."

"I don't think he invited me," Sindy said, before adding gently, "and I don't think that will stop him from hosting the Ball. He said he wanted to raise money. Sorry."

Ana stood up and stomped around her tent.

Money. She hated money. It seemed to be the one thing in the whole world that was guaranteed to turn decent people into conniving, dishonest, selfish, lying cheats. But if the King could get his hands on some, then he could find his water elsewhere, and then, once the giant steam engines were running, her small group of protesters would be about as effective as a glass shoe.

If only he would see that by cutting down the woods and expanding the city, he was drawing attention to their little home. The bigger Llanotterly became the more reason Cerne Bralksteld had to march on them. Ana, and indeed all the members of the résistance, were deeply afraid of Cerne Bralksteld.

They too had heard the whispers about forced evictions and villages burned to the ground; about the slave pits, buried deep in the stone walls of the city. The place where those who had fought and lost toiled in the manufactories, their skin burnt to a crisp from the boiling steam, their bodies held together by the bitter hope of death.

Ana had thought that the King's proclamation about selling the wood was just him showboating, trying to show the citizens of Llanotterly and their neighbours that he was the one in charge. Then, when it seemed he intended to continue in his madness, she'd thought that by moving out here and surrounding the widest part of the river, he might back down. But he hadn't.

This meant that she was still here, in an overcrowded camp in the heart of the forest, blocking the King's access to the only major water supply for miles.

It was a plan that, for all its functional simplicity, did not suffer from an abundance of longevity. During the day, it was quite jolly, but the fact was that there was only so long people could survive this close to nature. The whole drive of civilisation was, after all, to move human beings as far away from the natural world as bricks, mortar, clean water, cooked food and soft beds could manage.

The truth was that Ana wasn't sure exactly what to do about the fact the King was trying to raise money in order to work around her protest, but she would think on it and wait for guidance.

As it turned out, she wouldn't have to wait long.

Chapter Sixteen

There was a polite knock at the door.

"Come in, come in," shouted John.

Seven entered, bowing fluidly.

"No need to stand on ceremony, old bean, s'just thee and me, after all."

"As you say, my Lord."

The current King of Llanotterly was sitting on his bed, in a room with pastel papered walls on which paintings of his forebears stared down at him in silent recrimination. There was a thickly woven carpet on the floor, glazed windows and a large mirrored wardrobe along the back wall.

Seven stepped a little to the left, out of the reflection.

A small bronze and silver clock tick-tocked by the King's bed. John wound it every day, even though the old mechanisms were now well beyond usefulness. It had been bought abroad by John's father, Edward, when Llanotterly still had enough money to pay for a foreign education in the universities in Ota'ari, the First Kingdom. There the traditional lessons in arithmetic, astrology and ancient languages (the infamous three-As) were taught alongside more modern subjects like engineering, mathematics and the philosophy of elementis.

"Ah, S. Sit yourself down, fella," John said, pushing aside one of the piles of books littering his bed. "Got some matters to chew over."

"My Lord?"

John waited to see if he would take the invited seat, but as usual, the Adviser preferred to stand. "Been reading up on the steamers. Know anything about 'em, S.?"

"The technology was discovered in Ota'ari. Clockwork was the harbinger, but it is now the steam engines that power the worlds of agriculture, shipping and industry."

"Quite right, quite right," John said, smiling at his student. "The very first experiments were in Imi p'Antuf, a small place once, by all accounts. But do you know *when* all this malarkey went on?"

Seven didn't answer.

"Seventy years ago, old bean. Seventy years! Surprised me too, oh yes. Could've knocked me down with a feather and that's the truth of it. So, the question I asked myself was what, S.?"

"I would not presume to guess, your Majesty."

John leaned forward, causing the remaining piles of books to topple over, landing unnoticed on the thick carpet. He lowered his voice as if his bed-chamber were a likely den of intrigue.

"C'mon, S., it's not difficult. You know what's what."

For some reason, the Adviser's eyes wandered to the wardrobe.

"What's been the crack for the last seventy years?" John prompted.

"Pardon, my Lord?"

"Ehinenden, S.!"

Seven shook his head. "Apologies, Sire. I do not follow."

"Ehinenden, that's what, man!"

John watched as the Adviser frowned, trying to catch his gist. He wasn't disappointed.

"Ahh. Your Majesty refers to Cerne Bralksteld and the manufactories."

John beamed. "Indeedy. Thanks to the Baron it turns out Ehinenden's not really the Third Kingdom, more like *The* Kingdom. Ota'ari can't trade because of those paranoid Penqis, Voriias is too busy working over its own people and propping up Skjnelia. And Cairranbia's pretty much ruined now, thanks to Cerne Bralksteld taking all those people as slaves." John shook his head. "Hate the thought of slavery, S., though I'd be a damnable liar if I denied the benefit of it—look what the Baron's achieved off the back of it. Hellishly tricky business. My aunt used to say that slaves didn't know any better anyway, y'know, that they couldn't really catch on to what was happening to them. Be nice if she were right, eh, S.?"

John wasn't sure why, but he wanted the other man to confirm what his aunt had told him, even though he knew it was tosh. He could feel the need for reassurance inside him, like one of those pig's bladders the kiddies played sports with—all blown up in his chest, getting bigger and bigger.

Odd really, but there it was. There was just something about Seven that comforted. John always had the feeling he knew just what it was he wanted.

He waited for Seven to answer.

Come to think of it, he was taking his time about it. Unusual for him to not be quick off the mark. In fact, he looked dashed uncomfortable, like he was trying not to fart in front of a woman.

"You alright there?"

Seven shifted his weight, reaching up to touch the snake around his neck.

"Sire, you want me to tell you something we both know is untrue, and I find I cannot. I suspect they knew very well what turn their lives had taken, just as I am sure the current slaves in Cerne Bralksteld are aware of their fates."

The balloon in his chest deflated, but John nodded. He knew he'd been chasing smoke.

"Well, best we try and avoid any of that nonsense here," John said. "Baron's a nasty fella, and he wants more tax than we can pay. Llanotterly's a small state. We're farmers, builders, bakers. The whole of Ehinenden ain't much more than that, to be honest."

"And yet with the continuing rise of The Imperial City of Cerne Bralksteld, the fortunes of Ehinenden—Caer Marllyn, Marlais and Sausendorf—are changing, Sire, regardless of the region's historical preferences."

"Quite so, quite so. Seems like the world's on the cot," John sighed, frowning into the distance.

The clock continued to beat out its own paroxysmal rhythm, a series of missteps and dropped beats. John listened to the uneven ticking, which was not unlike his own Kingship: all wrong. He hadn't been sent to the right schools or universities. There hadn't been the cash. And his father should have lasted a good few years longer—now there was a lesson against fifty years of rich eating. So here he was, stuck with a near-bankrupt Kingdom with an immensely powerful, money-grabbing madman for a neighbour.

It really was a stinker.

"Got a lot on our plates, ain't we?" John said.

"...We... have, yes. Do not forget, though, that we have also much to our advantage. The docks in Sinne are yours, as is

Llanotterly itself. And the forests are our most significant asset. They are an enviable resource."

"If we could bloody well get at 'em. Which, as it happens, brings me to my point. We've still got to meet this wretched Ana woman."

"Sire?"

John stood up and walked over to his Adviser, putting his arm around his shoulder. "Of course, I say 'we'..."

He led Seven to his mirror. It was harder going than he'd anticipated. "C'mon man, no need to be shy. It's not going to bite. There we go. See? You're a handsome devil without that damn hood on."

"John?" A new note had entered the orchestra of Seven's accent.

"And you've got a way with words, damn right. More than once you've folded me like farthingale. So, I was thinking, y'see, that you could go down to that there camp on your tod, sort of thing, and speak to this Ana on my behalf. Do a bit of ambassadoring."

"Please, I am not—"

John patted him on the shoulder. "Course you are. I've got every faith in you, old soak. I couldn't wish for a better man."

If he hadn't had his hand on Seven's shoulder, John would have probably missed it, and even so, when he thought about it later, he really couldn't put his finger on what happened. He'd been speaking to Seven, trying to give the lad a bit of a pep talk, encourage him and so on, plus get this bloody Ana gel wrapped up, when the Adviser seemed to have a funny turn.

"You alright?" John asked. "You seem a little tense."

Seven gently ducked out of the King's arm and stepped away from the mirror. "I am quite well. If you have no more need of me...?"

"Nope, on your way," John said, feeling guilty for some reason. He studied Seven as he turned to leave, his hand already reaching for the silk hood at his waist. John's eyes started to sting.

"You know, S.," he called out, his vision blurry, "when you first rolled up here, I thought you were a rum fella, I don't mind saying so. But you've got a good head, and you don't mince your words. Been a delight having someone like you to take an interest in Llanotterly's wellbeing. Good show, old sport."

"Sire," Seven said, turning back into the room and bowing low before stepping out.

Seven stormed into his suite, slamming the large double doors closed. He paused for a moment, leaning back against the wood. His chest rose and fell rapidly and then began to calm.

He pulled himself off the door and padded towards his bed, his movements set to the sound of his jewellery. He landed heavily on the thick mattress.

Seven removed his silk hood and gloves, slowly flexing his fingers against the memory of the material. He folded the items up carefully and then tucked them, close at hand, into the waistband of his trousers.

To the eye of the invisible observer, it was in some sense a very minor change that overcame him when he entered the safety of his room, removed his protective clothing and allowed himself to relax. In feature, he was as he had always been: his eyes retained the same almond shape, and his jaw continued to be wide and square. His hair remained as tightly curled as a corkscrew and his shoulders broad, tapering down to narrow hips and a flat, strong stomach.

And yet if anyone had happened upon him now, in his natural state and too angry and exhausted to hide himself, all hell would have broken loose. It would have taken him a lot more than a bit of magic to set it right again.

He wondered that he ever thought he could manage such a task, surrounded by so many of them, bleating on and on about what they wanted.

And yet, was he so very different?

Was he not here now, entrenched to the point where the prospect of leaving—though of course possible, and it would hardly be the first time—felt very dissatisfactory?

Seven rubbed his temples in a way that suggested he was in pain, and indeed his forehead was caught in a frown which could have been discomfort.

It was John's fault, Seven told himself. With his good intentions and lack of confidence. Could he not see he was quite the most superior monarch this wretched place had seen in generations? Here was a human, such a weak thing, so mired in need and selfishness and fear, trying despite all of this to keep his people from harm.

Seven's fingers crept to the snake around his neck, looking for reassurance. Could he have resisted? What would have happened? With a stab of annoyance, Seven realised he could have refused if he'd wanted to.

"*Va*," Seven swore in the old language, shaking his head.

He was here now, was he not, and, for all that fate seemed determined to set obstacles in his way, every day, he got closer to his objective. Nothing would stop him, not John's earnest attempts at friendship, nor Ana's well-meant rebellion, nor the General Administration and its latest shill. There was no need for concern. Was he not just in his actions? Did he not strive for a greater good? He would be victorious.

He walked over to the large wooden desk in the corner of his chamber. It was Ehinen in origin, from the small Athenine forest in Marlais and thus extremely rare. The wood was thick and heavy, varnished to such a deep brown it was almost black. Carved woodland animals climbed up the legs and ran around the edges of the tabletop as if they had nothing better to do than look for a secret compartment or sneak peeks at the royal correspondence that littered its surface.

It was one of only two possessions that Seven had brought with him to Llanotterly, in addition to his charm and good looks and his strange ability to convince those around him he could make their wishes come true.

He rummaged through the desk's drawers and pulled out a sheet of crisp white paper and a bunch of pencils, wrapped with a red ribbon, which he untied carefully and laid on the desk.

He started to draw. He drew from memory. He had a good memory, something which, all things considered, was far from a blessing.

The pencils moved quickly across the paper, scratching back and forth in deepening shades of grey. He leaned low over the page, concentrating all his energy on his work.

The candles flickered and dripped wax, having nothing better to do.

Eventually, he lifted his head and looked at his creation. A young woman stared back at him from the paper, a slight smile playing on her lips. She looked as if she was about to say something, and that once she had, you would laugh. She was happy.

Seven stared at the picture, his strange eyes unreadable—eyes that, now he made no effort to mask them, were from edge to edge only the deep blue of the dead ocean.

He swallowed hard, as if he was trying to imbibe something foul-tasting but necessary, like a child sipping medicine, and pulled another sheet of paper from his desk.

Chapter Seventeen

Bea was waiting in Sindy's room. The eye of the imagination is no doubt focusing on one of two possibilities:

The traditionalist is probably seeing a small box room, with bare unpolished floors and a narrow, wrought iron bed, the springs of which squeak and stab in the night like a mouse with a vendetta. In the corner, there might be some hint at talents unused, like a piano or a dressmaker's doll.

Why not include a tattered sketch of the girl's dead mother on the old tea chest that serves as her bedside table? It can sit next to the stump of a candle, the wax cheap and dirty and given to filling the room with a greasy smoke that clings to clothing and stains the whitewashed walls. This room is barren and desperately sad.

Alternatively, some will have assumed the room is pink. It is, they might predict, a pink made up of a hundred different shades. Fuchsia curtains, possibly dotted with flowers or butterflies, drift lazily in the breeze, their carefully hemmed edges brushing against a soft cerise eiderdown that covers a coral sheet on a wooden bed whose frame is painted a gentle rose. A teddy bear, well-loved, missing an eye and with an amaranth ribbon tied around his ears, sits happily on the bed.

In fact, Bea was sitting in a slightly cluttered room that was in terms of colour palette neither the dismal beige of totalitarian poverty nor the headache-inducing pink of every shorthand description of a teenage girl. The walls were covered with plain, tasteful wallpaper. A small dresser sat in the corner near the window, its surface hidden under jars and pots of lotions and creams.

Bea eyed her bag. The Book was in there, causing it to bulge ominously.

She ran her hands through her hair, trying to ignore the enormity of what she was doing. There would be no getting out of it if the Redaction Department found out—this was definitely breaking with the Plot.

F. D. Lee

But what choice did she have? The introduction had gone spectacularly wrong, and she only had a few days before the Ball. All she needed to do was meet the girl, unofficially of course, and convince her to attend the Ball without an introduction. If she could do that, it would still be alright. Once the wedding happened and everything was Happily Ever After, this minor redraft would hardly matter. It probably wouldn't even make it into the Book, and then she could begin her training as a godmother.

Bea's train of thought was derailed by the sound of the front door opening. Sindy called out a general hello to the household and began climbing the stairs.

Bea covered the mirror on Sindy's dresser with a scarf and gathered her wits.

Sindy opened the door.

Bea smiled.

Sindy screamed.

Bea's wits made a dash for it in the confusion.

"Please! Don't be scared. I'm here to—I mean, I'm Bea. I'm your Fiction Man—, er, that is, your godmother."

Sindy opened and closed her mouth a few times, before replying, "but Mrs Morecombe is my godmother."

"No. I mean yes, I'm sure she is. But I'm your *special* godmother. Um. I'm a fairy, you see. Er. Ta dahhh!?"

Sindy continued to look uncertain. Obviously, a little more was needed.

"That means I'm here to help you."

This explanation wasn't helped by the fact that Bea, with her large bag at her feet and scraggly, homemade dress, looked not too dissimilar to someone who'd been caught mid-burgle.

"If you're a fairy," Sindy asked, approaching the question cautiously in case it turned around and bit her, "why haven't you got wings?"

Bea smiled, relieved—she knew this one.

"Because, you see, I'm a garden fairy. We don't have wings— that's the flower fairies."

"But I thought all fairies had wings and were a little more... er... little..." Sindy blushed crimson. "I mean you're quite.... That is.... I didn't mean you're... oh dear..."

"Well, garden fairies are a lot hardier than the other tribes," Bea said kindly. "Actually, any fae could be a godmother. Though you can try telling that to some people. It's like if your mother was a baker that wouldn't automatically make you a baker, would it? And, actually, I happen to think that fairies, especially garden fairies, are particularly well suited to being godmothers. Perhaps because godmothers are meant to be fair, ahaha?"

In the sight of Sindy's absolute mystification, Bea made the mistake of continuing. "Because, you know... we should be fair to the people we meet, I mean. Not fair as in pretty. You're the one who's supposed to be pretty. Not that you're not pretty..."

Bea stumbled into silence, wishing it had been higher up on her itinerary of must-see locales when going off-Plot with the heroine.

"What about the puff of smoke?" Sindy said, rallying much faster than Bea. "Shouldn't you have appeared magically? It's not very, um, 'godmothery' to lurk in people's bedrooms."

"I wasn't lurking. I was waiting."

"What's the difference?"

Bea waved her hand around airily. "Well, for one thing, I don't mean you any harm."

"But I don't know that, do I?" said Sindy, and Bea realised that although Sindy might be simple, she was not actually stupid.

"Noooo. No, good point. If I was here to hurt you, wouldn't I have done it already? I mean, it's not like I've come armed or anything."

Sindy's eyes moved from Bea to rest on her bag, which sat potentially stuffed with weaponry at her feet.

Bea could see that, as far as escapes went, the situation had received the cake with the file in it and was now industriously sawing through the bars to freedom. Which was why, reasoning that she might as well hang for a sheep as a goat, she did something else she had always been expressly forbidden from doing.

"Look, how about I show you how we travel into your world? It's sort of like magic. Then will you believe me?"

Sindy nodded, intrigued. Bea walked over to the dresser, pulled the scarf off Sindy's mirror and stared hard into the glass. Her reflection, picking up on her mood, glared back at her with equal intensity. Bea held out her hands, palm up, to the mirror's surface.

Nothing happened. In the reflection, Bea saw Sindy glance around nervously. A minute went by and then another, with no discernible change in the mirror. Just as Sindy opened her mouth to speak, the mirror took on an entirely new aspect. The smooth glass turned to an inky, milk-like texture, like it would make a 'glooping' sound if it were touched.

And then the mirror was no longer a mirror, but a window—a doorway.

Bea frowned in concentration, ignoring sludgy queasiness in her stomach the connection caused. Sindy leaned forward. She was seeing the Grand Reflection Station, a sight no character was ever supposed to see.

"Now can you take my word for it?" Bea asked, pulling her hands away from Sindy's mirror. The view of the Grand was swallowed by more inky blackness, and then the glass returned to normal.

"How did you do that? Is it magic?"

Bea rummaged in her bag for a mint leaf to chew. "No. Magic's not really anything." She saw the disappointment on Sindy's face. "Well, I mean, it's a special magic, I guess. It's to do with images. You just picture, *really* hard, where you want to be. That's why the older fae are better at it. They've been to more places, so it's easier for them to picture where they're going."

"Seems like magic to me. So why didn't you come in like that?" Sindy said.

"Because I'm not allowed to. I shouldn't even have shown you that. The Teller, *whocaresaboutus,* doesn't like my world and your world to get too close. But then," Bea added pointedly, "most people are pleased to meet their godmother. If you believe me, that is?"

Sindy gave it some thought. Happily, she appeared to reach the decision that if Bea was indeed a criminal mastermind, she probably wouldn't look like she was about to burst into tears of frustration.

"Do you promise you're not a burglar?"

"Yes. I promise."

"Alright. But I'll be checking to make sure nothing's missing."

"Fine, fine. Of course. Very sensible."

Sindy stepped further into her room, noticeably checking the top of her dresser and the little saucer of coppers by her bed. If she could have counted her possessions aloud without being rude, she looked like she would have done so. As it was, she had to settle for doing mental arithmetic, which meant she took on the appearance of a fish out of water.

A snide little voice in Bea's head pointed out that even now, when Sindy might lose a beauty pageant to a half-dead halibut, she was still unbelievably pretty.

It wasn't even that Bea was jealous. She knew she wasn't ugly, and anyway, the heroine had to be beautiful or else the story wouldn't work. It was just that Sindy was so pretty. She wasn't alluring, or sexy, or even attractive. She was just very, very pretty—even as she snuck with poor stealth towards her jewellery box to check everything was accounted for. She looked like at any moment, a little brown rabbit would hop onto her lap, or as if a bluebird was just waiting in the wings to join her in a duet. It was ridiculous. No one could be that wholesome.

Bea pushed the rogue thought down, to join all the other unwelcome whispers in the back of her mind.

"So, why are you here?" Sindy asked, her inspection of her room apparently concluded to her satisfaction.

Bea smiled her warmest smile and announced with no small flourish, "I'm here to help you marry the man of your dreams!"

"Will?!" Sindy cried out, her face lighting up like a thousand candles.

"Yes! No—wait. Who?"

"You're not talking about Will?"

"Who's Will?"

Sindy blushed. "His name's William, or some people call him Billy, or Buttons because his mum was a seamstress. He told me once he doesn't like those names, but maybe you only know him as Billy or Buttons..?"

Bea ignored the memory of the man from the kitchen. "I've never heard of him before this moment," she said, not exactly lying.

"Oh," Sindy said. "I just thought, when you said you were going to help me marry the man of my dreams, I thought you meant Will."

"Goodness no," Bea exclaimed, going once more for the flourish, "I'm going to help you marry the King!"

Sindy burst into tears.

"Feeling better?" Bea asked.

"Yes, thank you," Sindy sniffed, listlessly handing Bea her sopping handkerchief.

"That's alright. You can keep it."

"Oh. Thanks."

Bea took a deep breath. It was going to be much harder than she thought to get the story back on-Plot. "Come on, cheer up. You're going to be a Queen! How's that for a Happy Ever After? Every girl wants to be a Queen, don't they?"

"I don't know. Maybe."

"Think about how much better your life will be. No more pokey little cottage in the middle of nowhere. Dresses, and, and, shoes, and... um...clothes. And True Love. Your very own Happy Ending, married to a King. It's a Dream Come True."

Sindy's face crumpled. "I hadn't... I didn't mean to be ungrateful. I suppose I just always thought I'd marry Will."

"Well, you wouldn't have to stop being friends with him," Bea relented. "I'm sure the King could find him some work at the castle."

Sindy didn't reply; instead, she walked over to the window.

Bea nibbled at her fingernail. She could see the expression on her heroine's face as she stared through the glass. But Sindy really should see *why* it was such a good idea for her to marry the King— after all, what was the point of the story if not to improve her life?

Bea joined Sindy. She looked down at the garden and was surprised to see how beautifully it was planted. The majority of it was given over to a vegetable patch as necessity dictated, but someone had also planted little beds of wildflowers. They drifted on long stems in the late summer breeze and reminded Bea of things best forgotten.

"What about Ana?" Sindy asked suddenly.

"Who's Ana?" Bea asked, dragging herself away from the cliff of the past before she fell over.

"My stepsister. She's fighting the King at the moment because he doesn't understand 'the inherent dangers of drawing attention to our kingdom and is more interested in lining his own pockets and growing fat off the blood of the people'. If I marry the King, Ana will be very hurt."

The ugly sister. But she wasn't supposed to do anything until the Ball. Why was it all going wrong? Bea bit her lip as she worked out all the different permutations of what Sindy had said. After a moment, she gave up.

"You'd better tell me what's been happening," Bea said, already dreading what she was going to hear.

"…And so there's a Ball at the end of the week which he says Ana has to go to, but she refuses and I've promised her I won't go, but I've no idea what the King will do when she doesn't turn up, and there's no way I can go without her, either. Sorry."

Bea stared at the wall, hoping it might have some words of advice. It remained unhelpfully silent.

"Right," she said at last.

"Sorry," Sindy said for the twenty-seventh time.

"Right."

When Sindy opened her mouth to apologise again, Bea stood up and started walking around the room. Sindy joined the wall in keeping quiet.

"So. This is fine. It's fine," Bea said as she turned in circles. The bedroom wasn't really designed for dramatic effect, but Bea wasn't about to let that stop her.

She doesn't want to marry the King.

"Now then. Let's see about getting you to this Ball," Bea said very loudly and deliberately, despite the fact that Sindy was barely half a room away from her.

"But—"

"Really, how angry do you think your sister would actually be? After all, if you marry the King, I'm sure you can stop him cutting down the forest."

Sindy's eyes widened, making her look like a startled kitten. Rather ruining the effect, though, was the way she was also wheezing.

"Alright, maybe not," Bea said, taking pity on the girl.

She turned around the room again.

"How about this: I get the King over here again, and you explain to him that neither you nor Ana can make the Ball, but while he's here you both Fall In Love?"

"I don't think that would work," Sindy said.

"Why ever not?"

"I just… I don't know why he'd fall in love with me."

Bea paused her pacing to look at Sindy. She was a girl of such natural beauty and grace that it would have been easy to believe she had inspired every permutation of the Spring Festival, including the rather alarming ones involving poles, ribbons and raw eggs.

But she doesn't see it like that, does she?

And she doesn't want to marry the King.

"Well, it seems there's no way around it then," Bea said, much louder than was necessary for the little bedroom.

Sindy perked up. "Really?"

"It certainly appears that way, yes."

"Oh, wonderful!"

"Good, I'm glad you're on board."

"Thank you so much for helping me!"

"You're welcome. Now then, where's your sister's encampment?"

"We'll be so happy together—"

Sindy stopped, realising that, once again, something had happened which she wasn't entirely sure of. Unfortunately for both women, this kind of thing occurred so often that Sindy simply took the default position that she was somehow to blame for the miscommunication. If she hadn't, a lot of misery might have later been avoided.

"Ana's camp?" Sindy whispered.

"Exactly. I'll go there and convince her to attend the Ball."

"Oh. Yes. Of course."

"It's the only way to get this whole thing moving again."

"I see."

"So, then. We're agreed," Bea said in the face all the evidence. "How do I find your sister?"

Chapter Eighteen

Bea crept up to Ana's encampment as evening set in. She'd had to walk, which had taken much longer than she would have liked. The trouble with the Mirrors was that you had to use them. You couldn't, for example, go from the reflection in Sindy's mirror to a reflection in Ana's camp, you had to go via the Mirrors in the Grand, and Bea had no intention of straying so close to the GenAm.

Now she was finally at the camp, it wasn't what she'd been expecting.

From the way Sindy had described her sister's endeavours, Bea had built up a mental picture of something military: organised and hard, with little white tents in rows, and flags, and mud. What she was in fact seeing was a sprawling, haphazard mess.

Everywhere she looked, men and women were milling around, all engaged in some kind of task that was no doubt necessary but seemed to her to be being enacted more for appearances' sake than anything else. Someone was even whittling, for goodness' sake.

The general mood was quiet. In the distance, a guitar was being played; badly, but the thought was there. Nothing very much was happening, and the world seemed for once to have agreed to get to bed early and to leave all the drama and intrigue for tomorrow when it could be considered with a fresh head.

Bea hung around the edges of the tree line, unsure if she could just ask one of the background characters to introduce her to the ugly sister. She wasn't supposed to meet her, but then she shouldn't have met the King either, nor hid the involvement of the hooded man, nor introduced herself so early on to her heroine. She felt rather like a robber who would happily murder the restaurateur, but baulk at not tipping the waitress.

She was still dithering ten minutes later when the Probably-Yes-But-Possibly-Not-Anti appeared out of one of the nearby tents. Bea watched furiously as he sauntered over to a large wooden trunk and, reaching in, pulled out two earthenware jugs.

He ambled back towards the tent he had exited, stopping on the way to speak to one of the male background characters. They seemed to be sharing a joke. The man reached out a hand and touched the It-Really-Would-Be-Impossible-Luck-If-He-Was-An-Anti's arm with an awkward friendliness, and then quickly dropped his hand to his side, where his fingers continued to fidget.

Bea watched as the hooded Not-Quite-Ruled-Out-Yet-Anti said something to make the man smile. The conversation drew to a close, and the There's-Still-No-Conclusive-Evidence-One-Way-Or-The-Other-Anti clapped him on the back and went back into the tent. Bea noticed that the background character stared after him until the calico door fell.

She looked at the tent he had entered. Of course, the ugly sister could be anywhere in the hundreds of tents. The place was swarming with people, any number of whom could be of interest to him...

The chance of Bea's character being inside that tent was...

...*mortal gods...*

...Absolutely guaranteed, wasn't it?

Bea thought a very rude word and, careful not to draw attention to herself, crept to the back of the tent. Kneeling down, she gently lifted up the edge and pushed her bag through, with the Book inside it, before wriggling in after it.

A fire was burning in the centre of the tent. She could make out the shape of the It-Would-Almost-Make-It-Worthwhile-If-He-Was-An-Anti laying on his side by the flames. He had removed his hood and gloves, perhaps against the heat, perhaps to allow him to better converse with the skinny young woman with the prominent nose sitting next to him, who perfectly matched Sindy's description of her stepsister.

There was a lot going on between him and the ugly sister, but the thing that stood out—stood out more than the way they leaned into each other, stood out more than the spectacle of his beauty without the hood—was that he was blue.

Not blue in the sense of 'he was so cold his skin took on a bluish tinge'. For one thing, it was a pleasantly warm, early autumn evening.

No, he was actually *blue*.

His skin was the pale summer blue of cornflowers, and his hair was a mess of dark blue, tightly curled locks. His wide-set eyes were a deep peacock, with no whites and no irises. They were blue from lid to lash and lined thickly with kohl. Even his fingernails were blue.

Bea, like all the fae, lived in a world of ginormous trolls, yellow, spiky-scaled witchlein, and bony, black-toothed gnomes, but even she couldn't escape the nagging sense that this woman should have commented on the fact her companion was entirely *blue*. At least asked him if he wanted a blanket or something.

In fact, the ugly sister's lack of reaction was extremely annoying. Bea, in her effort to be recommended to the FME Academy, had dyed her green hair grey and made sure she only used dull colours when making her clothes, in order to better look the part. The Teller was very clear about how the fae presented themselves in his stories. But even if he wasn't, it was just something that was understood.

You worked at night when the shadows masked you, and you were little more than a dream. You hid in the forest or the mountains, away from the steam engines and the lamps of the cities, the things that would expose you, confirming you and stripping you of your mystery. You showed yourself rarely, and only to the ones who needed to see you. After the free-for-all that was the earlier Chapters, when babies were stolen, young men murdered and maidens locked away, the fae had had to learn to be very careful about their involvement in the lives of the characters, lest they turn still further away from their beliefs.

And yet here was this hooded fraud, wandering around blue and bold as he liked, and the ugly sister wasn't raising an eyebrow.

Bea crawled further into the tent.

There was no one else present, and, as luck would have it, the tent was also cluttered. Boxes, chairs, cushions and rugs littered the floor, offering Bea exactly the cover she needed. She settled down and began to listen.

"You are correct, Ana. The King is playing a dangerous game with the lives of his people," the Adviser said.

"You don't need to tell me. If Cerne Bralksteld decides we're getting too big… It doesn't bear thinking about," Ana replied, not only thinking about it in detail but discussing it at length as well.

"And yet I sense you think on this often. You are a very thoughtful and dedicated young woman. You strive. All these things I can see are true."

Ana nodded. She didn't see the point in refusing compliments when they were deserved. Although she hadn't imagined it would be the mysterious foreign man the King had taken on as Royal Adviser who would be paying them to her.

People said he had too much influence. They said he whispered in the King's ear at night and filled his head with strange ideas. Nobody knew where he came from, except that it was obviously somewhere *else*. Somewhere different. He wore a hood, they said, because the sight of him would cast a spell on you, making you do things you didn't want to do.

That was the problem, Ana told herself as she watched Seven lean forward to pull one of the terracotta flasks of wine from the flames. You couldn't listen to rumour. Sometimes people were so stupid. *Oh yes*, let's just cut down the forest, the main source of work for miles around, and give it all away to the Baron in Cerne Bralksteld, as if that'll sate him. *Oh yes*, let's just ignore all the ships that keep disappearing between Sinne and Ataji—although, sometimes it was the big O&P steamers that vanished, and that wasn't so bad, considering the O&P's business practices, but still.

People were very good at ignoring the facts or creating their own. It drove Ana to distraction.

Seven waved the flask at her.

"You shouldn't drink it that fast, it's not altar-wine," she said, pouring herself a generous measure. "Doesn't it burn your mouth, drinking from the bottle?"

"No. I am used to the heat," he replied, his accent for a moment thickening. "And there will be no altars or altar-wine remaining if Cerne Bralksteld invades."

"Exactly! But I don't know what we can do. If the King can find a way to power the tractus engines without using the river, I can't see how we can stop him. I can't really see how we can stop him anyway," she added. She probably shouldn't be speaking so freely to an agent of the establishment, but there was something very trustworthy about the Adviser. She could—begrudgingly—understand why the King was apparently so taken with him.

Seven leaned back, resting on his forearms. Ana shuffled around the fire to sit next to him.

"Honestly, I thought the King was an idiot. Or that he was just doing all this for show. But I guess I was wrong. What do you think?" She asked, placing her hand in the narrow gap between them.

"It is a shame you will not debate with him directly," Seven said, putting his hand over hers. "Of course, I understand the conflict it presents, but if you only would…"

Ana pulled away. "He's invited me to his Ball. He thought he could bribe me. That's hardly the behaviour of someone who's prepared to listen to dissenting views. You're a case in point, aren't you? He's only sent you here to cajole me."

"I understand your misgivings," Seven said gently. "And yet, I am sure if anyone could convince him, you are the one. You are right to raise these concerns. And, my Lady, I am not given to fawning. I will speak my mind, and in this I am certain. You and the King should meet."

He met her eyes, his own heavy-lidded from the fire-wine. They were such a strange blue, unusual against his warm brown skin. She'd never seen eyes that shade before… Ana pinched the bridge of her nose. She wasn't sure why, but whenever she tried to concentrate on his face, her head began to ache. The wine was probably stronger than she realised.

"You're not what I expected at all," she said.

Seven shifted under her gaze.

"Am I not?"

"No. You've got empathy."

"I do not follow."

The corner of Ana's mouth lifted. "It means that for someone so disgustingly good-looking you're actually quite thoughtful. You seem able to see things from both points of view."

"Of course," Seven said. "Empathy."

"And I suppose if I were to meet with the King, he'd have to at least listen…"

"Certainly. If you do go to the Ball, I am confident you will make him see reason." A pause. "You can utilise your empathy."

Ana cracked her knuckles. "Yes, you're right. This is my burden. I need to see it through, even if that means stepping into the lion's den."

"Exactly so," Seven answered, taking another gulp of wine.

He hadn't set out to drink so much of the strange, bittersweet fire-wine. However, Ana had proven herself to be quite charming, with her passion and her hostility, and he was against all expectation rather enjoying himself. She thought him to have 'empathy', a view that was unexpectedly welcome.

It would certainly explain some of his recent actions. He had refused to believe he could be slipping so fast or so far from himself, and now there was a reason for it. *Empathy.* And it made sense, did it not? Selflessness was the purview of the righteous, and he was, above all else, righteous.

Seven took another sip of wine and allowed his thoughts to lead him away from Ana's angry censure of the King. He was unsurprised to find himself instead thinking of Maria Sophia. She was always there, waiting for him to let down his guard. She hung in the air, danced on the water, crawled through the earth, always, inevitably, heart-breakingly, reaching out to him. She was his soul, torn from him, and he was nothing but a phantom, empty and waiting for her to—

"Look at that fire go," Ana cut into his reverie. "There must be a lot of sap in that branch."

Seven looked up. The fire was spitting, white-hot embers jumping into the air and falling, half-dead, to the floor. He ran his fingers through his hair.

"Huh. It's calming down," Ana said. "I wonder what that was all about. Anyway, that's what happened. He just disappeared."

Seven cursed his inattention and, ignoring the nausea it caused, dipped into his magic in an effort to find the right thing to say.

"This is the way of men, I fear," he said, rolling over to rest on his elbows so that he could look up at Ana.

"Oh yes," Ana scoffed. "Let's just absolve all responsibility, shall we? What would you know about anything, anyway?"

"I know what it is to be abandoned."

Ana lifted an eyebrow in surprise. "What happened?" she asked, leaning across him to get the other jug of wine, allowing her arm to brush against him as she did so.

Seven considered how to answer. It wasn't in his nature to refuse people when they asked him for something, and the instinct to see Ana's desire for knowledge fulfilled was strong.

"There was a woman. She was stolen from me," he said eventually.

"You mean she was taken by the slavers?" Ana asked, laying a comforting hand on his thigh.

"In a manner of speaking."

He turned to look at the fire, watching the flames as they danced across the blackened wood.

"So what happened? Where is she now?"

Seven looked round to see Ana staring at him, concerned. He moved closer to her, so his face was inches from her own. He reached up and stroked her cheek. "I am currently more concerned with your plight."

Ana leaned into the touch, her eyes meeting his. Seven shifted position, bringing himself closer to her.

He couldn't fathom what it was about Ana that had gained her such a fearsome reputation. Certainly, she was vocal and not afraid of disagreement, but neither was he. Her nose was big, and she had a boy's figure, all height and straight lines. Was that all it took? Or was it her self-assurance? She wasn't shy in expressing her wants, but that didn't make her an intrinsically wicked person.

Seven also knew what Ana didn't tell him, a gift of his nature that allowed him to sense what people needed, wanted, desired. Ana wanted a better world, and Seven, drunk and full of new-found morality, wanted to give it to her.

She smiled, sweeping her dull brown hair from her face in anticipation of what they both knew was going to happen next.

Seven reached out and pulled her down onto the itchy rugs and his hard body.

Bea didn't know where to look as the There's-Not-Much-Hope-Of-Denying-It-Now-Anti pulled Ana into what was one of the most passionate kisses she had ever seen—though she was forced to acknowledge that most of the kisses she had witnessed involved the grey area in which the hero is kissing what he at that point *genuinely believes* to be the dead body of his True Love.

They were not, thankfully, kisses designed to lead to anything further. *This* kiss, however, not only had designs on the near future—it had schematics and planning approval.

Bea backed hastily under the canvas. She stood in the encampment, warmed against the chill by the furious blush that was covering her entire body. There were perhaps something in the region of a hundred thoughts galloping through her mind with all the speed of racehorses on derby day, but the general gist was:

What in the five hells does he think he's doing?

Chapter Nineteen

"So what's the story?" Melly asked, tapping her cigarette on the edge of the ashtray.

After some disagreement, they had finally settled on meeting in a pub in the middle ring of Ænathlin. Bea hadn't wanted to sit in her flat, but she'd refused to go to any of the cheap dives by the wall, and Joan's house was ruled out as a meeting spot because it was too full of squabbling sisters to think in, and Melly... Bea wasn't actually sure where Melly lived. In all their years of friendship, the witch had never invited her or Joan to her house.

"I don't know where to begin," Bea said. "He's definitely involving himself in the Plot, but I don't understand why. He's done me a favour though, getting the ugly sister to the Ball."

"But he's a *you-know-what*?" Joan whispered over the foamy top of her beer.

"I think so," Bea answered.

Melly tutted. "I told you that days ago. What now?"

Bea flicked her fingers against her wine glass. It was so cheap, it thunked.

"I don't know. I can't ask Mistasinon any more questions about Anties."

The friends fell silent, all lost in their own interpretation of gloom. Joan drew pictures in the head of her beer. Bea fiddled with the stem of her glass. Melly smoked and tried not to cough.

"It's like that mouse," Melly wheezed after a particularly angry inhalation.

Joan pricked up her ears. "What mouse?"

"It's nothing," Bea said quickly. "It was a long time ago. I'd only just arrived in the city."

"She traded some silk—*silk!*—for this little clockwork mouse," Melly said, ignoring the huffs and rolled eyes of the fairy in question. "Silly little thing, it just went around in circles. But you were fascinated, weren't you?"

Bea gave a semi-shrug that might indicate that yes, she had found the little toy mouse somewhat intriguing.

"Fascinated," Melly confirmed. "Anyway, she got it home, and what did she do? Opened it up and pulled all the bits out. Just as you please, little bronze spiky wheels and the mortal gods know what else all over that table of hers."

"What did she do next?" Joan asked.

"I am here, you know," Bea muttered.

"Now here's the rub: she tried to put it back together," Melly finished triumphantly. She was a little disappointed when Joan failed to react in the way she had anticipated. The little tooth fairy tilted her head to one side, trying to visualise the scene the witch had described, and then back the other way. After a moment, she took a sustaining mouthful of beer.

Eventually, Joan said, "I don't understand what's so bad about that."

"Because it was wilful. No good comes of acting in such ways." Melly turned to Bea. "And now look at the mess you're in. Thinking you could work it out. The Teller, *whocaresaboutus*, has it all organised, that's why it works. And you broke that mouse," she added.

Bea folded her arms. "Yes, well, that's all well and good, but it doesn't work, does it? The Mirrors are breaking."

"Keep your voice down," Melly hissed.

Bea glanced furtively around the room. No one seemed to be listening to them, but you could never tell. Informers were everywhere. Joan shuffled on her seat.

"We should leave," Melly said.

They walked towards Bea's, subdued. The streets were emptying. Curfew was due to begin.

"The Mirrors really are breaking, aren't they?" Joan asked once they were safely away from the bar.

"I think so," Bea replied, dropping her voice. "The other day I ran into some fae. I think they were Anties—but the thing was, everyone else there seemed to agree with them. They were openly talking about the end of the Chapter."

"They think it was better back then," Melly said.

Bea looked up at her friend, shocked.

Melly was older than either Bea or Joan. She had let slip once, after a long night of drinking, that she had been working before the Redaction—a dangerous thing to admit to. Bea had asked her about it the next day, but Melly had denied everything, and then Bea had gone to watch another Plot.

"Was it?" Bea asked.

"What?"

"Better?"

Melly wrapped her arms around herself. Her voice was so low Bea had to strain to hear her. "It was… yes, in a way. We were free. We had control over our lives. Anyone could create a story, though of course, not all of them were any good. But yes, it was better, at times. Until the Mirrors started to crack."

"They're breaking now," Joan shivered.

Bea glanced over her shoulder. The spire of the GenAm glowed white in the darkness. It loomed over the overcrowded city, always visible, always reminding you what could happen if you stepped out of line.

"What I don't get is why," Bea said, and then wondered where the thought had come from.

"The Anties," Joan replied.

"I suppose so. But the Mirrors have only recently started to break—I mean actually break, not just crack," Bea said.

"And?"

"Well, I mean, the Anties have been around for ages."

Melly frowned in the darkness.

"Maybe it's taken this long for it all to build up?" Joan suggested. She didn't sound like she was convincing herself, let alone anyone else. Her voice dropped. "I heard there're no more spare Mirrors."

"They've been saying that for years," Bea said.

"They've not replaced the last one though…"

"Let's just get back to Bea's," Melly said. "I think we need to have a chat."

They walked on in silence.

Bea thought about her Plot. It wasn't just for herself, was it? She wasn't doing this just to prove a point, even if the point was one that needed proving. The Mirrors were what was important. Get the belief in, and the Teller would fix the Mirrors. Bea didn't know how he did it, but so far, he always had.

And it was an easy Plot. Three acts, no real obstacles to overcome except the ugly sister and a half-hearted Love Lost And Found at the end. If she could only make the Happy Ever After she could take her Book back to the GenAm, and there was no reason why they shouldn't let her train to be a godmother.

And then it wouldn't have all been for nothing. If she could make it work, she wouldn't be the selfish little fairy who had left her family after her father disappeared, just because she was angry and frightened and in pain, thinking she would find a better, safer life in the city. She wouldn't have to feel so guilty because all her Dreams Would Come True.

"We're here," Melly said.

Bea woke up from her thoughts and led her friends past the sleeping form of Ivor, his filthy arms splayed over the counter like the contents of a spilt chamber pot. They walked across the lobby, Melly's heels clicking on the floor. After what felt like a lifetime, they reached the relative safety of the staircase.

"So," Bea said, "what do we need to have a chat about?"

Melly sighed. "Look, you weren't there."

"Where?"

"Before the Great Redaction. You seem to think all the rules were written just to spite you. But when we could do what we wanted, we were uncontrollable," Melly said, resting her hand on the bannister and then pulling it away. She looked at her fingers, which were covered with a fine, tacky coating of something thick and pungent.

"It can't have been that terrible," Bea said. "How can being free to follow your dreams be bad? That's the basis for nearly all the Plots."

"Oh yes, freedom," Melly sniffed, wiping her fingers down the yellowing wall. "We were free, alright. Free to interfere, free to trick and free to frighten away all the characters."

"So what really happened?" Bea asked.

Melly paused on the step. "You know what happened."

"No one knows what happened."

"Let's get inside."

Bea hastily climbed the last few flights to her floor and opened her door. Melly and Joan stepped into her bedsit and sat on her faded sofa.

"Will you tell us?" Bea asked, grabbing a saucer for Melly, who had already lit a cigarette, to use as an ashtray.

"I'm not sure this is a good idea," Joan said, but she didn't make to leave.

"There isn't anything I can tell you that you don't already know," Melly answered.

"Yes, but if we already know it, then you're not telling us anything new," Bea said, thinking her way through the carriages of fear on the witch's train of thought. "And if we don't tell you what we know and what we don't know, then you won't know if you've actually told us something we don't know, and what you don't know we don't know won't hurt you."

Melly stared at Bea, her cigarette hanging from her lip in defeat.

"Did that make sense?" Joan asked.

"Yes," Melly said slowly, "but it probably shouldn't have done."

"So will you tell us?" Bea asked.

Melly sighed and crossed her legs, smoothing out the folds of her black skirt so that it hung like a lost moment.

"The Great Redaction happened because we lost our focus. We were too proud, too certain of ourselves. We've always used the characters' belief to keep the Mirrors open, but back then, we went too far. It started in the 5th Chapter when we stole babies and soured milk and killed cattle and worse, much worse. The characters did the only thing they could."

"They stopped believing," Bea said.

"It may be closer to say they stopped retelling. They started all their infernal experimentations. They built bigger cities. They watched the stars and played with numbers and tried to understand the world they lived in. Then they made those machines that eat the water. Now they can guarantee their harvests, travel the Shared Sea. They've got mechanical locks to bar their doors and lamp oil to keep the lights burning through the darkness. They didn't need our help anymore, and they didn't want our stories.

They stopped talking about us, stopped telling tales around the campfire. We were lessened."

"But all that stuff's ages old," interrupted Joan. "Everyone knows the problems with the Mirrors began with the King and Queen. That's the 7th Chapter, not the 5th."

"She's right," Bea said. "The King and Queen mismanaged the Plots, and the characters stopped believing. That's why they gave up their Chapter to the Teller. Everyone knows that. Don't they?"

"Does it matter? None of the old Narrators were any good," Melly said. "The Teller Redacted all the old stories because they didn't work. You weren't there. You don't know what it was like. We were falling apart. The city wasn't like it is now, even with the Mirrors and the Anties and the Beast. Back then, it was madness. We all thought Yarnis was going to come back, that there would be another war. And then the Teller came along. Yes, he brought the Beast and Redaction, but he also gave us the Plots, and they work. And he fixes the Mirrors, no matter what the Anties try. The GenAm keeps it all running. Even the white suits are useful, in their way. Look, we all know it isn't perfect, but what's the alternative?"

"Freedom," said Bea instantly.

"Freedom? The freedom to starve? To kill ourselves fighting over the few remaining characters who believe in us? The Teller Cares About Us."

"The Teller Cares About Us," echoed Joan, dutifully.

Bea kept her silence.

Melly stared at her and then shook her head. "Look. Whether you're a cabbage fairy or an FME or even the Narrator, it won't change the truth. The Teller, *whocaresaboutus,* took control and saved us. The blood and the bone were rewritten into Just Punishments and True Love and Wicked Old Witches and all the rest of it. And that's all there is to it. Yes, it's contrived and boring, but it's easier too. The characters accept these stories. The Mirrors are healing."

"But that's not true," Bea said.

"Well, no," Melly conceded. "Not anymore, because the Anties have started messing around with the stories. Which is exactly why you must promise me, Bea, that you'll report this Anti. I'll speak up for you, explain that you didn't realise what he was. Please, Bea."

Bea stood up and walked over to her window. She stared out at the night-time city, watching as the lights brightened nearer the centre. And somewhere behind her was the wall and beyond that the Sheltering Forest and her birthplace. She pressed her forehead against the cold glass, wondering if she was destined to spend her life caught between the place she'd run away from and the place she was running to, never quite escaping one nor reaching the other. It was exhausting.

But there was no denying it. She might have an Anti in her story. The heroine hadn't seemed at all pleased to meet her. Worse still, she'd gone against the Plot at every turn.

She turned back.

"Alright. I promise. This is too much. You're right."

Melly visibly relaxed.

The three friends chatted for another hour or so, covering safer and thus more boring topics until Melly made her excuses and left. Soon after, Joan stood up to leave as well, stretching her little arms in a yawn.

"Hold on," Bea said.

"Oh?"

"Joan... I'm not going to stop the story. I can't. No—please listen. How can I possibly stop it now? Do you really, honestly think the GenAm won't get the Redactionists involved?"

Joan lifted her eyebrows. "Well... not normally. But Melly said she'd speak up for you."

"But what good will that do? Melly's more senior than you and certainly me, but she's not a Plotter. She's not a Redactionist. Why would anyone listen to her? I'm up to my neck in it, Joan."

"But he's an Anti. If you report him, they might be grateful."

Bea shifted on her feet, a guilty look on her face.

"Bea?"

"It's not just him. There's more..."

"Why in the name of all things writ did you show her the Mirror?"

"I don't know—it seemed like a good idea at the time!" Bea cried. "I'd already broken the Plot by going to see her early. And she wasn't even happy about marrying the King."

"Well... I mean, would you be pleased if a stranger told you to marry someone you've never met?"

Bea shot her a death glare, powered in no small part by the fact she suspected Joan had a point.

"Perhaps they like being told what to do," Joan said diplomatically. "Isn't that why they believe these stories in the first place?"

"I don't know," Bea said, deflating. "I've never had direct involvement before. Maybe it's always like this."

"Well, you're right about one thing: you definitely can't tell the GenAm now. What do you know about the Anti?" Joan said, her tone of voice suggesting the heavy weight on the end of her conversational fishing line was going to be a boot.

Bea made a face. "He's smug and handsome. He knows it too."

"Is there nothing else? Didn't you say he sounded very old-fashioned? I'm sure that must mean something. And, I mean, he's blue. There's got to be something in that. I don't think I've ever heard of a blue fae before."

Bea dropped her head back and stared at the ceiling, trying to gather her thoughts. "I don't know. That's the problem. I don't actually *know* anything—we're not allowed to know anything." She sat up. "He did say something to the ugly sister that seemed strange. Not what I imagined an Anti to say, I mean. He said he'd lost someone."

"Was it your heroine? That might explain why he doesn't want your Plot to finish."

"Nooo," Bea answered, thinking of the ugly sister. "I don't think so."

"So who did he lose?"

Bea drummed her fingers on the arm of her sofa. "He didn't really say anything clear about it, but it sounded like he'd loved whoever it was."

Joan shook her head. "That doesn't fit. If he's so good looking and confident and charming, he can't be capable of loving someone. All the really good guys are a bit awkward or shy—you know, repressed. It's always the charming ones that end up being bastards. C'mon Bea, you know that."

"I suppose so."

"Alright then, how about we have a look in your Book? Perhaps there's something you've missed, you never know."

Bea cast her eyes over her small bedsit, looking for her bag. She was certain she'd dumped it on the floor when she'd come home, but there was nothing there. She climbed to her feet and turned around. She went to her kitchenette and opened the cupboards with increasing freneticism.

The Book. Where was the Book?

Panic rising, she dashed into the hallway and down the stairs to the front door, past the sleeping Ivor, and outside. She scrabbled around in the poorly lit street, but there was nothing.

It was no good. There was no escaping it. It wasn't in the house. It wasn't in the street. She didn't have her bag, and so she didn't have her Book. Could it have been stolen? Would she have left it somewhere? Pins jabbed into her, icy and sharp, making her skin itch. As soon as anyone opened it and saw the Book, they'd return it to the GenAm. She stood in the cold night air, trying to think.

When had she last seen her bag?

What had she been doing—

Bea froze.

She knew where her bag was.

Bea climbed back up to her room, each step heavier than the last.

"I've left my Book in the ugly sister's tent."

"Are you sure?"

"It's not in here or outside," Bea said, trying not to scream. "I had it in the tent with me. I left so quickly."

"Can you get it back?"

Bea thought about the cluttered tent, with its boxes and chests and cushions and throws. And everything else that she knew to be inside it.

"Probably," she said, dreading what she knew she would have to do, but dreading more the ramifications of losing the Book. "It'll be right at the back of the tent, not easy to spot."

Joan tried a smile. "Well, there you go then. Nothing to worry about. Just go back and get it."

Bea thought about going back into Ana's tent, knowing what was happening there. "Not now. In the morning."

"What about the Anti?"

"He won't be there."

"How do you know?"

"He's not the type."

"Well, if you're sure," Joan answered, sounding not at all sure herself but willing to let it go.

Bea pinched her nose, trying to overcome the panic still coursing through her.

"It's a shame you don't have any other clues, though," Joan said, wrapping her arms around her knees.

"Actually... there was something else," Bea said, remembering the paper Ivor had given her. "What do you know about the 2nd Chapter?"

"Not a lot," Joan said after a moment. "It's hard though to know what happened before the Teller, *whocaresaboutus*. You could always go and ask the Index to let you look at histories, but they never say much. You can't ask Melly. Not now you've promised her you were going to stop," Joan added reproachfully.

Bea nodded, glum. "That's that then."

Joan poked her friend in the arm. Bea looked up to see the tooth fairy was grinning.

"Not necessarily. I might know someone who can help. Get your Book back, then come and see me. The game is afoot!"

Bea gave her friend a puzzled look. "The game is a foot? What game? Whose foot?"

Joan thought for a moment. "I read it somewhere, I think. Maybe it's a hand?"

"Why a hand?"

"Everybody needs a helping hand, don't they?"

Bea shook her head. "What about 'best foot forward'?"

Joan tugged on her straw-like hair. "That's true. How about this: The game is definitely a body part of some description, quite possibly more than one, but either way all limbs are useful, so really we shouldn't discriminate either in favour or against them?"

Bea smiled and nodded, and wondered what would happen if she just turned herself in to the Redactionists.

Chapter Twenty

Dawn was breaking as Bea arrived at Ana's encampment. She paused on the edge of the forest, trying to quell the sense of unease slouching through her veins.

She needed to get her Book back and, if possible, she wanted to speak to the ugly sister. And if she saw the blue Anti again, she'd tell him what's what. That was all there was to it. That was all it was. It wasn't a big thing.

Of course, the title for 'most important thing right now' was being hotly contested, with shortening odds on 'how on Thaiana will Bea manage to get the heroine married to the hero'. However, as much as she was trying to ignore it, 'should Bea even be trying to get the heroine married to the hero' seemed to be coming up the inside lane with alarming speed.

Bea chewed her lip, thinking about love and weddings and Happy Ever Afters, careful not to make any sound as she crept towards Ana's tent.

Safely inside, she scurried behind one of the many boxes and, once her heart stopped racing, slowly peered over the top of the chest. She was met with the surreal and unwelcome sight of the muscular, blue Anti sleeping flat on his back in the centre of the tent, a thin blanket covering him. Ana was nowhere to be seen.

Bea started looking around for her bag, being as quiet as she could. The tent was circular, and she wasn't sure exactly where she'd come in. Still, it had to be here somewhere—it wasn't like she'd been asked to join in the more central activities of the night before. It couldn't have gone far.

She crept around the outer edge of the tent. She was certain this was where she'd been sat, but there was no sign of either bag or Book. She crawled back over to where she'd entered the night before. Perhaps the bag had got caught on a peg. It hadn't.

Muttering curses, Bea returned to where she had been eavesdropping and started searching again around the boxes and crates she'd hidden behind. Still nothing.

Her stomach trembled. She brought her hand to her mouth, overwhelmed with the urge to scream, throw up, or both.

There was a gap between two of the crates. It wasn't big, but it might be big enough… maybe the bag got kicked somehow…

There really wasn't any chance this had happened, but Bea was now at stage five on the panic-scale: blind hope. She lay on her side, her face pressed into the dust, and reached into the gap, praying to all the mortal gods she might feel the soft cotton of her bag against her fingertips.

"Ah. The fat little fairy. Imagine my delight."

Bea froze.

She looked up, and of course, there he was, sitting on the crate above her in all his blue, exotic glory, the sheet tied around his waist. How he'd managed to move so quickly, she had no idea, but his silence was accounted for by the fact he wasn't wearing any of his jewellery, except the snake necklace.

Bea pulled her arm back and got to her feet.

"I knew you would come," he said.

"And why's that? Because you told me not to?"

He had the gall to smirk. "That too. You have lost something, have you not?"

Bea felt the world stop. "You've got my Book?"

"I know where it can be found, yes."

"Well, you just better hand it over, that Book is General Administration property."

Bea was disappointed when her statement failed to have any kind of impact on him. She tried another approach.

"If you don't give me back my Book, I'll be forced to do something I'll regret." Well, that was true, at least. She really would regret having to go on the run from the white suits. "Don't you realise you're putting us both at risk of Redaction?"

"I fear I must contradict you," the Anti said. "You are yet to inform against me, is it not so?"

"Oh really?" Bea put her hands on her hips. "How do you know I don't have the Beast outside, waiting?"

"If there were a three-headed hound amongst the humans, I think we should both be in no doubt as to the fact."

"Look," Bea said in a tone of voice meant to be reasonable, "I'm not trying to be unfair, but you can't just go around taking what you want. So, if you give me back my Book and leave now, I won't report you. I'm asking you nicely, aren't I? Go somewhere else, ruin someone else's life."

The blue Anti pulled his legs up under him, sitting crossed legged and unmovable on the crate. "I have no intention of leaving. But perhaps we can resolve our disagreement. It would please me to do so."

Bea hesitated, unsure what to do. But she was stuck, wasn't she? She'd deviated from the Plot, shown her lead character the Mirrors, and now she'd let her Book fall into the hands of this creature. Telling the GenAm was an empty threat, not unless she wanted to join him on the Redaction Block.

Maddeningly, he was just sitting there, half naked, waiting for her to answer. He was also looking absurdly at ease and quite deliciously louche, two facts Bea was certain he was aware of. He looked like he would be happy to wait all day.

She tapped her fingertips against the flesh of her palm, which was tacky with sweat.

It's a rather remarkable trick of the mind that there can be a wicked little voice that whispers in your ear that you've done it before and nothing happened, so why not do it again? *Everything will be fine,* it says. *Things are bad now, but something will turn up. The good will prevail. You'll be rescued, you'll find the answer at the last minute.*

No one dies in a story…

"Alright, fine. I'm Bea, by the way, since you ask."

"And I am Seven. Now, let us discuss. As I have stated, I am not going to surrender," he held his hand up, silencing her before she could speak. "No, I am not, though you ask so nicely. I am resolved in my intention. This story cannot continue as your Plot would have it."

"So you *are* an Anti-Narrativist," Bea said miserably.

"Perhaps. I have not heard the term and know not its definition."

Bea gave him a sharp look, but he appeared to be serious. How was that possible? Everyone knew what an Anti was, surely and most crucially the Anties themselves.

"It means that you want to ruin all the Plots, that you don't believe The Teller Cares About Us. It means you're evil."

"I have been called worse." His eerie blue eyes fixed her with a long stare. "I found myself thinking about you last night."

"I—You—What?" Bea was completely wrong footed. It didn't help that she was pretty sure she knew what he'd been doing last night.

And then he laughed in her face, his white teeth flashing against his dark blue lips and gums.

"Yes, indeed it surprised me also. I am not a reflective creature, and yet recently I find I am empathying myself, empathying these humans—and now, of all unnecessary things, empathying you."

"Empathying? You mean empathising?"

The Anti's smile vanished. "I mean I am indecisive," he snapped. "And in your case, it will not do. So perhaps, madam, you might help me to understand this vacillation, and then I may return your Book to you. We shall engage in the old mannerisms, shall we not? A game of threes."

He laughed at this, though Bea could hardly see what was so funny. She fisted her hair. What was it about life that enjoyed making her miserable? What had she done to deserve this? And, the thought rising with the inevitability of a seesaw, what choice did she have?

"Fine. Three questions, and then you give me back my Book."

"What is your purpose here?"

"Seriously? That's your question? Easy. I'm here to do good. I'm making a Happy Ever After for these characters. When I've finished my story, there will be a wedding, and the whole Kingdom will rejoice because everything will have worked out as it should."

"That is as bold a lie as ever I have heard, and I believe I have heard many."

"You've got your answer. It's not my problem if you don't believe me."

The newly confessed Anti leaned back on his arms, his blue midriff stretching out like a cloudless sky. "I can see this is all very difficult for you. I can help you, you know." His voice dropped low. "Why not let me help? You need not fight so valiantly, you need not run so far and so fast, nor struggle so. Is it not exhausting?"

Bea stared at him, but her eyes were focused on something only she could see. For just a moment it seemed that she might be listening to him, and Seven leaned forward expectantly—

"I want my story," Bea said, suddenly refocusing. "Look, I'll make you a deal. I won't report you—not if you leave now and let me do my job."

Seven's nostrils flared. "And I decline, once again. Now, answer me this: The other day, when you unleashed the bear upon John and Sindy, what would you have done had I not been there to save them?"

Bea shook her head, her body tensing at the mention of the near-miss with the bear. "You answer me. Why are you here? Even if you don't care about me, or ruining Sindy's Happy Ending, don't you know the Mirrors are breaking?"

"A fair question, but you have nothing with which to bargain. I repeat, what would you have done?"

"What do you think I'd have done? I'd have saved them, of course. I was, in fact, going to save them, and then you interfered."

"I apologise. In the future, I will leave you to attend to any drug-addled bears we may happen upon. You are aware, however, that such an action would most certainly have resulted in your removal from your story?"

Bea stuck out her chin. "I'm not about to watch people die. There. That's three. My Book, please." She held her hand out impatiently.

Seven jumped off the crate, landing softly. Bea took a step away from him, but he ignored her, walking instead back to the centre of the tent.

"So, where's my Book?" Bea repeated, following him around the crates, keeping her distance.

Dropping his sheet unselfconsciously, he began to put on his bracelets and bangles. He did this far too slowly for Bea's comfort.

"You are quite irregular," he said.

"And what in the five hells does 'irregular' mean?" Bea said through clenched teeth, refusing to look away. She would have bet her life he was trying to embarrass her with his body, and she was damned if she'd give him the satisfaction. Still... if she blushed now, she'd save the Redactionists the trouble and go and throw herself in the river.

He picked up his white linen trousers from the floor. "You say that godmothers create happy endings, yet another would have left them, too afraid of reprisal to risk being uncovered. Another godmother would have sought refuge in the hallways of the General Administration, not a large stick."

"Yes. Well. We're not all the same."

He looked up at her. "Evidently not. Does it not concern you that your brothers and sisters in arms would have allowed their deaths?"

"Well, I... I've never thought about it."

"Perhaps you should? You are mistaken, by the way," the Anti continued in a muffled voice as he pulled on his tunic. "I have not said I wish to stop the story. And you, curious, concerned little godmother, cannot in good conscience believe that these stories are for the best. I know this is a falsehood," he finished, pulling his head free.

"You don't know anything about me."

"No, I know not *everything* about you. But I sense enough to know you have mistaken obsession with drive, guilt with injustice. I know you want to escape what you are, cabbage fairy," he said, reaching for his hood and gloves and tucking them into the waistband of his trousers. "Your desires are no different from my own, I simply have the courage to face them."

Bea stared at him, unable to believe the extent of his arrogance.

"Excuse me? I think I must have something in my ear. I could have sworn *you* just said courage. What courage does it take to hide behind hoods and pretty words and smiles? You don't impress me."

His strange eyes narrowed.

"Or frighten me," she added untruthfully, too angry to care. "You make some guesses—wild judgements, in fact—about me, and who in the five hells are you? Just some Anti who doesn't care about anyone but himself. You obviously have no idea about True Love or Happy Endings. You just want to get your own way. You're very quick to say I'm in the wrong, but you're the one trying to stop someone marrying a King. And what will you do when the ugly sister wants to see you again? You'll settle down with her and have little blue babies, will you? You're nothing but a liar and a hypocrite. Now. Give. Me. My. Book. Back."

Before Bea had any idea what had happened, he was on top of her, his icy cold arms wrapped around her, his hand clamped hard across her mouth. She tried to kick him or break free, but he had her too tightly, and she hadn't been expecting it.

She thought suddenly that this was the moment she was going to die. She didn't think about her life, about being a fairy, or even her friends or forgotten family. She just thought how badly she had misjudged herself and that—perhaps—it would be nice not to have to carry on.

And then she felt his chilly lips against her ear.

"Hold on," he whispered, and they disappeared.

...a rush of noise that sounded like sandpaper against her skin, that tasted vast and old and, though she was covered by something, hurt wherever it touched her...

She could feel something wrapped tightly around her.

Her mouth was covered. She took a long breath in through her nose. A warm, spicy-sweet scent filled her, reminding her of lazy, dream-filled summer days she'd never experienced but had always known were happening somewhere, to someone else.

She wanted to swallow, but her throat was so dry she wondered if it was still made of flesh and blood. A wave of sickening, boiling giddiness washed over her, and for a moment she didn't know what she was looking at. Her vision was filled with white and blue, and she wondered if she had died.

There was a voice, beautiful and deeply pained, telling her to breathe, telling her it would pass. It landed deep inside her, bypassing her ears to touch a part of her that made her feel desperate and needy.

Images spun in front of her eyes like a zoetrope... fractured, alive and silent:

Playing in the grass with Mustard Seed, her father calling for them to come home... The fires and the screams and her mother, crying... The GenAm, white and clean... Rags To Riches, Lost And Found... No one stopping her, no one telling her she couldn't...

...No attacks...

...No empty spaces by the fire...

...Happy Ever After...

"Can you... Please... I need...I wish..."

She began to panic. Her words were muffled. She couldn't breathe. She was going to suffocate. And then the voice again, rushing through her like blood and hope and desire, filling her veins, sighing promises:

"Breathe. Breathe, and you will be restored."

A thunderous rhythm, like the death roll of a thousand drums. Everything was blue. She pressed her head forward, brushing her forehead against the endless sky.

No, not the sky. Too hard, too cold, too empty. Ice. Hard and bitter and forgotten. Freezing, burning, refreshing. Ice, not new but old, hard as diamond, miserable as the space it came from.

The drums were beating too fast, too fast. Surely no one could keep up such a rhythm...

The ice was moving, shifting beneath her cheek, her forehead, her heart. Pulsing, in and out, in and out...

She groaned against the chilly surface, not wanting to lose it. It surrounded her. She pressed her lips to it, desperate, hungry for what she knew it could give her.

It felt like...

It was almost like...

As if someone were...

Bea frowned.

She had her head against the Anti's chest, her cheek pressed against him. Even though she could hear his heart beating, he felt cold and hard, as if there was no life in him. He still had his arms around her, his hand over her mouth.

Too late, she realised she was kissing the palm of his hand. She struggled against him as her senses returned. His hold was light, but it made no difference. Being in his arms was like being kept in by cold weather. Some part of Bea knew that if she could face it, she could leave, but somehow it just seemed easier to stay put.

"I am about to turn you around. Please do not take this as a slight. I enjoy being kissed," he said as he spun her around. His voice, normally so silvery, was rough and unappealing.

Bea kicked his shin, hard. He grunted, but neither let her go nor removed his hand from her mouth.

"Do you know where you are?"

About forty feet in front of them was a little garden, divided into sections for vegetables and herbs. It was still morning, and the wildflowers were turning their heads towards the climbing sun. Bea nodded grudgingly, recognising the heroine's garden.

"Watch," he whispered in her ear. He rested his chin heavily on Bea's head, his body against hers. He was breathing awkwardly: short sharp gasps of air pressing his chest into her back in jumpy movements.

Bea shifted her stance, ready to ram her shoulder into him, when she saw something that dislodged any thoughts of escape.

A beautiful blonde girl in a cheap dress was running through the garden, her skirts flying out behind her like angel's wings.

Bea stared as Sindy raced up to a young man in overalls. She was running so fast she stumbled but righted herself before she fell. Her cheeks were flushed, and her lips were trembling.

Bea stiffened.

"It is a shame you cannot hear them," the Anti said in her ear. Annoyingly, he seemed to be recovering. "I predict Ana has just informed her sister that they will indeed be attending John's Ball."

Bea stared. Sindy was waving her arms around urgently. The young boy grabbed her hands and held them in his own. She said something to him, but he just looked down at her, his expression as brittle as baked bone. He dropped his hands and turned away from her.

For a second Sindy stood, rooted to the spot, her hands hanging at her side. And then she brought them up to her face, hiding her expression from both him and Bea.

It's something else. It isn't because of me, Bea told herself, knowing as she thought it that it was a feeble thing.

Sindy must have said something. The boy turned and reached out to her, an ugly red blush blooming on his cheeks. He patted her on the shoulder, his hand lifting up and down in mechanical, juddering actions. But it was enough. Sindy dived into his arms, wrapping herself around his stocky frame. He stood frozen, and then, slowly, he put his arms around her and held her.

There was something so easy in their embrace. He stroked her hair and whispered words into her ear, words that Bea couldn't hear and realised she didn't want to. She was watching something deeply private and exceptionally beautiful.

She had the sensation that if she allowed herself to understand it, it would change everything. Everything she believed in and had worked for would wither and die. Everything she had told herself she didn't need, didn't want, that wouldn't make her happy, would take on a significance and consequence she had never imagined.

Bea's chest was tight. She couldn't breathe. The earth was spinning beneath her feet. There was a fire in her lungs, causing her throat to dry to a crisp. She watched as Sindy looked up at the boy, her arms wrapped around his thick middle.

Bea's hands gripped Seven's powder blue arm so tightly her knuckles whitened.

The girl, *her* heroine, *her* character, stood on her tiptoes, bringing her perfect face up to this dirty, stocky country boy…

Bea shut her eyes tight and brought her head back against Seven's face as hard as she could, gratified when he cried out in shock and pain. His arms dropped, and she ran on shaking legs from the sight of the two humans kissing in the dappled sunlight.

As soon as she was under the cool shade of the trees, Bea came to a faltering stop. She was feeling giddy and sick and, just underneath that, waiting for its moment, was a great chasm. She could feel it under her skin, waiting to pull her in.

She dropped to her knees, gasping for breath.

"Was not that informative?" Seven asked, appearing next to her. There was a smear of black blood on the underside of his nose, such as might have been missed by a quickly wiped hand.

She turned away from him, too angry to be upset, too upset to be angry.

She felt his hand on her shoulder.

She shrugged it off.

"It is understandable for you to—"

"Will you just shut up! Every beautiful girl dreams of marrying a King! It's what they're there for!"

"Still you persist in this ridiculous fallacy? What is it you believe will happen—that your girl will kiss John and instantly fall in love with him?"

"True Love—yes," Bea said. "That's what happens. That's why the Plots use it. Everyone knows that."

Seven snorted.

"Oh, and what do you know about it?" Bea said. "You're not a character. They like these stories. True Love and Happy Ever After."

"Love is not happy," Seven answered, his kohl smudged eyes darkening to a deep, midnight blue. "Love is painful. Love is sufferance and sacrifice and passion. It is the blood and the soul of life."

"You sound ridiculous," Bea answered back. "Love doesn't have to be so over the top. Love like that is just as bad, just as unthinking."

"Have not you gained insight from the scene before you? Can you not see what real passion is?"

"What do you know about anything? What can you possibly know?" If Bea had been a volcano, the locals would have started dashing around the house, gathering up their possessions.

"You show me things like… like… that," she continued, waving her arms in the direction of Sindy's cottage, "but you're just pushing this to get what you want! You're too good looking, and you've got all these clever little arguments, and you're so bloody pleased with yourself, aren't you? You might as well have 'villain' tattooed on your forehead."

A part of her, outvoted and ignored, was screaming at her to look at the way the Anti's hands had balled into fists, how he was now facing her, his body rigid. But she was angry and, underneath her anger, was the fear that everything he said about Sindy was right.

"You're nothing, nothing, nothing," Bea yelled at him. "You sleep with her sister, and you steal my Book, and you make all these wild accusations, and you seem to think you're somehow better and smarter than anyone else. But you're not, in fact, you're disgusting and selfish and cheap. It's no wonder the GenAm hates you so much. I understand now why they Redact creatures like you. No, Redaction's too good for you. *It wouldn't hurt you enough.*"

She glared at him, gasping for breath, daring him to fight back. He stepped forward, his mouth a thin line, his body casting a shadow over her. She steeled herself.

And then he looked away, saying something in a language Bea didn't recognise, a soft and rounded tongue that she imagined would be written to look sweeping and beautiful.

"Pardon?"

"I do not disagree with your insight," he said. "I wonder that you are unable to turn such clarity of understanding on your own actions. You have laid many accusations at my door, and yet what have I done that you do not so eagerly strive towards?" He met her eyes with his empty gaze. "I believed you sensed the truth of it, that you were better than the rest of them, that when you saw the reality of Sindy's feelings, you would revise your position. Clearly, I was mistaken."

"I'm not... What's wrong with them believing?" Bea asked, a note of pleading creeping, uninvited, into her voice.

"You do not sell belief, you sell 'belief-in'. Belief in true love, as if everyone were entitled to it. Belief in a simple solution to a complex problem. Belief in one type of person, one type of future."

"No, I don't. I offer people dreams, and hope, and, and, something to organise their lives with," Bea said, not sure why she was trying to convince him. "I don't make them into 'one person'.."

"Oh, no? Let me recall your doctrine: Kings, Princes and their ilk must marry girls whose only asset is their beauty. Not clever girls, not worthy girls, not girls who could rule. Powerful women, older women—like one day you will become—are nought but wicked creatures, consumed with jealousy and unfit to hold position. No," he said as Bea began to speak, "I am not finished. Let us turn our attention to the men. As long as the woman is something to be won, it follows only the worthy will prevail. It matters not if they truly love the girl, nor if the man is cruel or arrogant or unfit to tie his own doublet. As long as he has wealth and completes whatever trials are decided fit, he is suitable. For what is stupidity or arrogance when compared against a crown? The good will win and the wicked perish, and you and your stories decide what makes a person good or wicked. Not life. Not choice. Not even common sense. You."

Bea opened her mouth, but no words came out.

"*Va,*" Seven spat. "How could you possibly understand what it is to be so restricted?"

Bea shook her head. "No, no, no, I see what's happening. You're just trying to confuse me. That's obviously how you Anties work. You lie and twist everything up."

He reached out and grabbed her by the shoulders, squeezing them hard. "I have shown you only the truth, and you confound it to fit your needs. And if you, Bea, believe yourself to be above censure, you have not half the wit I credit you with. You are a wicked creature, as am I. All those futures, all those lives stolen— do you ever think on that? A shallow, vapid fantasy I may be, but *you* are dangerous and selfish and completely indefensible."

"Let me go," she shouted, banging her fists hard against his chest. "You don't know anything!"

The Anti lost control. "I know more than you could ever begin to understand," he shouted, his breath cold on her face. "You pretend to offer hope of a better life, but all you do is take! You are selfish and dictatorial, caring only about your quota and your Mirrors and damning your victims to the purgatory of prewritten futures! You know nothing of what it is to suffer!"

Bea wanted to destroy him then. Wanted to diminish him, erase him, make him small and insignificant. But right now, she couldn't think of a single thing to say to do so.

Seven dropped his hands from her like she was scalding hot. "This serves no purpose. You are not what I thought. Your Book is in the small carved box by Ana's bed. Do not say I do not fulfil a bargain."

And then he wasn't there. Bea stared at the patch of space where just seconds ago he had been, and where now there was only empty forest. She looked up in the direction she had come from, where Sindy and the human boy were.

She stood for a moment, lost. And then she began walking away from the cottage, back towards Ana's encampment to get her Book.

Chapter Twenty-one

Bea appeared through the Mirror, her bag and Book safely in her hands. She had found the Book exactly where the Anti had said it would be. Perversely this annoyed her; as if it would have been better that he'd lied about the Book's location, keeping it hidden from her. Still, here it was, and here she was, back in the Grand.

The station was once again full to bursting point, and the checkpoints were up. The red GenAm banners fluttered in the breeze of hundreds of breathing mouths. Bea normally didn't question them—she barely even read them anymore. They were just part of living in Ænathlin, like the dirt and the smell.

Now it was like she was seeing them as an outsider might; as she must have done once, a long time ago. She looked over the station and saw, like a new soul stepped into an old world, those same banners that had surrounded her for years:

"The Teller Cares About You"

"Carelessness Creates Crossed Plots"

"Anti-Narrativists Operate In Thaiana"

"The Redaction Department: Protecting Your Safety"

It was like there suddenly were a thousand tiny little messages hidden in the everyday humdrum of her life.

She bumped into the checkpoint, distracted.

"Sorry," she said, dragging her eyes to the brown-suited dwarf on the gate.

"I need to stamp your papers," he said, obviously unimpressed by her apology.

"Of course, of course." She handed him her Book and waited while he checked her in. When he handed the Book back, she headed quickly for the exit.

"Bloody fairies," he muttered as he waved the next fae forward.

Back in the safety of her home, Bea felt absolutely lost. She drifted around the room, picking things up, moving them to new positions and then changing them back again. She straightened out her bedsheets, organised her cupboards, and set the chairs under her table so they sat neatly. She wiped down her surfaces. She brushed the mud and leaves from her dress and went about fixing, poorly, a new hole in her skirt.

An hour and two pin-pricked fingers later, she felt no better than when she'd started.

She flopped down at her rickety table and buried her head in her arms. She couldn't help going over what the Anti had said to her, even though every time she replayed the morning's events, it made her feel heavy.

The Anti had said things which could—which should—be easily dismissed as propaganda. Except that he'd also *shown* her things she simply couldn't ignore. Things that she felt she should have seen herself. And, like a splinter under a fingernail, she couldn't easily shift the guilt she felt at the thought of Sindy marrying the King.

Bea groaned.

How was this possible? Her first ever character and she wasn't behaving like a character should. Sindy, who apparently had feelings and wants and desires that simply didn't fit. She was a beautiful, kind, young girl. She should want to marry a rich, handsome man and, Bea didn't know, have babies or brush her hair or whatever it was beautiful girls did when they married Kings.

But Sindy didn't want any of that. In fact, from what Bea could tell, all Sindy wanted was to be with the stocky boy she'd kissed in her garden. It wasn't a grand dream, certainly not the kind of Dream that should Come True. But then, Bea had the kind of dream that shouldn't come true as well.

She'd always believed that the Plots helped people. But now she couldn't quieten the voice in her head that kept saying 'but that's not exactly true is it..?'

She had certainly thought more than once that things could be better organised—that perhaps it would be wiser to select clients based on a little more than their ability to hold a note or look good in a raggedy dress.

She recalled one of the first stories she'd worked on. She'd taken on a Plot-watch from one of the other FMEs, an old, drippy-eyed woman who should have been jolly but was, in fact, merely sad. Bea couldn't remember her name now, but it had probably been something like Angie or Flo. Like all godmothers, she had been short and bosomy, with the telltale purple dress and grey bun. Flo, or maybe it had been Doris, had tried to liven herself up with a bright yellow sash that had disappeared into her rolls of fat like the last hurrah on New Year's Eve.

It had been in one of the faraoli in Ota'ari, the First Kingdom. On this occasion, like so many others, Bea's job had been to watch the story, making sure nothing happened to disrupt it. But as she'd waited, bored and frustrated, the unwanted and disturbing thought had occurred to her that the GenAm had selected this heroine because she had been the only one of age and who lived in a cottage that was remote enough to allow them to finish the task without risk of interruptions.

Of course, the girl hadn't particularly minded finding out she was the long-lost daughter of an old and gentle Sefipht, but Bea remembered thinking that that wasn't the point.

The Sefipht had died not long after being reunited with his daughter and seeing her married off to a young man who had more of an affinity with a fishing rod than with another human being. Doris/Irene had returned to orchestrate the wedding, collect her Book and scold Bea for being Bea, and that was an end to it, as far as she had been concerned.

Bea, on the other hand, found herself having to try very hard not to think about what was going to happen to all the citizens who now had as their rulers a girl who had never managed anything more advanced than a sewing kit and a young man whose idea of a sustainable food supply chain was to catch an exceptionally large fish.

Bea shook her head, dislodging the memory, and stomped over to her little window.

Her one-room apartment was divided into three sections by the rather ingenious use of imagination. One third of the room was given over to her narrow bed, another was the area she liked to refer to as her sitting room—a battered old sofa and a table with one leg shorter than the others—and finally, a section devoted to the kitchen. There was a shared bathroom down the hall.

What no amount of imagination, no matter how liberally applied, could give the flat was security. Ivor, brown-toothed and foul, would only really be good at stopping burglars who considered halitosis a serious deterrent—though, in particular regards to the gnome, Bea wouldn't have taken odds on how often this had actually worked.

Still, in deference to the possibility that the criminal underworld of Ænathlin were capable of securing a peg to their noses, she had taken to hanging her most precious possessions in a little bag out of her window. It was a trick Joan had picked up in one of the many detective books she'd stolen from Thaiana. Bea wasn't really sure how much help it actually was in keeping her belongings safe, but since she had nothing to trade for a strongbox, she took what she could get.

She leaned out of the window until she was all but hanging over the ledge and rummaged around in the bag. After a moment she fished out a small, corked glass vial and pulled herself back in.

Placing the vial carefully on her table, she left her room and walked down the musty hallway, as dank and dismal a corridor as ever imagined, into the rusty, shared bathroom. She grabbed a piece of tissue and walked back to her room, pulling the door closed gently behind her.

Very, very carefully she pulled the cork from the vial and, having placed the scrap of tissue over the rim, upended the bottle, letting the paper soak up a small measure of the clear liquid.

She put the cork back in the vial, placed it reverently back in the bag outside her window and took her tissue and herself to bed, where she got under the covers and lay sniffing at the doused paper, trying not to cry.

There was a noise at her door.

Bea could hear it through the covers. It sounded like someone was trying to open the door without forcing it. Groggily, she wondered why any burglar would be so considerate—a good kick would bring the whole door in, including the frame. And she then realised it was probably Joan—she'd said she'd go straight to Joan's house once she'd got her Book back, hadn't she?

Bea emerged from her blanket, her eyes screwed shut against the glare of the sun through her window. It didn't come. She let one eye creep open. Her room was bathed in the dirty orange of early evening. She must have fallen asleep.

The noise at the door persisted.

"Alright! Hang on!" She shouted.

The noise stopped.

Bea stumbled across the small space from her bed to her front door and pulled it open. "Oh Joan, I'm sorry. You won't believe what happened when I went to get—what in the five hells are you doing here?"

Mistasinon gaped at her from where he was kneeling in her hallway.

To say each was surprised to see the other was to miss an opportunity to use the word 'flabbergasted'. Mistasinon recovered first.

"...Hi," he said.

Bea stared at him.

"Hi," she said.

"So, um..." she added.

And then she slammed the door shut, leaning against it like it was the last line of defence between her and the hounds of hell.

"Are you alright?" Mistasinon asked through the wood.

"Yes, everything's fine."

"Oh. Only you shut the door in my face."

"Yes. Sorry. I was, um…" She looked around for inspiration, but nothing presented itself. "...naked?"

She heard Mistasinon laughing. She looked down at herself, still in her homemade dress.

"Am I really so awful to open the door to?"

"I wasn't expecting anyone, that's all. I've been working on my Plot."

"Of course. I didn't mean to disturb you. Let me explain."

Bea swore, but pulled the door open and stood in the gap.

"You've got a mouth like a sailor," Mistasinon said, gifting her with his funny, sad little smile.

"I don't think that's a compliment," she replied.

"It's not an insult, either."

"Why were you kneeling outside my door? It's not exactly business hours."

The Plotter bent down to pick up a polished leather satchel that had been resting by his feet. "I dropped my bag, I was picking up the papers." He tapped it against the door jamb but didn't open it. "I was out of the office this afternoon, working. I was heading back and thought I'd follow up on your story. The Second Act should be starting soon, and I figured I'd save you a visit to the GenAm. You seemed nervous the other day."

"Oh."

"But I shouldn't have just come barging over. I'll let you get on. I mean, unless…" He let the sentence hang in the small space between them.

"Yes?" Bea asked.

"Would you like to have dinner with me? If you're not too busy on your Plot?"

Mistasinon smiled anxiously, already embarrassed.

"Let me get my bag," Bea said. She had no idea why.

Chapter Twenty-two

Bea was relieved the streets were relatively quiet. They passed a few elves, one of whom shouted something at Mistasinon's blue suit and then darted down an alleyway, but otherwise, their journey was uneventful.

Mistasinon brought her to a tiny, plain café just a few streets in from her building. It was further away from the wall and thus somewhat safer and cleaner, but not so far into the city centre that the area was devoid of all local colour. The main hue being, currently, a pool of oily black blood outside the stairs up to the cafe.

"Careful," he said, gently steering Bea around the macabre puddle.

The café was nice enough, and it sold foods Bea had never tasted before, but which Mistasinon seemed to know quite well. There wasn't much on the menu, but he ordered what he could for them.

They ate in awkward nervousness, Bea forgetting her manners more than once as she allowed the conversation to drain away. She didn't know why he had brought her here or why she had accepted, and although it was impossible, she kept waiting for him to ask her about the blue Anti, Seven.

Mistasinon looked at her, his tawny skin warmed by the wall-mounted lamps, spluttering on the dregs of their oil. Then he smiled slightly. "I can guess what you're thinking."

Bea looked up in horror.

"You're thinking about your Plot."

"Nooooo, no, not at all. I was thinking about... um, isn't it strange that the heroines always end up asleep?"

"Hah. I've thought that too. It seems a little pointless, really."

"Pointless?"

"Well, of course, not pointless," he corrected himself.

The owner of the café, a fat dwarf with a stained apron, came up and hovered uncertainly.

"Do you want some coffee?" Mistasinon asked.

"Only if you do," Bea replied.

F. D. Lee

Mistasinon rubbed his neck. Bea thought he was about to say 'no', and then he nodded to the proprietor. She found she had to ignore the unexpected wave of happiness that washed over her. She had no idea where it had come from.

"So, have you travelled a lot?" she asked. For some reason, she was regretting the silence during their meal, and now it was nearly time to go she wanted to make up for it.

Mistasinon smiled his quiet smile and leaned back in his chair. "More than most. But it's always nice to be back in Ænathlin, even with the current troubles. Don't you find that?"

Bea thought about it. She'd always loved Ænathlin, not so much for what it was but what it *wasn't*. It wasn't, for example, where she had grown up.

"I remember when I first arrived here, I honestly thought I was dreaming. It just seemed so unreal to have made it this far. I suppose I always feel a little bit like that whenever I come back."

Mistasinon chuckled. "Yes, I know that feeling. I spent a long time in a very grim place, and I can tell you I'm grateful every day that I'm not there. So what made you want to be an FME?"

Bea took a sip of the hot, bitter coffee. "You won't believe me."

Mistasinon leaned forward, his eyes alight. "Are you a difficult person to believe, Buttercup?"

Bea threw an olive at him. Mistasinon's hand shot out, much faster than she would have expected, and caught it before it landed. For just a moment, she felt uneasy. And then he smiled at her and shrugged. He handed her back the olive, his fingertips brushing against the palm of her hand and a gentle blush colouring his cheeks. Bea laughed, and after a second so did he.

"So, are you exceptionally dishonest?" he asked. "Do I need to check my pockets before I leave you?"

"You know, I've always wondered about that. Why don't the humans, the characters I mean, notice all the things we take? The whole city's made of stuff we've stolen. I'm sure I passed a nest the other day that was made entirely out of teaspoons."

"The tompte's house outside the Baker's? The one on Blind Pin Alley?"

Bea nodded. "I know that once the characters knew we were real, and I get the reason why it's better for us to be… less real… but I do think they'd notice. They just explain it away."

"It's the belief," Mistasinon said. "It's difficult to really see something when you've always believed it to be a certain way. It's like, I don't know, suddenly being aware of the air. Not impossible, but why would anyone try? At least, until there's a problem."

Bea thought about the banners at the Grand, floating through her life like spider webs, keeping her in place without ever chaining her down.

"Bea?" Mistasinon said when she didn't reply.

"Sorry. I was just thinking. Well, I only hope they don't start noticing now, or I'll never manage to furnish my house."

Mistasinon leaned forward and poured her another small glass of the strong coffee.

"You do look at things in novel ways," he said.

"It was just a joke."

"I know that. Still… Do you want to know what I think?"

No. I don't even know what I think.

Bea nodded. "Sure."

"I think there are two of you. There's the one that wants to be a Fiction Management Executive, who writes letters instead of waiting to be recommended and takes any Plot-watch going. And then there's the cabbage fairy, the one who asks about the Cerberus and grows thickets and wonders about sleeping Princesses."

Bea pulled back, insulted. "I don't know what it is you're implying, but I'm serious about becoming an FME." She swallowed. "In fact, there's something I need to tell—"

"I didn't mean to offend you," Mistasinon apologised, interrupting her. He looked wretched. "I'm not very used to being with others. I've only ever really had one friend… Mortal gods. Look, sorry," he said dismally, giving up. "Of course you're professional. I quite understand if you want to leave."

Bea paused, feeling guilty. "I didn't mean to be rude. I'm just… I'm used to people saying I can't do anything."

"That wasn't what I meant at all. I'm certain you're the right person for this Plot. I wouldn't have given it to you if I didn't think you could do it."

She looked at him, trying to spot the trick. But the only thing she could see in his face was trust. He believed in her. He really did. And she nearly told him.

"So, how about you? Anything exciting going on?" she asked to change the subject, crossing and uncrossing her legs under the table.

"I'm not sure I'll do any better answering that question, but thank you for trying. Everything's 'exciting' at the moment, isn't it? I think we may have to ration the Mirrors."

"Ration the Mirrors? Isn't there something we can do?"

"We're doing everything we can, and they're still breaking. It's like they've all decided to go at once," Mistasinon said, rubbing his neck.

"My friend said it's been getting worse."

"And they're right. We've got as many FMEs as we have out, all running Plots, but it doesn't seem to be enough. We really need the stories. Oh—are you alright?" He leaned forward. "You've gone very pale."

"Oh. Yes. Definitely. Plots, Plots, Plots."

"Here, drink this," Mistasinon said, pouring her a glass of water. He waited for Bea to take a couple of sips.

"Perhaps..." Bea began, already aware of the mouldy taste of failure, "perhaps you need more experienced people on the stories...?"

"Please don't say that. I don't agree at all. I really wouldn't have anyone else but you on this story."

Bea looked up. "But perhaps I can't make it work."

"Bea, I'm certain you can. Don't listen to those other people. They're all monsters. Trust me." Mistasinon confided with a smile, taking a sip of coffee. "There's always another way, isn't there?"

"I guess so."

Mistasinon leaned forward on his elbows, closing the space between them. "Listen, do you know the story of the many worlds?"

"No."

"That's not surprising. It's not a real story—I mean, it was never a story we used with the characters. I suppose it was *our* story, the same way they have theirs. It was forgotten after the war."

"You know about the war?" Bea asked, curiosity pulling her out of her funk.

"Oh, no, no, no. The Teller forbids the old stories. How could I?"

"But you know about this story?"

"A little," he said. "Would you like to hear it?"

"What about the Beast?" Bea asked, remembering herself. "You know, they say that it likes to crunch your bones in your body before it delivers you to the Redaction Department."

"Oh, yes. The horrendous beast. What a monster he must be," Mistasinon said. And then he smiled again. "But assuming for a moment the Cerberus has more pressing matters, shall I tell you?"

"Well… I suppose if you're willing to tell it, I can admit I'd like to hear it."

"I knew you would," he said. "There used to be this story that Thaiana wasn't the only world, nor the Mirrors the only pathway. Once there were many others. A different path for a different world. Imagine it. There wouldn't be any need to ration our access to Thaiana, nor limit the Plots. We could even have new stories. There wouldn't be this constant scramble to keep the belief working."

"What happened?"

"They say the other pathways were lost during the Rhyme War. All except the Mirrors."

"So, if we could find the other pathways, we wouldn't need the Mirrors?"

"Exactly. Or at least, we wouldn't be so reliant on them. But it might just be a story. A myth." He rested his chin in his hand. "Can I ask you a question?"

She nodded.

"What would you do, Bea, if you could choose between something wrong but simple, or something right but difficult? Even if both choices would get you what you wanted?"

Bea looked at him sharply, but there was nothing in his expression that marked the question as anything but innocent. She chewed her lip. "Well, I... Well, I'd still do what I thought was right, even if it was harder."

"You wouldn't choose the path of least resistance?"

"Not if it was wrong, no."

"You should bear that in mind, Bea. With your story, I mean. I gave you this Plot because I like the fact that there's two of you, but I hope you'll listen to the cabbage fairy sometimes, too. Come on, I'll walk you home."

They strolled through the streets, neither one rushing to get back to Bea's building.

"I hadn't thought I'd see you today if I'm honest," Mistasinon said abruptly.

"Then why did you come to my flat?"

He lifted his large eyebrows and shot her a crooked smile.

"I thought I'd take the chance."

Bea dropped her eyes and began fiddling with the ties on her dress, making sure they hung at equal lengths.

"You like things to be orderly," he observed, watching her.

Bea dropped her hands. "I'm not a clean freak."

"I didn't mean it to be a bad thing. The friend of mine, he... he used to like things just so."

"Used to?"

"Yes."

Silence fell, and the odd couple had to wait awkwardly while it stumbled to its feet and moved on before they could speak again. The narrow streets were paved in pretty red stone. An imp was standing on a step-ladder, lighting the oil lamps that lined the pavements. It should have been a nice walk—romantic even—but it wasn't.

Bea couldn't help wondering if it would be easier to talk to Mistasinon if she wasn't currently undergoing a crisis of conviction and if he would stop saying things that made her think she was right to be questioning her Plot. Perhaps then she might be able to accept it when he was kind to her. Perhaps she might accept that not everyone was out to see her fail.

She hoped it was true.

"What are you thinking about?" he asked.

"Nothing. Just the view. The light makes everything seem more... magical."

They walked on. Bea watched Mistasinon from the corner of her eye. In defiance of the cool night air, he had taken off the jacket of his tailored suit and was now in a navy-blue waistcoat and a crisp white shirt. His hair, dark and a little too short, was brushed back from his forehead and shone like oil. He looked, to a casual observer, wealthy, idle and carefree. And yet his lips were drawn into a thin line, and his expression was darker than the encroaching shadows. Bea found herself wanting to ask if there weren't two versions of him, fighting it out in one body.

And then suddenly she was alone. She turned to find that he was a few paces behind her. He had stopped dead in the street, his fingers drumming against his forearms, staring at the imp lighting the lamps. When he spoke, his voice was oddly still.

"There was a story once about a view."

"A view?" Bea asked, walking back to him.

Mistasinon nodded, lost in thought. "I was staying in a small hotel in a beautiful city in old Ehinenden before the Kingdom split—the kind of place with more history than they knew what to do with, and the light... The light was..." he drifted off, eyebrows drawn together, his face caught between the shadows and the glow of the lamp. "I wasn't working on the story, not as such, but I was lucky enough to see it develop."

"What was the story?"

Mistasinon's fingers continued to drum as he spoke. "The heroine didn't know what she wanted, and the hero was lost and sad. She thought she wanted to marry someone rich. Handsome. And then the hero kissed her, and she knew. A kiss, and then love. I don't really understand it."

"I'm not sure what there is to understand."

"That's because you do. Understand it, I mean. I just wonder... Isn't it better to start as a monster and become a hero? Isn't that what creates belief? The idea that someone can change?"

"Change, Love, Rags to Riches."

He finally looked at Bea, his arms folded tightly across his narrow frame. "Do you think people can change?"

"I certainly hope so."

"You are being careful, aren't you? With your Plot?"

"Yes, absolutely. Very careful. Won't be long 'till it's all wrapped up," Bea said wretchedly.

Something intimate showed in his eyes, but when he spoke again, he was all formal efficiency.

"You should have Act Two wrapped up by Midnight on Saturday? That's the date of the Ball, I believe?" he said, thrusting his hands into his pockets, ruining the line of his suit. "That way we can have them married by Monday, Third Act done and dusted. There is some urgency, I'm sure you understand."

"Oh, yes. Yes. That's the plan," Bea said, confused. Something had passed between them, something she sensed had been extremely important, but now it was gone, and he was talking to her like it had never happened.

"I'll meet you after the Ball."

"That's alright. I can drop the Book off with an Indexer."

"It's no trouble," he said.

"It's no trouble for me either."

He looked away from her, clearly uncomfortable.

"I know the way from here," Bea said. "I can walk the rest of the way by myself."

"After the Ball, I could take you out. For breakfast. If you wanted to."

She blinked, unable to keep the surprise off her face. From the look on his, the invitation had thrown him as much as it had her.

"That'd be lovely," Bea's hindbrain answered before she had a chance to censor it.

Mistasinon relaxed. "Good."

They were nearly at Bea's building. It was easy to tell because the lamps were becoming further apart, and the streets darker and harder to see. Thus it was that Bea, too busy trying to watch Mistasinon from the corner of her eye, managed to trip, catching her feet on the uneven cobbles.

Mistasinon was fast. Where suddenly he had been a respectful distance, he now had her in his arms.

"I'm fine," Bea said, flustered.

"Are you sure? These pavements can be—"

"Honestly, it's nothing."

"You were hurt," he said, noticing the bruises Seven had left on her shoulders.

"Oh. Yes. I must have, um, landed badly," Bea said.

He looked like he wanted to say something more, but whatever it was he obviously decided not to. Instead, he brushed his fingertips over the little yellowy-blue bruises.

Bea looked up at him, aware of how tall he was, and of the way he was looking at her. She could feel the weight of him. Small goose-bumps danced in reels up and down her arms.

Mistasinon looked down at her, searching her face.

Bea's stomach jolted, hot and sharp but not at all unpleasant. He was going to kiss her and, Bea realised, she was going to kiss him back.

She met his eyes, conscious of the fact that everything she could see in his face he had to be reading in her own. He was so close to her now she could actually feel the air between them, as thick and heavy as water. His gaze flitted down to her lips and then lifted, his pupils wide and dark against the warm brown of his eyes, his fingertips still brushing the bare tops of her arms.

He leaned forward.

Bea tilted her head towards him.

She closed her eyes.

And then she felt him pull away.

Her eyes snapped open.

"Excuse me," he muttered. "You have an early start, as do I. I shouldn't have taken up so much of your time," and, not waiting for her to answer, he walked off, leaving Bea alone.

Chapter Twenty-three

Like Bea, night had fallen.

But the palace was still busy, castles never really going to sleep. The Night's Watch bled seamlessly into the Day's Watch, the Bakers and Dairy Men into the Chefs and Chamber Maids, the Stable Master into the Master of the Hound and so on throughout the day, every task executed with precision and efficiency so that the King would never realise it took so many people, all working around the clock, to make things run.

Bea's hand tapped against her hip.

She had to face up to it.

She had no idea how to find the Anti.

He'd always found her. It was like he could sense her. What kind of fae could do that? The tooth fairies, obviously, had a knack for finding the right pillow, and the higher level FMEs, the godmothers and witches and so on, were trained to spot the signs of a hero or heroine. But all Bea knew about the Anti was that he hung around the King, and so she'd decided to come to the castle in Llanotterly.

She didn't want to think about how many rules she was breaking, not when she had much more immediate concerns weighing on her mind. Like the fact she had just spent hours learning that castles were made up of more than Ballrooms and turrets full of spinning wheels. There was, she now knew, quite a lot of castle to a castle, and trying to find one person without uttering the words 'he's blue' was challenging, to say the least.

She almost laughed. All those times she'd wished so hard not to see him, and now the one time she wanted to, he was nowhere to be found. It was absolutely typical.

Of course, Bea thought, tiredness making her bitter, *if this were a story, I'd simply bump into him. I'd be here, walking around this garden, trying not to be spotted, and I'd turn this corner, around this bush here, and there'd he'd be, just—*

"Ha!" Bea laughed in triumph as her eyes landed on the now familiar sight of the hooded Anti. He was sitting on a stone bench, looking up at the stars. She was also pleased to note that he seemed quite wrong-footed by her arrival, though he recovered quickly.

"What a charming surprise," he said, not bothering to stand. "I would claim no knowledge of what I have done to deserve this, but I have committed many terrible acts. Still, the punishment seems disproportionate."

"Yes, yes. You talk very prettily, and you're very clever. That's not why I'm here."

The Anti lifted his right leg and placed it over his left, a sharp inhalation of breath accompanying the action.

"You've hurt yourself?" Bea asked, forgetting he was her sworn enemy.

He looked at her for a long time.

"Yes."

"You know, there are quite a few herbs in these gardens, if I mixed them up for you, they might be able to help."

"This from the creature that gave neat datura stramonium to a bear?"

Bea felt her new-found sympathy evaporate. "Fine, suffer then. That's not why I'm here, anyway."

Seven smiled behind his hood. "Of course. Very well. Please, proceed to shout and scream and call me liar. Though I beg you be brief. I am, as you note, unwell."

Bea took a deep breath and waited until she could speak to him in a normal tone of voice.

"Someone told me today that there are two paths. One's easy, and one's difficult. The easy path is to report you, but if I do that, I'll… Well. I'm not keen on reporting you. The difficult path is to try working against you to keep the story running."

"Fascinating. Did we not cover this earlier?"

"I think there's a third path," Bea said, trying not to grind her teeth as she spoke. "Tell me why you won't leave the story."

"You have been told."

"And I think there's more to you being here. You said to the ugly sister there was a girl. Who was she?"

"I wondered when I found your Book what you might have overheard. Tell me, did you only listen? It seems a waste if so."

"Tell me about the girl."

"Only recount? I am sure I could find energy enough to show you what you missed."

"That won't work. You're not going to embarrass me or throw me off by using sex."

"My dear, doubt not that were I to throw you in a sexual manner, the position most certainly would not be 'off'."

"Mortal gods, you're so vulgar. Can you not have a real conversation?"

"Why should I wish to converse with you?" Seven snapped. "You represent all that I abhor. These lives are nothing to you but another item to be crossed off your quota."

"You were more eloquent earlier. And you're repeating yourself."

"I am tired. And the point bears repeating."

Bea stopped. She had too much at stake to risk losing it over his arrogance and snide. This was her one chance to get everything back on track. She had to make him understand.

"You said a lot of things about me and the stories," she said slowly. "Some of which might have had some truth."

Seven turned his attention back to the night sky. Bea stared at him, his hooded head lolling on his shoulders. It hadn't worked. He wasn't listening. She realised she had no choice but to tell him the truth.

"This is my first story."

The Anti continued to sit silently, looking up at the stars.

"I want to be an FME, and if I do this story right, they're going to let me join the Academy to train. You kept asking me what I desire. I want to be something more than what I am."

The Anti turned towards her.

"And what are you?"

He stood and pulled his hood from his head, the moonlight hitting his blue skin, making it shimmer like ice, his hair falling in tight curls against his face. He seemed tense, his shoulders pulled back and his chest rising and falling in a controlled rhythm—as if he were about to say something which would cost him. Which was strange, because when he did speak, he said only:

"If you could wish for anything at this moment, what would you wish for?"

"What kind of question is that?"

"It is my question to you. What would you have of it?"

Bea looked at him, trying to ignore the way the blue orbs of his eyes made her feel. It was a stupid question, but there was something in the way he'd said it and how he was watching her that gave her pause. She thought about everything she'd always wanted, or said she wanted, and then spoke:

"I grew up in the Sheltering Forest. We don't get any protection there, and the orcs and gnarls come. I thought the city would look after me—you know the GenAm sends emissaries out to the Forest? 'Don't stay in the Sheltering Forest and feed the orcs' they say. Don't '*encourage*' them. And I listened. I believed in the safety of the wall and the Mirrors. But when I got there, they all hated me. Do you know what a fairy is in Ænathlin? Less than nothing, that's what."

Bea could feel the anger and resentment building in her like a fire. "But I'll be damned if I'll let them win. I'm going to show everyone that fairies can be more. What do they know about anything, anyway? All those stuck-up imps and brownies and the rest? They've never had to listen to ogres or orcs or gnarls in the night. They've never had to fight a day in their life. Never lost anything or anyone. You know what I used to wish? I wished they would all just—"

Seven tensed.

Bea wiped her eyes, which were stinging. When she pulled her hand away, it was wet with tears. "See? See how they make me feel? I won't let them have that much power over me. And now I've finally got a Plot, and I should be happy. I shouldn't be talking to an Anti or worrying about Sindy. But the truth is, I am. And there are things that don't make sense. No one else sees them." She thought of Mistasinon. "Or at least I don't think they do. I don't know. I suppose I'm saying that I don't know what I'd wish for anymore."

Bea took a deep breath. She was embarrassed to have cried in front of the Anti. She'd shown something of herself that she hadn't realised was there, and she was already regretting it. Seven shifted on the bench, making space for her, and Bea, to her surprise, found herself sitting.

F. D. Lee

"An honest answer," he said. There was a softness in his voice now, an acquiescence she hadn't heard before. She wiped her eyes again, roughly.

"Here." He handed her one of his silk gloves. "Dry your eyes."

"Thanks. So, will you tell me why you're here?"

"What has my history to do with you? We are not trading woes."

Bea dropped the glove like it burned her. "I just thought if we could understand each other, why this story is so important to us, we could work something out. But I forgot you're a total ass."

"An ass?"

"Yes. That's exactly what you are. You've come into my Plot, throwing all these accusations around, making me question everything, *everything*, I used to believe and now, when the tables are turned and I ask you why you're here, you refuse to answer. You're an ass. And I'm sorry that I bothered."

He cocked his head, his curls brushing against his face. Bea was annoyed that, even now, she couldn't help noticing how attractive he was.

"You are quite right," he said.

"I know," Bea said, sticking her chin out.

"You have asked me to reveal a truth to you, and I shall. However, I must first ask you to come with me. There is something I would show you that I believe shall benefit you."

"You have got to be joking. I shouldn't even be here now."

The Anti shot her a smile laden with all his charm. "Please, godmother—Bea. You have come to me, risking a great deal. Are you not intrigued as to where this third path you suggest might lead? No harm will befall you." Seven held his hand out. "You have my word."

Bea looked at him. Slowly she lifted her hand, every muscle in her arm fighting against the command.

"I have friends," she warned as she felt his cold fingers encircle hers.

"And you shall be returned to them."

Bea swallowed.

"Alright…"

He pulled her into his arms...

...the blood of the universe screaming through her veins, tearing her into a million pieces, the song of the worlds thrumming in her ears like the roar of a dying sun, but she was covered, protected...

...and they were in the hallway of what had once been a beautiful, grand mansion. A wide staircase swept in a graceful arc along the walls, its bannisters decorated by crumbling stone pillars that spoke of elegance, good taste and money. The floor was laid with a threadbare carpet, the colour of which had faded to the inky brown of the characters' blood when it dried. Large, empty windows invited the cool wind in, the torn and ragged curtains drifting in the breeze like seaweed. The mansion wore its history in tattered rags, whispering in your ear that once, before it had been degraded and brought low, it had been beautiful.

And in the centre of all this ruin stood Seven, his arms wrapped tightly around Bea, his chest rising and falling in short, pained movements.

Bea's ears were ringing, and her stomach felt like it was filled with sour cream, but she had been expecting it this time. She concentrated on breathing, letting the warm, musty air fill her lungs and calm her heartbeat.

It was difficult, and not just because she felt horribly queasy. There was also no escaping the fact that very certain parts of her body were pressed against equally definite parts of his. At least this time, she managed not to kiss his pale blue skin like some lovesick heroine. She placed her hands on his chest and tried to push him away from her, though in fact only managing to lever herself into a position any Ballroom dancer would be proud of.

"Why are you still holding me?" she asked, not unreasonably. "Where are we?" she added, taking in her surroundings in all their sinister glory. "How did we get here?" she finished, looking back at him.

Seven stared down at her, his ethereal eyes glazed and dull. "I moved us," he said and then, after a pause that was a fraction of a heartbeat too long, he released her.

"How do you do that?" she asked again, missing the way the Anti's step faltered as he walked towards the wide staircase. He collapsed onto the lower step, landing heavily.

"Magic," he answered.

Bea looked at him like he'd just claimed to have discovered the secret of turning iron into gold. "Magic couldn't move us like that. It's too weak for anything more than a puff of smoke or a parlour trick. That's why we have the Mirrors."

"You believe magic to be weak?"

"Everyone knows it. And anyway, it's not allowed."

"I am, as you informed me, an evil Anti-Narrativist, hells bent on the destruction of everything good and right with this world. What is it to me if I use a banned resource?"

"Fine. Don't tell me then."

Bea turned to leave. She realised how stupid she'd been, thinking she might be able to reach him. All that nonsense Mistasinon had said had obviously polluted her judgement. She started to look around for something reflective, but the window frames were all empty. She kicked around in the dust, hoping she might find a shard of glass.

"There is nothing here to transport you," Seven said in between deep breaths. "If I were to leave you, you would be forced to walk days to the nearest village, although I suppose you might find a puddle. Such a glamorous life you seek."

Bea glared at him, and then she noticed the way he was breathing. "You *are* sick. What's wrong? If you tell me, maybe I can help. I really am good at herbs. It's genetic," she added bitterly.

"As reassuring as that is, you need not exert yourself. My discomfort is momentary. Now, attend. I will give you your third path, though I suspect you will not wish to walk it. Once, the Queen of the Fairies resided here. Are you aware of her fate?"

"She was banished. Or Redacted. No one ever really said."

"Poor fairy. No wonder you are so conflicted."

"I'm not stupid."

"I said not that you were. You are, however, ignorant."

Bea gave him a filthy look, but she didn't try to leave. Everyone hated the fairies because of the King and Queen, and if he was going to tell her about the Queen, then she wanted to hear.

"Go on."

"The Queen is blamed for the Teller. It is an accepted lie that she and her husband were so out of control the Mirrors began to shatter, and thus the Teller was able to usurp them. This is not how he gained his power."

"What do you mean, 'an accepted lie'?"

"That it is not true, of course. Perhaps you were too quick to deny stupidity."

"Mortal gods, you're obnoxious."

"Again you insult me," he laughed. "I am more used to flattery, I will admit."

Bea bit her tongue. "So what about the King and Queen?"

"The King and the Queen's storytelling, though enthusiastic, did nothing to the Mirrors."

"Yes they did—they didn't manage the story. None of the old Narrators did. The Teller Cares—I mean, he made it possible for us to keep the Mirrors open," Bea said, not sure why she had corrected herself.

"As with all the Teller's chattels, you do not know your history." The Anti said this in the tone of voice a tax official might use with a small business owner who walks into the office with twenty years of receipts. It wasn't that he was displeased with her, but there was no denying the fact that she was causing him a lot of extra work.

"But that doesn't make sense," Bea said. "All my life, everyone's said that the King and Queen were the ones who broke the Mirrors. That's why they all hate the fairies. They got too close to their characters, especially the Queen. Their stories were out of control."

"And that is true. But they are not responsible for the Mirrors."

"Then who is?" Bea asked, trying to digest the information he had given her. "The Anties?"

"Ah, yes, the mysterious Anti-Narrativists. You fear the end of the stories. This is what you have been taught these 'Anti-Narrativists' desire. But how can they stop a story? Have you ever wondered?"

"They change the Plot, they interact with the characters, stop them believing."

"But the Chapters change, do they not?"

"Yes. They used to. But that was because the stories weren't strong. New ones were always needed. Until the Teller."

"What does that suggest?"

Bea started to answer and then paused. Even in the Sheltering Forest, she had grown up on the histories of the GenAm, which were very clear: The old Narrators didn't manage the belief. They got too involved, their stories were too close to the blood and the bone of life. They tricked and cheated, and the humans drew back as a result. The belief ebbed, and the Mirrors suffered. The Teller's Plots were simple, easy to run and generated enough belief to keep the Mirrors open, at least until the Anties had come along.

But if there had been different stories before, didn't that mean that there could be new stories after? And hadn't Melly said that the Mirrors had shown cracks before the Anties? It didn't make sense, not when you put it all together.

"What are you saying?" Bea asked.

"The breaking of the Mirrors is not caused by myself or these Anti-Narrativists you speak of, nor by any of the fae. Belief certainly revives them, and the stories you so enthusiastically peddle beget belief, that much is true. But ultimately so will any tale. Is not that freeing? Now you need not worry about my involvement in this story."

He smiled, obviously waiting for her delighted reaction. Instead, Bea felt a tightening in her chest.

"If what you say is true, then there's something very wrong with the Mirrors…"

"Perhaps. Perhaps not," Seven answered, resting his elbows on the step behind him. "I am being honest with you because you have been honest with me, and because I see how conflicted you are… and because you are different, like me."

Bea looked down at her hands, trying to find meaning in the lines that told the story of her life. She couldn't take in what he was saying.

"Why waste your life on a lie?" he said. "You have already admitted to feeling something when you saw the girl embrace the man she loves, the man from whom you would see her separated."

Bea kept her eyes fixed on her hands, unwilling to answer.

She heard him moving through the ringing in her ears, but when he took her hands in his own, she was so surprised she gasped. She dragged her gaze up, dreading what she would see reflected in his borderless eyes.

"You are distressed, and I can assure you it hurts me to see you so," he said softly. "Nevertheless, it should be obvious that changing the stories is not the cause of your woes. I am not your enemy. Let me continue my work."

Bea searched his face, trying to find some evidence that he was lying. He lifted his hand, holding her cheek in his palm. She felt him gently brush her skin with his cornflower blue fingers.

"But what about the Forest..? Ænathlin..? My home..?"

"What about it? Has it been such a good home to you?"

"That doesn't matter. There are thousands of tribes living there, all relying on the Mirrors to survive."

Seven dropped his hand. "And yet nothing you do here will prevent or facilitate their demise. You have accused me of instigating another civil war because you believe that changing the Plots, as you so unimaginatively call them, results in a lack of belief and the subsequent breaking of the Mirrors. Yet how can this be possible? Stories are rewritten."

"Yes, they can be..." Bea said, thinking about the changes she'd made. "But even so, the Plots are strong. They create belief. We need the belief to fix the Mirrors."

"And this is the General Administration's secret. Belief is a meek, guileless thing, attracted to its like. Love. Hope. Fear, naturally, is the greatest harvester. This is probably why there has been an escalation in the inevitable breaking of the Mirrors—the Teller attempted to erase the fear. Sensible, perhaps, but ultimately lacking sustainability, even with his stolen power."

"Stolen? No one could steal a Chapter. The Chapters change when a new Narrator has a stronger story. Belief decides." Bea paused. "Or, at least, that's what the GenAm says."

"Do you believe the General Administration in all things?"

"I... No. The GenAm thinks I can't be an FME, for example. I don't share that view."

"Ah, yes. The bullied little fairy, determined to become a bully herself."

"Why do you think I want to hurt my characters?"

He smiled, though there was no humour in it. "Experience?"

"If you hate me so much, why are you telling me all this?"

"You wish to know it. This is the true reason for your coming to me."

"What? No, it isn't. Anyway, why should I believe you?"

Seven shrugged. "Your refusal to trust me will not make what I say any less true."

Bea could almost feel the ground crumbling beneath her as he spoke. And she knew that if she asked the question that was running through her mind, she'd never be able to stand on safe ground again. But she could no more stop herself from asking it than she could stop breathing.

"But if the stories can be changed, then why would anyone live under the GenAm?"

"You suggest there is a fault with the General Administration? That people should seek to extract themselves from its shadow?"

"No! I—No, I mean, of course not—The GenAm—The Teller Cares Ab—"

"Calm yourself. They cannot hear you here. So, what is your conclusion? Are you satisfied?"

"Satisfied? How can I possibly be satisfied?"

"I have provided your answer. Fear begets belief. That is your third path. Abandon your fear of the General Administration and with it, your belief in their lies."

Bea stared at him.

"Will you take me back now?" she asked.

Seven cocked his head. "Have I not—"

"I'd like to go back now. Please."

Seven nodded. He opened his arms, and Bea stepped into his embrace. As she felt his cold skin against her own, followed by the lurching sickness of his so-called magic, she wondered if she would be able to travel so easily back to the life she had had before.

Chapter Twenty-four

Sindy stood at her kitchen sink, trying to keep busy. But as much as she tried, she couldn't forget the feel of Will's lips pressed against her own. Every few moments, she brought her hand to her mouth as if she thought she might find some evidence, other than the memory, that the kiss had happened. It felt like a lifetime ago. It was, in fact, only yesterday.

She swished the water over the plate. It was the same plate she'd been washing for the last five minutes.

She hadn't expected Ana would agree to go the Ball. But Ana had changed her mind and was now insisting they both attend. It was like magic. Or fate.

Sindy supposed it meant that the odd, chubby woman she had found in her room really was her 'special' godmother. But if that was the case, then didn't that mean that she had to do what she said? Sindy had grown up believing that all good girls would fall in love and get married, and she knew she should feel lucky to have a real-life fairy helping her, and that she had the chance to marry a King.

So why was it that she had woken up this morning feeling as if her whole body was made of stone? What would Ana do if she refused to go? Perhaps if she could explain that a fairy had told her she was going to fall in love and marry the King, Ana might listen?

Or she might laugh in my face.

Or she might want *me to marry the King.*

It would be a lot easier if she would just fall in love with the King. Wasn't that what happened—love at first sight? *But*, Sindy reflected, scrubbing the plate so hard it squeaked, *I have met him. And I'm not in love with him. I don't really think anything about him.*

Maybe he was in love with her? Perhaps he had hired the fairy? Ana said that nothing was beneath the bourgeoisie when it came to controlling the output of the common worker, and Sindy couldn't think of anyone more common than she was. If the King had decided he was going to marry her, what choice did she have, anyway?

But he hadn't seemed like he was that interested in her the other day. Was that normal? Sindy didn't know how Kings behaved when they were in love. Will had been quite shocked when she'd kissed him.

Just then the plate, surrendering to Sindy's rough handling, cracked. Sindy yelped in surprised. Red blood paled as it mixed with the water in the sink.

Sindy didn't panic at the sight of the shard of china sticking out of her palm. Instead, she pulled it carefully free and pressed a tea towel to the cut, applying pressure until the bleeding stopped. She lifted the cloth and was relieved to see it wouldn't need stitches. She took a slice of bread from the larder, pressed it against the cut to be safe, and wrapped her hand in a bandage.

Things were not going her way.

Lost in uncomfortable thoughts, Sindy gave up cleaning and followed her feet as they traipsed out of the kitchen and into the garden.

The truth was, she'd always thought that her life would be quiet and ordinary, even before she'd met Ana and seen first-hand what an exciting life could be like. She liked her life as it was. She enjoyed cooking, and she knew how to keep pigs and kill and pluck chickens. She knew her way around a medicine cabinet, could dress a wound, and recognise all three of the early signs of the hissing fever. She ran her house, and she was good at it. Running a Kingdom was probably the same, but Sindy didn't want to find out.

She wandered over to the apple tree at the foot of the garden. Years ago, her father had made her a rope swing, and she had never really grown out of it. It wasn't a particularly good swing, even she could see that. It was just a length of ship's rigging, brought back from Sinne, with a plank of wood tied lopsidedly on one end and the other wrapped a few times around the thickest branch.

It was impossible to sit on it in anything resembling a lady-like pose. Rather, Sindy had to gather up her skirts and straddle the rope in such a way that she could balance on the wood. But it had never mattered before. Now it would matter. She wouldn't be able to escape to the bottom of the garden and her rope swing if she were a Queen.

Sindy began pushing herself listlessly backwards and forwards.

But it wasn't just about her, was it? She would be very selfish if she had a way to improve everyone's life and she didn't take it.

And she was very lucky to have a fairy trying to make her life better. She hadn't heard of anyone in Llanotterly having a fairy helping them. There had been a girl somewhere off west, past Cerne Bralksteld even, who'd had one. Sindy couldn't remember now what had happened, but she was almost certain that the girl had died, or been frozen or fallen asleep. Something bad, anyway. The one thing that Sindy could remember was that it had been true love's kiss that had saved her.

Sindy had always imagined she'd meet someone nice, like Will, fall in love, get married and have children of her own. The King hadn't seemed very friendly the other day, and she didn't want to marry someone who frightened her just because he had money and was handsome. Sindy was pretty enough for two, and she much preferred Will's crumpled face and broken nose.

As for money, Sindy had never had any anyway, and Will had his parent's house. They could live there for the rest of their lives, cooking and eating and planting seeds, some in the garden and some in her belly. They would be happy and healthy, and they wouldn't need anything else.

Maybe she could have opened her own apothecary, or taught others how to tend to their sick. There were so many refugees now, they must need someone to help. It wasn't a big, grand dream like Ana's, but it had been hers, and now, she realised, it probably wasn't anymore.

Sindy couldn't stop the thought from spinning around and around behind her eyes, just as she sat spinning on her swing:

I don't love the King.

I love Will.

And then, with the same sharp pain as stepping on a wooden toy lost in a thick carpet, she thought that perhaps Will didn't love her.

She dug her feet into the ground, resting her golden head against the thick rope. The swing came to a stop.

F. D. Lee

They'd known each other for years, but he'd never actually said anything to her that might suggest he thought about her in the same way she thought about him. He'd always been kind to her, but he was kind to everyone. It was true he often spent longer in the kitchen with her than talking with her father or stepmother, and he didn't really seem to like Ana at all. He'd told Sindy once that he thought Ana was a bully, and he'd got very cross with her when she'd defended her stepsister. But did that mean he loved her?

She'd kissed him.

He hadn't kissed her.

Sindy could feel the rough edges of the hessian rope against her skin, scratching at her. Her hand throbbed from the cut on her palm. She looked over her garden, the garden she'd grown up with, the one she and her mum had planted flowers in when she was little. The one Will came and tended when he had free time.

She didn't know what to do.

Chapter Twenty-five

Joan lived in a tall, thin, mixed-brick building which was literally on the wall: the house's back wall *was* the wall.

Her family had, generations ago, looked at the sturdy grey brickwork that encircled Ænathlin and seen in it a fantastic investment opportunity for a large family with little status. The house itself had been made from whatever materials they'd been able to gather from Thaiana, making it a statement in post-modern eclecticism that hurt the eyes to take in in one go.

It was safer and certainly more comfortable to break the four-storey house into various subsections, such as the ornate rococo fronting above the door, or the jaunty gargoyles that hung from the gingerbread-like eaves. Viewed this way, each part of the house was well-made and sturdy, and reflected in it something of the taste of the person who had built it. It was a house made by committee rather than design, and, depending on your attitude, was either better or worse for it.

Bea stepped up to the heavy, wood-panelled front door and knocked loudly.

After a few intense moments filled with shouts and bangs, the door was opened by one of Joan's numerous sisters. She regarded Bea regally over the end of her nose. The effect was spoiled somewhat by the trail of snot dripping down to her upper lip, where it ended in a dry, greeny-yellow scab.

"Is Joan in?" Bea asked, kneeling down.

"Yeah."

"Could I come in and see her?"

The little fairy scratched at her hair, frowning at Bea over the top of her running nose.

"Aren't you that one that wants to be an FME?"

"Um. Yes."

The girl broke into a fit of giggles, causing little celebratory bubbles to form in her nostrils. "The cabbage fairy?"

"The very same," Bea sighed.

F. D. Lee

"Brilliant!" She grabbed Bea in a sticky hand and pulled her into the house. "Joan! Joan! Joan! Joan!" she screamed shrilly as she dragged Bea up the stairs.

"Mortal gods, what is it? If you've been in my wardrobe again Mags, I swear I will pull your head off and use it as a soup bowl— oh, hi Bea," Joan said, changing gears seamlessly as she appeared out of her room.

"Hi, sorry for barging in but—"

"Joan, it's the cabbage fairy!"

"It'll be the headless fairy in a minute," Joan said, pulling Bea into her room with one hand and slamming her door shut with the other. Joan's room was wood-panelled, clean and comfortable, if a little dark and sombre. The walls were covered in her obsessive drawings of anatomy, plant leaves, types of mushrooms, knots and lock mechanisms.

"Sorry about her. You're quite famous, you know that?"

Bea didn't know. "Famous?"

Joan grinned. "Yeah, at least amongst the fairies. You know, trying to get your own recommendation and everything."

"But I don't know any other fairies apart from you."

"Oh well," Joan smiled, jumping up on her bed, "you're quite famous for that too."

Bea opened her mouth and then decided she probably didn't want to know anything more about that statement. So? She was famous, was she? Great. At least that meant she'd draw a crowd when they Redacted her. Bea smiled. See? She was keeping positive.

"You said you might know someone who can give us some information about the 2nd?"

Joan pulled a face. "About that…"

"Please Joan, no more bad news… What's happened? Have they refused to help?"

"Oh no, no, they haven't refused—"

"Thank the mortal gods for that—"

"Because I haven't asked them yet."

Bea closed her eyes. "What's wrong?"

"Nothing! No, honestly. It's just I thought you might want to know…" Joan let the sentence drift off.

Bea opened her eyes. Joan was sitting on her bed, fiddling with the nail heads in her heavy boots. She looked more uncomfortable than Bea had ever seen her. She sat next to her on the bed.

"Joan, you don't have to do anything you don't want to. Seriously."

"No, I don't mind. But you might."

"Me? Joan, what is it?"

"My friend, the one who might be able to help us, she's a Raconteur."

"What? How in the Land do you know a Raconteur?"

Joan gave a sort of half smile, half grimace. "I met her years ago. She was just starting out then, but she's got her own dragon's den now." Joan paused. "In the centre."

Bea whistled through her teeth. This she had not been expecting. She knew Joan made friends quickly—she was a very easy person to get on with. She had the knack of talking to people she'd just met as if she'd known them for years, something Bea had always ever so slightly envied. But to be friends with a Raconteur? And one with her own den? That seemed too far-fetched, even for Joan, and Bea said as much.

"Well, we weren't exactly friends. And I haven't seen her for years. But I thought, if anyone's going to know about blue men and old Chapters, it'd be Delphine."

Bea shook her head. "But the Raconteurs all work for the white suits—hells, they entertain at the Redactions."

"Not all of them. That's like saying all fairies prance around in the stems, scattering fairy dust and making daisy chains."

Joan said it mildly enough, but Bea felt suitably chastised.

"Alright, sorry. It's just, I mean, a Raconteur. You really know a Raconteur? Mind you," Bea added, smiling, "I have always wanted to meet one. I never thought I'd be able to afford it. I've heard they know all the old stories."

Joan grinned. "So, what do you say?"

"Well," Bea said, "what else could go wrong?"

Joan rapped her fist against the door of The Golden Claw. Bea couldn't hide the fact she was nervous, though she was trying to. She stood up straight and put on a nonchalant air as if this was just a regular morning for her. Joan, too, seemed to be affected—or at least, her stream of happy burble had slowed to a trickle the closer they had come, and now she was standing silently, every now and then rubbing the toe of her heavy boot against the back of her other leg.

Bea brushed down her dress for the tenth time and tried to prepare herself for whatever lay inside. Dragon's dens were by all accounts strange, opulent places, the air scented with opium, calaris root and fenlandriz from the large glass smoking pipes glued to the lips of those customers who had enough wealth to gain entry. Trade power wasn't the only necessity, however. You also needed courage.

Dragon's dens were dangerous places if you didn't have the will to manage what they offered you. The Raconteurs were there to guide their clients through the stories, to give those who could trade for it a little taste of something forbidden so that they didn't ask for more. But if you demanded too much, the white suits would find out, and then you wouldn't want anything ever again.

The thought hadn't escaped Bea that The Golden Claw probably wasn't the best place to start asking questions about unreported Anties, but what choice did she have? To distract herself, she looked up at the sign hanging from the eaves. It was painted with a curving slash on a shield, in hard blocks of colour like the heraldry that used to be popular in Ehinenden.

"It does look sort of like a claw," Bea said to Joan as they waited.

Joan looked up. "Oh that? I don't know... The old one had this smoke trail, twisting and turning. If you looked at it right, you could see the dragon."

"Really? I wish I'd see that."

Joan scratched her head. "Ah, well. Times change. That was when—"

The door creaked open, revealing a pair of brown, heavily dilated eyes.

"Yes?"

Joan leaned forward, tilting her head upwards. "I'm here to see Delphine," she said, speaking slowly and clearly.

The eyes blinked against the muted sunlight. "She doesn't take visitors. You can make an appointment."

"That's alright, I mean, I haven't got an appointment, but I know she'll see me."

"That's what they all say."

The eyes fell back behind the door, but Joan was ready. She stepped quickly forward, shoving her booted foot in the jamb. The door bounced harmlessly against it. There was a pause while Brown Eyes tried to understand why the door wouldn't close.

"You can't do that, I need to close the door," came a plaintive voice.

"I know. Sorry. But I promise she'll see me. Tell Delphine it's Joan ó Cuilinn."

"Let me close the door and I will."

"Yes, I will. Definitely. But could you just let me hear you tell her? Shout? Then I'll move my foot. Sorry."

Bea waited, trying hard to remember to breathe, while Brown Eyes thought about it.

"Alright," she said through the crack in the door, and then the message was loudly shouted that someone called Joan was waiting.

Joan pulled her boot away, and the door slammed closed.

"Joan ó Cuilinn? Your name is Joan 'Holly'?" Bea asked.

Joan giggled. "It's the clan name. We weren't always tooth fairies."

Bea joined in. "Holly's alright. My brother's called Mustard Seed. I think my mum must have hated us."

"Mustard Seed and Buttercup Snowblossom? I think you might be right."

Just then, the door opened again, and the same pair of rheumy brown eyes blinked at Joan from the darkness.

"You can come in," they said, opening the door. Joan slipped in easily, but Bea had to squeeze through the narrow gap Brown Eyes had allowed them.

The inside of The Golden Claw was almost exactly what Bea had imagined. The floor was dotted with yielding, well-cushioned beds that sat on short legs and were smothered in beautifully sewn blankets of soft velvets and silks. Even at this early hour, a dozen or so guests of varying tribes lounged on them.

Tall, slender tables abutted the beds, each with only enough space on their surface for one bulbous glass pipe to sit, its trailing hoses dropping off the edges like octopus arms. Each table was made of brass or silver plate and decorated with little tiled patterns. Either they came from Ota'ari, The First Kingdom, or they were extremely good reproductions. In fact, the whole room seemed to be inspired by Ota'ari, which suggested that Joan's friend Delphine was doing well for herself if she could afford to trade for such frivolities.

The light was dim and hazy, in part due to the sticky brown smoke from the pipes and in part because there was no natural light. Oil lamps burned on the walls, their orangey glow reflected in the little mirrors that were sewn into the large wall hangings, each one depicting one of the Teller's Plots.

A flower fairy floated in front of one, her wings a blur and her soft turquoise and purple hair fanning across her shoulders with all the flashy beauty of peacock feathers. She was tracing the line of the characters with her delicate fingers, a happy smile on her face. Bea scowled at her out of habit.

Brown Eyes led them carefully across the lounge, stepping as neatly around the beds as a politician avoiding an honest answer. Bea had to struggle to keep up with her guide whilst at the same time not stamping on any of the patrons. She had never been a clumsy or heavy-footed person, but compared to Joan and Brown Eyes, she might as well have been an ox.

"I've got to stay by the door," Brown Eyes said as they reached the foot of the staircase. "You can go up by yourselves—the room with the red door. Delphine says you can have the freedom of the house after you've finished if you want."

"Thanks. Sorry about the door," Joan said absently, eyeing the staircase. "Don't they look steep?" she said to Bea once Brown Eyes was out of earshot.

Bea looked up at the staircase. It seemed perfectly normal to her.

"Joan, are you sure about this? We can still turn back."

"Nope. Onwards and upwards," the tooth fairy said, and began climbing.

Bea followed, eyeing her friend with concern. She'd never known Joan to be anything other than good-natured and easy-going. She was utterly unfazed by Melly's anxiety or by Bea's stubbornness, no matter how often this caused the two friends to come to harsh words. She got on with everyone and was always the first to laugh it off if something didn't go her way.

Bea remembered Joan had once spent two days sitting outside some child's bedroom window in the biting snow, only to find out later that she'd been in the wrong place. Bea had been astonished and then, later, very impressed by how quickly Joan had taken to telling the story herself, laughing at her own misfortune.

But there was no mistaking the anxiety that shrouded her friend. She watched as Joan's pace slowed to a dawdle the closer they got to the red door. She kept rubbing at the back of her neck, and her shoulders were rigid.

"Joan—I think we should leave," Bea whispered. "I'm sorry I brought you here. Let's just go home."

Joan turned around and attempted a smile. "Ah, get away with you. She knows we're here now. Besides, you want to know more about this Anti and so do I. C'mon."

And with that, Joan knocked on the red door.

Chapter Twenty-six

"*Entrer*, Joan," came Delphine's voice. She sounded rich and bored and was sporting an affected Marlaisan accent.

Bea shot Joan a questioning look, who rolled her eyes in return. Joan pushed the door open and walked in, her head held high. Bea swallowed, rolling her shoulders to get rid of the tightness there. This was it. She was finally going to meet a Raconteur.

The room was dim, but not dark. There were oil lamps in the wall, set to burn low, and a hurricane lamp on a stand by the bed, a red scarf draped over it, casting strange shadows across the room. Bea resisted the temptation to rub her eyes, instead waiting for her vision to adjust.

Slowly, she began to make out the image of a woman sitting neatly at an armoire with her back to them, daubing perfume on her wrists from a small glass decanter. Bea could see her face in the polished bronze that rested against the wall. Her short hair was curled around her face in soft waves, and she wore little green gems in it that sparkled like jealousy. Her eyes were round and misleadingly innocent, her face oval with a pointed chin and plump, heart-shaped lips painted a dark brown.

So this is a Raconteur, Bea thought. No wonder they could charge so much for their time.

"I wondered if I'd ever see you again," Delphine said casually, not bothering to turn around.

"You said that you didn't want to see me again," Joan replied with a little laugh. Bea had never heard Joan laugh that way. It was like she was trying to seem unaffected, as if the Raconteur had said something offensive to her.

"It's a terrible person who listens to what we say rather than what we mean," Delphine answered, fluffing her hair. "So, who is this?" She turned her eyes in the bronze, acknowledging Bea for the first time.

"This is my friend." Joan hesitated. "Bea."

Delphine spun around on her seat to face them, crossing her legs in a way that accentuated her plump thighs and narrow ankles, and let out a dismissive puff of air from the corner of her mouth.

"This is the cabbage fairy? Humility is a hard lesson, but I wonder that you need to teach it in such a cruel manner."

"She's my friend, that's all."

Delphine blew out another puff of air, ruffling the hair around her collar bone. "This is how it begins."

"Delphine," Joan said, a note of warning in her voice.

"*Non*, you have come to me, Joany. You do not get to set the tone."

"Joan?" Bea asked. There was something wrong, and it wasn't what she had expected to be wrong. The air between Joan and the Raconteur vibrated with the tension of unspoken words.

Delphine narrowed her eyes. "I do not want to hear her voice," she said to Joan.

"I don't care what you want," Bea said, pulling herself up to her full height. "This was a bad idea. Come on Joan, let's go."

Joan scratched again at her hair. She looked wretched. "It's alright, just... just let me do the talking."

Delphine smiled triumphantly. Bea sensed that she'd just lost a competition with the Raconteur, a competition she hadn't known she'd been playing, for a prize she didn't understand. But she trusted her friend to know her own mind. Plus, she hated to admit, she wanted answers.

"Fine," Bea said, folding her arms. "But the moment you want to go, you say so."

Delphine leaned forward on her elbows conspiratorially, talking directly to Joan. "How are you? Your hair has grown."

"I'm good, thank you. Busy."

"And your family? Your mother?"

"She... She's better off now," Joan said.

Delphine cocked her head, waiting to see if any more information would be forthcoming. "Well then," she said in a business-like tone when it became clear Joan wasn't going say any more, "I suppose I must ask why you're here, since I assume you have come for a reason. So be quick—my time is precious."

Bea frowned at the sudden change in the Raconteur but kept her silence. Delphine was an adhene, a famously spiteful tribe, and it could just as easily be her nature that made her sound suddenly so cold. Or, more likely, there *was* something there, but Bea had no idea what, nor why Joan's voice had thickened at the mention of her mother. She squirrelled the thought away, to ask Joan about when all this madness with the Anti was finished.

"I know it's been a long time," Joan said to Delphine, "and you don't owe me anything, but we were friends once, and I thought perhaps—well, I hoped you might be able to give me some information about the 2nd Chapter."

"Are you in trouble?"

"No, no, no, not at all," Joan said quickly, and then, in a formal sort of tone that didn't suit her, "but we're having some difficulty, and we've been led to believe that we might find answers from the 2nd."

"You shouldn't go poking your nose around. There is danger in the air."

"That's why we need to find out what's going on. It affects a story. We need the stories right now."

"We? You and this cabbage fairy?"

Silence. And then Joan turned to Bea. "I'm sorry, Bea, but I think we should go. It was a mistake coming here. I don't know why I thought she'd help me," she said, shaking her head. "Apparently, time doesn't heal all wounds."

Delphine walked over to her bed, fingering the silk canopy that hung from the masts. The adhene were not known for being ugly, but even by their lofty standard, Delphine was a sight to behold. There was something about her, whether it was her round face and cloudy hair or her curved hips and narrow waist, which seemed to hint at all the things she would share with you, the stories she could tell you. There are, in short, some women who wear short skirts and stiletto heels to create allure; Delphine merely needed to smile.

She smiled at Joan.

"Darling one, it is not about helping you or not helping you. You of all people should know what's coming."

"What do you mean, 'you of all people'? Are you laughing at me?"

"Not at all. You are a detective, are you not?"

Bea started. Joan was hugely secretive about her dream to become a detective. Of course, the adhene were liars and tricksters, but this part of Joan's life was a truth, a precious secret she kept from the world because she was afraid of being mocked for it. Bea had known Joan for two years before the tooth fairy had admitted to it, and even then, Bea was certain she only told her because she knew that Bea's own dream was even more impossible. Whoever this Delphine was now, she had clearly once been someone Joan trusted.

Joan shook her head. "I didn't do that in the end. I was needed at home. I'm a good tooth fairy," she added defensively, although Delphine hadn't said anything.

"So you are still the secondary character, little Joany? The sidekick?"

"Why do you always have to be like this?" Joan said.

"Why not? You will not even think these things, and you hate me still for saying them."

"I don't hate you."

"Really? You have come here, after so many years, for my help, not for me. Traditionally we would play the game. Three questions, three guesses, three riddles. Which would you prefer?"

"You've never been a traditionalist," Joan said.

"A fact of my life that used to frighten you, I remember," Delphine answered. Bea watched as the colour drained from Joan's cheeks and then flooded back in a hot red blush.

The conversation was jumping between Joan and Delphine so quickly Bea couldn't begin to understand what was being said, let alone what wasn't. But she didn't need to. She could see the look on Joan's face, and no amount of information was worth it.

Bea put her arm around her friend. "Let's go." Delphine shot her a look full of hatred, but Bea was beyond caring. "I'm sorry you don't like me, Delphine, but to be honest, you can join the queue. Joan, if she's just going to upset you, we don't need her help."

"Ouf. She is angry, isn't she Joany? I suppose that's something in her favour," Delphine said grudgingly.

Joan stepped forward, letting Bea's arm drop from her shoulders. "Please, Delphine—Delphi. We need your help."

Delphine pursed her lips. When she spoke next, there was a new note in her voice, one Bea hadn't expected: fear.

"Joany, the city is dying, and it will not be a quiet death. She will try to take us all with her, and it is always the good little sidekick who dies first."

Joan shrugged. "No one dies in the Teller's, *whocaresaboutus*, Plots. Well, except the parents, and that's before the story begins."

Delphine shrugged. "Very well. Sit down, both of you. But I will say again, you should not be asking these questions, not at a time like this."

"Thank you," Bea said. "We need to know about the 2nd Chapter. Can you tell us anything?"

"Very little. I am old, but I am not so old."

Joan flopped down on the stool by the armoire. "You don't know anything at all?"

"Take heart, my love. I said I know little, not nothing. The 2nd was the time of the *djinn*. Genies, in the new tongue."

"The genies had a Chapter?" Joan asked. "That doesn't make sense. Everyone knows they were stupid, clowning things. All you had to do was wish for more wishes. That's a loophole in their story big enough for a hoodlelump to jump through."

"Ah, this is what everyone knows, is it?" Delphine frowned. "So why not ask everyone? You came to me."

"She's right," Bea said. "Haven't you noticed? It's always 'everyone knows this' and 'everyone knows that', and how often do they actually know anything? It's all the old ones, keeping secrets, and us just bumbling along, swallowing the shi—I mean," she said quickly, remembering that Delphine could report her if she said too much, "we don't think to question because the Teller Cares About Us. How could the genies have had a Chapter and no one know about it?"

"The genies were, I believe, one of the first to be targeted by the Great Redaction," Delphine continued. "The Teller Cares About Us, as you say, but he also cares about order and control, yes? The genies were the epitome of everything he despises. They were wild things, telling tales based on the desires of the characters, desires which relied solely on the judgement of the one who happened to rub the lamp."

"You don't approve?" Joan asked, picking up on Delphine's tone.

"Their stories were for themselves, not the Mirrors."

"What do you mean?" said Bea.

"Certainly *sometimes* a good little character would find a lamp, and would not be so corrupted by the strangely endless possibilities of three wishes that they ended up causing more harm than they ever imagined. *Those* stories fostered belief and were retold, but they were few and far between. Most of the genie's tales showed the characters exactly who they really were, not when they were despised and degraded, not when they'd reached the gutter and been given licence to look at the stars. No, the genies showed them who they were when they were *invincible*. The characters, they try to forget stories like that."

Bea nodded. "That... makes sense."

"Ah, yes. You see the problem, cabbage fairy," Delphine said, something like approval in her voice.

"What happened to the genies?"

"Perhaps the Teller Redacted them. And yet, you don't see any dead-headed genies, do you?"

"How would you recognise one?"

"Their looks, for one. They were said to be prettier than the elves, prettier even than the adhene, or so it goes. The characters trust beauty, do they not?"

Bea looked at Joan, who shifted her head slightly, giving her an almost imperceptible nod. She needed to know more. She'd have to risk it.

"The man in my story is very handsome. He's also blue."

"Then this creature could be a genie. They did not hide as we do. Arrogant creatures."

"So why is he trying to ruin Bea's story?" Joan asked. "Even if he is a genie, why would he bother? It sounds like any genie should be too frightened of the Teller, *whocaresaboutus*, to risk exposure."

"Well, there was a story I heard a few years ago. A ridiculous thing, not even worth retelling. Or so I thought at the time."

F. D. Lee

"Can you tell it to us?" Joan asked quickly. "I can pay for the tale. I've got some teeth on me."

Delphine blinked her wide, round eyes. "Ah Joan, Joan, Joan. Such cruelty—you should have been a Redactionist."

"I just thought... you said your time..."

"Put away your teeth. I will help you on your quest. Oh, don't look so surprised, my love. How can we learn the value of saying no if we didn't occasionally say yes?"

"I wasn't surprised. I just didn't want to assume you would. That's all."

"I can afford to help a friend."

"Oh," Joan said, looking awkward again. "Well, I'm pleased you're doing so well."

"As am I," Delphine answered neatly. "Now. There was a story, as I said, hardly an anecdote, but perhaps it will aid you. Some years ago, a human woman fell in love. They do so love to fall in love, don't they? Still, this story was unusual for two reasons. Firstly, this man she loved, they say he was charming, confident, and that he made all her dreams come true."

"All the heroes are like that," Bea said.

"But this was not a Plot. So, how could a human ever live up to the standards of a hero, without us to aid him? Perhaps—"

"He wasn't human?" Joan and Bea said in unison.

"Exactly. Now, to the second unexpected thing. She didn't marry him. She married a Count or some such title. Unusual, *non*, to turn down such love? I wonder if something about this hero scared her. What do you think?"

Bea felt a glimmer of understanding. "Ever since the King and Queen, it's been expressly forbidden for the fae to get romantically involved with humans. But I heard him say he'd loved someone and lost them. It must be the same person—how could it not be?"

"Narrative Convention is certainly on your side," Delphine said.

"What's Narrative Convention?"

"The Teller's stories all have the same ending because he will not allow us to deviate from the Plots. But once, the stories followed their own path. Maybe again, who knows? The Mirrors are breaking, are they not?"

Bea and Joan glanced nervously around, but they were safe. A Raconteur wouldn't allow themselves to be watched—at least, not easily. The bronze was polished to a dull gleam, and so would interfere with any image the GenAm tried to pick up, assuming they were watching. And like Mistasinon said, the Mirrors didn't pick up sound. Plus, there was nothing illegal in seeing a Raconteur. They were probably safe.

"Do you know what happened to this girl?" Bea asked.

"As I said, she married someone of The Third Kingdom. That is all I know."

Joan stood up. "Thank you. We'll let you get on with your business."

Delphine nodded her head. "You're welcome. But Joany—"

"Yes?"

"If he is a genie, you must not get in his way."

"Why?"

"They are dangerous. They are not like us, they do not belong in the Land any more than they belong in Thaiana. There is nothing they want or need, except the stardust."

Joan leaned forward on the stool. "Delphine, what do you mean?"

"Take my advice and walk away from whatever you are caught up in. You and your cabbage fairy. The end is coming."

F. D. Lee

Chapter Twenty-seven

Ænathlin had always been a city designed to add to its own madness. The streets wound in circular patterns that could only be called normal by those who had a penchant for experimenting with two-dimensional infinities.

The city was awake and teeming with life, if such a gentle expression could be used to cover the chaotic energy of the walled-in city, overpopulated by hundreds of tribes of the fae, all hoping to find a way to survive.

At every level, someone was trying to trade for something. Shops and market stalls spilt into the streets, gnomes and dwarves and all the tribes that had once held the stories in their hands, reduced to trade and barter to survive—a survival that was becoming increasingly difficult, judging by the sudden hike in prices.

Tomptes, wyrewens and sprites, tribes that had always managed to find a pathway through the maze of rules the Teller had created, were now running businesses out of crates and barrels, eking out a living by selling services only the very small could offer. Bea had even seen a kelpie pulling a rope to work a grinder, its black hooves raising sparks and tail hanging in wet tendrils. The kelpie, a tribe of water horses, rarely allowed themselves to be employed outside the services of the GenAm, which at least appealed to their sense of dignity. It was, or had been, an arrangement that suited everyone. The kelpie had too strong a penchant for fresh meat to ever be truly welcome anywhere.

If it carries on like this, Bea thought as she side-stepped a troll, *the gangs will come back*. The threat of Redaction and fear of the Beast had kept the city peaceful for hundreds of years, but the deal was that the Teller's Plots maintained the Mirrors. And now that deal was in danger of breaking.

Bea and Joan walked away from the centre, towards Joan's house. Bea wanted to ask Joan if she was alright, and about what had happened between her and the Raconteur, and why Delphine had decided to help them in the end, and how she had met the adhene in the first place.

But she couldn't think where to begin, so instead, she said, "Thank you. For helping me."

Joan smiled. "Get away with you. It was no trouble."

Bea lowered her voice. "Do you think he really is a genie?"

Joan stopped dead in the street. "Tooth and nail, Bea, are you serious?"

"What? I don't understand—"

Joan grabbed Bea by the arm and pulled her down an alleyway. It wasn't empty—before curfew, nowhere in Ænathlin was empty, but the only other fae were a couple of goblins, rooting through sacks filled with offcut material. They were behind a haberdashery; what was scrap here would have value by the wall, and the goblins knew it. They wouldn't pay two fairies any attention. Still, Joan pulled Bea as far away from them as she could.

"Does it matter if he's a genie?" she said. "He's either that or an Anti or probably both! Who cares what he is? He's dangerous. You heard Delphine."

"I was just asking—"

Joan took a deep breath, her little hands pumping fists at the ends of her arms. "No. No, you weren't asking. You were hoping. I could hear it in your voice. You were hoping I might say no. Or that it didn't matter. Bea, I'm sorry, but maybe Melly is right. Sometimes we don't get to follow our dreams."

Bea shook her head, searching Joan's face. "You don't mean that."

"Yes, I do," Joan said. "We all have to face up to it sometime."

"What's that supposed to mean?"

Joan sighed and leaned against the wall. "I'm not trying to be mean, Bea. I do think you can become an FME, I really do. But this isn't the way to go about it."

"I don't know what you're talking about. I haven't said anything about anything. I only asked if you thought what the Raconteur said was true. They're storysells after all, always looking for the highest bidder." Bea knew she was being spiteful and childish, but she couldn't help herself. Joan was supposed to be her friend. So was Melly, come to that. But they were both telling her to give up, to go home. To forget it all.

"Oh really?" said Joan, an unexpected edge in her voice. "And you're so brilliant, are you?"

"I'm not a quitter."

"You quit on me when I needed you."

Bea blinked. "What? When?"

"My mum died last year. She got sick, and we couldn't trade for the right herbs. You weren't here then, but you've been back nearly a week, and you haven't asked either Melly or I what's been happening in our lives. You're obsessed with this whole FME business. It's made you selfish."

Bea felt her throat dry. She looked in horror at her friend.

"I didn't know... how...?"

"The usual way," Joan said, the anger ebbing from her voice to be replaced with tiredness. "She was sick when you left, that's why I was so busy getting teeth. I thought at the time perhaps you hadn't realised, and then you took on that long Plot-watch, and when I saw you at the Contents Department you were so excited..."

"I'm so, so sorry," Bea said, reaching out uncertainly and placing her hand on Joan's shoulder. She didn't know what to do.

"It's alright," Joan said. "I'm not really cross. Well, no, I am. A little."

"I'm so sorry, Joan. I wish—I don't know what to do..."

"She was old. The iron got in her blood. So it goes. But you don't have to run behind her, Bea. You're my friend, and I don't want to lose you either."

"Some friend. You're right, I've been so caught up in my own life, my own problems. Oh, mortal gods, Joan, I'm so sorry."

"Bea, listen to me," Joan said, meeting Bea's eyes for the first time since the conversation began. "You are a good friend. When I first met you, I was in trouble, and you helped me. You didn't judge me or ask questions. You took me as I am, and you always have. I've still got the spyglass you bought for me, and I remember how you helped me hide my Thaianan detective books when they did the sweeps a few years ago. You're brave, Bea. You don't know it, maybe, but you are. And you're moral, too. But yes, you've become..."

"Selfish."

Joan shrugged. "Maybe. I don't know if that's the right word. You've never really explained why you came here, or why it's so important to you that you succeed in the GenAm, and I may not be a detective, but I pick things up. I know what it's like to lose someone and the guilt that goes with it."

"Joan—"

Joan waved her hands. "You don't have to tell me if I'm right or not. I'm just saying it so you'll know I'm not writing you off. But this business with the Plot, Bea, it's all wrong. A heroine who won't marry the hero, an Anti who's a genie... even the way you got it is weird. You weren't recommended, were you? Who even is this Mistasinon—what tribe is he? Where does he come from? And I think you're more worried about your heroine than you let on. I know you think this is your only chance, but please, get out of this story."

"But how can I? Even if I wanted to, the Redactionists will have my head."

Joan sighed. "That I don't know. But there must be a way, and if anyone can find it, you can." She smiled. "You're the fairy who changed the Plots, remember? Just find a way out, and then leave all this FME stuff alone. At least for a while. Take a few years off."

"I... yes. Alright. I'll finish this Plot and then think. How's that?"

"That's all I ask," Joan said, sagging with relief.

Bea realised how difficult it must have been for Joan to say the things she had. She wanted so much to say something to make it better, but she didn't know where to begin. She looked at her friend, returning her smile. But there was something in Joan's eyes which Bea was only now seeing, and she wondered how long it had been there.

Chapter Twenty-eight

King John looked up to see his Adviser slouch into his private study, a greenish tinge to his normally healthy complexion. John blinked as his eyes started to tear-up. Bloody candle smoke.

"Where've you been? It's almost 6 bells, man."

Seven walked slowly up to the throne, his movement heavy. Nevertheless, he bowed low to the King.

"Lord, I apologise most sincerely. I was delayed unavoidably."

"What's this? Unavoidably, you say? Explain yourself, S."

To John's surprise, Seven sat at his feet. "I was in town, my Lord. I wanted to ascertain the mood of the citizenry. There is a general optimism regards the Ball. Tension appears lower between the natives and the refugees. You were right to suggest such an event."

"Yes, yes, well, well," John said, slightly mollified. "That took all day, did it?"

"I also made another delivery of food and supplies to the encampment, my Lord. Anonymously, as you requested," Seven said.

"And the rest? Something's up, fella. You look like hell."

"I am simply tired after a long day. One it seems full of wasted effort. I thought you would be pleased, Sire. But I am sorry if I have overstepped myself. It was unconsciously done."

John puffed his cheeks up, but after a moment he released his anger with a pop. The Adviser was looking at him with such sincerity, John felt guilty for questioning him.

"If you say so, S. Poor show not letting me know you were planning to be out gadding around. Had things for you to do today." John said, walking over to the table with the map.

John's private study was, unlike the majority of the castle, quite cosy. The old Kings and Queens of Llanotterly had shared one vision for the castle, and that was that it should intimidate. This had translated itself in a number of ways, from King George's Penqioan red, gold and jade pillars and wall paintings of dragons and fish that stretched over the ceilings in the south wing, to the wooden panels, trophy heads and sombre portraits in the main throne room, which were the taste of John's father, Edward. Even Queen Margaret, a woman best remembered in the folk song 'Old Red Meg', had found time to furnish the castle in velvet and gilt.

John, however, hadn't been left enough money to afford to put his mark on the castle in any great way. Still, he had done the best he could with what he had. The King preferred collecting cheap antiques to commissioning, but he had a good eye and, although there was nothing in the room that necessarily matched, the overall result was both warm and welcoming.

He stared down at the map, where the black figures that represented his workforce remained insultingly still. Little wooden tiles, painted white to represent Ana's encampment, were dotted around the main arc of the river.

"Not much of a kingdom. What isn't field is forest, what isn't forest is field. No great cities, no empire."

"I confess I am not sure I follow your line of thought, my Lord."

"I could just kill them. Round them up and hang the lot of them."

Seven joined his master at the table.

"You could," he answered.

"It's what father would have done. Well, I say father. My aunt Constance, she was the one really. Power behind the throne and all that. The old man didn't last long after her, and that's a fact."

"So why have you not?"

"Not what?"

"Killed them, my Lord."

"Dash it all, S. I'm not going to start hanging me own people for having an opinion. Some might find their way into the dungeon, I suppose, but I'm not my father. Or rather, my aunt. Look at this map here."

Seven did so.

"Land's jolly powerful, you were right there, old sweat," John said. "But so's money. No need to invade us if we're paying up, what?"

"No, my lord. This is why we endeavour to sell wood from the forests."

"Yes. But these ones here," he pointed to the white tiles, "reckon I'm inviting trouble. Making a splash. Might be they're onto something. Sit still and the Baron gets us, stand up and the Baron gets us. Wish there was some other way, old bean."

Seven winced, brushing his fingers against the snake necklace he insisted on wearing. The man looked like he was about to lose his lunch.

"My Lord, do not forget the Ball. Perhaps, there, another route might be discovered. We know not."

Poor fella, John thought. *Working all hours, running around. Strain's starting to show.* He offered him a wide smile. "Quite right, old sport. S'always darkest before dawn, what? So then, best get on with the arranging. Where's that list…?"

Much later, Seven entered his suite. Yawning, he turned around and locked his doors, a habit so ingrained he wasn't even aware he did it.

Stepping into his rooms, he allowed himself to relax. He was concerned with how exhausting he was finding everything, but he reminded himself that he hadn't exactly slept the night before, nor had he planned to use so much magic that day. Still, it was worrying how much it was hurting him.

He leaned back against the door. His eyes settled on his desk, but after a moment, he shook his head and headed instead into the small washroom attached to the main chamber. He turned on the brass taps and watched the water pour from their mouths like vomit. He splashed his face and started to feel better.

He looked up into the space where a mirror should have been. He'd had one of the staff remove the glass the day he'd taken up residency in the castle, but that wasn't to say he had no mirror at all.

The second piece of furniture that Seven had brought with him, other than his carved wooden desk, was a tall mirror. The mirror itself hadn't been anything special, only really the fact that it was full length making it noteworthy. Until, that is, Seven had purchased it.

He had, at great personal trouble and expense, taken the mirror to Ataji, a bustling faraoli in Ota'ari and still the spiritual home of steam- and clockwork-powered machinery. There he had hired a bald, smiling little man to customise the mirror to Seven's personal requirements.

It had taken the human a week to add to the mirror the series of valves and cogs that would ensure that if anyone stepped through it, they would receive a rather unexpected and inhospitable welcome; a welcome that would allow Seven to make his escape.

That will allow Maria Sophia and I to make our *escape,* he corrected.

And then he found himself wondering whether he might also be able to take John with him. It would be harder to hide with two humans, but not impossible. And he was certain the fairy, Bea, had not reported him. She wanted too badly to overthrow her oppressors, something he couldn't help but respect. And if the GenAm were to discover him, he could always leave his lamp hidden for a few more years. It would hurt him, true, but he had managed thus far. Yes, he perhaps could escape with both Maria Sophia and John…

His thoughts were interrupted by sudden, violent stomach contractions, and before he knew what was happening, he was throwing up into the sink.

It was ten minutes before all he could taste was bile. He slid slowly down the edge of the counter, his eyes watering and his nose stinging. He wiped his mouth with the back of his hand, closed his eyes and waited for his throat to stop burning.

Eventually, he climbed to his feet and reached for the small pot of toothpowder he kept by the sink, listlessly dipping his blue fingertip in the dust, and started to clean his teeth, brushing away the acidic taste of his stomach. He spat. A thick, black glob landed with an ugly sound against the white sink. Seven dipped his finger in the mess, bringing it up to his nose and sniffing it.

Blood.

He frowned, absently rubbing his bloody fingers against his thumb. The Ball was in two days; all he had to do was hold on a little longer.

And make sure nothing happened to disrupt his carefully laid plans.

Chapter Twenty-nine

Bea stood in the trees, watching all the people go in and out of Sindy's cottage with rising dread.

There was a constant stream of men toing and froing outside the door, all carrying heavy, serious equipment like axes and hoes. Bea also recognised a number of Ana's encampment milling around, all equally burdened. There was a tall woman, with a hairstyle that must have weighed more than she did, sitting on a water butt and fanning herself. She was crying loudly, while other women bustled around her, offering her cups of tea which she kept batting away. The one person who wasn't there in all of the hubbub was Sindy herself.

Bea moved around the tree line towards the back of the house, a knot forming in her stomach. Here she found yet more men and women, all full of industry. There was an older man handing out woodcut prints to two soldiers, who were nodding their heads as they listened to him. One of the soldiers said something that upset the man if the way his skin flushed red and his face disintegrated was any clue. She had the feeling he was Sindy's father; there was something about the way he handled himself that reminded her of her character.

She chewed her thumbnail, looking for Ana. Now she thought about it, the two people she would have expected to be here in all this furore, Ana and the boy Will, were absent. Maybe that meant that her initial suspicion upon seeing these people, all armed with weapons and panic, was wrong. Maybe this was some human ritual she didn't understand.

Surely if something had happened to Sindy, Ana and Will would be here?

Bea arrived at Ana's encampment and immediately noticed the difference. The other night there had been a relaxed ambience, with people playing music, chatting and laughing. Now there was a tension in the air, thick and heavy against her skin.

She crept through the forest to the tent she recognised as Ana's, a sixth sense telling her that today was not the day to be discovered by some random human. Her seventh and eighth senses asked her whether she was prepared to acknowledge that whatever was happening was probably her fault.

She crawled under the covers and into the tent. It was empty. She moved around the crates by the edge and into the centre of the space. The firepit was unlit, and with the tent door closed, it was hard to see anything. She started to poke around, looking for some clue about what was going on.

It didn't take Bea long to realise that there was a lot more to detective work than she had realised. She wished Joan was with her. She was just about to give up when light suddenly filled the tent.

There is a scene that is often used in westerns, in which the stranger walks into the crowded saloon and the music stops, all eyes turning on the intruder. This was exactly like that only, obviously, different.

Ana and Will stared at Bea in her dirty, patchwork dress, her silver hair falling out of its bun in tangles. Bea stared back at them, mouth opening and closing like she had just been asked to name all the Penqioan Emperors, in reverse chronological order, by height.

"Who the hell are you?" demanded Ana.

Bea waited for her brain to supply some words. Unfortunately, nothing seemed to be forthcoming.

"You've got until the count of five to explain what the hell you're doing in my tent, or I'll—"

And then Will pushed past Ana, waving a crumpled woodcut of Sindy in Bea's face.

"Have you seen this girl?"

"Um, yes, I saw her a couple of days ago," Bea said.

Ana moved faster than Bea had ever thought a human could, grabbing the front of her dress in her fists, forcing Bea to look up and meet her sludgy green eyes. Had Bea been of a lighter build, Ana would probably have lifted her off her feet.

"Do you know where my sister is?" she demanded.

"Er, no. But I think I know who's taken her," Bea said.

"Taken her? No one's taken her. She's run away. She left a note and everything," Will said. "She said she couldn't stay here anymore, but she didn't explain why."

Bea looked at Will's sickened expression, and at Ana's anger and fear. For some reason she couldn't understand, the memory of her brother rose in her mind. She hadn't thought about Mustard Seed in years, hadn't had time, hadn't allowed herself to think of what she'd left behind when she chose to escape her life in the Sheltering Forest.

But now, looking at Will and Ana, she saw him perfectly. The way his head had dropped the night he accepted their father was never coming back. His silence for weeks after the funeral. For the first time, she wondered if he had also tried not to cry when he realised *she* had left as well. Bea swallowed, and it hurt.

"I've had enough of this," Ana snapped. She tightened her grip on Bea's dress. "I want to know exactly who you are and how you know my sister, and I want to know now."

Bea took a deep breath and peered around Ana to address Will. "Would you believe I'm your, um, godmother?"

The room fell silent.

Ana let go of Bea's dress.

It had taken Bea about an hour to explain the basic principles of godmothering to Will and Ana, and she still didn't seem to be getting very far. It was like they'd never even heard of a Rags To Riches story.

"But I haven't got a birthmark," Will said again.

Bea smiled her best smile. "I know that. That's why I've got this red ink with me."

"Why does he need to have a strawberry birthmark again?" Ana asked.

"Because he hasn't got a mysterious sword," Bea replied, trying to sound patient and not annoyed. "There has to be some mark of destiny if we're going to pull this off."

"Riiiight. Oh yes, and he's selfish enough to have known both his parents," Ana said.

Bea was beginning to seriously dislike her. Ana was the sort of person who was so sharp she'd end up cutting herself. Bea was rather ashamed to find herself wishing she could be there to see it happen.

"I didn't say he was selfish—I just said it would have been helpful if he'd been sold at birth into some kind of menial job, like a swineherd. That's all."

"But I still don't see how any of this is going to get Sindy back," Will said. "That's all that matters right now."

Bea softened. "Yes. I know. But you see, it doesn't work if you just, I don't know, meet someone and get on with them and then, what, fall in love and get married? That's not how Dreams Come True, is it?"

"No... I suppose not..." Will said.

She'd been surprised to discover he wasn't all that good looking. She knew he wasn't rich, but she had been working under the assumption, she now realised, that up close he would at least be handsome. He wasn't ugly, though—just very regular. He was neither tall nor short, and his skin was tanned from hours working in the sun. His nose must have been broken at some point and set slightly crooked. He had sleepy brown eyes and an open face. He was completely unremarkable.

"But, if you don't mind, whose dreams do you make come true?" Will asked. "Because the last time I saw Sindy, she was very upset. She kept on asking me if she was selfish."

Alright, not completely unremarkable then.

"Yes. You're right," Bea said. "Forget the birthmark. The other problem is, I don't know where Sindy is any more than you do. If she was younger, I could ask my friend to help."

"So ask her," Ana said.

"She won't be able to. Not unless Sindy still has her milk teeth. She's a tooth fairy, you see."

Ana shook her head. She looked like she was about to laugh. Or murder someone. "A tooth fairy. Of course. What's next? Trolls under bridges and three little bears? Do you think we're complete idiots?"

"You're just too old, that's all. And cynical," Bea added. "It's not my fault people stop believing in fairies when they grow up."

"And I suppose none of this is your fault either?" Ana snapped. "Some fairy you are. You've got no more of an idea how to find her than we have. You're just wasting time trying to get Will to pretend to be some Prince. You do realise there are wolves in the forest and bears? Not to mention Slavers. What if Sindy's on a slaver wagon already? She'll never survive in the Baron's manufactories."

Will turned green. Bea had never seen anything like it, and she had recently spent time in the company of a blue genie. He fell to the ground on broken legs, his face buried in his hands. Bea knelt down next to him, placing her hand on his shoulder. He said something she couldn't hear.

"Pardon?"

Will lifted his head up, silver trails of tears running down his face. Bea recoiled instinctively. Looking at him felt like she was witnessing someone's soul screaming.

"I've lost her, haven't I?"

Bea threw her arms around him. She could feel his warm, wet tears on her shoulders, seeping through the material of her dress. "No, no, no."

"Yes I have," Will sniffed. "I didn't... I wasn't... and now she's dead..."

Bea realised she had no choice. The mortal gods knew what would happen, but she couldn't let these people suffer like this. "Look," she said, "maybe there is a way. Can you think of anything Sindy might have taken with her? Something important to her?"

Bea didn't want to think about what Melly would say when she asked her to help find a lost heroine on a Plot she'd promised she wasn't going to continue working on. But Melly was a witch, and witches were good at finding heroines who had hidden themselves.

Will grabbed Bea's hands in his enormous ones and kissed them. "She wears a necklace—it's a charm. I gave it to her when my mum died, I wanted Sindy to have it. She wears it all the time, and I know she looks after it. It's a little glass slipper."

Bea thought about it. She didn't know how Melly's witchiness worked, but it had to be worth a shot. "Yes... maybe that would work."

"You're going to use a glass slipper to find her? She could be anywhere in the whole Kingdom," Ana said. But there was an edge of hope in her voice.

"Alright." Bea got to her feet. "I'll go home and ask my friend to help us. At least if we know where she is, we can make sure she's safe. I'll meet you at Sindy's cottage—can you make sure no one else is home?"

She didn't add that she had no idea how she was going to get Sindy back, if they found her at all.

Bea arrived in the Grand to find the checkpoints still up. She joined a queue and waited, tapping her fingers against her Book, safely held in her bag. It took an hour for her to reach the front of the line, and by this time she had worked herself up into a sickness of nerves. Melly might refuse to help her. Sindy could be dead already. Ana was right—it was all her fault.

She finally reached the brown suit at the checkpoint. She was so caught up in her own thoughts that at first, she didn't register what he said.

"Ssso?"

Bea jumped at the sound of the brown suit's slithering voice. He was a witchlein, not a tribe anyone wanted to run into unexpectedly. The witchlein were fearsome creatures, despite their small size. Sharp toothed with razor-thin scales over their yellow skin, they had, before the Redaction, been amongst those fae who had used fear to keep the belief rolling in. Now they used their skills to the same effect, only with a different audience. It was extremely unusual for one to be working for the Contents Department—if they were employed at all by the GenAm, they worked with the white suits.

"I'm sorry?" Bea said, trying to hide the way her skin prickled at the sight of him.

The witchlein hissed at her, baring his needle-point teeth. "Ssstupid fairy. When doesss your ssstory finisssh?"

"Tomorrow evening."

"Right," his said, giving her a hard look. "And your FME asssssignment isss godmother. Why have you been in Thaiana today?"

Bea met his glare and raised him an eyebrow. "Because I've been checking to make sure my Plot is running smoothly," she said. It wasn't a lie, after all.

"A ssstory thisss ssssimple doesssn't need to be checked," the witchlein said around his teeth. Under different circumstances, Bea would have been impressed.

"Why not?"

"Becaussse the Mirrorsss are breaking. No unneccesssary travel permitted." He stamped the inside page of Bea's Book with ill-concealed glee. "You can travel there on *Sssaturday* night. Not before."

"But—"

"Next!"

"Now listen to me," Bea said, ignoring the growing discontent of the queue behind her. "I very much nearly happen to be a godmother, and as such, I think you—"

"If you don't like it, take it up with her," the witchlein said, nodding over his shoulder. Bea peered around him.

Standing on a platform, high above the crowds, was the blonde Redactionist Bea had seen the day she'd arrived back in Ænathlin. She was scanning the Grand, eyes narrowed as she focused. Every now and again a tompte would zip through the air to stand on the railing of the platform, no doubt updating her on the goings-on below. The Redactionist would nod or shake her head, but she never once stopped scouring the Grand. Bea didn't want to think too closely about what she was looking for, just in case the very act of thinking it brought her to the attention of the white suit.

"Well?"

Bea swallowed. "I think I'm alright."

"Thought ssso," the brown suit said, smiling smugly.

Bea said something obscene.

Luckily, there was no one in the Sheltering Forest to hear her. She was looking for Melly's cottage, and she wasn't having much luck. She was a good hour away from the wall, and still hadn't found the right path. Of course, she hadn't expected it to be easy, but she was beginning to think that something, or someone, was deliberately causing her to lose her way.

She made a face and stomped further into the woods. She hadn't been back in the Forest for years, not counting the wobble she'd had the night she'd first realised she'd been changing the Plots. It didn't feel like home. It should have done, but it didn't. The trees were darker and thinner, and they twisted and turned in patterns that reminded her of broken spider webs. They whispered to her, their leaves rattling high above her head, telling her to go back where she came from.

"I can't," Bea muttered. "I've got business here. Anyway, this is where I came from."

A cold breeze brushed against her skin. Bea wrapped her arms around herself, wishing she had her cloak. She'd forgotten how cold it was outside the city. The wastelands beyond the Sheltering Forest did nothing to regulate the climate of the Land, and the chill of desolation threaded through the trees.

"Look, I don't want to be here either. Trust me, there are people in this Forest I don't want to meet, and I don't just mean gnarl raiding parties."

An apple dropped from overhead, landing heavily on the dank, brown carpet of leaves and mulch. It shone red, despite the hazy light.

Bea sighed. "For goodness' sake, do you think I was born yesterday? I'm a garden fairy, not a bloody imp—garden, you know? Fruits and vegetables? I know a poisoned apple when I see one."

The Forest wailed, leaves and twigs falling on Bea as the trees shook violently. She flung herself to the ground, covering her head with her hands. Something heavy hit her shoulder, causing her to flinch. She rolled, catching her dress on the rocks and stones that had suddenly risen up through the undergrowth. She came to a stop on her back, opening her eyes just in time to see the branch rushing towards her, sprigs outstretched to scratch her eyes out.

Bea shifted quickly to her left, rolling on her damaged shoulder and rising to her feet. A white-hot jolt of pain shot across her back and down her arm, but she didn't have time to acknowledge it. The branch came back the other way, hitting her head and throwing her off balance. She skidded forward, landing on her chin.

No time to check the damage. Bea pushed up into a starting position and launched herself forward just as the branch slammed down on the spot where she'd been.

Tears blurring her vision, Bea ran on. Her chest burned, her muscles screamed. Still the Sheltering Forest attacked her. The ground underneath her shifted and moved, roots dancing below the leaf cover, causing her to stumble and fall. Every time she hit the ground, the trees would slam their branches into her until she could barely stand. Faltering, her pace slowing with each step, Bea stumbled on.

"Why are you doing this?" she cried, her voice raw as she gulped air into her exhausted lungs. "I'm one of yours! This is my home!"

The Forest stilled. Bea looked around her. Perhaps it hadn't recognised her? There had to be a reason why it had turned on her. The Sheltering Forest had always protected the fae. During the Rhyme War it had been their greatest ally—so what was happening? What had changed?

Bea wiped the sweat from her forehead. When she pulled her hand down, it was sticky with black blood. Gingerly she brought her fingertips up to her head, feeling around her hairline. She winced as she found the wound.

"Why are you—" Bea began, but she was cut off by a low, creaking sound. The kind of sound that makes you think there's someone on the stairs. The kind of sound made by wood trying to be quiet. The kind of sound Bea really, *really* did not want to hear while an entire Forest went to war against her.

She jumped just in time.

The tree smashed into the ground, missing her by inches. What caught Bea was not the tree, but the hail of splinters that exploded outwards from the impact of the dry, old trunk hitting the ground.

There was a ringing in her ears.

Night was closing in…
She was cold.
Bea fell.

Chapter Thirty

"Sleeping Beauty awakes," Melly said. "Can I get you anything?"

Bea ran her tongue over her lips. It felt like she was licking sand. "W't'rr?"

"Hang on."

Some fae were able to read emotions—it wasn't exactly the same as being psychic, but the few who were truly adept, like the genies, weren't far off. Bea was not one of those fae. But right at this moment in time, she was one hundred per cent certain that the second she opened her eyes, she was going to be shouted at. She kept them closed.

Melly's footsteps receded into another room.

Right.

The Sheltering Forest had taken it upon itself to try to kill her. And now she was with Melly. That was a definite improvement even if the witch's tone had been decidedly unimpressed.

Bea ran through what she could remember, which was basically being annoyed, frightened and, finally, in a lot of pain.

That was interesting. She didn't hurt now. Tentatively she tilted her head, wincing in anticipation of the agony from the cut on her brow and the damage to her shoulder. She felt queasy for a moment, and her shoulder was tight, but other than that, she was fine. In fact, she felt no worse than after a night of drinking—better even, given some of the morning afters she'd experienced.

"Come on, then. Up and at 'em," Melly said, walking back into the room.

Bea cracked open her eyes. The witch was carrying a large glass of red wine in each hand. She supposed she hadn't really expected water. She pulled herself upright, ignoring the momentary dizziness the action caused. She was in a cosy living room, warm and full of the evidence of a long life. There were large wooden dressers with glass doors, and when she peered at one, she was surprised to find a series of china shepherdesses and dancers; another one was full of glass animals. Still feeling dizzy, Bea couldn't put her finger on what it was, but there was something odd about the space.

"Why did the Forest attack me?" Bea asked, taking the offered glass.

Melly sat on an old chair, shifting a pile of knitting carefully onto the already over-crowded coffee table. It seemed to Bea she was taking as long as possible before having to answer her.

"It doesn't like outsiders," Melly eventually admitted.

"But I'm not an outsider! I was born here—and anyway, Ænathlin isn't outside. If anything, it's inside the Forest."

Melly frowned and took a long sip of wine. Bea was just about to repeat herself when the elf said, "The Forest is angry with Ænathlin. For hundreds of years, it's protected us from Yarnis' soldiers, mostly at its own expense, so that we could look after the Mirrors. And now we've welched on our side of the deal. You can't blame it for being peeved."

"Oh," Bea said, feeling somewhat chastised. "I hadn't thought about it like that. I guess the Forest must be frightened it'll become like the wastelands."

"Something like that."

"But that still doesn't explain why it attacked me. I'm one of the Belgae, we look after the Forest."

Melly looked uncomfortable. "I suppose you've been gone too long. Or you've changed too much. It didn't recognise you."

Bea flinched. That's what you get for trying to be someone different—you become someone different. "Oh. Right. How did you find me?"

"The Forest told me there was an intruder, but it didn't sound like an orc or a gnarl, so I came to investigate. When I saw it was you, I called it off and brought you here."

Bea tried to ignore the flash of anger she felt as Melly spoke. Melly had been living in the Forest for hundreds of years, if not thousands—Bea had no idea how old Melly really was. She, on the other hand, was barely eighty and had spent the last twenty years of her life trying to pretend the first sixty hadn't happened. She shouldn't be jealous that the Forest trusted Melly and not her. She *was* jealous. But she knew she shouldn't be.

F. D. Lee

Taking a large gulp of wine, Bea took another look around the room. She almost forgot to swallow.

Criss-crossing the walls of Melly's cottage were strange black snakes made of metal. Bea could taste the iron, even over the red wine. They clung onto the wall in haphazard lines and angles, like something from the crazed dreams of an overworked geometry teacher. Suddenly, one of the snakes let out a high-pitched hissing whistle, causing Bea to nearly choke to death.

"They do that sometimes. It's perfectly safe," Melly said, sipping her drink.

"What are they?"

"I don't like fire," Melly said, her tone so casual it was anything but. "The pipes keep the house warm, so I don't need a fireplace. I got the idea from the steam engines the characters use. Though I'm not sure I got it quite right," she added as another hiss cut through the room.

Bea stood up and walked over to one of the so-called 'pipes'. Gingerly, she reached out and touched it. It was warm. More confidently, Bea pressed her palm up to the metal. The iron, hidden behind black paint, made her hand sting, but the warmth was so comforting it was worth it. The heat and the wine began to work their own kind of magic. Bea started to relax.

"Bea, exactly what are you doing here?"

Well, she thought, *it was nice while it lasted.*

"I need your help."

"What's happened?"

Bea whistled through her teeth, dreading Melly's reaction. "I've lost my heroine."

"What? I thought you said you were going to hand the Plot back?"

Bea squirmed. "Yes. Sorry. I didn't mean to lie to you, but I can't hand the Plot in because I... I made changes to it."

Melly put her wine glass down.

"I think you better start at the beginning."

Bea told Melly about Sindy and Will, and changing the Plots, and showing the girl the Grand, and how she'd promised she would find Sindy again, and the fact she didn't have an ending to her Plot.

"Right," Melly said when Bea had finished.

"So you see, I need you to help me find Sindy. I can't do it myself, and I don't think Joan would be able to. But you're a witch, and I thought, well, witches are always finding heroines when they're hiding. Do you think you can?"

"I can, but I don't think I should. This is exactly the sort of thing the GenAm expressly forbids. You changed the Plots, Bea!"

"I didn't mean to. I just—I saw ways to make them run better. And why not? I didn't do any harm."

"What about the Mirrors? Are you seriously saying you think you did the right thing?"

"Melly, please. Whatever I did or didn't do doesn't matter now. You must see I can't return *this* Plot, not with it all messed up? I'll be Redacted for sure. This whole thing is such a mess," Bea said, flopping back down on her seat. "You know, the reason I wanted to be an FME was to make more of myself than everyone thought I was, but I think all I did was lose me. I didn't know Joan's mum died. I didn't know, and she just assumed I was too busy to tell me." Bea's voice cracked. "I've lost my past, and I don't have a present to replace it with."

But if she was hoping for sympathy, she wasn't going to get it.

"What about the Anti?" Melly asked. "Where does he fit into all this?"

"Um. Well. There've been a few developments there as well…"

Melly smoked while Bea told her about Seven, how she thought he was love in with a human and that was why he was in her story, and that he'd told her changing the stories doesn't cause the Mirrors to break. Finally, she told Melly what he'd said about the King and Queen, and how they weren't responsible for everything that had happened to the Mirrors.

"He said that, did he?" Melly asked.

"Yes. I mean, I know it's hearsay, but I think he's right. At least, about the Mirrors. If you think about it, it doesn't make sense. Stories changed all the time, once. And Mistasinon knew I'd made changes when he took me on, and it didn't bother him."

Melly leaned back in her chair, crossing her legs. "What *is* breaking the Mirrors then?"

"I don't know. But the most important thing right now is finding Sindy, making sure she's safe and working out some sort of Happy Ending. The Mirrors can wait." Bea rested her chin in her hand, her lips pursed. "I've got to finish the Plot. Not just because of Sindy, but because sooner or later Mistasinon will want to see my Book."

"Have you completely lost your mind?" Melly cried, her green eyes searching Bea's face for any sign her friend had momentarily misplaced her senses and any second now she might find them behind the proverbial sofa of self-preservation.

"If I don't, the Redactionists will want to know why not, won't they?" Bea said, shaking her head. "And on top of that my heroine is still lost, miles away from her home. I've made up my mind, Melly. But I need your help."

"Bea, you need to drop all of this, now. Forget your Plotter and the Anti—they'd forget you fast enough, trust me. I know the type."

"Mistasinon's done nothing but help me, and Seven…" here Bea floundered somewhat, but managed at least to say, "…is very passionate about his beliefs. And I agree with him. If this Plot has taught me anything, it's that we—the GenAm, FMEs, all of us—cause harm to the humans. Sindy could be lying dead in some slave pit now, all because of me."

Melly stared at Bea in much the same way a palaeontologist might stare at someone who'd suggested that all those old bony type bone things buried in the hills were only some kind of cosmic practical joke.

"How can you think like this? None of these people… Look, your Plotter works for the GenAm. He's a company man, he doesn't care about you. And the Anti doesn't care about anyone but himself. He's got you convinced he's sympathetic to these characters, but believe me, he's not. The Anties are the ones causing all the trouble!"

"Maybe they are. But it doesn't mean that what he said was wrong. Come on, Melly, you must have thought it sometimes. Look at you—you're the least wicked person I know, and it doesn't matter how many cigarettes you smoke or how much black you wear. You're not a nasty person. I know you feel it too."

"Oh really? Well, don't you just know everything about everything suddenly?" Melly said sourly. "Bea, this is suicide; this is worse than suicide—you might as well be Redacting yourself. Listen to me. I'm your friend, I've got your best interests at heart."

"If you're my friend, help me. Tell me where Sindy is."

"Bea, you need to think about this—you should've been thinking about all this from the beginning. This is that bloody Anti, polluting your mind," Melly said, her tone becoming hard where moments ago it had been conciliatory.

Bea slammed her hands into the sofa cushions. "Mortal gods! I'm sick of everyone telling me what to think, what to do, who to be!"

"And what has this Anti told you exactly?" Melly countered, brushing her auburn hair over her shoulder. "That someday, if you work hard enough and believe in yourself, all your dreams will come true? That you can run around doing things just as you like and not get caught? That you can still have your story?"

"Yes, alright, what you're saying... it isn't wrong. But I *do* agree with him, and even if I didn't, I still need to finish my Book and get Sindy back. I'm not going to leave her out there."

"Just listen, Bea. Whatever he's told you, whatever you believe... you need to stop all this. Your charming Anti is a genie."

Melly looked at Bea triumphantly.

Bea wrung her hands.

"Er. Yes. I know."

"What?"

"I know he's a genie. And I know they had a Chapter. How did you know?"

Melly reached into her sleeve and pulled out her black cigarette case, angrily lighting another cigarette. She glared at Bea. "I can't stop now, alright? It's the leaf, it gets into your blood." She took a pull on her cigarette, blowing smoke through her teeth. "I know about the genies because I'm older than you. I remember them from before the Great Redaction. They didn't bother with us much, to be honest. I didn't know they'd had a Chapter though. Who told you that?"

"A friend of Joan's. A Raconteur."

Melly's eyebrows shot up. "Really?"

Bea allowed herself a smile. "That's what I thought. In fact, I think they might have been an item, once."

"You don't say? Joan and a Raconteur? Good for her. I've never liked the way you fairies are treated." Melly sighed, releasing the tension in her shoulders. "Look Bea, the thing about the genies is that they were expert at the time. They perfected it, really." She said this with something that sounded to Bea a little like admiration.

"Perfected what?" Bea asked, leaning forward and taking a sip of her wine.

"Greed. Desire. Fear. All the things that make a good story. Reward, sometimes, too. They tell you what they know you want to hear, and then they make you think you can have it."

"They granted wishes," Bea said. "Doesn't that mean the whole point was to give people what they want?"

Melly flicked the ash off her cigarette as she thought of the best way to explain. "Does anyone really know what they want? Maybe they think they do, but the reality is often very different. The genies thrived on it—on the tricks and the cruelty and the misdirection. It was a game to them."

"Seven says that we all play games with the characters. He says we ruin lives."

"Seven, is it now? Well, he'd know. How much damage can be done with some pretty eyes and flowery words?"

"You're right about that. He definitely has an effect on the humans."

"Only on them?" Melly asked.

"I certainly don't care about his looks," Bea said, betrayed somewhat by the memory of a naked, muscular blue body that sprung up in her mind. "I just happen to agree with him. That's me, my opinion. I know it is."

"Look, just think about him for a minute: isn't it strange that you meet the only Anti in the whole of Thaiana that has some kind of credible reason for doing what he's doing?"

Bea couldn't deny it.

"And then, that he can help you do what you think is right while at the same time allowing you to get what you want? Isn't that a bit much?"

"Coincidences happen all the time."

"*In the stories.* Coincidences we *ensure* happen."

Bea thumbed the rim of her glass. Melly had her there, and they both knew it.

"Genies," Melly said, "are designed to give people what they think they want. Just think, haven't you seen it?"

"He's very charismatic."

"But is he? Really? You said yourself that when you actually listen to him, he isn't very nice at all."

"He hasn't granted any wishes," Bea said.

"I don't know about that, but I do know he'll say exactly what you want to hear. He's manipulated you. That's what they do."

"He said he'd suffered because of the story."

"Bea, of course he did," Melly said, more gently. "You're… you're soft. You might have been trying to be hard. I think what you said earlier, about Joan's mum and everything… Yes. You've not been a very good person recently. But we all make mistakes, we all behave badly at some point. But you're not a bad person. And the genie, he'd know that. He'd know that you'd be sympathetic to a broken heart."

Bea picked up her wine glass and, taking a long gulp, drained it of its contents.

"You were right. I should have reported it all at the beginning and dropped the Plot. But I didn't, and, rightly or wrongly, I've seen things now that I can't ignore. And I don't believe Seven's manipulated me. I'm not saying he's a good person, but I'm not stupid, and I agree with him about Sindy and the stories. I think I always have done, that's why I buried myself so deeply in them, so that I couldn't see the detail. Does that make sense?"

Melly grunted.

"But even if I didn't agree with him, I still can't walk away from all this now. There aren't really any options," Bea finished, standing up from the sofa. "If you won't help me, I'll just have to find someone who can."

"Oh, for the love of… Fine. I'll come to Ehinenden with you," Melly said. "I'll find this girl, and I'll help you finish your Plot, too."

Bea didn't even try to hide her relief. "Oh, thank you!"

"Well," Melly said, fishing another cigarette from her case, "one of my best friends is determined to rebel because she's the first fae to grow a conscience in hundreds of years. It seems to me my choice is to sit here and watch you get Redacted or try to help you."

"Oh Melly, thank you," Bea said again. "We'll get the Book finished, hand it in and then I promise I won't ever get into such a mess again. I'll listen to all your advice, and I won't—"

"Let's not get too far ahead of ourselves," Melly said, smiling faintly.

Bea sat forward, only now remembering the problem at the Grand. "We'll need to find a way to sneak into the Grand. They're rationing the Mirrors now."

"Ahhh, now here I think I can help," Melly said. "What about the Happy Ending?"

This time it was Bea's turn to smile. "I think I might have an idea…"

Chapter Thirty-one

Bea yawned, unwilling to shake off the warm blanket of sleep. Yesterday, when Melly had outright refused to take them back into Thaiana until today, which was Saturday, which was also incidentally the day of the Ball, Bea had been furiously impatient. But the witch had held her ground, stating that Bea smelled dreadful, her dress was filthy and she looked, quite frankly, exactly like she'd been attacked by a forest in the middle of the night, none of which was going to help her inspire a Happy Ending.

Needless to say, Bea had been more than a little upset by these comments. Now, however, after having had a long bath the night before and slept soundly in the witch's wide, well-sprung spare bed—so different from her own narrow cot—Bea had to admit that Melly had been right.

She lay in bed, looking up at the ceiling, trying to organise her thoughts. Melly had said a lot about Seven, and try as she might, Bea was finding it very hard to ignore.

Was he a handsome stranger? Check.

Did he seem to offer her a way to get her heart's desire? Check.

Did she feel a strangely powerful sense of trust in him? Check.

Melly said the genies were expert manipulators, but whether that actually meant she was completely unable to make up her own mind in Seven's presence, Bea stubbornly doubted. She'd seen the way the humans acted around him, and she was certain she wasn't like that. She based this on the fact it was impossible to suggest the time she'd spent with him had been a hazy cloud of happiness and agreement, a thing she now found extremely comforting.

The second reason Bea doubted that Seven posed quite the threat that her friend feared was because she was sure there was something wrong with him.

If she accepted he was a genie, that meant he had certain gifts. All the fae tribes had things they were good at, after all. Bea, a garden fairy, could talk to plants. It was always a bit hit or miss as to how much sense she'd get out of them—a carrot, for example, tended to get confused if you started asking it what it thought about the nature of existence—but for better or worse it was her talent. Flower fairies could fly, goblins could work metal. Genies... if what Melly and Delphine had said was true, it seemed genies could do things most of the fae could only dream of.

But every time Bea had seen Seven use his 'magic', as he called it, he'd seemed sick afterwards—the first time she'd met him, after he froze John and Sindy, he'd gripped his stomach like he was about to vomit, and Bea was now of the mind that the nosebleed he'd suffered in the woods was a result of moving them both and not, unfortunately, of her head-butt. And he'd told her he wore the hood and gloves so he didn't have to hide himself in front of the characters. Bea was certain that he couldn't use his gifts, though she had no idea why not.

She rolled over.

Regardless of his abilities, or lack thereof, the fact remained that she agreed with Seven's assessment of her Plot, even if he was an Anti and now a genie. And whatever Melly said, she was also certain he'd been telling the truth when he'd spoken about the girl he'd loved. It just didn't seem possible that anyone could fake the kind of pain she'd seen on his face.

And it just didn't make sense for him to lie about it. If he was an Anti, and if he did want to ruin her story, why not just kill her characters? Or her? He was physically stronger than she was and, even if it did hurt him, he could have just whooshed her a thousand miles away. But instead, it seemed like he wanted her to understand his point of view.

Mind you, Bea thought, *getting someone to agree with your point of view was probably much more effective than killing them.* Just look at the GenAm—they'd found a way to stop the fae having any kind of thoughts, let alone dissenting ones, and all without a single execution...

Bea kicked the covers off, telling herself she was too hot and she'd been in bed too long, at the same time knowing that she simply couldn't stand her own thoughts anymore.

She padded over to the washbasin in the corner of the room. The water was warm and clean, two luxuries she seldom got to enjoy at home. She washed well, scrubbing under her nails and behind her ears and all the other forgotten little places. Next, she rummaged around under the stand until she found some charcoal and a bag of hazel sticks, selected one from the assortment, squashed its end into frays, and began to clean her teeth.

Finally, she brushed her hair using one of Melly's silver-backed brushes, taking her time, remembering to count the strokes as her mother had taught her. There were no mirrors in her bedroom, not unusual in Ænathlin, but for once annoying.

Now clean and tidy, she looked for her dress. It wasn't on the floor where she'd dropped it the night before, slightly drunk and very exhausted. Nor was it draped over the armchair or hanging in the wardrobe.

Bea walked over to the bedroom door and opened it just enough to call downstairs without exposing herself. Melly's cottage was not big; a short staircase ran up the centre of the house, separating the kitchen from the living room and the two bedrooms upstairs. There was a small wash closet off of the kitchen, not quite an outhouse but not exactly an in-house either.

"Melly, where's my dress?" she called.

There was the clatter of plates, and Melly's face appeared around the edge of the wall at the foot of the stairs.

"I threw it away," she answered matter-of-factly.

Bea stood, dumb, at the top of the stairs.

"Pardon?"

"It was nothing but rags. You could hardly wear it to a Ball. There are plenty of other dresses in the wardrobe in your room. One of them's bound to fit. Hurry up, I've made breakfast."

"Come on, Bea, it's getting cold!"

"You're going to laugh at me!"

Melly sighed, slammed the plate down on the counter, and marched to the bottom of the staircase.

"For goodness' sake. It's your time you're wasting, I'm perfectly happy to stay here all day, but I thought you had things to do?"

Melly rolled her eyes as an avalanche of swear words tumbled down the stairs. She was about to ask Bea exactly how she managed during her meetings with her character not to swear, considering her almost addictive propensity for it, when Bea appeared through the bedroom door to stand on the landing.

Melly's jaw dropped.

Bea folded her arms across her corseted bosom, her expression daring the witch to laugh at her.

Melly smacked her lips, trying to think of the right words.

"It's certainly very... it's a lot more, er, shiny than I'm used to seeing you in. I mean, I wonder if it's quite necessary to wear such a wide skirt? But the corset certainly... accentuates... you. Not that it doesn't suit you," she added quickly. "All that glitter really makes it. Oh, and the butterfly motif. Very stylish. I just... is it the most, uh, practical thing you might have chosen...?"

"It's traditional," Bea glared.

"Yes, yes, it's definitely that," Melly said, the corner of her mouth dancing like a music box ballerina.

"I could hardly wear one of those black dresses. I *am* a godmother. Sort of."

"No, no, I can certainly see your predicament."

"And I'm going to a Ball. I'm sure lots of the guests will be wearing something similar."

Melly hid her mouth behind her hand and nodded.

"Are you laughing?"

Melly shook her head quickly, her shoulders shaking.

"Do you have a mirror?"

"It's behind you," Melly wheezed.

Bea shifted herself around, so she was facing the wall. There was only a painting of a forest. It was large, certainly, and extremely detailed, but it wasn't a mirror.

"Where?"

"It's behind you."

"No, it isn't."

"Oh, yes it is."

"Oh, no it isn't."

"Oh, yes it is."

Bea swung back around, her expression thunderous.

"Will you stop playing silly beggars?"

Melly fanned her face with her hand as for some strange reason—that had absolutely nothing to do with Bea's enormous pink and gold dress—she was finding it hard to breathe.

"Come and have some breakfast," she managed to splutter out after two tries. "Then I'll show it to you."

Bea descended the stairs. Or at least, she attempted to. It really was a very wide skirt. They finally made it to the table with a couple of heaves and one broken plate.

Melly's eyes were fixed on Bea as she concentrated on buttering her toast.

"What?" Bea asked.

"Nothing, nothing."

Bea reached for some jam. "Where did you get this from? I haven't seen jam in ages."

"Oh? Ahh, I made it," Melly said, her voice higher than normal. She coughed.

Bea placed her knife on the table and looked up.

"Right, come on. Out with it."

Melly leaned back in her chair, her arm resting against the back. Her eyes were sparkling with unspent laughter.

"I just didn't realise you had quite so much hair, I suppose."

"My best-kept secret."

"You've certainly managed to make it very big."

"Well, I didn't want the skirt to feel left out."

"No danger of that, I think," Melly replied, straight-faced.

"Do you think the butterflies are a little much?"

"Well, I think a lesser person might have stopped at the corset, but personally, I believe you can never have too many glittery butterflies."

"My thoughts exactly," Bea nodded. "That's the real reason the Mirrors are breaking, in my opinion. No one has the courage to really go out there and make use of glittery butterflies."

The two women looked at each other. Bea, always ready to see the funny side, cracked first.

"I think it suits you, actually," Melly said, once they'd finished laughing. "Maybe not quite the colour. Or the glitter. Or the butterflies. Or, in fact, the dress. But it's nice to see you in something well made. Right then. I guess we'd better make a move."

"How are we going to sneak in at the Grand?" Bea asked.

"We're not. Just wait here."

Melly stood up from the table and manoeuvred herself around Bea to disappear up the stairs. Bea spun around on her chair, craning her neck to see where the elf had gone. She couldn't see anything, though she could hear what sounded like her friend lifting something heavy.

A moment later, Melly walked back into the kitchen, the painting of the forest from the landing in her arms. Bea quickly moved aside the breakfast things, and Melly placed it carefully on the table.

"That's a painting," Bea said, confused.

"No. It's a Mirror. A Mirror-mirror."

"But... how do you have a Mirror?"

Melly shrugged. "I found it one day. I just thought, well, why not? Anyway, is this where we need to be?" She held her hands over the surface. The image rippled thickly, reverting to the black milky texture of a blank Mirror.

"Gosh, you did that quickly," Bea said, surprised.

"Ah, well. I'm old," Melly replied. "Where shall we start?"

"How long will it take you to find Sindy?"

Melly thought for a moment. "Well, if she's wearing this charm you spoke about, that'll help. If I can get into her room, even better. Usually, I've met the heroine earlier in the story, you see. But I can ask the animals as well."

Speaking to animals wasn't a witch thing, it was an elf thing. However, given the fae's abuse of the natural kingdom in Chapters gone by, very few practised it now. Unlike the humans, the animals had never stopped believing. They remembered the hunts too clearly.

"Are you sure? Will they help?"

Melly nodded her head. "Probably. I helped the Great Stag once, and he remembers."

Another mystery to be solved. Bea was beginning to realise that she wasn't the only one who had been keeping secrets in her little friendship group. The thought didn't make her feel any better.

"If it won't take you long to locate Sindy, we should probably go into the town first. I'll need some supplies if we're going to make this Happy Ending work. I can hardly turn up at the GenAm and ask them for a whole new wardrobe. At least without having to answer some questions first."

Melly nodded. "Agreed. How are you getting the girl to the Ball?"

"Damn. I hadn't thought about that. Do you think there'll be time for me to come back here? That way, I could still go through the Mirrors on schedule and set up the coach."

Melly pursed her lips. "This is getting complicated."

"What choice do we have?" Bea asked, already feeling exhausted. *If I get through this with my head,* she thought, *I really will set up a vegetable stall in the markets. I'll steal some seeds from Sindy's garden and grow cabbages in the dirt behind Ivor's ears.*

"So, to town first, then your heroine's house, then back here, then to the GenAm. I told the Forest not to give you any more trouble."

They had too much to do and too little time to do it. If this really were a story, they'd be guaranteed a Happy Ending, considering the odds they were facing. Bad luck, then, that this was real life. Melly closed her eyes, her hand resting palm out just above the Mirror. The thick, gloopy surface rippled again, and an image of Llanotterly's main square appeared.

"Off we go then," Bea said.

Chapter Thirty-two

"So how do you want to do this?" Melly asked, closing the connection to her Mirror, back in her cottage.

Bea tugged at her ear thoughtfully, trying to work out the best use of their time, while Melly looked around for something to cover the mirror. However unlikely, it didn't do to risk observation by the GemAm, let alone when travelling illicitly into Thaiana.

The Ball started in eight hours. They needed to get a new dress, meet Ana at her parents' cottage, find out where Sindy was so Will could go and get her—assuming she was alive and easily gettable; Bea wasn't sure what they'd do if she wasn't—and then Bea had to get back to Melly's cottage, and from there to the Grand to go through the Mirror officially, thus getting her promissory slip for the coach. The GenAm, when the Mirrors had started breaking a few hundred years ago, had taken to keeping the larger Plot items in troll caves in Thaiana. Bea needed the note to get the coach; even Melly couldn't talk her way around a thirty stone troll.

"How about we split up, get everything we need, and then meet in an hour?"

"Sure," Melly said. She held out her hand.

Somewhat confused by this sudden formality, Bea shook Melly's hand.

Melly raised a quizzical eyebrow.

"What?" Bea asked.

"You need to give me some money. How exactly do you expect me to trade, otherwise?"

"Ah," said Bea. It hadn't occurred to her that the humans used bits of metal in exchange for goods and services, a system that to her seemed very abstract.

"Yes," replied Melly.

"Tricky," Bea added.

"Very," Melly agreed.

"You don't have any…?" Bea asked, hopefully.

"No," said Melly, dashing said hopes.

"You wouldn't consider—" Bea began.

"No," Melly said.

"You don't know what I was going to say," Bea protested.

"Yes, I do," Melly answered. "Your face said it for you."

Bea kicked at the dusty floor.

"There is someone who could give us some money... But you're not going to like it."

"If you're about to suggest we ask the Anti—"

"Can you think of anyone else? He works for the King. He's bound to have some. I expect there are pots of it sitting around the castle."

Melly looked like she'd bitten into a lemon.

"Or you could wait here, while I go...?"

Melly's expression didn't improve. "Here?"

Bea joined Melly in surveying the room they'd arrived in. It wasn't exactly hospitable. They were in a basement with no natural light save a few limp beams of sunlight staggering through a low gutter-window. There was an old mirror leaning against the bare stone wall, which was how they'd entered the room, a rocking horse that had lost one of its runners and numerous crates covered half-heartedly with a cloth. The air tasted of mildew. On the plus side, it didn't seem to be a room that was much used. On the minus, it was clear why.

"No, perhaps not," Bea conceded.

"Why don't I come with you to meet this mysterious man who's so enslaved your good sense?"

"It's not like that," Bea said crossly, picking up the witch's suggestive tone. "I just agree with him, that's all. Why do I have to be infatuated by him in order to think he has a point?"

Melly tutted, but didn't answer.

"Right then. To the castle," Bea said, hoping she sounded more confident than she felt. They walked quietly up the stairs to the basement door, and Bea pressed her ear against the wood.

"I can't hear anyone," she whispered.

Melly stepped forward and listened. After a couple of seconds, she nodded her head in agreement.

Bea turned the handle and pushed the door. It refused to open. She tried again, this time leaning her weight against the wood. The door remained steadfast.

Melly reached out, took the handle with a slight smile and pulled. "Sometimes things aren't as complicated as they seem," she said sweetly as the door swung inwards. Bea glared at her.

They stepped into a small, empty kitchen. Bea looked around, spotting another doorway. She walked past the range, ignoring the faint buzz on her skin from the iron, and cracked the door open.

"There's a hallway and what must be the front door," she whispered over her shoulder. "I think we're in someone's house. Does that mean we're actually in the town? Are you sure you've brought us to the right place? Melly?"

She turned around to see why the witch wasn't answering, only to find her rooting through the kitchen cupboards.

"What in the worlds are you doing?

Melly looked up.

"Nothing." If the expression on the witch's face had been asked to take the stand, no jury would have acquitted her.

Bea gave her a look.

"Well, I've never actually been in a character's kitchen before. I tend to see throne rooms or bedrooms. It's interesting. You can learn a lot from what people put in their cupboards," she added defensively.

"C'mon," Bea said, shaking her head.

Melly closed the cupboard door regretfully, and they snuck through the hallway and out of the house, into Llanotterly.

The town was buzzing. Everywhere they looked, people were bustling about, busy as bees, no doubt getting ready for the Ball. The streets were cleaner than in Ænathlin, though this wasn't exactly a difficult thing to achieve. There were public toilets in the back rooms of cheap pubs that were cleaner than Ænathlin. Even so, it seemed to Bea that Llanotterly had been scrubbed to within an inch of its life and then scrubbed again.

Bunting ran in swathes from house to house and shop to shop, all along the street. There was a baker's a few doors down, its doors swung open. The smell of baking bread and cakes drifted towards them with the lazy amble of a tourist with nothing to do and nowhere to be. A milk cart rattled past, its rotund driver humming a merry tune. Three young women, one blonde, one auburn, one brunette, came out of another shop, waving ribbons around their heads and laughing gaily at some private joke. A handsome soldier in red livery smiled at them, calling out a compliment to the brunette as she passed.

It was impossible, and Bea said as much.

"It's the story," Melly replied, standing amongst the lightness and frivolity like a raven, her auburn hair a bloody waterfall. "Unlike the Anti-Narrativists, the characters understand how things are supposed to work," she said archly, pulling a cigarette from her case.

"Don't do that here, you'll attract attention," Bea said, scolding the beautiful elf-turned-witch who was dressed head to toe in black with an antlered crown on her head, Bea's own glittery dress with its hooped skirt and butterfly motif shaking in time with her wagging finger.

"Oh yes, of course," Melly said, dropping the cigarette and stubbing it out under the sole of her boot.

"Right then, let's get to the castle and find Seven."

Bea scanned the pretty street. There was a gentle stream of people heading further into the town, all laughing and joking. She lifted her eyes to take in the tall walls and short, fat turrets of Llanotterly Castle. It was well made, built for defence rather than for aesthetics. Yet, in the spirit of the day, long banners ran from the crenels, and the merlons were festooned with even more bunting. Nevertheless, as jolly as the castle currently was, there was no disguising the heavily armoured guards that walked along the parapets, long spears in hands and, if Bea wasn't mistaken, broadswords glinting at their backs.

"I suppose the town square is that way," she said, nodding her head in the direction the people were moving.

"Best if we go the other way then," Melly said.

Bea nodded, and they headed off against the crowd.

"You what?"

"Washer-women," the fat one in the pink and gold meringue dress repeated.

"You don't look like no washawoman," Gabe said resolutely, trying to ignore the evil eye the tall one was giving him. She looked like a crow who'd discovered the make-up box. To be honest, neither of the women were what he would call 'normal'. But it was a holiday. Free beer and roast pork attracted all sorts.

Gabe sighed.

He'd been on guard since six, and he wasn't even supposed to be working today. Not that he minded helping out the Kingdom, no, no, no, but he was already feeling peeved he'd been given the back gate, far away from all the sights, smells and jugs of ale that he knew were being passed around at the front drawbridge. And now there appeared to be two women who could only be escapees from the psycarium in Cerne Bralksteld trying to get into the castle.

"How do you know what washer-women look like?" the fat one demanded.

Gabe rubbed his chin, giving the question due consideration before answering. "Well, me mum's a washawomen. So's me sister." He paused, rubbing some more at his stubble, and then continued. "N' me wife. Me daughter ain't, but she's only two, so I figure that's a bit young, what with the lye. And where's your basket 'n' soap 'n' all that?"

She looked at him in surprise and then turned to the red-headed one, who shrugged.

"It's inside," the fat one said, turning back to him.

"Why'd you leave it inside?"

"So we wouldn't have to carry it?"

Gabe curled his lip in confusion. "Ain't you worried the other scrubbers'll nick it?"

"They wouldn't do that, would they?" she asked, clearly aghast at such failure in the sisterly work-force.

"Yeah, yeah, course. S' half a mark for'a good chunk o'soap to buy it, and if you nick it, you don't need to risk your own skin coz the other bugger's made it."

"That's horrendous."

"Tell me about it," Gabe answered meaningfully, leaning on his spear. "That's the trouble with being a washawoman. You don't get paid by the crown no more, get paid by the load. Saves 'em money, which young John sends off t'Cerne Bralksteld quicker'n a sailor on shore leave slips a skirt, alright, but then back here we gots the girls all fighting each other over who gets to wash a hanky on account of needin' the money coz prices've gone up due to unforeseen demand from them refugees. S'not a sustainable fiscal system. Any fool can see that."

"So why does the King send the money away?" the fat one asked, seeming to momentarily forget her hurry.

"Where you been? Taxes, innit? Don't pay the taxes and we're next on the Baron's hit list. Still, ain't right to set workers against each other." He leaned forward conspiratorially. "That's why them lot gone into the woods. They reckon that if young John starts cuttin' down the trees, sellin' the wood, the Baron will just want more an' more. Which might be right, or it might not," he finished, doffing his cap as socio-economist and resuming his role as a guard. "I ain't King or no insarhgent. I'm a guard. And you two ain't no washawomen."

"Yes we are, I promise," the fat one pleaded. Behind her, the redhead rolled her eyes.

"Oh, for goodness' sake," the redhead muttered, shouldering her way in front of her friend.

"Please, sir. We're, ahaha, guests to the Adviser," red simpered, her voice infused with a tone so suggestive it insisted.

Gabe had to ignore the other one, who was having some kind of coughing fit.

"What sort of guests?"

"Very special guests."

Gabe looked from one to the other, trying hard to work out exactly why the King's weird foreign Adviser would want two such bizarrely dressed women as visitors, each one attractive in their own way, nor why he would have sent them to the back gate....

...*Oh.*

"Oh," Gabe said.

"Yes, exactly," Melly confirmed with a wink. "Now can you let us through?"

Gabe looked wretched. Now more than ever he wished he'd been put on the front drawbridge.

"Well, y'see, I can't. You ain't got no ticket, and though I'm not a man to judge another man, 'specially not the Adviser to the King, I got very clear orders, and it's more'n my life's worth to disobey 'em on a day like today. Ole Hendry got a right whopping just the other day for letting someone in what he shouldn't't've. Here, that was a washawoman, too," Gabe added, suspicion momentarily overcoming his discomfort.

"But if the Adviser doesn't see us, I think he'd be very disappointed," the thin one purred, twisting a lock of red hair around her finger as she spoke.

"Er…"

"Very, *very* disappointed."

Gabe's Adam's apple jumped in his throat. "Hang on."

And with that he disappeared into the castle, making sure to lower the small portcullis behind him.

"Special guests?" Bea asked, studying the witch very closely.

"That's what I said," Melly answered, her expression carefully blank.

"*Special guests?*"

"Are you suggesting we're average guests?"

"Somehow I suspect that, in this context, 'special' does not mean the opposite of average."

"Oh, I don't know," Melly said with a dry smile.

Bea's reply was interrupted by the sound of the guard's heavy footsteps returning, accompanied by a faint jingle that she instantly recognised. She wondered for a second if the ground would do the decent thing and swallow her up, but the earth, as is well known, is no gentleman when it comes to saving a lady's blushes.

"…I have not the time for these insinuations."

"M'lord, m'not suggesting nothing. See f'yourself."

The portcullis rattled into life, lifting upwards in jerky movements.

"Are you unaware this is the day of the Royal Ball? There is much to be done, none of which concerns two harlo…. Ah. Yes." Seven faltered, coming to a sudden stand-still as he reached the two fae.

He leaned against the stone wall, crossing his arms, his expression mercifully hidden behind his silk hood. Bea ignored the burning in her cheeks as he looked her up and down.

"My sincerest apologies, young guardsman," he said, his voice alight with mischief. "I forgot I requested these two lovely women to, ah, what was it again?"

"Er. 'Do your washing'. M'Lord."

Just when Bea thought it couldn't get any worse, Seven sniggered. There was no other word for it. It was certainly not a laugh. It was short and dirty and completely at her expense—it was, without doubt, a snigger.

"Ah, yes. Quite. It appears I have been very dirty," he said. "I wonder which of you two fine women will be undertaking the bulk of the chore?"

Bea could guess what his expression was behind the safety of his hood. There really seemed to be no limit to the Anti's brashness. She wondered that so many of the human women kept falling for him. He was so arrogant. It wasn't at all attractive.

"I think that task must fall to me, sir," Melly flirted, and then added, catching the guard's eye with a giggle, "I am more experienced than my friend."

Bea gaped at Melly, completely unable to stop her jaw from dropping. Seven's hood also centred on the witch, but where Bea was doing her best impression of a startled kitten, Seven's silk-covered head spent appeared to be focused on her crown.

"Well, let us see, shall we, what you are able to accomplish," he said, ever the gracious host. "Please, ladies, follow me."

He offered Bea his arm, which she ignored. She scuttled past him, trying hard not to blush as the guard gave her a very enthusiastic thumbs up.

Seven led them across the gardens towards the south wing, slipping between the hurrying servants as they prepared for the Ball. For some reason, Bea had only thought about Balls in terms of the Ballroom. She was quickly discovering that hosting one was a very large undertaking.

The castle heaved with people, especially here. The Penqioan inspired south wing was Llanotterly Castle's most famous asset, and John intended to use it to its best advantage to wow his guests.

The jade and gold statues, the intricately painted wallpaper, the impossibly large chandeliers—everything was being worked on by a veritable army of servants. It was like walking through an ants' nest on a public holiday.

Seven led them through it all and up the sweeping staircase to his floor as if everything happening around him was commonplace. Something caught Bea's eye, and she paused for a moment to look out of one of the large windows into the front courtyard, where soldiers were stood in little lines practising some kind of ceremony.

"It is not what you were expecting?" asked Seven over her shoulder.

"No... I never thought so much work would go into something like this."

Seven put his hands on her shoulders and steered her away from the window. She could feel the chill of him through the thin silk of his gloves. Considering how cold he always was, she wondered that he was comfortable in such thin clothing.

"Come, we shouldn't idle in front of glass," Seven said, reaching his arm around her shoulder like a lover. Bea looked up at him, startled. He was leaning on her.

"Are you still sick?"

"Bea, come on," Melly called impatiently from further up the hallway, her expression cloudy as she saw the way the Anti was fawning over her.

"I am quite well," Seven said, but he didn't shift his weight, and Bea realised she would have to put her arm around his waist if she was going to support him. She reached around him and held him steady.

"This Ball is designed to attract investors," he continued, stroking her shoulder affectionately as they caught up with Melly. Bea didn't miss the look the action elicited from the witch, and she supposed he'd done it deliberately. For just a moment she wondered what would happen if she refused to play along and let him drop.

"It is in everybody's interest Llanotterly be seen at its best advantage. You thought perhaps the only purpose was for your story?" he asked.

"I don't know. I suppose so," Bea replied. "The guard said the King gives all their revenue to Cerne Bralksteld."

"So he does," Seven nodded.

"Everyone seems very frightened of this Baron."

"Cerne Bralksteld's the stronger city," Melly said. "They're right to fear it."

"Your friend is correct," Seven said amiably, making sure Melly saw him place his free hand over Bea's, which rested on his waist. "It would be a foolish ruler who tried to stand up to such an enemy. And yet, in his way, this is what John hopes to do."

"Then you're right. He is a fool," Melly answered.

Seven looked towards her, his expression hidden in the shadow of his hood. "You would submit?"

"I'd save myself and my people."

"Perhaps that is what the King believes he is doing. The manufactories are the death of hundreds, and the lives of many thousands more. Such corruption will not be contained for long. Evil metastasises. And, if I may be so bold, I suspect that you might not surrender so fully. After all, are not you here now? My dear little godmother must surely have apprised you of my nefarious intent?"

Bea waited for Melly to react, but she just turned on her heel and continued down the corridor.

They didn't stop again on the way to Seven's room, arriving without further incident. As soon as they were through the doors, Seven let his arm drop from Bea's shoulder, and she stepped away from him. She doubted anyone who didn't know to look for it would have noticed the way he wobbled.

"Welcome to my lair," he said, sitting heavily on his bed. He removed his hood and shook out his curls. "Would you be so kind as to close and lock the door?"

"Is this necessary?" Melly asked, but she did as he requested.

"Regrettably. I would not have us disturbed."

"You seem to be quite good at getting what you want. May I?" Melly asked, pulling her onyx cigarette case from her sleeve and placing a cigarette between her lips.

"Please, allow me," Seven said, standing up. He clicked his fingers, and a small flame appeared at their tips. Melly raised an eyebrow but leant forward, inhaling deeply.

"An unusual skill," she said.

"I have others," he replied, sitting again on the bed, leaning back on his arms.

"Right, what in the five hells is going on here?" Bea demanded, watching them watching each other. "You're like two cats waiting to see which one'll jump first."

"A very well-chosen simile," he said, winking at her, which annoyed Bea. He was actually trying to conspire with her. "Your friend is a witch, I assume?"

"You've told him about me?" Melly asked, aghast.

"No, nothing," Bea denied hotly.

"You wear your vocation like armour, my Lady, unaware it causes you to shine on the battlefield. And you know what I am, do you not? I assume you have informed against me to Bea? What sugared untruths have you fed her, I wonder?"

"None."

Seven laughed then, filling the room with the golden sound of his amusement. He pulled himself to his feet with the help of the bedframe and walked to his desk, where he poured three glasses of a rich, amber liquid. He handed one each to Bea and Melly with a little bow.

"My Lady, you are everything I had hoped you would be," he said. He appeared in good spirits, but Bea noticed that when he moved, he kept one hand on the bedstead or the desk, as if he needed the support.

"But look, our mutual friend is growing angry with us," Seven said, misunderstanding Bea's frown as she watched him. "Perhaps we should discuss our deceits later."

"You can forget that," Bea snapped. "Everyone's got some secret it seems—quite honestly, I doubt there'd be time. Now, I've been told you're a genie. Is that right?"

Seven inclined his head.

"There," Melly said. "I told you. You can't trust him. Genies are only interested in themselves. They're selfish, cruel hedonists."

"I understand I am also an Anti-Narrativist. I wonder I do not simply burst into flames."

"See? See how glib he is?" Melly said, stabbing her cigarette in the air. "No one good is that confident. Or that clever."

"I'm not sure Seven's ever actually said he's good."

"I have not," he confirmed.

"Aha! He admits it!" Melly announced.

"I fail to see how I can be both a liar and a character witness."

"You'll not fool us with your pretty words, *djinn*."

"Nor would it appear with logic," Seven answered.

"Let's get the money and go," Melly said to Bea.

Bea pinched the bridge of her nose. She could feel a headache coming on. "I want to talk to him."

"What could he have to say you'd want to hear?"

"*Aef atesh yvon*," Seven said, yawning pointedly. "Why do you not organise these things before beginning? Now, mistress godmother, for what purpose do you require money?"

"To buy material for a dress," Bea said. "Do you have any?"

He nodded, went to his desk and produced a small bag that hung heavily from the little strings he held it by. He walked back to Bea and placed it in her hand, closing her fingers around it.

"There is enough here to buy the finest silks. This is for Sindy, then? You are determined to see your story through?"

Bea didn't dare look at Melly. "No. I think you're right. But I don't want to be Redacted either. I have another idea to finish the story, one that will make everyone happy—even you. But I might need your help."

"Oh?"

"Sindy's missing. She's run away. I think—I hope—she's just hiding somewhere we can find her. But if she isn't... if she's been taken on a slaver ship..."

"You wish me to return her to you?"

Bea nodded. If she was right about him, what she was asking was that he cause himself untold pain to help her. She wouldn't blame him if he said no. She'd hate him, but she wouldn't blame him.

Seven looked down at her, his endless blue eyes darkening as he studied her face. Bea held her breath.

"Fine. I will do this for you—"

"Thank you."

"After the Ball. That is my condition. Do you agree?"

Bea thought. If Sindy was in trouble, leaving her there any longer than necessary was unforgivable. On the other hand, if Seven kept his promise, he'd be able to bring her back in a matter of moments. On the *other* other hand, she had no guarantee that he'd stick around after the Ball.

"You have my word," he said.

He'd never lied to her.

"Agreed," Bea said. "A bargain made?"

"A bargain made," he confirmed. "Is that all? If so, I must beg you excuse me. I have been engaged all morning, and still, there is more to be done before tonight."

"Are you... Will you be alright? We can look after the King at the Ball if you're feeling, um, under the weather," Bea said. She realised as she said it that she meant it. She would look after John for him.

Melly huffed. Bea ignored her.

Seven somehow managed to roll his eyes, a trick which, had Bea had more time, she certainly would have asked him about.

"Your concern underwhelms," he replied, whatever moment of rapprochement between them over. "I am the King's Adviser and must attend. Go now. I will see you and your marvellous dress this evening."

Bea glared at him, secretly relieved. It was easier when he was nasty. "Ha bloody ha. At least after tomorrow, we can get back to our normal lives. What more could possibly go wrong?"

Seven and Melly looked at Bea in horror.

"It's not her fault," Melly said quickly, taking Bea by the arm and unlocking Seven's door, pulling them out of the room. "No one tells them about Narrative Convention anymore."

Chapter Thirty-three

Bea hung around the edges of Llanotterly town square, trying not to notice the stares from the humans as they busied themselves around her.

The sun was sitting low in the sky, and the atmosphere was slowly changing from one of frantic preparation to one of frivolity and boozy high-spirits. A roaring bonfire was burning in the centre of the square, encircled by four large spits already occupied by the multiple carcasses of fat pigs. The sweet, smoky smell of cooking pork filled the air, mingling with the warm scent of autumn leaves, baked cakes and bread, and melting butter.

A child ran past, skidded to a stop and turned to stare at Bea, a candied apple attached to his fingers with the dual adhesive of sugar and enthusiasm. He seemed to be confused by the sight of her in her grand dress and, for a second, he looked like he was going to turn back and speak to her, but something changed his mind. He ran off, into the crowd.

She glanced down at her corseted chest, brushing the hard boning with the tips of her fingers. When she'd seen it in the wardrobe, she'd chosen it because it was such a traditional kind of dress, and the rest had all been black. But the truth was she felt the absence of her raggedy, patchwork dress as keenly as ice against an exposed tooth.

"Any joy?"

Bea looked up. Melly was watching her, a gentle expression on her face. Bea let her hand drop back to her side and, with a little difficulty, lifted her skirts up high enough to reveal the hessian bag safely tucked between her feet.

"Not much," Bea admitted miserably. "I could only get red. Hardly the colour for a heroine. Please tell me you had better luck?"

Melly's smile curdled, and Bea felt her heart drop.

"I found some black silk—don't, I knew you'd look at me like that. I did try to find colours. There just isn't anything left."

Bea pinched the bridge of her nose. "I know. The seamstress I spoke to said all her best material was bought months ago. This is a disaster. She can hardly show up to a ball dressed for a funeral. She needs to make an impression. Mortal gods, she needs to undo the impression she's already made."

Melly squeezed her friend's shoulder, but she didn't have anything to say.

"Come on," Bea said, her voice as heavy as her dress. "We'd better get to the cottage."

"I thought you said you'd be here this morning," Ana grumbled, opening the door for Bea and Melly. "What in the Five Kingdoms are you wearing?" She exclaimed as the perspectives of Bea's dress clicked into place.

"It's called a ballgown," Bea answered, a very explicit look on her face.

"We could house a family of five under that skirt. The butterflies are nice though," Ana added.

"Hmm," Bea said, not entirely pleased to be mollified.

Ana stepped to the side, trying to make room for Bea and the dress to pass through the narrow front door. It wasn't an easy fit. Ana stood somewhat helplessly in the hallway while Bea struggled to pull herself in.

"You must be Ana," Melly said, leaning around Bea with her hand outstretched.

"And you are?" Ana asked, taking the witch's hand in her own.

"You can call me Melly. Well met," Melly answered, returning to the task of getting Bea into the house. "Could you perhaps…?"

It took three goes to get Bea through the door, with Ana pulling and Melly pushing and Bea steering. They were now sitting in the little living room that Sindy had met John and Seven in earlier in the week.

"Thanks," Bea said, panting.

"That's alright. I didn't like that vase anyway," Ana said, equally breathlessly. "So… would you like a tea? Or perhaps something stronger?"

Bea found the energy to smile. "I've heard a lot about your brain," she said, "and I think I can see why. That is a very good idea."

Melly simply nodded, too exhausted to speak.

Ana disappeared into the kitchen, returning a few minutes later with a bottle of honey wine and a plate of mushroom sausages.

"I probably shouldn't eat if I've got to dress up later, but I'm starving so hang it. The universe helps those who help themselves, after all, so I'm helping myself to Mum's wine and Dad's dinner."

Bea smiled, taking a sip of the cold wine and feeling better for it.

"Where are your parents?" Melly asked, selecting a sausage from the plate.

"With Will. He's taken them to Sinne to try to find Sindy. When are you going to find her?"

"Do you know when they'll be back?" Bea asked, dodging the question.

"Probably around ten, eleven. It's only an hour's ride, and they won't want to be out late," Ana said, rubbing the ball of her shoulder uneasily.

"What's happened?" Bea asked.

"They didn't want to leave the house. Will—he had to tell them there was a slaver ship in dock, and that he'd heard a rumour they were looking for young girls. You know. It was awful. I really thought her dad was going to cry. Even Mum showed some reaction."

The room fell silent, no one sure what to say.

Bea shook her head, more unwilling than unable to believe what a mess everything had become. There were some very dark, hard truths forming in her mind.

"What an unforgivable thing to tell a parent," Melly whispered at last.

"And what should he have said?" Ana snapped.

"I don't know—that she was staying at a friend's house?"

"For two days? Without word? There are bears in the forests and wolves. Not to mention the normal dangers facing a girl alone in the world. Slavers are just one of the fears our parents have been living with since she went missing."

"Well, why didn't you just tell them that she was on an adventure?" Melly asked, confused. "She could've gone off with the local swineherd to find a missing sword or something. I've used that one plenty of times."

Bea thought Ana had reached her capacity for anger the day before, when she'd tried to explain about birthmarks and True Love, but it turned out she was wrong.

"I beg your pardon? You've 'used that one'? Hasn't it ever occurred to you that all the people who get left behind are frantic with worry? What do you think happens? They just stop existing because you've come along and started playing story-time?"

Bea kept quiet. New thoughts and old memories were rushing through her mind.

"None of this was my idea, by the way," Ana spat. "I didn't even want to go to the Ball, but the new Adviser talked me into it, and now your friend is insisting I go as well. I should be helping find Sindy. And as for all this godmother stuff, well, so far it doesn't seem to be much more than manipulation."

"No, no, no," Melly said, shaking her head. "Our job is to make you happy. You're characters. We give you stories and you... just be happy. We help you achieve your dreams."

"Well, I'm yet to see you do anything that actually helps me achieve *my* dream, and to be honest, I don't think you even know what it is."

"You want to marry the King," Melly said, resting her arm on Bea, who'd gone very pale during Ana's speech. "And my friend Bea is a very good, very experienced godmother. She'll get your sister back and have you married and settled down before you can say 'I do'."

Melly looked from Bea to Ana, an encouraging smile on her face. It didn't survive long.

"What?" Ana shrieked. "Is that what this is all about? You seriously think I'm going to marry that idiot? No. This ends now. You said you'd find Sindy but all you've done is eat my food, smash up my house, and nearly tricked me into marrying someone. I'll go and get Sindy myself, and you can shove your story up your arse. You can leave now."

Melly looked at Bea helplessly.

Bea stood up.

"You're right."

Ana glared. "I know I'm right."

"Good. You should know that. It's important. I'm going to get Sindy back. I promise. But if I do, will you still go to the Ball?"

"No, I won't," Ana said.

"Look, I don't want you to marry the King. Not anymore. But I do want you to go to the Ball because I think you need to speak to him about the woods and Cerne Bralksteld. I'll have to confess I broke the Plot and face the consequences."

"What the hell are you talking about? What consequences? What 'plot'?"

"Bea, don't..." Melly warned.

"No, Bea, do," Ana retorted.

Bea held up her hands. "You see, Sindy was supposed to marry the King, but I didn't know she was in love with Will. I was going to force her to marry John. It's my fault she ran away—"

"Excuse me?"

"I know. I'm sorry. But Melly will find her, and I'll get her back. And then I thought I could get you to marry John. It made sense in a way, you two have such different opinions. But I see now it's no different, not really. It's the Plots. They control us as much as you."

"Bea, stop it," Melly said urgently.

"No, this has gone on too long," Bea said. "And it's bullshit. The Mirrors, the Plots, all of it. And now some poor old couple are riding across the country to try to stop what they think is their youngest daughter from being sold to slavers! It's not good enough! We thought we'd got rid of the blood and the bone, but we just changed it. It's still there, it's just all dressed up as morals and true love and the good being good and the bad being bad, but life's not like that. Not for them or for us. It's got to stop."

Bea searched Melly's face, trying to find some sign that her friend understood what she was saying, that she might even agree with her. She didn't know what had happened to Melly, what or who she'd lost, to make her so afraid of the GenAm. Hells, maybe nothing had happened, and being scared to death was the only sensible reaction to an organisation that could wipe your memories as easily as fingerprints from a looking glass.

Maybe, Bea thought, *I should have considered sooner why that prospect doesn't frighten me as much as it does Melly?* But it was too late for reflection. She had run too far and, just like when she'd left home, it was too late to turn back.

"What the hell did all of that mean?" Ana said, breaking the tension.

Bea turned to look at her. "I… it's a long story," she said.

"But you're still going to bring Sindy back, and you don't want me to marry the King?"

"Yes. And No." Bea said.

"Good. Now then, how about your friend here finds where Sindy is, while you and me have a little sit down and you tell me exactly what all that meant and then, if I believe you, I'll go to this Ball for you."

"You'll still go?"

Ana nodded. "Yes, probably. It makes sense for me to try to break terms with the King. We can't really hold him up much longer, so I might as well have some say in what happens next. Why are you looking at me like that?"

"Well, that's a lot to take in," Ana said, trying to take it all in.

Bea, once she'd begun explaining, had found she couldn't stop. It was like a dam, shored up for years, had finally burst.

"I'm not sure what to make of it all, to be honest with you," Ana added. "I suppose that explains why everyone always expects me to be an idiot or cruel or whatever. Can't be ugly and nice, it seems."

Bea shifted in her seat, embarrassed.

"I'm not going to marry him," Ana restated.

"That's your choice," Bea said, knowing with absolute certainty it was. There had to be a moment when the story ended, when she had to stop reading from the Plot and let real life begin, and that moment was now.

In the space of a week, she'd achieved her dream, only to realise it was a sham. She'd met the evil villain and discovered that, although he was dishonest, arrogant and very smug, he probably wasn't as wicked as she'd been led to believe. And, if she hadn't been in trouble with the Redaction Department before her confession to Ana, she certainly would be now. She'd also no doubt blown any chance she might have had with Mistasinon.

But none of that mattered. She'd realised the truth, not just about herself but about the world she had idolised and fought to be a part of. It wasn't a nice truth, but at least it was hers. That mattered. She wasn't sure quite why it mattered, but she knew it did.

"I've found her," Melly said, coming down the stairs.

Ana jumped to her feet. "Is she safe?"

Melly looked uncomfortable. "I… I think so. She's not far away. She's in a cave, I think. Somewhere dark. Look, I've only got a glass shoe to work with! I'm pretty certain she's fine."

"Not good enough," Ana said. "I'm sorry about your story and your Mirrors and everything, but I'm going to find her. If she's in a cave, she must be on the coast."

Bea stood up. "I'll get her. Melly, can you get started on Ana's dress?"

"What? How are you going to get her?" Melly asked.

"Don't worry about that. I… I'll get help."

"You're going to ask him, aren't you?"

Bea shrugged. "Something like that. Please, will you get Ana ready? Ana, I'll have Sindy back soon. I promise."

The look on Ana's face suggested she didn't place a high value on Bea's promise, but she nodded. "You've got an hour."

"I won't need that long. Melly—the dress, please? We're going to be late as it is."

"Fine. But I hope you realise how dangerous he is," Melly said. "Come on, Ana. Let's see what we can do…"

Bea took a detailed account from Melly of the cave she'd seen and then clambered up the thankfully wide staircase to Sindy's room. It was as she remembered, but then she realised Sindy probably hadn't been back since they'd been there together. With a stab of guilt, she recalled Sindy's tears when she'd told her she would be marrying the King and not Will.

F. D. Lee

Bea glanced over at Sindy's mirror and thought about what she was going to do. Was it nerves or guilt that made her stomach tense and her throat dry? Probably both.

Travelling by Mirror was never a pleasant experience, so the mortal gods knew what this was going to be like. She'd travelled twice with Seven. She could remember the feel of it. She really wished she couldn't, as it felt like being crushed by the beat of the universe, but there you go. She was pretty sure she could do this. Pretty sure. And someone needed to do it. If Sindy was in danger, she couldn't wait until after the Ball to get her back.

Someone had to make things right again, and since she was the one who'd broken it, it stood to reason she should be the one to fix it.

Bea took a towel from the wardrobe and covered Sindy's mirror, just to be safe.

Here goes.

She thought about the little glass slipper that Sindy wore because she loved it and because it reminded her of the person she loved. That might help if she kept it in mind.

Bea closed her eyes, levelled her breathing and thought about her first and last heroine, picturing her in the cave Melly had described, trying to build a connection. After a moment or two, she felt a tug in her stomach, the odd little heaviness that, when using the Mirrors, told her she had a link.

Bea took a deep breath.

This is really going to hurt.

Her stomach clenched, causing her to fall forward, a scream already escaping from her mouth as she…

…the noise was no longer a hum but a roar, a furnace of molten hot sound that crashed into her, searing her skin and her blood and bone until it reached her soul, exposing her and stripping her away, burning her, melting her…

…landed hard on a cold, stony floor. A bright flare of pain shot through her, spreading outwards from her chest in an arching, spitting inferno… black and white spots in her vision… she reached up to her eyes, feeling a strange, sticky hotness there…

Her stomach convulsed. She pitched forward to throw up, the sharp taste of bile stinging her throat and nose. She closed her eyes, hoping somehow the action would stop the violent spinning that caused every gloopy, soft, damp organ in her body to churn. It felt like someone was reaching into her with a red-hot iron poker and stirring.

"You're bleeding! Oh my! Here, here, let me…"

Bea tried to focus on Sindy's voice. She felt something wiping at her mouth, her nose, her ears, even her eyes, and everywhere it touched, she became aware of more of the hot, sticky liquid.

She started to lift herself up if nothing else but to get her away from the stench of her own vomit. The screaming, scratching wail in her mind rose, her stomach pitched again, and she buckled forward, vomiting wine and stomach acid. It was like she was melting from the inside out.

Sindy caught her and heaved her backwards.

"Sindy?" Bea wheezed, "…Are you alright?"

"Am I…? Yes, yes, I'm fine. But you're… I don't know what you are. Where did you come from?"

"Your house," Bea said. She wiped her mouth, ignoring the blood that spotted her hand. She wiped it absently on her dress and then realised what she'd done. "I'm here to rescue you."

Sindy inched backwards, a fearful look on her pretty face.

"I'm not going back," she stated with something like firmness.

"No, look, I'm not—"

"I'm not marrying the King. You can't make me. I'm going to stow away on one of the steamers and make a new life for myself."

"Sindy, I…" Bea paused, trying to think what she could say. She wondered if she could simply take her by force. She shook her head against the thought, a shock of pain stabbing her temples in retaliation. That was the old her.

"I'm sorry, Sindy," Bea said with difficulty. "It's my fault you ran away."

Sindy chewed her pink lip, unsure.

"I shouldn't have tried to… make you marry someone you don't know… and don't love," Bea choked out, a screeching siren ringing in her ears. She couldn't focus. She felt her chest heave and her throat constrict. Her mouth filled again, and she swallowed it back. "But please come… home now. Your parents are frantic, and Ana, and Will—Will's so… worried about you, Sindy. You must come back with me."

"I…"

Bea held out her hand, which in most circumstances, given its current state, wouldn't have had the desired effect. But as beautiful as she was, Sindy was a country girl, and she understood blood and vomit better than most people would have credited.

And Sindy wanted to go home. She didn't like the cave. It was cold and damp, and she'd already run out of food. She missed her family. She wanted to see Will again, even if he didn't love her back. She reached out for Bea's hand and…

…a strange humming buzz against her skin, like the tickle of the rain, if the rain were made of the roll of a drum, the soft, insistent susurrus of creation surrounding her, making her feel giddy and sick when it touched her…

…found herself sitting on her bed, back home. Everything was as it had always been, except that there was a fairy in a large dress on her bedroom floor, stone dead.

Chapter Thirty-four

"Please someone! Come quickly! She's dead, she's dead!"

Sindy didn't wait to see if anyone heard her. She flew back into her room and rolled Bea onto her back. She spent a few seconds rearranging Bea's arms and then reached her fingers into her mouth to check nothing was blocking her air. She heard footsteps on the stairs and felt a quick sense of relief. She wasn't alone.

She leant forward and breathed deeply into Bea's mouth, fearing as she did so that she was already too late. She pulled back and began to beat a rhythm onto Bea's chest with her clenched fist, counting under her breath.

"Bea!" Melly cried from the doorway.

"What happened?" Ana demanded.

"I don't—" *puff puff puff* "—know."

"Sindy, can you do it?" Ana asked, wrapping her arms around Melly, who was shaking.

"I don't know," Sindy repeated, bringing her lips to the godmother's, sharing her oxygen.

Melly cried; wild, hysterical sobs that made the house sound like a newborn was announcing its entrance into life rather than an old elf fearing her closest friend's exit from it.

"Can't you do something?" Ana asked. "Magic or a spell?"

"No," Melly wailed, "we're not allowed to!"

"For God's sake! Your friend is *dead*. Do something!"

"I don't know. The Teller—" Melly gulped around her tears.

Ana slapped her, hard.

"Listen to me," Ana said as Melly stood frozen in shock. "You're a witch, right? Do some magic."

"That's just my job," Melly said, panic still threaded in her voice. Her eyes were fixed on Sindy, leaning over Bea's body. "I'm an FME like Bea is… was… *ohgodsohgods*… witching is just what they assigned me after the Redaction."

"So you can't do anything magical at all?"

"No. Yes. I mean, elves can heal people—but we're not allowed to in front of the characters… Anyway, I can't do anything if she's dead." Melly's voice cracked. "I can't bring someone back from the dead!"

Sindy looked up from Bea's still body, her hands pumping her chest. "Look, if I can get her breathing again, *then* you can do something? I don't know what happened to her, but," she pressed her mouth back over Bea's, breathing in and out in short breaths, before lifting her head and continuing, "she was bleeding and throwing up. It was like she'd been poisoned and beaten."

"She's dead, she's dead, I told you I can't bring back the dead!" Melly sobbed.

Ana took Melly by her shoulders and looked her in the eyes. "If Sindy gets her breathing, what can you do?"

"I don't know—"

"Will you try?"

Melly's eyes darted to the covered mirror on Sindy's dresser. "Yes. Yes. If she's breathing."

Ana turned to her step-sister. "Right then. We've got a plan."

Sindy, her actions heavy with doubt, brought her lips once more against Bea's.

Mistasinon stood by the entrance to the Grand, looking for Bea. She was over two hours late. He glanced up at the viewing platform. Julia, the blonde Redactionist, was looking directly at him. He looked away.

He'd have to go up there soon and explain his fears to her. Not for the first time, he wished he wasn't on his own.

He couldn't believe Bea had given up. Something must have happened to her. He knew she'd come through the Mirrors yesterday; she was recorded by the Contents Department. He closed his eyes and tried to relax. This was no mean feat given, firstly, the feeling of Julia's cold blue gaze on him and, secondly, the reaction of the fae to the further rationing of the Mirrors. The latter was less of a problem. Mistasinon was used to shouting. Mistasinon was used a lot of noisy things.

He let his mind wind out, the same way he had in the Index, the night he'd found the Books Bea had Plot-watched.

He sniffed the air.

Opening his eyes, Mistasinon looked up at Julia. She tilted her head, questioning him. He ignored her and headed for the Mirrors.

Bea's lungs spluttered back into life. Sindy leapt back, and Melly sprang forward, landing heavily next to her friend, hands already outstretched and ready.

Green light spread from the witch's fingers into Bea.

Bea's body jumped, but she didn't open her eyes.

Melly, tears pouring down her face, sent another burst of healing into her, and again, Bea's body jumped. But her eyes remained closed.

Melly took a deep breath, closed her eyes, and sat very still. The two step-sisters stood watching, clutching each other, too frightened to speak.

Melly's breathing slowed. The strange green light spread further up her arms, getting steadily brighter until Ana and Sindy had to close their eyes. There was a loud thrumming noise, a deep bass sitting in their stomachs, unsettling and alien.

When the sisters opened their eyes, Bea was blinking slowly. Melly was leaning heavily on her elbows, a thick, black substance running from her nose.

"You saved me," Bea whispered.

Melly reached forward to grasp her friend's hand. "Oh Bea, oh Bea, oh Bea… you died, Bea, you died…"

Bea slowly sat up, swearing loudly and clutching her head. Melly laughed, a sad wet little sound that was for the four present the happiest thing they'd ever heard.

"I think I'd like some more of that wine," Bea said. "And a sausage," she added as an afterthought.

They stood in the dusky sunlight. Bea was on her third sausage and second glass of wine and was feeling much better. Melly as well seemed improved, though Bea had noticed she was moving a little slower and more carefully.

"It's too late to go back, isn't it?" Bea asked.

Melly nodded.

"So, we don't have a coach."

"No," Melly said. "But we do have a dress."

Bea smiled. It was nice to hear her friend say 'we'. It almost made her feel like she hadn't nearly died. "You fixed me up very well. I've got a bit of a headache, but nothing worse."

Melly shrugged.

"You'll have to tell me how you became such a good healer, you know? And where you got that Mirror from."

"Wait for the sequel."

Bea laughed. "Touché."

Melly fell silent. Something was obviously playing on her mind. To her shame, Bea found herself hoping the witch would keep it to herself. It wasn't that she didn't want to know, but the truth was she was exhausted. Dying was not the rest she had been led to believe it would be, and she still needed to attend the Ball and find an ending to her Plot, which was thickening faster than curdled milk.

Bea took another sip of wine. "What's wrong?"

"I was thinking…"

"Yes?"

"Did you notice, Sindy brought you back to life with a kiss? I thought that was quite fitting."

Bea laughed. "That's pretty brilliant."

"I thought so," Melly smiled, but it didn't last long. "Bea, about the coach. We'll never make it to the Ball on time without one, and you've been, uh, resting for hours. There's no way you'll make it back to the Grand from my house."

"You're right. And I can hardly turn up through one of the official Mirrors."

Melly reached out and squeezed Bea's shoulder. "You tried, Bea. I'm sorry."

"Don't be. I think I've got a way around it," Bea mused, taking a thoughtful bite of her sausage. "But I'll need one of those pumpkins."

Ana gave Sindy one last hug.

"You don't need to worry about Will. Trust me."

Sindy twisted her hair in her fingers. "Do you think so?"

Ana smiled. Sindy had been crying, but where any other girl would have had puffy, red eyes and blotchy cheeks, Sindy's blue eyes sparkled, her cheeks were flushed a faint pink, and the little purple shadows under her eyes simply made her look fragile and in need of protection. But there was a glint of determination in those same eyes that made Ana wonder if Sindy wasn't just as maligned by her looks as she was.

"Yes. I'm sure. Right. We'd better find out what new mess those two mad pixies have made."

"They're not pixies. Bea's a fairy, Melly's an elf."

"Melly's a witch." Ana thought for a moment. "Bea's a pain in the arse."

Sindy giggled. "Weren't you listening? Those are just the jobs they do. And, also, did you know that you don't have to be a fairy to be a godmother?"

"What?"

"It confused me too when Bea told me. But I think I understand now. Just because it seems like you should be something, it doesn't mean you have to be. Still," Sindy sighed, "I really did think fairies would have wings and stuff. It's a bit disappointing."

"You have to be the only person alive who would say something like that, after everything that's happened," Ana said ruefully. "Come on."

They left the kitchen and walked through the house. They heard the argument before they saw it.

"It's still too orange!"

"Well, what do you expect me to do about that? There was only half a tin of whitewash in the shed."

"It looks like someone dropped it in flour."

"For the love of—can you at least do something about the leaves? They're getting caught in the wheels."

"Yes, yes, I heard you the first time. Pumpkins aren't exactly the easiest things to talk to, you know. It keeps asking where the manure is. It's very single-minded, in that respect."

"If I didn't know better, I'd say the pumpkin wasn't the only one here talking shi—"

"Oh my," Sindy breathed, staring at the coach.

"You can't be serious?" Ana added, markedly less enthralled. She was the one that was going to be riding in it, after all.

Bea and Melly stopped their arguing as Sindy and Ana stepped into the garden.

The coach was... unique. The smell of hot pumpkin, on the other hand, was uncomfortably familiar. Apparently coaxing a root vegetable into expending enough energy to expand to the size of a two-horse carriage created a lot of heat. Even in the garden, the night was dark and full of starch.

Bea had done her best with what she had, and in fact had managed pretty well, given the circumstances. The coach had wheels and a little door and windows, even if it was somewhat rounder than the traditional model. And, as Melly had been keen to point out, orangier. Long reins—well, alright, vines—trailed from what Bea was now enthusiastically calling the driver's box but which Melly kept on insisting was a giant leaf rolled around a root, and were currently being attached to the livery. Here, even Bea was prepared to admit, however, they had encountered something more of a problem.

Ana and Sindy's parents were not wealthy people, even allowing for the endless business trips Sindy's father took. They had one horse, which they were using to travel to Sinne with Will. As a result, Bea and Melly had had to pull in the understudies, as it were.

Gertrude the pig grunted happily from her position at the front of the hitch. Behind her was Gussie the cow, who was somewhat less impressed. She chewed her cud and wondered, in the way of most cows, what she'd done to deserve all this.

"Oh look!" Sindy cried when she saw them. "How lovely! I wonder—" and with that, she ran back into the house.

Ana folded her arms across her chest. "A pig and a cow? I'll certainly make an entrance."

Bea walked around the coachkin, mouth already open to form the words 'what would you have done, used magic mice?' when they died in her throat.

Bea stared at Ana.

"You look... amazing," she said, trying to hide the wonder in her voice.

"No need to look quite so surprised."

Bea had no idea how Melly had done it. She hadn't bothered trying to cover up everything Ana didn't have, something which Bea suspected she would have done if she'd been left with the task of seamstress.

Instead, Melly had created for Ana a floor-length gown in red silk that ran in straight lines up her slender body and ended in a high neck. There were no sleeves; instead, Ana wore long black gloves. Her hair, which Sindy had brushed so hard it shone, was up in a neat, simple bun. She wore a small tiara, her lips were painted soft red, and her eyes were lined with black kohl and framed with thick, sticky mascara. Bea wondered if they'd dropped a little lead infusion into her eyes, or if they sparkled like that naturally and she'd never noticed.

"Wow," Bea said.

"Thanks," Ana answered, her voice drenched in sarcasm. "Your friend has a good eye," she added, nodding her head to Melly. Bea was certain she could hear a touch of admiration in Ana's voice.

A faint blush coloured Melly's cheeks. She pulled a cigarette out of her case and lit it with a match struck against the house. "You're very kind," she said, drawing on her cigarette in embarrassment. "I used to be quite creative when I was younger. I suppose you never forget how. Of course, if you wouldn't mind pretending to be at least a little bit scared of me, I'd appreciate it."

"See?" Ana said. "That's the problem with all these stories you peddle. Everyone feels like they have to perform some role. But I don't need to marry the King to have my voice heard." She walked up to Melly, taking the elf's shoulders in her hands. Melly looked like she was about to faint. "You're a funny, wonderful, creative woman, and the way all the little bunnies and birds helped make the dress... If you're really a wicked witch, I'm Gertrude's uncle. And who says that you need to be wicked to be a witch, anyway?"

Melly was saved from further embarrassment by Sindy, who ran out of the cottage trailing ribbons. "Come on!" she shouted, throwing bundles at the other three. "Coach, you shall go to the Ball!"

Thirty minutes later, and the coach was looking better. Sindy was able to achieve what neither Melly nor Bea had managed, which was to gentrify it. She succeeded mainly because she did all the work while the others argued, but she didn't mind.

Gertrude had ribbons tied to her ears and around her tail. Gussie was eating hers.

"That's probably the best we can hope for," Ana said, surveying their handiwork. "We need to go. It's already going to be close to midnight before we arrive."

"Alright then," Bea said. "We'll get Ana and the King talking, find Seven to let him know we've got Sindy back, and see if we can work out a Happy Ending before Mistasinon wants the Book back, agreed?"

Ana and Melly nodded their heads.

"Good. Let's get this bloody Ball over with, then."

It was not the most magical speech ever given by a godmother, but the three women clapped anyway.

Chapter Thirty-five

Seven stood behind the throne, as far from the maddening crowds as he was able. He wasn't wearing his hood at the King's insistence, but to some extent the swarms of guests kept him hidden. There was so much for people to see that, in fact, very few bothered giving him more than the cursory glance his beauty required. And John was right—he couldn't very well meet and charm potential investors with his face covered.

He waved at one of the waiters, drawing the boy's attention over to the dais on which the throne sat. He darted quickly up the shallow steps and presented a tray of small glasses of sparkling wine from Dirkbrock, a distant town in Sausendorf. Expensive wine, well suited to the opulence the crown had created. Seven took a glass and instructed the boy to return with a bottle.

The snake at his neck glittered as it caught the light, its flat, diamond-shaped head resting with grim threat above Seven's collar bone. It seemed it was waiting only for its moment to sink its teeth into his smooth, cold flesh. He scanned the room again, looking for her.

The Ball was in full swing, if such a small word could be used to describe the hundreds of guests filling the Ballroom and spilling out through the wide, glass doors into the palace gardens. The high, star-painted ceiling glowed from the light of thousands of candles as the chandeliers turned on clockwork mechanisms, casting dancing shadows over the party.

The jewels at the throats, wrists and in the hair of the women sparkled like cats' eyes amongst the movement of the guests as they flitted from group to group, gossiping and exchanging intrigues. There were even a couple of Cultivators from Cerne Bralksteld, invited to show the Baron that John held no secrets from him.

In the centre of the dance floor, the band played, turning without cessation on their steam-powered platform, the guests dancing around them like love-addled mayflies on the last night of summer. Rice liquor, untouched by all but the most experimental and now horizontal of guests, was imported by O&P steamers from Penqioa, a fact which raised a number of eyebrows among the more miserly guests.

More popular, though in fact no less expensive, was the ale. Ehinen in origin, it hadn't travelled so far but was exceptionally well brewed and oaked. There was also fire-wine, a drink that made Seven think of Ana, although most guests' palettes had long ago lost the ability to differentiate the Morismontre from the Risebek.

Seven had worked hard to guarantee John's Ball would be elegant, ostentatious and impressive, and he had surpassed himself. If it didn't result in trade agreements, the Crown would certainly end up bankrupt.

The boy returned with the bottle of wine. Seven took it and waved him away, sipping the wine from the neck, confident in the knowledge his beauty would forgive his behaviour. And if not, what would it matter? They would no doubt attribute his poor manners to his foreignness. And after tonight, he wouldn't have to worry about what any of them thought of him, anyway.

The trumpet sounded. He looked up at the staircase to see Ana and her entourage enter the Ball. John excused himself from his conversation, hopping down the steps from the throne to stand next to Seven.

"That her then?" he asked out of the corner of his smile.

"Yes, Sire."

"Looks smashing. Hope that's not a bad omen. Got enough empty, pretty heads 'round me, present company excluded, of course."

"Of course," Seven answered with a ghost of a smile.

"Well, best you go offer up the intros, old sweat. Can't be seen to be pandering to the opposition, what? Get her up here, and then I'll see if I can't find five mins for a quick chat."

"Your Majesty."

Seven glided towards the three women with all the grace and determination of a shark. He reached them just as Ana stepped off the staircase, and, bowing, said, "I am delighted to see you. I had been concerned that perhaps you would not be attending."

He held his arm out for Ana, who gazed at it for a moment before taking it.

"And miss all this?" she replied, taking in the room. There was a definite hint of wonder in her voice, though she tried to hide it.

"This is nothing compared to the beauty you bring. I am ashamed of my feeble efforts," he said, smiling lazily at her.

"Thanks. My dad always said it didn't matter how you looked if you could say the right things, but I always wanted to be prettier."

Seven could tell she hadn't planned to say so much. He ignored the sting in his stomach as her need reached out to him.

"I have yet to see anyone so lovely," he said, threading his fingers through Ana's and bringing her hand to his lips, dropping a kiss on her knuckles.

Ana stared at him, her expression unmistakable. She coughed, flustered. "I don't know why you need so many candles. It's giving me a headache."

"Ah. Yes. You should go," he said to Ana, releasing her. "The King awaits."

For just a moment, a look of absolute fury passed across Ana's face, but then she seemed to remember herself. She stepped back, and Melly was next to her in an instant. She took Ana's arm in her own and whispered something in her ear that made her laugh.

"Excuse me?" Seven asked, puzzled.

"Melly's going to chaperone Ana," Bea said. "She doesn't need an introduction to talk to the King, not really. And it'll save you both any, um, unnecessary stress."

Seven looked from Bea to the still, watchful face of the witch. He inclined his head graciously. "I see. Very well. Enjoy the Ball."

Melly led Ana off. Seven noticed the way Ana kept glancing over her shoulder to look at him. He wondered briefly how it made the godmother feel, and then he wondered why he cared.

"You do not accompany them?" he asked.

"There's no point."

"Ah?"

Bea sighed. "I thought Ana might be my new ending. I'd planned for her to marry John. You know, a royal wedding. And she'd be a good Queen, you can't say she wouldn't be. But she doesn't want to. And no—I'm not going to force her. But it means I haven't got a Happy Ending."

Seven stood silently, watching as couples began to take the floor. He lifted his eyes to the top of the Ballroom, where he could see Melly and Ana waiting in line to be formally welcomed by John. He touched his fingertips to his necklace, reassured by its weight.

"You believe the story must end in a certain manner for it to have been successful. I know this is not the case."

Bea snorted. "You've never wanted me to finish this Plot—I thought you'd be pleased. Or at least sarcastic."

"It was never my intent to hurt you, as I have stated. Frequently."

"Anyway, it doesn't matter what you or I think. It's what they think that's important."

Seven nodded. "Perhaps you would take a walk with me in the gardens, in order that we might take full advantage of the fact we are free of our chaperone?"

Bea's lip twitched. "Full advantage?"

"My dear, I know not what your tone implies. Like all godmothers, I suspect you are thinking of *romance*. I am shocked."

Bea laughed.

Encouraged, Seven continued, "I forgot earlier to comment on your latest foray into the world of fashion. As the hero of your story—"

"The hero?"

"Please do not interrupt. As the hero of your story, it is my duty to inform you that in general, this new dress is well. The corset is certainly striking, and never before have I been privileged to see quite such an excess of skirt. I do feel, however, please forgive me, that the staining detracts somewhat from the whole."

Bea and Seven stepped into the gardens. Braziers burned along the gravelled pathways, interspersed by tall spinning tops, their cogs ticking in a soft undercurrent to the sounds of the band. They were not alone, but the atmosphere was calmer, and the cool air felt good after the heat from the candles.

"Really? It's the rips I think are the problem," she said, looking around her.

"No, no. Honesty forces me to disagree," Seven continued, keeping to the shadows where he could, watching her watching the other guests. "Some of those rips are extremely promising. I find myself most intrigued by the one above your right thigh, and the fraying around your décolletage is quite distracting. No, I am of a mind. It is the stains that present the issue."

"Thanks," Bea said, stopping to sit on a stone bench.

Seven ran his hand over his necklace. He'd always been the one in control, the one to twist and lead the humans into whatever tale amused him. But now he sensed he was part of someone else's story, and thus not so privileged. It was interesting. He left the shadows and sat next to Bea.

"You look nice too," she said.

"I look not unlike those black and white ice birds from the Fifth Kingdom, but the King insisted. He is surprisingly rigid in some areas. He takes exception to my hood," Seven added in a disapproving tone.

"Someone I know... he always wears suits," Bea said, her cheeks glowing red. "I think he looks good in them."

Seven grinned. "I would suggest it is the person beneath the suit whom you believe so pleasing to the eye. In my experience, clothing is just another shackle. The witch wears black, does she not, because that is the colour a witch wears."

"I suppose," Bea muttered, fingering one the butterflies hanging from her dress, an expression on her face that Seven couldn't intuit. "Do you know what the stains on my dress are?"

"I do not."

"It's blood. My blood."

Seven shifted his weight, suddenly uneasy. He couldn't gauge the direction of the conversation—the godmother's desires were unchanged, and yet the way she was with him, and the things she was saying, didn't match his experience.

"Aren't you going to ask how it got there?" she asked.

"I assume you will tell me. You do seem inclined to involve me in your every mishap."

"I got Sindy back. She was in a cave, near Sinne."

"That is some five miles from here. How were you able to retrieve your young lady and arrive here in such good time?"

"I copied you."

"Pardon?"

"I remembered travelling with you, and the sound of the drums, and then I was there. I brought her back too. That's where the blood came from."

Seven's laconic attitude crumbled. He stared at Bea in disbelief.

"Of all the things I have witnessed, all those people I have had dealings with, you are by far the most—you impossible, idiotic, *stupid* fairy. You might have died."

A thin smile flickered across Bea's face.

"I did. I died. No one dies in the Teller's Plots, but I did. And the thing is, I don't think I care. I don't even care if they Redact me—I don't think I ever have. I think that's what I've always wanted, you know? What other reason could there be for what I've done? All the way through, I've made choices to lead me here. It's not fate, is it? And it sure isn't a Plot, because that's all a pack of lies. That's what you told me, isn't it?"

She put on an imitation of Seven's accent. *"Wherefore and hence shalt thou realise thine whole existence doth be but a falsehood?* Well, you were right. Everything is arranged for us—no, it's worse than that. We arrange it for ourselves. Happy Ever After, True Love, Rags To Riches. It's a con, and we all buy into it. We play our little games with these people here, and if they don't let us, or they stop believing, or try to fight back? We'll just change the rules. The game stays the same. So you know what? I honestly don't think I'll mind being Redacted. What you don't know can't hurt you."

Seven tilted his head, his voice softening. "And thus you are obliged to remember."

"Huh. I thought the whole point of genies was to tell us what we wanted to hear."

Seven fell silent. He didn't comprehend why, but for some reason, he felt the need to help her understand. It was very irregular, but there it was. Besides, soon he would have his prize, and then he could leave all these humans and fairies behind him, so what harm was there in exploring this odd new sensation?

"The night before last, you came to me, demanding to know my purpose. Would still you like an answer?"

Bea shrugged.

"When The Great Redaction began, the genies had greater reason than most to fear it. Some of my brethren fought back, but not I. I ran. I found a forest far from people and civilisation and the hateful eyes of the Teller and his Beast and lived, if not well, then quietly and safely for hundreds of years. This was my life, and I settled into it. Until one night, I heard a scream and, against my better judgement, I went in search of the source of the cry. I found a girl, collapsed on the earth, her dress torn and her head bleeding. Slowly and as quietly as I was able, I approached her. My fear was great, yet I did this thing."

"What happened?"

"She was the most beautiful woman I had ever seen. Her hair was black as ebony, her lips red as human blood and her skin white as the new-fallen snow. We loved each other to the detriment of all else. Every sense was awakened, every moment a dream. We were the world, entire and whole unto each other, all its wonders shared between us. And then she became entangled in a story, one which I could not stop. I loved her, and I am in no doubt my feelings were returned. Yet I am to believe that it was True Love when she was poisoned and encased and stolen from me?"

Bea reached out and very gently touched his arm. Seven gave a little groan that quickly became a chuckle. "Are we comforting one another?"

"Maybe. Why not?"

"Ha. Yes. Why not?" Seven looked up at the stars. "Maria Sophia was everything to me. She brought into my life something I had never before known, and now I cannot live without. She created me as the sun creates the day, as the moon creates the tides. She is more myself than I am. Without her, I know not how to live. And tonight, she attends this Ball. It has been the work of years to prepare myself for this moment. You know not the danger being here presents to me, not only from the humans and their wishes but also from the General Administration. But tonight, I will see her again, and when I do, the spell she is under will be broken. She will remember me and love me again."

"I don't know what to say."

Seven smiled. "Truly, this is a night of wonders."

"Ha bloody ha. What has this got to do with me?"

"When I decided to carry out my plan here in Llanotterly, I was concerned, naturally, about interference from the General Administration."

Bea nodded. "We're always warned not to engage with anyone we suspect of being an Anti. I should never have spoken to you that first day."

"I had planned to kill any member of the General Administration on sight."

Bea tried to pull her hand away, but Seven grabbed it in his stronger one. "Please, do not be afraid."

She tugged her hand free but didn't leave. Instead, she thought for a moment. "So why haven't you killed me?"

"There are many reasons. You are unlike the usual General Administration puppets, that is one. You desire so much, which is always attractive to my kind. You are conflicted, and that intrigues *me*. Perhaps, however, I did not kill you because I have changed. And, Bea, this is why you must not submit to Redaction, nor to despair. You too have changed, and who knows where such change will carry you?"

"But what if it carries me somewhere even worse?"

"Indeed it might. And yet, mistress godmother, what if it does not? Enough. We are here, and it is now." He stood, pulling Bea up with him.

Bea smiled. "You're refusing to grant my wish, aren't you?"

Seven laughed. "*This* wish, yes. Perhaps, one day, you will come to me with another. Now, this is of far greater importance: can you dance?"

Chapter Thirty-seven

Ana was frustrated. She'd barely had a moment to talk to the King. It wasn't his fault, she grudgingly admitted. Every time they got started, some new person would need to be formally welcomed. She turned to John, who was looking out at the Ball with an expression of absolute misery on his face, his chin resting against his knuckles.

"What's wrong?" she found herself asking.

He sighed. "Look here, tell me what you see."

"I see your subjects, my Lord—"

"Quite right, quite right—"

"Until the Baron forces them into the manufactories because you've drawn his attention to us."

John shook his head. "This was a mistake."

"So you're giving up? Why am I not surprised?"

"For goodness' sake. I meant trying to sort all this out here was a mistake. Can hardly hear myself think over this racket. But let's talk brass tacks," John said. "Baron of Cerne Bralksteld will invade, sooner or later, and that's a fact. Not much we can do about it, far as I can see."

Ana scowled. "There's always a way."

"Well, I'm buggered if I can think of it," John said. "What do *you* suggest?"

Ana took a seat next to the throne. "Don't draw his attention to us by expanding. He'll see it as a threat."

"And how do we pay the tithes without the tax?" John asked.

"Stop paying them."

"And then he invades, and we die."

"We've got people, children, in our camp that he's near tortured to death in his manufactories."

"And I've got people in my kingdom who he'd actually torture to death if I stop paying him."

Ana drummed her fingers, trying to think. The trouble was, she could see the King's point of view. She hadn't expected it, but there it was. Llanotterly did have to keep paying the Baron. But she was right as well. The more they expanded, the more the Baron would want, and the bigger he grew, the more people would die.

"It seems like all we're doing is putting off the inevitable," she said.

"Yes," John said. "Quite frankly, I'd hoped you might have a little more to add."

Ana thought about it.

"Well," she said slowly, tasting the idea on the tip of her tongue, "I might be able to suggest something. But it's not very... ah... moral."

John looked up. "Less moral than keeping slaves or threatening to invade if we don't cough up the dosh?"

Ana smiled one of her rare, genuine smiles. "More moral than that. Alright. How about this? My father was a pirate. He went missing years ago, but I still know some of the boys he did business with. If we could perhaps, ahh, reconfigure some of Llanotterly's imports and exports, we could get money in without attracting attention."

John shook his head. "We'd never be able to explain where the money was coming from."

"So sell the forest, just not so much. What do you think?"

John started to answer when the trumpeter broadcasted the arrival of another guest.

"The Count Henri Laurent Ghislain of Cierremont, the sixth city of Marlais, middle county of Ehinenden, the Third Kingdom of Thaiana," announced the page at the top of the steps, "and his Countess, Maria Sofia."

John turned back to Ana. "I think you might be on to something, that's what I think. Let's discuss it with my Adviser in the morning. No, stay here," John said when Ana stood to leave.

"Why?" Ana noticed the way some of the pages were eyeing her and added, "My Lord."

"I think it might be an idea for you to meet some of this lot, that's why. They're a slippery bunch, and you're a sharp girl. Just keep your eyes and ears open. God knows where S. has got to—ah no, there he is, catching flies on the dance floor. Not like him to lollygag," John said, a note of uncertainty in his voice.

Ana followed the King's line of sight and, after a moment, found the Adviser in the crowd. John was right. Seven was standing like a statue in the middle of the dance floor, oblivious to the fact he was interrupting the dancing guests, staring at the newly arrived Count and Countess as they made their way down the staircase at the other end of the Ballroom.

Suddenly Ana felt uneasy. She searched the crowd, trying to find Bea, but she wasn't anywhere to be seen.

"Excuse me a moment," she said to John.

She left the King and walked as calmly as she could over to Melly, who was standing on the edge of the dais, glaring at the crowds.

"Do you know where Bea's gone? She's not with the Adviser anymore. I think something—"

"Hush," Melly hissed through her teeth.

"Excuse me? Did you seriously just 'hush' me?"

Melly glanced quickly at Ana, before returning her gaze to the crowd. "Yes. Something's happening, but I don't know what. I can feel it... something's coming."

Ana peered at the room. "There are guards on every door and a standing army outside. Although it's probably more of a leaning army now," she conceded, thinking about how much free beer the citizens of Llanotterly could get through. "Do you think it's the Baron? Is he coming?"

"No," Melly said. There was a film of sweat on her skin. "And it won't matter how many guards are stationed at the doors."

"Why not?"

Melly looked at the far wall, glazed doors along its length to allow access to the gardens. "They won't be using the doors."

The band has ceased playing.

It struck Seven as odd that they would, considering there were still couples dancing. Perhaps they hadn't realised the music had stopped?

He didn't glide, not anymore. He wasn't even sure he knew where his feet were, or any other part of him. He knocked into the

F. D. Lee

heavy shoulder of a woman from the Six Points whom John had gone to a great deal of trouble to get here. She turned her red face towards him, insulted by such unaccustomed mistreatment, but when she saw his beauty, she went back to her conversation, settling to disparage the poor breeding of Llanotterly.

Seven watched Maria Sophia as she made her way through the crowds towards the throne. She was as beautiful. Her skin seemed to glow, reflecting back the candlelight like porcelain. She looked every bit as fragile and lovely as he remembered.

The image of her lying dead in her glass coffin filled his vision. He could still remember the hollow, raw, *futile* sound of his voice as he begged her to wake up, his face pressed against the glass, his thick, black blood smearing against the clear surface, mixing with his tears.

But as much magic as he'd used, he hadn't been able to wake her. For three weeks he'd returned to her living grave. He'd sat with her, telling her stories, sharing memories with her of their time together and his life before The Great Redaction. He'd begged her, quietly, softly, to *just wake up.*

And then one day she had.

Seven watched her now as Maria Sophia turned and smiled up at the tall, dark, handsome man on her arm, whispering something in his ear that made him laugh. A knot of fire twisted in Seven's stomach, so hot it burned him. He fixed his gaze on the man, a shadow of a memory brushing against his consciousness. And then he had it.

He had only ever seen the man at a distance, on the day Maria Sophia had married him and become the Countess of Cierremont. Seven hadn't been at the ceremony, but he'd seen the new couple when they'd stood on the balcony of their turreted castle while he had stood in the market, hidden under his hood.

That was the first night he had ever been drunk. When he'd come to outside the boundary of Cierremont, hazy memories of trying to convince the revellers to wish for their new Countess to die in a series of increasingly painful ways had clogged his memory. His ribs had been broken, his left arm fractured and his body a mess of bruises, all no doubt courtesy of the drunkenly patriotic locals.

And now she was here. In Llanotterly. She had returned to him.

He stepped back as Maria Sophia and her man walked past him. Someone came up to speak to them, a guest he should have known but couldn't place. Seven's mind had shattered, broken into sharp shards at the sight of her.

He could only see Maria Sophia's back, but the patrician face of the guest they were talking to seemed serious. Somewhere Seven knew he should be paying attention to this rigid, humourless man. But he couldn't focus, not when he could see the curve of her spine. Not when he could remember so clearly what it felt like to run his fingers over her, to press his lips to her, to love her and cherish her and be inside her.

The tall, austere man leaned forward and spoke to the Count, who shook his head, laughing loudly. Maria Sophia stood up on her toes to whisper something to her husband, Seven's stomach twisting anew as he saw her lips brush against the man's ear. The Count shrugged his wide shoulders, and after another round of head shaking and laughter, they said goodbye to the white-haired man and continued their journey towards the throne to formally thank John for the invitation.

Seven stepped into pace behind them, his mind racing. She was here and the world, for so long ugly and deformed, was all at once itself again. She was taking a glass of sweet wine from one of the waiters. She was smiling. She was breathing. *She was here.*

Maria Sophia was an island of such colossal importance within a sea of inconsequence that it seemed impossible the Ball was able to continue its empty existence.

She was on the steps now, a few feet from John and Ana and the witch. Seven realised all he had to do was walk up behind her, reach out his hand, touch her shoulder and—

What?

What would occur?

Seven's step faltered.

The woman above him had tumbled out of his dreams and now stood like a half-waking ghost, a photograph double-exposed, showing him in one moment the fallacy of his past as it bled into his future. The image of Maria Sophia had grown too large for him to bear. He had made it so. In his industry and creativity, he had transformed her into something so wonderful that the very fact she might now be anything less terrified him almost as much as the prospect she might exceed it.

Seven turned. He had made a mistake. He never should have come here, never should have mixed and meddled with these creatures. What a fool he was—he had put himself in the eye of the Teller and the General Administration for something he now knew he would never have the courage to take.

It was time to run. Time to hide. He would recover what remained of his lamp, and he would leave this—

"Albelphizar!"

Seven froze.

She had called him.

Chapter Thirty-six

Sindy tried to work out what she was going to say. A couple of hours ago, when Ana had told her how frantic Will had been, she'd felt certain of his love, but now her confidence had drained away.

What if she told him how she felt and he rejected her?

What if she never told him and he did love her?

The noise of the coach as it approached the cottage shook her from her thoughts. She ran to the front door, took a deep breath and opened it.

Her father, when he saw her, burst into tears. He ran across the garden and gathered her up in his arms, dropping kisses on her golden hair. Even her stepmother hugged her, though she was also quick to bring attention to her nerves, which had suffered dearly.

Sindy took her father's arm, explaining to her parents that she had been trapped in a cave and that a huntsman had found her and brought her home, all the while watching Will watching her from the driver's seat of the coach. He didn't welcome her. He didn't even wave or smile.

Sindy's heart cracked.

Inside the house, she sat with her parents for another hour or so, repeating the story she and Ana had devised, hugging and kissing them and being hugged and kissed in return. Eventually, they went to bed, and Sindy promised she would follow soon.

She padded through the kitchen and out to the garden, the night air cold on her skin. She shivered and walked towards her little swing, trying hard not to cry. When she started crying, she'd probably drown in her tears.

When she got to her swing, she realised she didn't want to sit on it. It was a swing built for someone who didn't exist: a permanently young girl who would never grow old, never be strong, never be more than her father's daughter and her husband's wife. A weak girl.

If she'd been stronger at the beginning, none of this would have happened. If she'd refused the godmother, then she wouldn't have needed to run away and frighten her parents. She wouldn't have kissed Will and completely ruined their friendship. She looked around the garden, her eyes landing on the axe. She picked it up; it was heavier than she'd expected, but not so heavy she couldn't wield it.

She walked back to her swing, lifted the axe and hacked at the rope. It didn't break in one go, but with each swing of the axe, it frayed a little more until the wooden seat was suspended by only the faintest length of twine. Sindy shifted the weight of the axe in her hand and looked at the remains of the rope. She swung hard, and the seat fell to the ground with a clatter.

"Why'd you do that then?"

She turned, the axe still in her hands, her blonde hair wild and tangled. Will was standing behind the house. She must have walked straight past him.

"Why didn't you welcome me back?" she countered, panting.

He detached himself from the cottage, his wide, normally open face marred. "I didn't know what to say," he admitted, reaching her.

"You should have said something."

"I know."

They stood in silence, staring at each other.

"Could you possibly put the axe down?" Will asked after a moment.

"Oh, yes... goodness... sorry."

"You didn't go to the Ball," Will said in a tone of voice he probably hoped was casual.

"Why would I go to the Ball? I ran away to avoid going to the Ball."

Will looked surprised and then embarrassed. "Really? I thought perhaps it was because of me..."

"How could you think that?"

"Well, you see, the other day when you, ah, you kissed me, and you seemed upset, I didn't know what to think. But then I met this woman who said she was my godmother... But that didn't make sense. You're the kind of girl who gets a fairy helping her. You're the kind of girl who marries Kings," Will said wretchedly, kicking his feet in the dirt, unable to meet her eyes. "I guess I thought you didn't know how to say goodbye to me, and then I thought something had happened to you... Sindy, we've always been mates, if you want to marry the King, I'm happy for you."

Sindy looked up at him, his weather-beaten face staring at her in confusion. He wasn't handsome. He wasn't rich. But he was hers, and she loved him. She pulled him forward, although in actual fact she more pulled herself towards him. It didn't matter. What mattered was that she was the one doing it. She realised that Will would never lead her.

She took his left hand and placed it on her waist and threaded the fingers of his right hand through her own. She rested her head against his wide chest and began to lead him in a dance.

After a moment, Will rested his head against hers, and they danced without music in the bare moonlight of her little garden.

Mistasinon eased his way through the Ballroom, blending in reasonably well in his blue suit and waistcoat. His tatty satchel ruined the look somewhat, and his frame, which was slender for such a tall man, drew attention, but on the whole, he was unremarkable. He wondered if this had been the Teller's intention all along. In Ænathlin, his tan skin and height drew the eye like a wolf amongst sheep, but here with the humans he was just another face, slightly unusual but nothing more.

A young boy offered him a drink from a silver tray, but Mistasinon shook his head, and the lad wandered off.

He scanned the room without interest, taking in the band on the spinning podium, the food and drink, and the guests showing off their beauty. Not for the first time, he wondered how strong the genie was, and what it would be like to see one again. They were extremely perceptive, he remembered, which might cause problems, especially if Bea were present.

His gaze swept over the dance floor. He came to a stop when he saw her.

Mistasinon couldn't see the blood or rips in Bea's dress. From where he stood, he could only see the way the corset highlighted her shape and the sparkle of the sequins as they glittered in the candlelight. She was dancing with an exceptionally beautiful man.

His eyes fixed on the couple. Bea was dancing well, though it was the man who now had his attention.

A foul taste filled his mouth, and Mistasinon realised he'd bitten his lip so hard he'd drawn blood. He pulled the handkerchief from his waistcoat pocket and wiped at his lip before any of the guests would notice he bled the wrong colour. He waved one of the waiters over and took a glass of wine from the tray, swilling it around his mouth before swallowing it.

He made to step forward and then stopped. He looked up at the large gilded clock hanging above the arched entrance to the Ball. Mistasinon stood as the music of life flowed around him, the instrument of his agency muted.

Then, turning his back on Bea and Seven, he walked away. Guests were still arriving as he climbed the stairs to exit the Ball, but he passed by them without drawing attention. He moved against the crowd until he could slip down another corridor and be, finally, alone.

Closing his eyes, he took a deep breath in through his nose. Colours filled his mind, momentarily overwhelming his limited new senses. He leaned against the wall and concentrated. After a moment, he found what he was looking for. He opened his eyes and followed the smell of the genie towards his room.

Bea couldn't believe it. She was dancing at a Ball with a handsome man—although it wasn't actually the person she wanted to be dancing with. She mentally stepped away from the noxious thought, landing right in the next one, which asked why she had agreed to dance with Seven in the first place.

She turned her head to the side to watch the other couples as they spun around her, the women's dresses spread out like chrysanthemums.

"You are enjoying yourself?" Seven asked, his breath brushing against her hair as he spoke.

Bea, her eyes level with the golden snake around his neck, shook herself out of her thoughts. "We should see how Ana and John are getting on."

"That is no answer."

"And Melly. I just left her. Although I think she's probably been to more Balls than I've had hot dinners."

"The witch delights in a challenge?" Seven said, a smile in his voice.

It struck Bea that once she would have found the same comment annoying, but she knew better than that now. He was hedonistic, cruel and self-important, but at least he was reliable in it. And, she couldn't help adding, he might also be honest and decent.

"I'm almost having fun," Bea relented. "This is definitely the way to spend your last night before being dead-headed. I just hope the white suits don't go after my Plotter or my friends."

"You are being overly dramatic. Or overly selfless. In either instance, it is extremely boring."

Bea glared at him. "I'm not being boring. I'm accepting my fate with dignity."

"You are running away."

"Alright, fine. Maybe I am. And what you said just now… thank you. For trying to help. But it doesn't matter. I still don't have an ending. No ending—no Book. No Book—no Bea."

Seven pressed his hand against the bare skin of her back, pushing her against him as they danced. As always, his touch was cold, despite the heat. He looked down at her, his handsome face seemingly impassive. His blue eyes were lined with kohl, as isolate as a cloudless sky, but Bea was getting better at reading them: with Seven she had to look at the muscles around his eyes and the position of his eyebrows to see what he was thinking.

And that was when Bea realised she could see something in his expression she probably shouldn't be seeing, at least not directed at her. Yet there was no mistaking the way he was holding her, one hand resting on the small of her back, pressing her against him, the other now at the nape of her neck.

"What about Maria Sophia?"

He shrugged. "I love her. Wanting you does not diminish that."

"Yes, it does. Anyway, I don't fancy you."

"I am aware you pine another, but I do not believe this results in your being unattracted to me. Take heart—if you are determined to sacrifice yourself upon the altar of martyrdom, you may as well find pleasure while you are still able."

Bea opened her mouth to tell him that she didn't 'pine' for anybody when he kissed her. She hadn't been expecting it, and he took advantage of her shock. His lips and his tongue, when she felt it against her own, were cold as stone.

She didn't mean to kiss him, but such was Seven's skill that she was responding before she realised what she was doing. Bea could feel the power of him, the chill of his body against the increasing heat of her own, and she realised anything they did together would probably be the best experience of her life, and that it was all wrong.

He pulled back, puzzled.

"You do not enjoy my attention?"

"It's not that. It's only—" Bea began and then stopped. She'd seen something, *someone*, who she really shouldn't have seen climbing the stairs.

"Yes?" Seven asked, frowning.

"I have to…. Just wait here. I'll be back," Bea said, pulling out of his embrace.

Seven watched as she disappeared into the crowds. He had no idea what he had done to cause her to run away, and then it didn't matter.

Maria Sophia had arrived.

Chapter Thirty-eight

Bea peered around the corner and then ducked back. There was no mistaking that narrow frame—it was definitely Mistasinon. But what in the worlds was he doing here?

Her first thought was that he had come for her. But as the initial wave of panic ebbed, she'd realised he was heading towards Seven's room, so she'd followed silently behind. She was very good at being quiet, something an unthinking person might find surprising given her proportions. It was a skill learned through years of living in the Sheltering Forest, always on the lookout for orcs and gnarls, and later honed as a result of all the Plots she'd watched. Bea peered around the corner again. Mistasinon was kneeling outside the genie's door, rummaging in the tatty satchel he always carried with him.

Without warning, he froze, Bea's heart not far behind him. He sat still, his back to her and his arm lost in his bag. She watched, not daring to move, as he took a deep breath in through his nose. He sat quietly, breathing deeply, for what felt to Bea to be a hundred years.

And then he went back to rummaging in his bag as if nothing had happened. He pulled out a bronze ring from which hung five oddly shaped, flattened sticks, and held it up to study it. Bea watched as he brushed his fingertips over the keyhole in Seven's door.

He put his eye to the hole like he was trying to spy into the genie's bedroom. Then he turned his attention back to the bronze sticks and, after a moment or two flicking between them, chose one that to Bea seemed to be a bit pointier than the others. He slipped the stick into the keyhole and then, leaning into the task, began to wiggle it around. Bea wasn't sure what she expected to happen, but when nothing did, she felt almost as frustrated as Mistasinon did, if his quick expulsion of breath was anything to go by.

She was just trying to decide whether she should confront him when he stepped back from the door. He put the sticks back in his bag, which he placed carefully at his feet. Next, he took off his blue suit jacket and waistcoat, and then, of all unexpected things, he started unbuttoning his shirt.

Bea considered pulling her head back around the corner, but she very quickly squashed that thought. If she was going to ignore all the things she shouldn't do, surely that included ignoring the fact she shouldn't be watching Mistasinon undress? That was just parity. She had always thought herself a very fair person.

She was surprised to see a dapple of light brown hair across his chest, disappearing down his stomach and under his trousers. The fae, as a rule, didn't grow body hair. Even the trolls, who were generally considered a boorish tribe, only grew hair on their fingers and in their ears. Body hair was limited to humans and animals.

Mistasinon rolled his shoulders, shifted position and then, in a movement so fast Bea wasn't sure she saw when it began, he slammed himself, shoulder first, into Seven's door.

Bea yelped in shock, but the sound of the wood creaking covered her cry. She quickly pulled her head back behind the wall and listened as Mistasinon hit the door again. This time there was the loud crack of thick timber splitting.

Silence fell. Bea swallowed and waited for her heart to slow down. When she was reasonably confident it wasn't about to beat its way out of her chest, she peeped again around the corner. Mistasinon was gone, his shirt, jacket and waistcoat no longer on the floor, nor his satchel. Seven's bedroom door was also markedly absent. All that remained was a splintered hole, edged with jagged pieces of broken wood. It looked like it had been hit with a battering ram.

Bea bit her lip.

It was only Mistasinon—sad-eyed Mistasinon, with his lopsided smile and kind words. He was her Plotter. He'd taken her to dinner and, she was almost one hundred per cent certain, flirted with her. She liked him. But then he'd also just broken down a solid wooden door. And, she remembered, he was fast. Very fast.

She glanced behind her. The Ball was still going, which meant that Seven was still out there.

How did the wishes work? Would he hear her if she called to him?

She would just have to hope he would.

Bea released her lip and stepped through what had once been Seven's door.

Mistasinon was on the floor, his top half disappearing under the bed. Around him various drawers and cabinets hung open, their contents spilt across the floor.

"Looking for something?" Bea asked.

Mistasinon backed out from under the bed. He had replaced his shirt, the crisp, white sleeves rolled up to his elbows. His satchel was sat on top of the bed, his jacket and waistcoat presumably stuffed inside. Some madness caused Bea to notice how the white shirt seemed to suit him more than the dark blue of his Plotter's uniform.

"What are you doing here?" he asked.

"I was going to ask you the same thing."

"I came to see if you were alright. You didn't report in at the Grand."

Bea raised an eyebrow. "I don't think that's true."

Mistasinon stood for a moment, his hands flexing at the end of his arms. And then he flopped down on the bed.

"I—it's complicated," he said.

"I'm beginning to think everything is," Bea answered. "What are you doing?"

"Will you sit down?"

"I'd rather stand."

"Please?"

Bea rolled her eyes but grabbed the chair from Seven's desk and pulled it over to the bed. She set it down in front of Mistasinon and sat, her large skirt billowing up around her.

"So why are you here?"

"I'm, um, looking for something."

Bea took a moment to glance pointedly around the room. "I can see that. What are you looking for?"

Mistasinon rubbed his neck. His hair, normally slicked back, had fallen loose from his exertions and hung over his eyes, softening his wide forehead. "There's another fae here," he said slowly. "In addition to you, that is."

Bea leaned forward on her elbows. There didn't seem much point in being coy, not any more. "You mean the genie?"

Mistasinon frowned. "Yes. How did you know?"

"It wasn't hard to put it together," Bea said breezily. "So, what is it you're looking for? And why don't you just ask him for it?"

Mistasinon sat on the edge of the bed, his knees brushing against the thick material of Bea's skirt. "I know you must have a lot of questions, but this really isn't the time to explain. It's almost midnight." He shot her a relieved smile. "And now you're here, you can come back to the Grand with me."

"Are you mad? I need to be here, with my Plot." She didn't add that Melly was downstairs in the Ballroom. She didn't want to get her friend into trouble. "What's going on?"

"Honestly, it'll be easier to explain once we're back home. Give me ten minutes to have one last look around and then—"

"I just told you, I'm not going anywhere."

"Um. Well, I'm your Plotter and a GenAm official. You need to do what I say, or else—"

"No, I don't," Bea said. She was beginning to realise that whatever was going on, it was about a hundred times worse than anything she'd imagined up to this point. "You just tell me why you're here and how you know about Seven. I'm not frightened of you."

Mistasinon snorted. "Everyone's frightened of something."

"Redaction doesn't scare me either," Bea said, annoyed.

"What about the Cerberus? A 'monster', that's what you said, wasn't it?"

"So what? The Beast *is* a monster. But it's not here, is it? It's just you and me."

He was only a few inches from her. She could feel the tension in him, like the whisper of air on skin in what should be an empty room. Then he spun around on the bed, reaching for his satchel.

"Don't," Bea warned.

He sighed, but he turned back to her. "I'm not about to pull out a sword, Bea. I just wanted to put my coat on. We're wasting time. It's twenty to twelve."

"Why are you so worried about midnight?"

"I, we, have to be back by Midnight."

"With this mystery object you're looking for?"

"Ideally, yes. Bea, I... I waited for you at the Grand. I waited too long when I should have been here, hunting. I thought you'd given up. I hoped you had." He offered her one of his rainy smiles. "I should have known better. But thank the mortal gods, you're here now—I mean, here with me. That is, that you followed me. I mean, mortal gods, what do I mean? I mean, you can come back with me, now that you're here. That's all."

Bea felt herself wanting to return his smile. If someone had asked her half an hour ago, she would have said he was nice. Perhaps even her friend, or something more. Certainly trustworthy. But now...? Now she wasn't so sure.

"Why weren't you surprised when I said Seven was a genie?"

Mistasinon pulled back. "I—does it matter? We need to leave."

"What's happening at midnight? I'm not leaving until you tell me what in the five hells is going on."

"Why are you so determined to stay?" Mistasinon said, his expression souring. "You've lost control of your Plot."

"How do you know that?"

"Are you staying for him?"

"What? Who?"

Mistasinon stood up. "Are you staying for him? For 'Seven'?"

Bea stood as well, her skirts knocking her chair to the floor with a loud crash. "Why on Thaiana would you think that?"

"I saw you dancing with him."

"And? He's not a character. No rule against dancing with another fae, is there? Stop distracting me and tell me what's going on."

"Let's go, and then I promise I'll explain ev—"

"Now. Explain now."

Mistasinon looked like he was about to scream. He took a deep breath, obviously trying to gather himself. Bea very quickly tried to work out how far away she was from the hole in Seven's door. There was something about the way Mistasinon was acting that suggested he was very near the end of his patience, and Bea was suddenly absolutely certain she didn't want to see what would happen if he reached it.

"Fine," he said. "But then you're leaving with me. The Mirrors use magic to work."

Bea stared at him. "But that doesn't... I mean, what have the Mirrors got to do with Seven? Anyway, magic isn't..." she was about to say strong enough, but she knew better than that. "I mean it's banned."

"You've been told it's weak? Useless? Haven't you thought about why something that the GenAm says is laughably weak is also banned?"

Bea opened her mouth to stand up for herself, but she knew he was right. She hadn't thought to question it. She'd gone along with the GenAm's line on magic the same way she'd gone along with everything else the Teller told her.

"It's not weak at all," Mistasinon continued. "But it is difficult. Only the very, very old can use it with any real level of accuracy or success, and even then, if they aren't careful or they overuse it... It'll kill them."

Bea thought about her own brush with magic and shivered. "And the Mirrors use magic?"

Mistasinon nodded. "A lot of magic. If we were to try to travel through the Mirrors by ourselves, 'under our own steam' as the characters would say, we'd never survive it. Certainly not given how reliant we are." He glanced at the clock. "Bea, the time..."

"Explain faster. If the Mirrors use magic, how do we use them without killing ourselves in the process?"

"Belief."

"Belief?" Bea nearly laughed. "So the GenAm was telling the truth?"

"Belief is a kind of magic all of its own. Belief can change reality, lives, the world, just as magic can. But belief can only do so much." Mistasinon was growing increasingly restless. "Bea, we must go."

"What about the Anties? Are they even real?"

"Yes. In a manner of speaking," Mistasinon said. He started walking towards Seven's mirror, standing covered in the corner of the room.

"What have the Mirrors got to do with Seven?"

Mistasinon reached Seven's mirror. "I wanted to find his lamp. But the GenAm... they want something else from him."

Bea felt coldness trickle through her veins. "What does the GenAm want from him?"

Mistasinon met her eyes. "I think you know."

"Say it."

"They'll use his magic to repair the Mirrors."

"You mean they'll wish him to death. That's why there are no Redacted genies, isn't it? The GenAm murdered them all, to keep the Mirrors going." Bea shook her head in disgust, unable to look at him. "Only... what? The GemAm ran out of genies? And the belief isn't enough, that's what you said. That's why the Mirrors have been breaking more. Did the Plots ever work?"

"Yes, the stories work, but without magic, we need so much belief, and the characters are changing. They have all those machines, all that light... They explain everything away." Mistasinon put his hand on the cloth covering Seven's mirror, not noticing the pressure plate at his feet nor the way the blade distorted the shape of the material.

Bea felt sick. "Mortal gods. Was this your idea? Get some idiot fairy no one would care about to do your dirty work?"

"No, no," Mistasinon said, stepping away from Seven's mirror, towards Bea. "Please. This isn't what I wanted—I thought I could find another way. But I've run out of time. And we really don't want to be here when the Redactionists come."

Bea stepped backwards, towards the broken door. "You knew all about me before you'd even met me. You knew how much I wanted to be an FME. You put me on this story deliberately, didn't you? Mortal gods—you kept me on it. All those times I came to you, ready to quit, ready to tell the GenAm about Seven, you always said something to keep me on it. Some little secret to make me trust you. I thought you believed in me. But you just wanted me to keep him here. You used me to entrap him."

Mistasinon stepped closer to her. "I didn't mean it the way you're making it sound. I knew you would intrigue him. They're attracted to desire. I wanted him to trust one of us, and when I read your Books, I realised you were the only one—"

"The only one who would be stupid enough to think any of this was real?" Bea felt her back hit the broken door.

"No, no, no," he said. "You've got it all wrong."

"Oh really? What part exactly? The part where you lied to me, or the part where you manipulated me, or the part where you're trying to make me a murderer?" Bea reached down and grabbed a lump of broken wood, waving it in front of her. "Don't come any closer."

Mistasinon stopped. "Bea... I should have told you what was happening. I wanted to. But I didn't know where to begin. Please, we must leave now."

"I'm not going anywhere with you. I'm going to warn Seven."

Bea lifted her arm to swing the lump of wood at him. She heaved it around with all her strength, the wood whistling through the air towards his midriff. But he was fast, so fast that by the time her swing had finished its arc, he wasn't there. He was underneath her, lifting her easily over his shoulder and moving back towards Seven's mirror. Bea screamed and kicked him, beating his back with her fists. But if he felt it, it didn't slow him down. He reached Seven's mirror in a matter of seconds, and with his free hand, pulled off the cloth.

A troll burst through the mirror and landed foursquare on the pressure plate below. Her huge, heavy feet pressed the plate down, and before she knew what had happened, the viciously sharp blade Seven had paid so much money for swung round, slicing into her chest. A shorter tribe and it would have taken their head.

Mistasinon threw Bea off his shoulder, causing her to land with a heavy thump, hitting her head. Bea stared, blinking at the troll, her vision fuzzy. The troll was screaming, a low baritone that made the floor shake. Black blood spurted from her chest in a fountain.

"Get out," Mistasinon shouted at her, circling round to stand between the troll and Bea.

The troll pressed her hand against her chest, blood spilling between her fingers. She looked up at Mistasinon. "You," she growled. "You did this to me."

Mistasinon rolled his shoulders, his eyes fixed on the troll as she lowered her head, ready to charge him.

"Bea, run, now!"

Bea shook her head, trying to clear it. "What about you?"

"Go, go," Mistasinon shouted. "I can—"

He was interrupted by the troll as she ran at him, her heavy body and thick skull perfectly designed to shatter the bones of any smaller creature, a category that included almost all the fae and certainly all the humans.

Mistasinon jumped aside at the last moment, twisting in mid-air to land on the troll's back. Bea watched in horror as he crawled across her body until he was on her shoulders, his hands pressing down on either side of her head, his teeth bared like a snarling dog.

Bea, clutching her head in her hand, pushed herself through the hole in the door, her skirts ripping further on the splintered edges. She landed poorly, twisting her ankle. She lifted herself to her feet and began running down the hallway, towards the Ballroom.

She heard the clocks begin to strike twelve, and then the sound of screaming.

Chapter Thirty-nine

"Albelphizar!"

"Maria Sophia," Seven said, turning. She stood on the middle step of the dais, looking down at him. She was smiling. She reached out her hand.

Seven stared at it. She wasn't wearing gloves. If he took her hand, he'd feel her skin against his own. He swallowed. When he had known her, her hands had been rough, the skin that on every other part of her body was as soft as melting snow was, on her palms, calloused from years of household tasks. He shivered as he remembered the blissful contradiction of her touch on his body.

"Very well," she said, pulling her hand back.

Seven jolted. "I am sorry—I did not mean to offend, I only... It is good to see you."

Maria Sophia smiled again, all upset forgotten. "I knew it was you, you know?"

Seven stepped closer to the dais. "I do not follow."

"I knew you were the Adviser here. Even with the new name—which, by the way, I don't find in the least bit amusing."

"I chose my name for you. It is a token of what was taken from us."

She looked away.

"Maria Sophia," he whispered.

She smiled quickly, warm and slightly embarrassed. "Like I said, I knew you'd be here. I should have trusted my instinct. If I had, I certainly wouldn't have—"

Seven bounded up the stairs, bringing himself level with her. "Do not say you would not have come. A love such as ours will not be denied. I know you still feel it, I see your longing to be with me."

"No, no," she laughed, her features relaxing, "I was only going to say I'd have worn a nicer dress—yellow really isn't my colour. Still so dramatic, Alb?"

Maria Sophia again lifted up her slender hand for him to kiss, and Seven felt the breath die in his throat. He could smell her. He caught her hand in his, and softly kissed her knuckles, his eyes closed against reality as he once again felt Maria Sophia's skin against his lips. He turned her hand over and began kissing her palm and the tips of her fingers.

"Alb…"

He groaned low in his throat, continuing to drop kisses on her hand, refusing to hear the worried tone in her voice.

"Albelphizar, don't," she said gently, pulling her hand away. "My husband will be finished talking to the King soon."

"Let him see. I care not."

"You might not," Maria Sophia laughed, "but I do."

"You care so much what these people think of you?"

Maria Sophia's laughter drifted into a sigh. "You never did understand these things."

"I need only understand my feelings for you."

"So you do still love me?"

Seven looked into her brown eyes with his blue ones—his true eyes, not the misty hallucination the rest of the humans projected onto him, but the eyes he knew she could see and understand.

"I have never stopped loving you," he said. "Of all the things I have done, of all I have caused to pass, the lives I have ruined and saved, loving you has been the defining of me. It is both the most painful and least regrettable action of my existence. I have been dead these fifteen years past, and I will die again if you forsake me now."

"You should be careful with a declaration like that, Alb. Someone might hold you to it."

"You believe I jest?"

"No. I know you mean it."

Seven looked around. Ana was with the witch, both women leaning into each other like schoolgirls sharing secrets. John was still talking to the Count, Maria Sophia's husband. The world was ongoing. It seemed unreal.

"But you do not love me," he said, pulling his gaze back to Maria Sophia.

"Alb, it's not that simple—"

Seven rubbed the snake coiled around his neck. "It is the simplest thing in all the worlds. We are destined for each other. This is the miracle of our love. You think that man will do for you? He will not. He is less than a shadow of myself, as every other woman is a shadow of you. They are but trees offering brief shelter from the storm, yet ultimately so easily torn from the earth. Our love is the very earth itself. It is the foundation of my life, Maria Sophia. I am born of our love, as are you. I do not accept—"

Seven heard the explosion before he felt it. The windows and glazed doors along the far wall of the Ballroom shattered into a mist of tiny shards. He leapt forward, covering Maria Sophia's body with his own as the glass flew through the air. He could hear screaming, and the pounding of feet on the marble floor as guests ran for their lives.

He lifted his head, peering over the top of his forearms. In the centre of the Ballroom was an ogre, surrounded by witchlein. All were dressed in white suits.

Ana put her hand up against the invisible wall. It was definitely there, even though she couldn't see it. Her eyes focused beyond her fingers, onto the Ballroom. Below her on the dance floor, a woman was screaming, blood pouring down her face and matting her hair. Ana watched as she fell to her knees, her hands dancing around the large shard of glass impaling her thigh. People were running past her, crashing into her, no one bothering to stop.

Ana pulled her gaze away, trying to take in the whole Ballroom. What she saw was a nightmare.

The floor was slick with blood as the guests, almost all of whom had been in the radius of the windows when they exploded, stumbled over each other to escape. To the left of the dance floor stood a monstrous creature, five times the size of even the largest man. She watched as it knuckled its way across the room towards them, casually sweeping people out of its way like so many paper dolls. It roared and raged when some wannabe hero took a run at it, only to be reduced to a broken and bleeding pulp.

"What the hell is that thing?" she asked Melly, not looking away.

"….og'e…."

"That's… Ogres aren't…" Ana stopped herself. Why not? She was trapped in some kind of solid, invisible bubble with a witch at a meeting with a King that had been arranged by a fairy. She was learning a lot today, but a massacre hadn't been on the curriculum.

She turned to Melly. What she saw did nothing to reassure her.

"Good God! What's wrong with you?"

Melly was on her knees on the floor, her skin waxy and covered in sweat, her hands biting into the material of her dress.

"...m'g'c..."

Ana looked back at the Ballroom. The ogre was getting closer, its lumbering gait unstoppable. A movement caught her eye, and she turned in time to see a man being, yes, being yanked down to the floor. She blinked. Surely she'd imagined it? He'd been standing, advancing on the ogre, and then he'd... it was almost like his legs had bent and broken under him. Ana scanned the room, and then she saw it again. This time it was a woman. She was drawing a sword—God knows how she got it past the guards—and then she was crumpling towards the ground as if all the joints in her body had snapped.

Ana narrowed her eyes. "What are all those little spiky things? They keep... my God... they're swarming... Melly! What the hell is happening?"

"...r'd'ct'on..."

Ana spun around and knelt by the witch. "Re-what-tion? What's happening?"

Under the slick of sweat, there was now a definite yellow tinge to Melly's skin. "Re...dac...tion..."

Ana reached out to Melly but pulled her hand away as if it had been burned. "You're freezing cold!"

Melly turned to look at her. Blood was trickling out of her nose and eyes, black rivulets running down her waxen face. "...keep...safe..."

"Keep safe?" Realisation dawned. Ana slammed her fist against the invisible wall that surrounded them. "You're doing this?"

"Can't... see... us..."

Ana stood up. "Stop it right now! We need to help them—we need to... oh God, no, no, no!" Ana forgot all about Melly as she pressed her face against the witch's shield. "Stop it! Run! It'll kill you! Stop it! No! No!"

But it was no good. No matter how much she screamed, he couldn't hear her.

Outside the safety of Melly's magic, John ran towards the ogre, a large sword raised above his head.

Chapter Forty

Bea shoved her way through the guests as they fled the Ballroom, her head throbbing from being thrown out of the way of the troll by Mistasinon. She couldn't see anything, and all she could hear was the frantic pounding of a thousand people as they pushed and shoved against each other.

She was too short, too small, too late.

The mob thickened, and for one terrifying moment, she thought she was going to be crushed. Someone slammed their shoulder into her left ear, causing her stomach to lurch as pain shot through her head. Bea closed her eyes, pulling her arms up to cover her head, and continued forward.

And then, like a cork from a bottle, she was suddenly freed from the mob and stumbling down the staircase and into the Ballroom. She righted herself, reaching her arms out to get her balance. The skirts and butterflies of her gown were lost, sacrificed to the struggle to reach the Ballroom. Her hair hung in long knots, dark grey with sweat and matted with blood. A bruise was already darkening on her cheek, threatening a black eye.

The Ballroom looked worse.

The witchlein swarmed around and over the bodies, no longer trying to hide, overwhelming the few humans who still stood. Bea knew she would wake up in the dark to the sound of their hissing—if she survived, anyway.

On the far side of the room, near the clockwork podium where a lifetime ago the band had played and she had danced with Seven, an ogre let loose a bellow. Bea felt the noise hit her in the chest and covered her ears against it, screwing her eyes shut. When she opened them, the monster was moving towards the throne. She couldn't see Ana or Melly anywhere. A flash of blue and her eyes landed on Seven. He was on the steps, his body bent over someone she didn't recognise. Why wasn't he doing anything?

Bea didn't have time to wonder. Free from the bonds of her heavy skirts, she ran towards the ogre, all the while knowing she had no idea what she would do when she reached it. And then something caught her eye, a flash of light reflected from the candles as they continued to spin on their clockwork mechanisms above her head.

Bea skidded to a halt, not daring to think about what the slippery substance beneath her feet was. Scrabbling against the floor to gain purchase, she snatched the sword from the cooling hand of one of the guests.

Around her the witchlein hissed.

"John!" Seven screamed at the King as he ran down the stairs. He lifted himself up, about to grab him, when he felt soft hands on his jacket, pulling at him.

"No! Save me!" Maria Sophia begged.

Seven turned back to her, his expression an agony of indecision. "I must aid him, he will not survive—"

"No, Albelphizar, please! Don't leave me!" She reached her hands up to his face, her skin brushing against the golden snake around his neck. "I wish for you to save me!"

The magic shot through Seven like spears, pinning him in place, causing him to gasp in pain as the wish took hold. And then, hot on its tail, was the inevitable wave of pleasure, the impossible, longed-for warmth that came with the pain. Seven barred his teeth against it, groaning as the magic coursed through him in waves, shocks of pain closely followed by tingling sparks of pleasure. For Seven, who had for so many years lived in self-imposed denial, it was as if the universe had opened itself to him. He heard the music of the nine worlds, the song of his home, the drumbeat at the centre of time.

The empty blue of his eyes filled with stars and he was, once again, himself.

John stepped in front of the ogre, broadsword clasped firmly in his hands. He'd trained with a rapier, of course, but he'd always found it easier to manage the weight and heft of a broadsword. His aunt had hated it and had discouraged the ability. John's lessons with the palace guard had been his one boyhood rebellion, and his aunt had never found out.

He didn't like being King.

He'd never wanted it, never asked for it. But he'd tried to do it right, tried to find answers to impossible questions. He didn't know how to deal with the Baron in Cerne Bralksteld. He didn't know what to do with the refugees. He didn't know how to negotiate or be diplomatic.

He adjusted the balance of the broadsword.

But *this* he knew.

He let loose a bellow and charged at the creature in front of him, the sword raised above his head and ready to lunge.

The ogre turned at the sound of John's rage and blinked stupidly at the King. And then it picked John up, barely flinching as the broadsword pierced its hand, and threw John away as if he were nothing.

The last King of Llanotterly hit the wall with a heavy thump and slid to the floor, a red trail of blood smearing the surface as he fell. He landed in a wet heap.

Ana screamed as John flew across the Ballroom and smashed into the wall.

"Let me out of this thing now!" she shouted, turning on Melly.

The witch coughed, blackness showering the floor as she did so. She was on all fours now, hunched over in pain. She shook her head.

"…no…"

Ana turned and slammed her fists against the barrier, ignoring the way Melly convulsed with each hit. And then she stopped.

"Oh. My. God."

The ogre bit the hilt of John's broadsword in its teeth and pulled it from its hand. And that was all the attention it paid to Llanotterly's King. It turned instead to the real prize.

Why had that tiny blonde imp told such a tale of this blue fae? He was nothing. He cowered over his woman like a child in his mother's skirts. Even the characters had tried to defend themselves.

The ogre spat. There were no wars anymore, no warriors to earn them.

Feet landing heavily on the once pristine floor, it stomped the last few paces to the foot of the dais, looming over the whelp and his strumpet.

"I am come for you, *djinn*."

The genie stood in one movement, his star-filled eyes as beautiful and devoid of empathy as the universe.

"You will give yourself up, or I will take you. It makes no odds to me," the ogre said. Maybe the whelp would fight after all? It had heard about genies. This was going to be good. It lifted its fists, ready to smash.

The genie took a step forward. The ogre was aware of the pain before it felt the cold. It raised its hand to its face, a frown marring its heavy brow. Its fingers were turning black, and skirting around the edge of the darkness was more pain than it had ever known. The genie stepped down from the dais, growing in size as he did so. When he was stood in front of the ogre, he was twice the height of the monstrous creature.

"*Dhfi, orhgr. Abakes ih ju,*" the genie said.

The ogre backed away, tripping on the bodies beneath its feet. Not fast enough. The genie was growing still bigger, and with its increased size, so the coldness entrapping the ogre grew. The ogre's legs were caught now, the bitter chill coming off the genie catching its limbs in a vice. The ogre stumbled and hit the ground as one of its legs shattered under its weight.

The genie had made it barely three paces from the foot of the dais, and already his head was nearly touching the ceiling.

The ogre grinned. "*Abak ij, djinn.*"

Seven reached out his hand, condensation running off it like steam, and lowered it toward the ogre's face. Maria Sophia's wish danced through his veins, turning reels in his soul. He was once more all that he was. He lowered his hand, ready to capture the ogre's head in his freezing grip—

"Albelphizar!"

Seven felt the wish pull at him, scratching his skin from the inside, and turned to see the first witchlein jump on Maria Sophia, its sharp-scaled hands reaching for her eyes. Forgetting the ogre, the wish moved him in a heartbeat to Maria Sophia's side and back to his normal size.

Seven pulled the witchlein off Maria Sophia, picked her up in his arms, and vanished.

Bea stood rooted to the spot as she watched Seven change.

She could feel the cold from where she was. The ogre clearly didn't stand a chance. Already she could see the frost-rot crawling up its skin, and Seven was still a good five feet away from it. She dragged her eyes up from the sight of the ogre to look at the person she thought she had finally understood, and realised the extent of her ignorance.

And then Seven was standing over the monster, his enormous blue hand outstretched. Bea wanted to close her eyes, but she couldn't. The cold was biting at her now, stinging her lips and making the ends of her fingers pinch. How the ogre was still alive was beyond her.

She wanted to shout. She wanted to call Seven's name and tell him to stop, but the words died in her throat, dried up and useless. In the corner of her eye, she could see the red smear of John's blood on the wall.

And then the woman shouted something, a word Bea had never heard before, and Seven turned. No... no... It was like he was pulled back to her, and in the next moment, he appeared at her side, pulling the white-suited witchlein off her.

Seven and the woman disappeared.

Bea blinked.

He'd left her.

The ogre screamed in rage and pulled itself forward to where Seven and the woman had been, black fingers snapping with the effort, splintered leg dragging behind.

It was at this moment Melly and Ana appeared in the centre of the dais.

Melly was collapsed on the ground, Ana kneeling over her. The ogre roared, blinded by pain and fury, and reached up what remained of its hand to crush the witch and the ugly sister, when suddenly it toppled forward.

Bea rubbed her arm. It was years since she'd thrown a spear, and the sword had been much heavier. But it was a skill you never forgot, not when you grew up in the Sheltering Forest. Aim for the heart, throw hard, don't miss. She smiled as the ogre slumped forward, the hilt of her stolen sword sticking out of its back.

Fairies weren't good for anything, was it? Bea started to laugh.

And then she threw up.

"Bea!"

Bea looked up, confused. The pounding in her head had returned, the adrenaline wearing off all too quickly. Ana. Ana was shouting at her, waving her arms. Bea took a step forward, trying to hear her over the ringing in her ears.

"Bea!"

She blinked. There seemed to be stars everywhere. That couldn't be right, could it? And then her right leg exploded in pain. She looked down to see a witchlein climbing her leg, its sharp scales digging in to the flesh of her thigh.

The pain brought her back. Bea pulled the witchlein from her leg and ran to the dais. It was only when she reached it that she realised she didn't have a weapon.

"What's wrong with Melly?" she panted, watching as the witchlein drew closer. They were wary, probably unsure whether Seven was going to come back. Bea didn't hold out much hope that their caution would prove justified.

"She did something, put an invisible wall around us. It made us invisible too," Ana said in a rush. "I told her to stop, but she wouldn't, and then she lost consciousness, and it came down. What are we going to do? There's at least thirty of those little bastards."

Bea bit her lip. She looked around for a weapon, but there was nothing. The witchlein were closing in, hissing in anticipation.

"Bea? What are we going to do?"

"I think, Ana, we're going to die."

Bea stepped in front of Melly and took Ana's hand.

"Here it is, then," she said. "The end."

Chapter Forty-one

"Stand down! Stand down this instant!" Mistasinon screamed from the top of the staircase.

The witchlein froze. They backed away from Bea and Ana. Mistasinon ran across the Ballroom, making easy work of the distance. He stood in front of Bea and Ana, glaring at the witchlein.

"This has gone too far," he said.

"It wasss only what ssshe asssked usss to do," the nearest one hissed. "You sssaying we ssshould ssstop? Isss that official?"

Mistasinon gave a curt nod of his head. "It is."

The witchlein shrugged its spiky shoulders. "On your head be it."

Mistasinon turned just in time to catch Bea as she collapsed.

Bea kicked her legs, banging her heels against the floor.

She'd been home for two days and hadn't left her bedsit. This wasn't through personal choice, but rather was the result of the brown-suited troll from the Contents Department stationed outside her door.

She wasn't a prisoner. She just wasn't exactly encouraged to leave. The cupboards had been stocked, and someone had made the bed. They'd even provided her with some new clothes. She had a couple of pairs of trousers and tunics, as well as a new dress. The dress was in most respects exactly the same as her old one, only much better made than anything Bea could have managed. She suspected it was the work of brownies—expensive then, unless they were already employed by the GenAm.

Bea was wearing the dress. She was slightly cross with herself for it, but she also figured if she was going to be Redacted, she might as well look nice while it happened. Or they might do things the old-fashioned way and just execute her. Bea had spent a lot of time over the last two days weighing up the options, and she still hadn't decided which one she preferred.

There was a knock at the door.

Bea didn't bother getting up, and sure enough, a moment later, the door opened by itself.

"Great," she said. "It's you."

Mistasinon stood in the doorway, the picture of awkwardness.

"You're letting all the heat out," Bea said.

"Oh. Sorry."

He stepped into the room, closing the door behind him. Bea took a moment to look him over. He was back in his blue suit or one just like it. His hair was neat again. He wasn't covered in blood. She supposed that wasn't all that surprising, but once you've seen someone take on a troll with their bare hands, you tend to have different expectations.

But then, she'd killed an ogre. Admittedly, she was pretty certain her sword had only finished the job Seven had started, but that didn't matter. She allowed herself a small smile and hoped that Mistasinon was thinking about the ogre too.

"How's Melly?" she asked, not bothering to stand.

"She's fine—no, honestly. She's old, so the magic didn't hurt as much as it might have done. She's been taken off all her active Plots, and the GenAm is still giving her ration tokens. She wants to see you."

"So why can't she?"

Mistasinon shook his head. "Bea, I'm sorry—"

"Don't you dare apologise to me. What about Ana and John?"

"Your characters? The woman's none the worse for wear. In fact—"

"And John?"

"Well, he's still bedridden, but—"

Bea's façade cracked, and she allowed herself a sigh of relief. "He's alive?"

"Um… yes. Bea, when the ogre attacked him…. They're quite delicate, the characters. You know that, don't you?"

"What are you saying?"

Mistasinon dropped his eyes. "It broke his spine. He's alive, but he'll never walk again."

Bea sank back into her sofa. "Mortal gods…"

Mistasinon stepped forward hesitantly, but when Bea failed to bite his head off, he joined her on her sofa.

"It's not your fault Bea."

She looked up. "No, it isn't. It's yours."

Mistasinon nodded. "I know you're angry with me. You've every right to be—"

"I don't need your permission."

"No, I didn't mean... I just... I've been trying to help you. The last couple of days. I finished your story."

"What? How?"

"Well, your character helped actually. Ana, the one with—"

"With what? The nose? Don't you dare insult her."

"Bea... I was going to say the one with the very determined attitude. Please. I want to make things better."

Bea glared at him, but after a moment she nodded.

"So. Um. Yes. Ana helped me finish your story," Mistasinon continued. "She's appointed herself as the new Adviser to the King. I mean, the King approves of course, but I think it was her idea more than his."

"How is that an ending? My Plot was a Happy Ever After. A crippled King is hardly a '*nice*' ending, is it?" Bea spat the word. She didn't care if he knew she didn't believe in the Plots anymore. And, when the white suits had finished with her, it wouldn't matter anyway.

Mistasinon smiled. "I took a leaf out of your book."

Bea looked blank.

"I changed the Plot," Mistasinon explained. "It's a Rags to Riches now. Ana told the city that the old Adviser was a wicked foreign sorcerer and that he conjured the ogre to kill the King. When it went wrong, he disappeared. She's being credited with breaking the spell and saving the city."

Bea couldn't keep the shock out of her voice. "But that's not what happened—Seven wasn't trying to kill John. He liked John. And there were people there, they saw what happened."

Mistasinon shook his head. "Bea, it's better this way. The characters like stories, they make life easier for them. Try to understand. The genie was foreign—he was strange. But a familiar kind of strange, if you see what I mean. The kind of strange that's easy to believe is evil. But an ogre and a whole scrabble of witchlein? That's *strange* strange. To be honest, even if Ana hadn't blamed the Adviser, they probably would have come to it on their own."

"But it isn't fair—" Bea caught the pleading tone in her voice and started again. "It isn't *right* to blame him. He didn't do anything wrong."

Mistasinon sighed. "Either way, he's gone now."

"You don't know what happened to him?"

"No. He took one of the guests with him. Do you know why he might have done that?"

Bea shook her head firmly. "Not a clue. I guess because he's 'evil'?"

Mistasinon ignored the sarcasm in her voice. "That's disappointing. There have been some suggestions about how to keep the Mirrors going without him, but I had hoped…"

"You'd hoped I'd help you kill him? No chance. I don't mind being Redacted, but I'll run before I help you murder someone, even if it would save the Mirrors. You'll have to set the Beast on me."

He flinched. "I was never trying to murder the genie."

"So what were you trying to do?"

"I wanted his lamp. The magic's in the lamps, I think. And, I don't know… I wanted to speak to him. I thought he might know something about the Mirrors, something we don't know."

"What?"

"I don't know," Mistasinon answered, smiling softly. "That's rather the problem."

Bea looked him up and down. "You know, I'd almost believe you. If it wasn't for the ogre and all the witchlein and the maimed King. Apart from all that, your story is *really* plausible."

"None of that was my doing. That was the Redaction Department."

"Well," Bea said, rubbing her temples. Her headache was coming back. "I suppose I can ask them myself soon enough."

"You're not going to be Redacted. I told you, I've been helping you."

"How can you possibly stop them Redacting me?"

"I finished your story. I handed your Book in myself. They've got no reason to Redact you, and the Redactionists aren't really in a position to start throwing their weight around, not after that fiasco."

Bea stood up and walked over to her kitchen. She poured herself a glass of weak beer from the jug. "None of this makes any sense," she said, sipping the drink. "I know it doesn't. But every time I ask you a question, you're going to slip out of it, aren't you? You'll say something that seems like you're answering, but actually, all you're doing is telling me what I already know."

"I got you a place at the FME Academy."

Bea stared at him, stunned. *Well*, she thought, *that was something I didn't already know.*

"I'm not joining the Academy. And they can't possibly want me. I hid an Anti. I changed the stories."

Mistasinon stood up and joined her in the kitchen.

"Bea, there are two ways through this. The first is to join the Academy and pretend everything went as planned. As we planned, remember? You did it. You finished a story—and very, very well. Monsters and evil Advisers? Rebel outlaws saving the King? The belief is pouring in from that region, and it'll spread quickly enough. Or you can go out that door and turn your back on it all, and just hope people don't start asking questions or that the Redactionists don't start seeing you as someone who isn't a team player. I'm not going to make the choice for you, Bea. It really is up to you. But…"

"But what?"

"You've got friends, Bea."

"You wouldn't?"

"Not me, Bea, not me. But the Redactionists?" He searched her face with his large, brown eyes. "Please, Bea. Join the Academy. Isn't this what you always wanted anyway? Think about it like this: your dream has come true."

Chapter Forty-two

Bea stood in the chill sun.

Winter was approaching. She thought about her family, out there somewhere in the Sheltering Forest. Winters were always hard in the Forest, but now she couldn't help wishing she was with them.

She was standing in the open square outside the GenAm building, the Teller's spire stabbing at the sky. There were about thirty other fae with her, waiting to be signed up for the Academy, all from different tribes—although, unsurprisingly, she was the only fairy. Bea was also the only one who hadn't been recommended by an established FME. But she was *also* the only one who had finished their very own story. It was obvious no one knew what to say to her. Bea didn't mind. She didn't want to talk to anyone anyway.

The ceremony itself was quick. All they had to do was repeat the words, their hands on a Book. But the GenAm had decided to turn the occasion into a celebration. There were Raconteurs in the crowds and beer, meat and bread were circulating. Everyone seemed delighted by the sudden show of largesse. All except Bea.

Her full name was called and, accompanied by sotto voce giggles from the other recruits, she walked, head up and back straight, to the Head of the Plot Department. The Head Plotter was a boggart who sat slumped in her seat, not saying a word when each of the new recruits came to kneel in front of her and declare their oath.

Bea dropped to her knees, her only aim to get the whole thing over with as quickly as possible. She opened her mouth to begin when a creaking voice called out to her. Bea looked up. The whole audience joined her. The Head Plotter had spoken.

"Stand up, fairy."

Bea stared at her.

"Up. Up. Up," the Head Plotter repeated. Her voice sounded like it had been trapped in a cave for thousands of years.

Bea stood up.

"Bow," the Head Plotter commanded. "Let the others kneel, fairy. You've finished a Book. You've brought in more belief than we've seen in years. *You* bow. Now get on with it."

Bea swallowed. Her eyes darted over the audience, looking for Melly or Joan to reassure her this was really happening. She knew they were out there somewhere—they'd met her before the ceremony began to wish her luck—but the only person she could see who she recognised was Mistasinon, standing behind the Head Plotter. He smiled at her. Bea glared at him.

Why was he here? Probably to make sure she went ahead with it. What would happen if she turned and ran? Would the Beast really be sent after her? She doubted it. Only Mistasinon knew she didn't believe in the Plots anymore, that she didn't want to be here. And whatever he said about the Redactionists, if she did run away, it would probably be put down to her being a feckless fairy, and quickly forgotten.

…But then, the actual Head of the Department has just spoken out loud, to her. It was unprecedented. And maybe she could do some good if she was on the inside? She knew now that the Plots could change, didn't she?

Plus there was Seven. Bea had spent a lot of time thinking about him since he'd disappeared. If she was an FME, she'd have access to Thaiana. She might be able to find him, warn him that the Redactionists were after him.

Mistasinon was still watching her. Well, everyone was watching her—but it was his eyes she was aware of. She avoided looking at the space she knew he occupied, and instead dropped a low bow, the kind Seven would have been proud of, and spoke her oath to the Plot Department and the General Administration.

"Look at you! A real FME!" Joan cried, engulfing Bea in a bear hug. Bea laughed and hugged her back.

"Well, a real *trainee* FME. And it's thanks to you. And you, Melly," she added, smiling at the elf over the top of Joan's head. Despite her current reprieve from witching, Melly was still wearing black, a cigarette hanging from her fingers. Even that made Bea smile.

"You did ever so well!" Joan said. "I can't believe you made it all work out! Everyone's talking about you! Imagine finishing a Rags to Riches on your first ever Plot!"

Bea wiggled out of Joan's embrace. "Well... you know it wasn't exactly—"

"That was exactly what happened," Melly interrupted sharply. "Bea, you've navigated your way out of difficult waters, but you're on the ocean now. Keep your eye to the horizon."

Bea nodded.

"Oh, for goodness sake," Joan huffed. "Let's not start all that again—honestly Bea, she's been so miserable today. Come on, Melly—tell her!"

"Tell me what?"

Melly smiled. "We've got a surprise for you."

"A surprise? What is it?"

"Well, Bea, firstly it's a surprise—you do know what a surprise is, don't you?" Joan asked, punching her arm playfully. "Come on, we need to get to the Grand."

"The Grand?" Bea asked, dumbfounded.

Joan grabbed her hand and began pulling her through the crowds, away from the GenAm buildings and towards the Grand Reflection Station. Melly followed, laughing.

"We're going through the Mirrors? But they're still rationed?" Bea asked as they arrived at the front of the queue for the checkpoints.

"You've got a friend in high places, it seems," Melly said, showing a slip of paper with a gold seal to the brown suit, who waved them through.

"What? Who? Oh no, you didn't ask Mistasinon for a pass?"

Joan grinned. "We didn't have to. He offered it to me this morning. This was his idea, actually. I definitely think he's keen on you, Bea," Joan continued, oblivious to the way Bea had turned pale. "I'm not sure he'd be my type, but he's got a nice smile, hasn't he? I tried to work out what tribe he's from, but you're right, he does look odd. Almost like one of the characters, but he's very thin, isn't he? And tall. Still, I can see why you like him. Suits are always attractive, aren't they? Oh look, we're here! Come on, off we go!"

Bea looked up at Joan, who was now standing in front of one of the functioning Mirrors. In fact, there were a lot more Mirrors open than the last time she'd been here. Something must be working, Bea thought. Could it really be her Plot? Out loud, she said, "Where are we going?"

Melly pushed her from behind. "You'll see, come on."

Bea chewed her lip. She didn't like the idea of Mistasinon giving her gifts any more than she liked the idea of him helping her. But Melly was sensible, and she knew what had really happened at the Ball. If she thought it was alright, it was probably alright.

Bea stepped through the Mirror and into Thaiana.

The wedding was spectacular. Sindy looked radiant, and Llanotterly Castle was resplendent in banners and flags. Even Will had managed to brush up well and had spent the whole ceremony grinning and surreptitiously tugging at the sash over his chest. When the friar told him he could kiss his new bride, Will had blushed crimson and then whooped with joy. Sindy had been laughing and crying throughout.

The whole town turned out to watch, including the rebels from the woods. Really it was a small wedding by state standards, but everyone was buoyed up by the bride and groom's happiness, and later, when the beer and bards came out, it was almost as if the castle hadn't been attacked by an ogre a little over a week ago.

Bea was, against all her expectations, actually having a nice time. She enjoyed watching Ana organising everything, though she was pretty certain the ones being organised were less enamoured with the fact. It was good to see Llanotterly in such good hands.

John didn't make an appearance—he was still being carefully monitored by his physician. But he sent a decree and awarded the young couple a smallholding on the outskirts of town. Melly had admitted after the fourth pint of Ehinen beer that she was helping to heal John, with the GenAm's permission no less. Bea didn't know how she'd ever repay the witch for everything she'd done but was determined to find a way.

She helped herself to another mug of beer and wandered away from the crowds to catch her breath. She had just found a quiet spot in the castle gardens to sit and gather her thoughts when Sindy peered round one of the hedges.

"I thought it was you," Sindy said.

"You thought right. Congratulations."

Sindy smiled. "I wanted to say thank you."

Bea nearly dropped her beer. "Thank me? Whatever for? I nearly caused you to run away from home."

Sindy came and sat next to Bea. "But you came and got me back. And you helped Ana. At the end of the day, I'm married to Will now, not the King or anyone else. You gave me exactly the happy ending I've always wanted." Sindy suddenly leaned over and gave Bea a quick hug. "You're definitely my favourite fairy. And my favourite godmother."

"How many others do you have?" Bea laughed.

Sindy blushed crimson. "Oh, oh, oh, I didn't mean—"

"I know what you meant, I'm just teasing," Bea said, patting Sindy on the arm. "Thank you."

Sindy smiled, but she looked anxious.

"What is it?" Bea asked.

Sindy wrung her hands in the folds of her dress. "I don't know how these stories work or what will happen next. My mum and dad were happy, but then Mum died. And I don't mind my stepmother but… you know… I don't think she and Dad are very well suited. Not really. Do you think Will and I…?"

Bea put her arm around Sindy's shoulders.

"You and Will will be perfect together. You'll never get anything done because you're both far too kind and too gentle, but you'll be happy when you can be, and when you're sad you'll help each other. You'll fight, and you'll make up, and you'll be even stronger as a result. You're both going to live Happy Ever After."

Bea had no guarantee what she was saying was true, but she knew it was exactly the right story to tell.

Bea's Story Continues in

The Academy
The Pathways Tree series book two

Available now in paperback, e-book and audiobook

**How far will Bea go to do the right thing—and is she prepared
to face the fearsome, three-headed Beast to it?**

Bea's Back! But life at the Academy isn't all it's cracked up to be.
Being the only fairy is bad enough, but then rumours of a ghost
spread, setting everyone on edge. And when people are afraid, it's
never a good time to be the odd one out.

So Bea is determined to keep her head down and not, absolutely
not, draw attention to herself. That is until she comes face to face

with the so-called ghost. Bea quickly realises that things at the Academy are a lot more complicated than they first appear—and that's before an unwelcome face turns up, begging a favour...

"I literally couldn't put it down, fantastic!"

"This sequel is beautifully written, witty, dark, funny and remarkably complex ... Just read it—you won't be disappointed."

Join my Readers' Group newsletter!

Get access to bonus unpublished material and deleted scenes, early access to new titles, and information about special offers. As a subscriber, you can also join our secret Facebook group.

Thanks

I would very much like to thank the following people for all their help and support. Writing is a lonely business, and one riddled with self-doubt. If it wasn't for the people below, you wouldn't be holding this book in your hands. Blame them!

Firstly I want to thank my brother, Jon, for whom this book is dedicated. He read and re-read all the early drafts, and spent hours on the phone telling me where I was going wrong, talking about my characters and helping me to imagine Thaiana and Ænathlin.

He was always honest, always positive, and always treated this like a real thing. In the same vein, I'd also like to thank my mum, who, throughout my life, has always told me I *can*, and without this foundation, I doubt very much I would have ever begun to write, let alone finish, a book.

I also want to thank my husband, James, for… well, everything really. He has put up with losing his wife to the writing of this book, has loved me and looked after me, and always believed in me. I love him, every day. I'd also like to thank my dear friend Miranda, who has been my guru and pathfinder in the daunting world of Do It Yourself. Miranda has rescued me when I needed rescuing, complimented me when I needed complimenting, and shouted at me when I needed shouting at. This is the recipe of a true friend—and I can't wait to pay her back! #occupytheniche

I would also like to thank Liz Rippington and Kelly for their proofreading, comments and enthusiasm, all which were very gratefully received! Thanks too to Brett Hardman, who did a developmental edit for me and produced an incredibly thorough and thoughtful report, and gave me such good advice. I'd also like to thank Cornerstones for introducing me to Brett, and happily recommend their services. Thanks also to Jane Dixon-Smith for my beautiful cover and memes.

Finally, I would like to thank *you* for reading my book, and all my friends for showing me such support and encouragement.

Printed in Great Britain
by Amazon

42337560R00178